Nina Singh lives just outs̲i̲d̲e̲ ̲B̲o̲s̲t̲o̲n̲ ̲w̲i̲t̲h̲ her husband, children, and a very m̲a̲l̲f̲u̲n̲c̲t̲i̲o̲n̲s̲ ̲Y̲o̲r̲k̲i̲e̲. After several years in the corporate world she finally followed the advice of family and friends to 'give the writing a go, already'. She's oh-so-happy she did. When not at her keyboard she likes to spend time on the tennis court or golf course. Or immersed in a good read.

Having written over ninety novels, **Tara Taylor Quinn** is a *USA TODAY* bestselling author with more than seven million copies sold. She is known for delivering intense, emotional fiction. Tara is a past president of Romance Writers of America and is a seven-time RITA® Award finalist. She has also appeared on TV across the country, including *CBS Sunday Morning*. She supports the National Domestic Violence Hotline.

HER BILLIONAIRE PROTECTOR

NINA SINGH

HER MOTHERHOOD WISH

TARA TAYLOR QUINN

MILLS & BOON

First Published in Great Britain 2020
by Mills & Boon, an imprint of HarperCollinsPublishers,
1 London Bridge Street, London, SE1 9GF

Her Billionaire Protector © 2020 Nilay Nina Singh
Her Motherhood Wish © 2020 TTQ Books LLC

ISBN: 978-0-263-27877-4

0420

HER BILLIONAIRE
PROTECTOR

NINA SINGH

For Becks, for all the joy you've brought us.
And the way you guard us in your own way.

CHAPTER ONE

ADAM STEELE KNEW he was in the right line of work. But days like this, he wondered if perhaps he should have gone in a different professional direction. He had no right to complain. Providing personal security for the A-listers of the world as CEO of Steele Security Services had certainly provided him with all sorts of riches, both material and personal. But every once in a while, an assignment arose that he just knew was going to be a giant pain in the—

Before he could complete the thought, the elevator pinged and the shiny stainless steel doors swished open. Adam entered the empty elevator and punched in the number to the top floor.

Assignments borne of requests for personal favors always made him wary. That personal connection often led to complications and distractions. And distractions could be deadly in his line of work.

He should have turned Brant down as soon as his friend had asked to see him. Instead, here he was at Terrance Technology headquarters about to meet with his old friend and the senior Mr. Terrance to personally discuss why they were suddenly interested in his services. Something told him it would be a meeting he would ultimately regret.

But Brant didn't often take no for an answer. Adam had learned that during the years they'd served together and even before that. They'd been friends since middle school. And he remembered his friend's character well, even though those days seemed like another lifetime.

Adam tried to avert the images threatening to invade his mind by focusing on the view of the greater Dallas metropolitan area outside the glass elevator as it took him up. Images of war-torn buildings and hot desert...

Brant made his home mostly in Manhattan these days. The fact that he'd made this trip simply to see Adam face-to-face said a lot about the importance of whatever it was he wanted to discuss.

The elevator finally came to a stop and the doors opened with a smooth swoosh. A statuesque blonde woman immediately stood up from behind a long, cherrywood desk across from him. Her tall heels clicked loudly on the heavily varnished floor as she approached him. She looked like she could be gracing the runway at a high-end fashion show. Adam would know; he'd been in charge of security for several such shows in the past.

"You must be Mr. Steele," she said through a brilliant, ivory-white smile. "I'll walk you to Mr. Terrance's office. They're waiting for you."

Adam gave her a slight nod before following her past her desk and down a wide corridor.

"Can I get you anything? Coffee? Or water?" the woman asked over her shoulder. "Something else?"

Adam didn't miss the flirtatious flip of her hair as she added that last part, nor the implication in her tone. Any other time, he might have pursued her invitation. Right now, he had too much on his mind.

"No. Thank you."

Her small shrug was barely noticeable as they reached a tall wooden door that stood slightly ajar. With a small knock, she pushed the door open and motioned for him to step inside.

Two impeccably groomed men in well-tailored suits immediately stood up from behind an elegant desk as soon as he entered. They had the same eyes in shape and color. Anyone who gave them a thorough glance would easily conclude that they were father and son.

Brant stepped up to him with a wide grin and he suddenly found himself in a tight embrace. "Adam, man. It's been way too long." Brant stepped back to study him. "You're still as ugly as I remember."

Adam laughed. It was a wonder the two of them had become such close friends over the years despite the odds. Brant was a prodigal son, born into wealth and a loving family. Adam had been abandoned and discarded when he was barely a teen. If not for the decency of a well-off uncle who'd begrudgingly taken him in, Adam would have no doubt found himself in the foster system instead of the ritzy town where he'd grown up. A town where he'd known he didn't fit in.

"Nah. You're just too pretty for your own good." Adam rebutted. The teasing words held a minutia of truth. Brant had the reddish-blond, blue-eyed looks of a Renaissance angel. Though somehow, he carried such features without looking the least bit angelic. In fact, he bore the sort of rugged looks that most men worked hard to achieve with hours in the gym and intense grooming.

"So I've been told," Brant responded. He motioned to the older man behind him. "You remember my father."

Adam reached over the desk with his hand out. "Mr. Terrance. So nice to see you again."

"Please, call me Edward. We are all adults now, after all," he said as they shook hands.

"Very well," Adam agreed, though it would take some getting used to.

All three sat down with Adam facing the other two men across the desk.

Brant took a deep breath, making it clear any catching up or chitchat would have to wait. "I'll begin by saying this might be a lot to ask, especially given that as CEO you don't personally do fieldwork anymore. And considering that you know the person in question."

That last sentence sent warning bells ringing in Adam's head.

Brant continued, "But I find the need to ask it, anyway."

Adam crossed one ankle over his knee. "Maybe you should just tell me what this is all about."

Brant inhaled sharply and looked away toward the wide window. He appeared visibly shaken. "It's Ani."

Adam tried not to react visibly to the name. It wasn't easy, despite his professional training. "Your younger sister."

"That's right."

"Has something happened? Last I heard, she was on her way to being the next international musical phenomenon." Anikita Terrance was a musical prodigy, a world-class pianist at the young age of twenty-six.

Brant nodded, pride clear in his eyes. "That she is. In fact, she's been asked to perform in Paris. Then Brussels. A one-woman concert."

"She got her talent from her mother," Edward added, the sadness thick in his voice and clear in his expression. They'd lost Brant and Ani's mother over a decade ago after an unexpected and short illness.

"Is she in trouble in some way?" Adam asked.

Brant snapped the pen he'd been holding in two. Adam didn't think he was even aware of doing so. The action spoke of far more than concern for a sibling. Brant was downright angry. Brotherly protectiveness could be a hell of a force, and Brant had always been fiercely protective of his sister, particularly after their mother had passed.

"I'm afraid she is," he finally answered, his voice shaky. "Through no fault of her own. And I trust you to be the one to get her out of it."

Ani bit down on the groan of frustration churning at the base of her throat as she entered the high-rise building in central Dallas that housed the family business headquarters. As much as she loved her brother and father—they were the only family she had, after all—this meeting was sure to be an exercise in patience.

She knew what they wanted to talk to her about. And she knew they only had her best interests in mind. Still, she couldn't help but feel they were simply blowing the matter out of all proportion. As usual. Famous people received disturbing messages all the time. Or near famous, in her case. She was hardly a household name. She was only just starting to receive some recognition for her playing.

All the more reason for Brant and her father to get a grip already. Yes, she'd received some anonymous notes and emails from someone claiming to be her only true love, her soul mate. They hadn't been overtly threatening. But Brant and her father had had a bit of a panic when the last note mentioned that her secret admirer would show himself when he felt the time was right. And that afterward, they would live happily-ever-after when he whisked her away. It was enough of a threat that the two significant males in her life were now up in arms about her "stalker."

Hence the reason she'd been summoned to her father's office to discuss it all this morning.

Ani liked to think she wasn't naive. Of course, she'd

heard horror stories about seemingly innocent correspondence from admirers turning suddenly dangerous and nefarious. She just didn't think her case warranted such alarm. Not yet, anyway.

The elevator finally reached the top floor and Ani exited with a resigned sigh. Best to get this over with. The sooner she could smooth over Brant and her dad's ruffled feathers, the sooner she could focus on practicing and rehearsal for her upcoming performances in Europe. It had been a pure stroke of luck that a previous act had canceled a couple of dates on their tour. Ani's manager had been at the right place at the right time.

Her father's secretary gave her an easy smile as she waved and walked past the circular desk in the main lobby. She appeared to be handling several phone conversations at once. Her father hired no one but the best. Ani returned the smile and entered her father's office.

To her surprise, Brant and her dad weren't alone. Another man rose immediately from his chair across Dad's desk and approached her. Tall and dark, the man could be straight out of the pages of *Polo Magazine*. Dear heavens, he was certainly fit. His expertly tailored suit failed to hide the muscular frame underneath. She couldn't quite place it, but she knew him from somewhere. He had a strange sense of familiarity about him.

He held a small notebook in his hand. Understanding dawned. One of Dad's employees was apparently a fan of hers. He certainly didn't look like the typical enthusiast who attended piano performances, but what did she know? She was so new to all of this.

With a polite smile, Ani reached over and took the notebook from his hand. A strange sensation traveled through her core as her fingers brushed his. It was the barest of contact, lasting less than a second. Yet she felt a physical tug that could only be described as longing. A curl of heat formed around the vicinity of her belly, then moved lower. How utterly silly. Had it been that long since she'd enjoyed the company of the opposite sex?

She forced herself to push away the unsettling thoughts and scribbled her signature on the page, then added a musical note symbol. She handed him back the notebook.

He simply stood silently. Then he blinked at her. Not even a thank-you. Was he that starstruck? And why had the room suddenly gone completely quiet?

Ani glanced at her father in confusion. He was rubbing his forehead. Brant, for his part, looked somewhat amused. Clearly, she had missed something.

Well, if no one else was going to break the silence... Ani summoned another smile. "It's always nice to meet a fan."

Brant let out some sort of sound behind her. Not quite a laugh, but pretty close.

Her father cleared his throat. "Ani, he's not quite a fan."

The stranger lifted an eyebrow, his gaze solidly fixed on her face. "On the contrary," he began. "I enjoy Ms. Terrance's music immensely."

There was no mistaking the slight hint of teasing in his tone. Ani wanted to sink into the floor and disappear. Whoever he was, he was most definitely not here for her autograph. She'd clearly gone ahead and flattered herself. No wonder Brant looked as if he wanted to break into laugher.

The stranger stepped closer to her and Ani had to stifle an urge to move away. The man had much too strong an enigmatic pull. And she had no doubt that he was now laughing at her inside.

"But perhaps I should introduce myself," he announced. Ani's confusion and embarrassment grew as he continued,

"Or reintroduce myself, as you clearly don't seem to remember who I am."

But his name echoed in her head before he could utter it. *Of course.* Suddenly, the missing puzzle piece fell into place. Adam Steele.

How could she have not known immediately? Brant and Adam had been buddies since middle school who'd then served overseas together. He'd been a guest in their home and Ani had always felt like an awkward and clumsy teen around him. In turn, he'd seemed utterly unimpressed and annoyed by her mere presence. Probably because she stared at him like the besotted schoolgirl she'd been at the time. Apparently, her body had recognized him before her mind had, judging by her intense physical reaction.

She distinctly remembered one afternoon when she'd headed down to the family swimming pool unaware that Brant had Adam and a few other friends over for an afternoon swim. She'd barely made it onto the patio in her newly purchased two-piece swimsuit when Adam had suddenly leaped out of the pool. Not even bothering to dry off, he'd uttered some kind of excuse about why he had to leave right then.

Now, heat warmed her cheeks as she vividly remembered being unable to look away when he'd stormed past her, his chiseled chest and tanned, broad shoulders dripping wet. He hadn't even spared a glance in her direction as he'd stormed off.

Ani felt the embarrassing sting of the moment as if it had happened yesterday. Looking at him now, it was little wonder she hadn't recognized him right away. Any hint of boyishness or youthful features had vanished from his face. His ebony hair was now cut shorter than she'd ever seen on him. A dusting of dark stubble ran along his angular jawline. His eyes were harder.

Ani tried to shake off the memories. How stunningly, cringingly cliché. She'd embarrassingly had the hots for her older brother's friend. He'd been so out of her league. Unlike most of Brant's neighborhood friends, Adam had always seemed distant and unapproachable with an aura she'd be hard-pressed to describe, much rougher around the edges than the others. The perfect swoon bait for an awkward teenage girl who had no real female influence around her.

No wonder he had been her very first crush. Clearly, she hadn't outgrown it. And she'd just made a complete fool of herself upon seeing him again.

He had to wonder if she was playing some kind of game. She couldn't really be that much of an ingenue. That description certainly might have fit Anikita Terrance all those years ago. But she'd done some growing up in the meantime. It chafed his ego a bit that she hadn't guessed who he was. And didn't that make him all sorts of foolish?

She'd thought he was here for her autograph!

In all fairness, he'd had an advantage over her, knowing who she was and why they were all here in her father's office. He had to admit, he might have very well been unable to recognize her if their roles had been reversed.

Anikita was no longer the bespectacled, gangly, awkward teenager she'd been when he'd last laid eyes on her. Just how often had he good-naturedly teased her about those thick glasses and tight ponytail?

He had nothing to tease her about now. The thick glasses were gone. Her thick, satiny red hair hung in soft waves around her face and over her shoulders. Gone were the frizzy, tight curls. And the shade was so much richer. She had inherited the most striking looks from both sides of her heritage. Dark, almond-shaped eyes from her Singaporean mother and fiery red hair from her American father. It made for a stunningly striking combination. Adam cursed internally. He was so not the type to wax poetic about the color of a woman's hair. Not normally, anyway.

He'd felt inexplicably drawn to her all those years ago. Probably because she had never questioned his background or asked where he came from. And also probably because she was one of the handful of people in this town who didn't manage to make him feel completely out of place in their well-heeled circle of friends. She and Brant had been the only ones who hadn't, in fact.

He'd also managed to see beneath Brant's little sister's geeky exterior to the attractive young woman hovering underneath. And man, had he been right. Anikita Terrance was a stunner all grown-up.

A stunner who was currently staring at him with confusion. *Focus.*

Brant suddenly approached to stand between the two of them. He looked nervous. "Adam, sorry. We haven't really had a chance to discuss all this with Ani just yet. Her schedule has just been so busy." He glanced down at his much shorter sister. "Also, she's been a little resistant to the idea."

"What idea?" Ani asked.

Adam pinched the bridge of his nose. Great. Just great. She really had no idea why he was here. Hadn't been expecting him at all. What had Brant and his father been thinking?

His friend must have sensed the frustration humming through him. "You have to understand, Adam. We weren't even sure you were on board. Then by the time Ani found some time to come in, Dad and I never got a chance to actually tell her."

"Tell me what?" Ani demanded once more.

Brant inhaled deeply before addressing his sister. "Adam owns a private security firm now."

Adam watched her facial features harden as she put two and two together. "Do you mean to tell me you're trying to keep me secure with a bodyguard?" Saying she was resistant to the idea certainly seemed to be the case, judging by the murderous look she threw at her brother. She turned just long enough to shoot the same glare at her father, who merely shrugged.

"Adam's the best there is," Brant insisted. "I'd trust him with my life, sis. And yours."

"You didn't even discuss it with me, Brant. You had no right to make such a decision." Ani didn't give her brother a chance to respond before turning back to face Adam. "I'm sorry you had to waste a trip out here, Mr. Steele. My brother and father seem to have exaggerated my predicament. I have no need for personal security."

So formal… She wasn't using his first name. For some reason, that rubbed him the wrong way. It had been bad enough when she hadn't even remembered who he was.

"You've been receiving anonymous messages from a stranger," Brant argued.

She glared at her sibling. "They've hardly been threatening."

"Not yet, anyway." Adam felt compelled to jump in.

"He's got a point, Ani. Just listen—"

Adam cut Brant off before he could continue. "I'll leave if you like, Ms. Terrance." Two could play the formal game. "But would you mind if I asked you a couple of questions first?"

She released a deep sigh and leaned back against her father's wide mahogany desk. "I suppose. It's the least we can do given how we've wasted your time today."

Her tone gave every indication that she was merely indulging him. How generous of her. It shouldn't have irked him, but it did. He was used to dealing with some of the wealthiest, most privileged individuals on the planet. He'd seen more than his share of spoiled, entitled behavior. But coming from her, it sent prickles of irritation along his skin. He'd thought he knew her better.

"Do you have any idea who the sender might be?" he asked her.

She shook her head. "I get correspondence all the time."

"Has anyone else been as regular with their contacts as this admirer?"

She paused before answering. "No. He is the only one who emails regularly."

"How often would you say he does?"

"At least three times a week. He uses different addresses. But the sign-off is always the same. He calls himself Ani's Admirer."

"I see. When this all started, did you receive these messages with the same frequency?" When he'd first walked in, Adam had been convinced he wanted nothing to do with this assignment. That he was only here to indulge the request of a friend. So why was he now actually trying to convince Ani to hear him out?

He knew the answer, though he loathed to admit it. The moment he'd seen her, his protective instincts had kicked into high gear. The thought that she might actually be in some kind of danger wasn't sitting well, though he'd sworn to himself he wouldn't return to fieldwork. He didn't miss it at all. And the people who worked for him were more than capable without him.

But Ani was acting as if she were doing him the favor. He was downright foolish to continue standing here rather than accept the out she was giving him and simply walk away.

"No. At first he only sent them once a week or so," Ani answered.

"So things have escalated."

She crossed her arms in front of her chest. "I would hardly call a few emails an escalation."

"Have you at least changed your email address?" He couldn't seem to help the accusatory mocking in his tone.

This time, her irritation was obvious in the tight gritting of her teeth. "Of course I have. He seems to have somehow discovered what it was changed to."

"So he's determined and skilled."

The other two men in the room gasped with alarm. But Ani wasn't moved.

"Have you answered any of these emails?" Adam continued.

"Of course not."

"And what happens if he grows impatient?"

"Impatient?"

He nodded. "If he gets frustrated at your lack of response?"

"I guess we'll have to cross that bridge if we come to it." Adam didn't miss the emphasis on the *if*.

"Unless it's too late."

She defiantly lifted her chin. "Regardless, I do not need a personal bodyguard at the present." But her statement this time sounded a bit less certain, her voice wavering ever so slightly. "I simply don't see a need at this point."

He really didn't need this. So why wasn't he walking away already?

Ani stood glaring at him. Adam half expected her to stomp her foot before he gave her a small, affirmative nod. "If you say so, Ms. Terrance."

Ani had to resist the urge to stomp her foot. She most certainly didn't need a bodyguard. And she definitely didn't need him to be the overbearing, overly smug man that was Adam Steele. What nerve, to ask her if she'd taken the most basic precautions. What exactly did he take her for?

Brant and her father had really gone too far this time.

"Ani, please hear us out," her father pleaded. She hated that strain in his voice, hated that he was so worried about her. He overworried. He always had. Ever since the loss of her mother.

Adam turned to the other men. "Could we have a moment? Anikita and me. Alone?"

Ani started to protest but couldn't seem to summon any words. No way she wanted to be alone with him; her insides were quaking just being this close to him in the same room. She was likely to blither like an idiot if he got her alone. How could she not have gotten over a silly schoolgirl crush after all these years? Adam Steele may have changed in appearance, but he was still treating her like a pesky, ignorant child.

But her father and Brant didn't even hesitate. They swiftly walked out the door, shutting it quietly behind them.

"Your father and brother are very worried about you," Adam began as soon as they were alone.

She'd thought often over the years what it might be like to run into him. The scenario currently before her had never once crossed her mind.

"They tend to worry excessively."

"Maybe so. But I know your brother well enough to sense that it's different this time. He's very concerned."

"That's because he's used to having me near home. Where he or my father can keep an eye on me. I didn't even go away for university, I stayed in Dallas. They're both out of sorts because I'll be traveling to perform. That's all there is to it."

He shrugged. "You might be right. But I'm not the type who can live with myself if Brant's concern turns out to be warranted and I just walked away."

"Even if I'm the one asking you to?"

"I'm afraid so. And then there's your father."

Sweet honey on a cracker. Why did he have to go there? "So Brant told you?"

"Only that Edward had a health scare a couple months ago."

"His heart. He's being monitored very closely. By the finest cardiothoracic specialists in Dallas."

"Still, the last thing he needs is the added worry and stress about the safety of his only daughter."

Ani felt her resolve deflate like a pinned balloon. Of course she'd thought of all that. Had almost entertained the idea of canceling her mini performance tour. But ultimately, she'd decided against canceling. If she knew her father, the thought that he'd held her back from her dream would be no less traumatizing for him than his actual concern about her traveling.

She stood and rubbed a hand down her face. "Does it…? I mean, can we…?"

He merely quirked an eyebrow at her.

Better to just say it outright. "What I'm saying is, does it have to be you?" There. She'd just gone ahead and blurted it out.

A muscle twitched along his jaw. She'd hit a nerve. No doubt he was insulted by her question. Ani had a sudden urge to cry. What must Adam think of her? He probably took her as a spoiled, rich dilettante used to getting her own way, with how she was behaving. She'd actually signed an autograph for him thinking he was a fan, for heaven's sake. Adam no doubt thought her a snob with a superiority complex.

It was so far from reality.

The truth was, her sanity would be sorely tested if Adam Steele was the one guarding her. The two of them together as she traveled for her two performance dates. In close quarters. How in the world would she even be able to concentrate on her playing? He had no idea the affect he would have on her. The havoc he might wreak on her equilibrium. As much as she wanted to deny it, and as much as she wished it weren't so, he still had an effect on her. Just as he had when they were kids.

She'd only laid eyes on him again about thirty minutes ago and already she was behaving uncharacteristically— less like the accomplished musician she was and more like the silly schoolgirl who'd been shooed away at every turn.

Adam's answer was abrupt, and hardness rang in his voice. "You'll have a full detail. A team of professionals. But I'm the one in charge." Clearly, there'd be no arguing that. "As competent and highly trained as they are, all of those professionals work for me."

"I see."

"I'm the best there is." There was no bragging or conceit in his voice. Simply a matter of truth he had no qualms stating. "Trust me, I'm the man you want at the helm."

That was it. She had no response. But she wasn't about to fold completely either. "In that case, I'll agree to a trial run."

"What's that supposed to mean?"

"You have to realize this was all thrown at me unexpectedly. I have to wrap my head around it somehow."

"What do you suggest?"

"You accompany me to the first venue. The Le Trianon theater in Paris. After that trip, I need to have a heart-to-heart with my brother and father. Perhaps bring the Dallas authorities in, see what they have to say."

He studied her. "I know what they're going to say. Would you like me to tell you?"

She simply shrugged.

"They're going to say they'll put their cybersecurity guys on it. But your case will be low priority. As you said yourself, so far you're only dealing with a couple complimentary emails. After that, they'll tell you that without any specific threats or any kind of leads to go on, there isn't much they can do for you."

Ani had to fight the urge to bristle at his smug tone. "Nevertheless, it's all I can agree to at this point. You and your team accompany me to the first performance. After that, the four of us will revisit this whole matter."

He gave her an exaggerated nod that bordered on a slight bow. He was mocking her. "As you wish, Ms. Terrance."

She managed to stammer out a resigned thank-you, despite her annoyance. The man bothered her on so many levels.

I'm the man you want...

Little did he know, that was what scared her the most.

"Is this really necessary?" Ani asked in a defiant tone as she begrudgingly let Adam into her apartment.

"I'm just going to take a look around. Get a feel for your surroundings." He stepped past her through the doorway. "I'll study the outdoors on my way out when I leave."

He'd been satisfied enough by the footman at the high-rise building's entrance and the solid lock on her apartment door.

Her place wasn't quite what he would have expected. A grand piano sat in the corner. Music books were strewn about all over the floor. A book sat open on its face on the cream-colored couch that was the centerpiece of the room.

Behind the piano was an open doorway that led to a small kitchen. There was a pet bed next to a water dish, and a feed bowl against the wall on the opposite side.

"You have a dog?"

She nodded. "He's at doggy day care for a few more hours."

"Good. It's good to have a pet around, under the circumstances."

She released a small laugh and her eyes lit up with amusement. For an insane moment, Adam wished things could have been different between them. That he was somehow here to pick her up for a date and they were merely getting acquainted, learning about each other.

Maybe in a different universe.

He squashed the useless pining. Meaningful relationships with women weren't in his cards.

"He's hardly a guard dog," Ani said. "He's about twelve pounds."

Adam returned her smile. "Still, any dog is useful for alerting their owner to unexpected visitors."

She laughed again. "Right. You might change your mind about that when you see Snowball. He's more likely to lick any visitors with boundless affection."

A twelve-pound dog named Snowball. Clearly, they weren't speaking about a German shepherd or a Doberman.

He made his way to the window. Her blinds were open. Anyone in the building across the street would have an easy view into her apartment with the right eye gear. He would have to address that further with her at some point. Once they got past this trip to Paris.

He pulled his notebook out from his back pocket. "Does anyone else have a key to the apartment?"

"Just the building manager."

"No one else? A friend? The person who waters your plants?"

She shook her head. "No."

"A boyfriend?" Why was he holding his breath after asking that?

"No. I'm not seeing anyone seriously. Certainly not serious enough to share my key."

The unknotting at the base of his gut was not due to some sort of relief at her answer.

"Are you seeing anyone at all? On any dating sites? I'll need names if so."

She visibly bristled. "Is that really necessary? We seem to be getting into some personal areas here."

"It's my job to get this personal, Ani."

"Not yet, it isn't. Your assignment hasn't even begun."

"I beg to differ," he countered.

She planted her hands on her hips. "And I beg to argue."

Adam blew out a deep sigh. He wasn't going to debate the point with her. The time would come soon enough when she could no longer deny his involvement. And whether she liked it or not, he'd considered himself on the clock as soon as she'd walked into her father's office earlier.

"Nevertheless, we need to go over some ground rules."

Ani crossed her arms over her chest. "What sort of ground rules?"

"You need to keep your phone on at all times, so that I can track it."

She glared at him.

He continued, "Please forward me your password so that I can monitor your emails."

Her jaw fell open. "Some of those messages are personal."

"I'm sorry if this is uncomfortable for you. But some things are nonnegotiable."

She visibly gritted her teeth.

"Furthermore, don't make any sudden changes in plans. I need to know where you are and what you're doing at all times."

"You can't be serious. The tour hasn't even started yet."

He ignored that. "Do you have any plans for the rest of the day? When do you leave to pick up your dog?"

"He's getting dropped off here later by the day-care staff," she answered. Adam could have sworn she hesitated before she answered. "Why?" She wanted to know.

"I told you. You're not to go anywhere without letting me know exactly where you're going and the timing."

A tinge of red appeared on her cheeks. "This is preposterous. Please tell me my father and brother didn't agree to any of this."

"It just so happens they did."

Before she could argue further, he made his way down the hall to her bedroom.

"Hey, wait a minute," she protested behind him.

He halted in his tracks at the urgency in her voice. "Is there a problem?"

She brushed past him, rubbing against his shoulder in the process. A delicate flowery scent tickled his nostrils as she moved by. "I wasn't exactly expecting company. Give me a chance to pick up some things."

Adam leaned back against the wall. He felt off balance, out of sorts. This wasn't how his usual gigs worked. Never before had he been assigned a VIP who didn't want his protection. Not to mention, he'd been out of the field for the better part of two years. It was all throwing him off. Not at all how he liked to run his game. Even the smallest mistake could be too costly.

He should have asked her for permission before trying to enter her bedroom. She probably had all sorts of personal items lying about. After all, it was probably where she undressed.

He made certain to stop that train of thought completely in its tracks.

He entered the room when she gave him the okay moments later. The shades were pulled wide open here as well.

"Do you keep these blinds open mostly?"

Her mouth formed a tight thin line. "Only when I want natural sunlight. That's their purpose after all, isn't it?"

"At all times? What if you're not dressed?"

Ani gasped.

"Did it ever occur to you that someone might be watching?"

"If you're asking if I prance around the apartment naked with my shades wide open, the answer is no. Obviously."

Adam bit out a curse. Again, he found himself redirecting the path of his thoughts. How utterly, shamefully unprofessional. What the hell was wrong with him? He'd convinced himself that he could handle this assignment because he owed it to his friend.

One thing was certain, he had to refocus and pull it together or he was bound to make a mistake. His new VIP was distracting him like none other before.

He knew firsthand and all too well exactly how costly distractions could be.

Ani watched Adam leave her apartment twenty minutes later and blew out a breath as she shut the door behind him. That had gone even worse than she'd anticipated.

He sure seemed to take up a lot of space. His mere presence in her living quarters had made her edgy and tense. She was too aware of all the pure masculinity he exuded. And when he strode into her bedroom, she'd wanted to kick herself for the wayward thoughts that had shot through her head like a mini movie. If someone had told her years ago that Adam Steele would be standing in the middle of her bedroom, she would have offered to sell them a bridge.

More was the pity, considering the frustrating reason for his presence.

She had to stop thinking of him like that. He was only a temporary fixture in her life for the next few weeks. For all the wrong reasons. Once her two-city performance tour ended, Adam would go back to being the unreachable, distant teenage crush from her past just as he'd been all along. Nothing more.

Well, he may think his responsibility toward her had already started. But he was wrong, as far as she was concerned. She hadn't agreed to any of this. And she still had a few days of freedom left before the tour started and Adam became an unwanted presence in her daily life.

She hadn't really lied to him earlier about her plans for the day. She'd simply answered only the question about having to leave to get her dog. That part of it was completely true. Snowball was due to be delivered to her later this evening by one of the doggy day-care staffers. As far as the rest of it, that really wasn't any of his business. Not yet.

She waited several moments after he'd left before returning to her bedroom closet. She slipped off the summer dress and replaced it with her most comfortable pair of jeans and a soft cotton blouse. Pulling her hair up, she secured it in a large tortoise shell clip.

Then she sneaked out of her apartment.

Adam had just finished making some cursory notes outside about Ani's block when he saw a familiar figure exit her building. He watched as she strode confidently to the street and hailed a cab.

What the…? It couldn't have been more than twenty minutes since he'd left her apartment. Where exactly was she going?

Better question was, why hadn't she mentioned her plans to leave?

Was this about a man? She'd been quite hesitant to answer his questions about dating. Perhaps she was going to meet someone right now. But why the secrecy?

Without hesitation, he jogged to his parked car and began to follow her. Every turn took them farther out of greater Dallas. Chic boutiques and swanky restaurants gradually gave way to boarded up buildings and graffiti brick walls. About four miles later, the cab came to a stop.

Adam pulled up behind them and parked his car as Ani exited out the passenger side of the taxi. When she noticed his presence, her surprise quickly collapsed into an expression of clear anger. She stomped her way over to where he stood next to his car.

"What are you doing here?" she demanded.

"I could ask you the same question. I thought you said you weren't going anywhere the rest of the day."

She narrowed her eyes at him. "No. I said nothing of the kind."

Adam pinched the bridge of his nose. Great. Now she was arguing semantics with him. The truth was, she'd deliberately misled him. "You were less than forthcoming."

"Never mind that. Did you just secretly follow me?"

Adam couldn't help a bristle of irritation. She had a lot of nerve stepping out on him like this and then acting as if she was the affronted party. "If it had been a secret, you wouldn't have any idea I was here, sweetheart."

The deep red flush of her cheeks deepened. "Don't call me that!"

Her demand took his ire down a peg. She was right. It

was highly unprofessional of him, past history or not. "We should talk about that, by the way," he told her.

"About what, exactly?"

"How you didn't even notice there was a car trailing you all that time. You need to be more aware of your surroundings."

She countered with an exaggerated eye roll. "You had no right to follow me."

"I beg to differ. What are you doing here, anyway?" He glanced up at the sign hanging above the doorway of the gray stone building they stood in front of.

Plano Street Youth Center.

"I hardly see how it's any of your business. Now, if you'll excuse me."

She turned on her heel but Adam stopped her departure with a gentle but firm grip on her elbow. She seared him with a look of outrage.

"Sorry, Ms. Terrance. Not so fast. You may think our association hasn't started yet, but you'd be wrong. It started the moment I left your father's office earlier today after signing a contract. Now please answer the question. What are you doing here?"

She tugged her arm free with so much force, Adam worried for a moment that she might actually topple backward. "See for yourself. If you must." With that, she strode toward the entrance.

Adam released a deep breath and slowly counted to ten. Then he took a moment to pray for patience. He had to make sure to maintain an emotional distance here. The guilt would eat him alive if he failed in his duty yet again.

He followed her inside.

CHAPTER TWO

SHE JUST HAD to get through this trip.

Ani settled into the soft leather seat of the private jet they'd boarded moments before. Adam's jet. He'd insisted they take his private aircraft to Paris rather than follow through with the travel plans the tour management company had made for her. Controlling to the last.

As if she didn't have enough of that in her life.

How hard would it be? She would be plenty busy. Between rehearsing and performing, she had more than enough to keep her mind off her complicated feelings for the man accompanying her. He'd made her so angry, following her to the youth center three days ago. But then he'd sat there patiently for hours while she worked with the kids.

He'd driven her home afterward and mumbled what might be described as an apology, for upsetting her about being followed, explaining that he was only doing his job. He almost sounded conciliatory, regretful. It was a side of him she hadn't really seen before nor expected to see.

Now, she tried not to turn and stare at him behind her. He sat at a round conference table with his crew. Two other men and two women. They appeared to be going over procedure with open blueprint plans of the concert hall spread out in front of them.

It was all so unnecessary. Much ado about nothing.

Moira, her manager and dear friend, approached, providing a much-needed distraction. "You should try to get some rest," she suggested, sitting down in the leather seat next to her.

Like that was possible. Ani's nerves were stretched much too thin thinking about her bodyguard. The fact that she had one still felt like a foreign notion.

"I'll try," she fibbed. "How's Snowball?"

"Resting comfortably in his pen in the back. He seems very unexcited about his trip." She waved a hand at their surroundings. "Not too shabby. This certainly beats flying commercial. Even if we would have been traveling first class. Your fella coming along seems to have its benefits."

"He's certainly not my fella, Moira. Just a friend of my overprotective and paranoid brother. The brother who thinks I'm in unacceptable peril and I need a big, strong crew of babysitters to accompany me on my first trip overseas."

"Well, I'm not going to complain. I'm not sure why you are either." Moira glanced behind them. "That's a whole lot of handsome sitting in one spot."

Ani shrugged. "I haven't really noticed."

Moira rolled her eyes. "That's what I mean. You never notice. Men are staring at you all the time. And you won't give anyone the time of day."

"I don't really have time to give. I would think my manager would appreciate such focus on my craft."

Moira nodded. "Sure I do. But I don't exactly want you to behave like a nun either. There's more to life, you know. When was the last time you even went out on a date?"

Ani sighed. She wasn't really in the mood to talk about her social life. Or lack thereof. It had been bad enough trying to ditch Adam's questions when he'd been the one asking. "Let's just say my last boyfriend wanted more than I was ready or willing to give." She'd found herself gradually acquiescing to more and more of his requests and increasingly resenting him for it.

"I see," Moira said, as if she hadn't heard the story before. She glanced behind them once more. "But have you ever seen such a gorgeous group?"

One of the men looked up as if sensing Moira's attention. They shared a smile. Moira's cheeks turned pink. Ani had never seen the no-nonsense businesswoman flush before. This might be an interesting trip in more ways than one.

"I think you might need to go get some ice water from the minibar, Moira."

The other woman fanned her face. "Not a bad idea. Can I get you anything?" she asked, standing.

"No, thanks. I'm good."

That description was short-lived. Adam came to sit in the seat only moments after Moira had evacuated it. Would Ani's heart ever stop missing a beat whenever the man approached? He was dressed casually yet professionally in a crisp black T-shirt and pressed khaki pants.

"Ready for takeoff?"

She wasn't ready for any of this. It was hard enough to accept her new reality. She was actually a performing artist with an audience. All the years of hard work and training would finally amount to a career she might be proud of. But it was a demanding one. And now she had the complication of Adam Steele to contend with on top of it all.

"Not really. I'm also not so sure I'm ready for all the rest either," she admitted, surprising herself somewhat. So far, she hadn't actually discussed her anxiety about the mounting pressure of her career with anyone, not even Moira. No, the only way she'd even voiced any of it out loud was during one of the many imaginary conversations she still had with her mother before she began her warm-up whenever she practiced. "It's all a bit scary," she added.

He turned to face her, and for an insane moment, she thought he might actually reach out and touch her. But his hands stayed firmly by his side. "You can feel safe with me. I won't let anyone get near you."

He'd misunderstood. She hadn't been referring to her so-called admirer. Maybe she was being naive about the potential for danger in that respect. But she was so used to Brant and her father blowing things out of proportion where her well-being was concerned.

"It's not that. Not really. I guess I just never stopped to think how overwhelming all of this would feel. Not until it was too late to back out."

Adam studied her face for several beats. "Listen, Ani. You deserve this," he said, surprising her. "You deserve your success. I know you can handle it."

Perhaps he did understand, after all.

He hadn't meant to say all that.

Adam shifted in his seat and wondered why he'd said any of it. His words were too personal. He wasn't here to be Ani's friend—he was here to protect her. His only excuse was that he'd been reading about her over the past couple of days. She was an instant celebrity, totally unprepared for the sudden glare of the spotlight. In interview after interview, she mostly recounted how dreamlike her life had become, how out of place she felt in this new world she found herself in. She wasn't exactly a pop star gracing the pages of music websites, but her pure raw talent and striking good looks had caught the attention of music lovers all over the world.

Another recurring theme in those interviews was how

she wished her mother was still around to support her and
to celebrate her success.

"Thank you for saying that," she finally replied. "It
helps to hear it."

"You're welcome."

The air between them grew awkward. It behooved him
to change the subject to less personal matters. "How long
have you been volunteering?"

"At the youth center? About three or so years. I performed in a charity event for them, and afterward a lot
of the kids came up to say how much they'd enjoyed my
playing."

"So you ended up volunteering to provide piano lessons." It didn't surprise him in the least. "That's quite a
gift you're giving those kids."

A genuine smile of affection graced her lips. "Those
kids give just as much in return. Just watching their hard
work and joy from learning to play enriches my life in so
many ways."

He wanted to tell her just how much she must mean to
those kids. She probably had no clue. He'd spent hours and
hours at just such a center as a kid himself. His mother had
left when he was barely a teen, and with no father around,
he'd been foisted off to live with his aunt and uncle at the
age of thirteen. That was when he'd met Brant and all the
other kids in that rural town just outside of Dallas, Texas.
Most of them were friendly enough, but there were always the snobbish few who kept reminding him that he
didn't fit in.

And they were right. He'd never really belonged.

But there was no use in getting into all that with Ani.
Again, it was much too personal. She was simply his job
for the moment. Nothing more.

So why was he still sitting here next to her when he

should be going over more details with his crew? Why did he want to spend the bulk of this flight in this chair chatting with her as they got reacquainted? It made no sense.

But he wanted to know what her life had been like in the years since he'd last seen her. How had the opportunity to play in Paris come about?

Why there was no significant other accompanying her on this trip?

It was a question that he had to eventually ask, from a professional standpoint. He needed to know if a past boyfriend might be behind those mysterious emails. But Adam had to admit his curiosity ran deeper than that. He hadn't stopped thinking about her since the day in her father's office.

That was completely irresponsible and unacceptable. Adam had way too much baggage for the likes of Ani Terrance. He had way too much baggage for anyone. She was a musical talent on the verge of a career most people could only dream about. And she'd already dealt with enough heartbreak and loss in her life.

He had nothing to offer someone like her, couldn't risk the inevitable failure of letting her down as he would most certainly do. Judging by his history.

I can't let you keep holding me back. The feminine voice echoed in his mind as if he were hearing it again this very moment.

"Looks like we're about to take off," he told her, pushing away the wayward memories. "Make yourself comfortable." He stood to leave and go back to join his crew.

"Wait!"

The urgency in her voice gave him pause. "Is something wrong?"

She bit down on her lip. "It's just—I don't fly that often.

And I don't seem to see Moira. It's just as the plane lifts off the ground. After that, I should be fine."

"You don't want to be alone at takeoff."

She ducked her head with an embarrassed smile. "It's silly, I know. Once we're in the air, I'm sure I'll be totally fine. I just…need a distraction."

How was he supposed to deny her request? Adam sat back down and the relief in her sigh was clear. "It's not silly, Ani."

"Thanks."

The plane began its taxi journey and Ani's hands gripped the armrests so tight that her knuckles turned white. He had to resist the urge to reach over and take her hands into his, to try to soothe her anxiety.

"Is this the part where I should distract you?"

She gulped and nodded. "Please."

"Tell me more about the kids you teach. What are they like?"

The tension seemed to melt away from her face. It was replaced with an affectionate, soft expression. "They're so amazing. They each have their challenges with the lot they've been given in life. But none of that seems to have deterred them from reaching for their goals and dreams. They leave me in awe most days."

A sudden sadness appeared in her face as the plane took off. "In many ways, the time I spend with those kids leaves me feeling closer to my own mother." She looked away quickly but not before he caught the slight sheen of tears in her eyes.

"How so?" he prodded, not even caring that they'd somehow broached yet another subject that was much too personal. Why did discussing all this with her feel so natural?

"It just reminds me of all the times I sat beside her as a little girl on the bench while she played." She swiped at her cheeks with the back of her hand. "I like to think she'd be as proud of me as I am of those kids at the center."

Adam couldn't help it. Despite all the reasons to avoid touching her at all costs, this time, he did reach over and take her hand in his.

"I have no doubt of it, Ani. How could she not be?"

So much for keeping her distance from Adam.

Ani couldn't believe what she'd shared with him back on the jet. He'd held her hand. She rubbed her palm over her wrist. She could almost still feel the warmth of his touch.

That tidbit about how volunteering at the center helped her remember her mother wasn't something she'd shared with anyone. Not even her brother or father. And not Moira, who happened to be riding up the hotel elevator with her right now.

They'd arrived in Paris to a beautiful, sunny day. Ani should be elated. She'd always wanted to visit this city. And here she was, under circumstances she would never have dreamed for herself. About to perform for a French audience full of people who'd paid months in advance for the chance to see her.

But all she could think about was the man who'd accompanied her here.

Moira must have somehow read her mind. "You seem off in a distant place," she began as the elevator moved upward. "Any chance you're thinking about a tall, dark-haired bodyguard who happened to sit with you for most of the flight here?"

Ani avoided looking at her friend. "I was nervous about flying. He was just being a gentleman, trying to ease my anxiety."

Moira huffed. "That man gives off all sorts of vibes, but gentlemanly is not one of them."

Luckily, the dinging of the elevator spared Ani the need to answer. When they reached her suite, three hotel employees were already there with her luggage, her equipment, and Snowball. The dog perked up in his pen when he saw her, his tail wagging furiously with happiness.

"Look who's awake," Ani cooed, lifting her devoted pet. Her thank-you was a flurry of sandpaper-tongue licks. "You were a good boy on the plane. Yes, you were. Who's my good boy?"

Moira giggled at the spectacle, no doubt because of the exaggerated voice Ani was using to greet her pup.

The sound of someone clearing their throat behind them had Ani halting midnuzzle. She could just guess who it was standing in the doorway. The throat clearing was quickly followed by an all-too-familiar masculine voice: "Hello."

Ani quickly put Snowball back in his crate, to the animal's deep upset judging by his immediate yelping.

"Uh, hi. I was just…saying hi to my dog."

Moira giggled again. Ani resisted the urge to give her friend a small nudge.

"Can I come in?" Adam asked, still standing in the doorway.

Ani nodded.

"I just want to take a quick look at the room, check out the locks, that sort of thing." Adam strode into the suite with his usual air of authority. She could have sworn she saw one of the bellhops give a small bow at his entrance.

"Sure thing."

"I was just leaving," Moira announced and followed the hotel employees out the door. She firmly shut it closed behind her.

Traitor.

Ani swallowed the ball of apprehension lodged in her throat. It was one thing to sit side by side with Adam in a jet full of others. But being alone with him always seemed to throw her off balance. And now they were alone in a luxurious hotel room overlooking the Seine. She wondered how many couples must have honeymooned in this very suite. Her mind brought up all sorts of unwanted images, all of them starring a very sexy and brooding bodyguard who happened to be staring at her dog at the moment.

"What's that?" he asked, pointing to where Snowball sat still whining in his crate.

"*That* is my dog. Snowball."

Adam looked over at her and crossed his arms in front of his chest. "You are a liar, Ms. Terrance."

Ani bit back a gasp. "What's that supposed to mean?"

"That is clearly a rabbit or hare of some sort."

It was only then that she noticed the tiniest tug of a smile around his lips. She thrust her hands on her hips in mock offense. "You must apologize to my fierce and loyal guard dog at once."

"You mean your guard bunny?" He pointed down at Snowball once more. "Look at those ears. Only bunny rabbits have ears that long and pointy. And he's as cottony white as any rabbit I've ever seen."

"Well, I never." Ani leaned down and picked up her dog. "We don't have to listen to this, do we, Snowball?" She made an exaggerated show of walking away.

Only, Snowball had other plans. He practically leaped out of her arms toward Adam.

Adam caught the animal just in time. Impressive reflexes, though she shouldn't be surprised. It was Adam's turn to be on the receiving end of wet doggy kisses.

"*Et tu*, Snowball?" How many traitors were in her orbit, anyway?

"Oh, yeah. He's definitely fierce, all right," Adam said

in a muffled voice as he unsuccessfully tried to duck from all the canine kisses.

Ani couldn't hold back the laughter any longer. Come to think of it, she couldn't quite recall the last time she'd so much as giggled, let alone indulged in a good, hearty belly laugh, what with the pressure of the tour, the stress of knowing her brother and father were so worried about her and the sorrow of missing her mother during such a momentous time in her life. But somehow, in this moment, she was finally enjoying some humor.

She threw a glance at Adam who was now playfully nuzzling the dog, and had to admit what she didn't want to face. He was the reason she was finally enjoying herself.

The last time Adam had interacted with a dog, it was a German shepherd trained to sniff out explosives. He hardly knew what to do with one this small and…energetic.

"Looks like you made a new friend," Ani said after a steady stream of laughter.

He set down the dog and studied her. "I really hope so, kitten."

The amusement dropped away in an instant. So she remembered; he saw it on her facial expression.

He hadn't meant to call her by the name he'd used for her all those years ago when they were both kids. Back then, he'd been mocking her. He'd been all kinds of a jerk as a teen. Mostly to cover up the hurt and embarrassment of his existence. Unfortunately, Ani had been one of his targets.

What kind of name is that? Anikita? I can't pronounce that. I'll just call you kitty. Or kitten. Or maybe kitty cat.

He ducked his head with embarrassment at the memory. "Listen, I was kind of a jerk to you when we were younger. I should apologize for that."

"No apology necessary. It was a long time ago."

"Maybe. But I shouldn't have been such an—"

She held her hand up to stop him before he could continue.

"I guess I took it as some sort of compliment." She looked away as a pink flush crept into her cheeks. "You didn't seem to have any kind of nickname for anyone else. It was almost a term of endearment as far as I was concerned. Silly, I know."

Adam reached over to run a finger down her cheek. He couldn't seem to eradicate this strong urge to touch her. "Only thing silly about it is that you apparently gave me way too much credit. You should have given me a hard smack across the forehead."

She snorted. "As if. You were much bigger than me. I wouldn't have risked the potential retaliation."

Adam felt the color drain from his face. He prayed she was joking. A tremor of horror traveled up his spine. She couldn't have ever thought that way about him, ever thought that he might strike her or any other woman for that matter.

It was bad enough that his error in judgment had caused such injury and suffering. He would never get over the guilt. An image of Tonya's bruised and damaged body assaulted his mind, and his blood ran cold.

"Are you okay?" Ani asked, as if sensing his discomfort. Her eyes held his for countless moments. Neither one seemed able to move. He thought he might have stopped breathing.

"I would never have so much as touched you, kitten. Not under any circumstances."

A knock sounded on the door before he could say any more.

Ani didn't tear her gaze away from his. "I should get

that," she announced, but stood still where she was. As if waiting for him to concur.

He was about to tell her to ignore it, that they had some things to discuss. But the knock came again, louder this time.

Ani studied him a second longer before releasing a deep sigh. She turned away to get the door.

He finally came to his senses and stopped her with a gentle grip on her elbow. "Let me."

A look through the peephole revealed a well-heeled, tall man in a designer suit and hair slicked back within an inch of its survival. A pair of piercing blue eyes and angular cheekbones rounded out the look of a native Parisian son.

"Were you expecting someone?" Adam asked Ani over his shoulder.

"I was told someone from the theater might stop by upon my arrival. Just to go over some things."

Adam opened the door a few inches.

"Bonjour," the man said with a smile. "My name is Philippe Penault. I'm here to see Mademoiselle Terrance. I'm with the Le Trianon theater," he added with a thick French accent.

There was no doubt the man was exactly who he said he was. Adam stepped aside to let him in. Philippe didn't hesitate to make a beeline to Ani and landed a small peck to the back of her hand.

Adam watched as the two exchanged introductions and pleasantries. The man was the epitome of sophistication and elegant charm. Qualities Adam would never hope to have. Something tightened in his gut as he watched Ani smile at the stranger, displaying a rudimentary knowledge of French. He knew a bit himself, having owned property in France for the past several years now.

Still, he felt a bit like the help watching his employer

with a guest. Which was essentially an accurate description...

No matter how much money he had now or how successful he'd become professionally, Adam knew when he didn't fit in. Just as he hadn't as a kid in that tiny little town he and Ani had grown up in.

Now, Philippe was asking Ani to accompany him to a nearby café to discuss her upcoming performance in his theater. Adam interrupted before she could answer.

"I don't think that's a good idea," he declared in English. There was no way he was letting Ani out of his sight in this city. And somehow, he didn't think he'd be extended an invitation by Philippe.

Ani's jaw dropped. "Why ever not?"

Adam crossed his arms in front of his chest, bracing for the argument sure to follow. What kind of question was that? Didn't she know he had a job to do? He was in charge of her security detail. That responsibility included things like not letting her wander around an unfamiliar city with a man she'd literally just met.

His irritation had nothing to do with how handsome this Philippe was. Nor the way he was looking at Ani as if she were a delicate piece of pastry he couldn't wait to get alone to himself.

Jealousy had nothing to do with it, he reassured the nagging voice in his head. He was simply doing his job.

Adam spoke French. Maybe not fluently, but enough to hold a pretty steady conversation with the rep from the theater. Ani glanced at him now sitting at a nearby table scrolling on his smartphone. They'd agreed to head to a nearby sidewalk café. She and Philippe sat alone going over some of the details about her performance tomorrow night. Adam's eyes may have been on his screen but Ani had no doubt his attention was laser focused on her.

She'd stood and watched with her mouth agape back in the hotel room as he'd explained to Philippe, mostly in French, that he was in charge of her security and he wasn't about to let her out of his sight. He certainly hadn't asked her for any say in the matter.

She wasn't sure whether to be furious, embarrassed or downright impressed with his communication skills. The man was a constant source of surprise. And a frequent source of pure, unfiltered frustration.

Focus. Ani forced her attention back to the tablet Philippe had set down on the table between them. They were going over last-minute details to ensure a smooth performance, hopefully resulting in glowing reviews. She appreciated that the venue was going the extra mile to ensure she had a successful night. This was her career, after all. At the least, she owed this man her full, undistracted attention. But her gaze seemed to constantly drift to her dark, brooding bodyguard who sat a few feet away.

Several of the tables around them were occupied by couples who appeared completely enamored with each other. Old and young alike. Paris certainly seemed to be the city of love as reputed. Many of them held hands. One couple kept feeding each other pieces of cake.

It had never occurred to Ani before that she wanted that experience with someone. She wanted to sit at a romantic café by the Seine as the lights slowly flickered on around the city with the Eiffel Tower looming like a majestic steel mountain in the distance. She wanted to have her lover offer her a piece of his fruit crepe, then slowly wipe her lips with his napkin. Afterward, they would hold hands as they entered their small apartment. Then later they would indulge in a night full of passion in each other's arms.

Ani reached for her sparkling wine and took a long sip.

Heaven help her, Adam was the man she was imagining in all those scenarios. Though he hardly seemed the type to delicately feed a woman cake. In fact, the very notion was almost laughable.

An audible giggle actually escaped her lips. Adam even looked up, gave her what could only be described as a glare.

What was wrong with him? What did he have against amusement, anyway? He'd seemed happy enough when she was laughing about Snowball back in the hotel room when they'd been alone.

She looked up to find Philippe studying her questioningly. "*Pardon*, mademoiselle," he began in French before adding in accented English, "You appear a bit distracted. Is everything all right?"

Ani wanted to kick herself. This was her career, for heaven's sake. Damn Adam Steele for the way he was distracting her from something so important.

"I'm so sorry, Philippe. I don't mean to drift off."

He gave her a charming smile. "But it is I who should be sorry. You must be exhausted after your long day of travel." He powered off the tablet. "That is enough for now. I have no doubt you'll be magnificent tomorrow night. Please call if you need anything in the meantime."

The man had barely pulled his chair back when Adam materialized by their table. He was certainly fast on his feet. Yet another talent.

"Finished?"

"*Oui*," Philippe answered. "Do you two know your way back to the hotel?"

"We'll manage." Adam sounded somewhat dismissive and needlessly curt. What was his problem all of a sudden? They seemed to have had a minor truce starting during the flight and then later in the suite with Snowball. He'd even called her kitten and apologized for giving her the nickname to begin with. Now he was acting surly and annoyed all over again.

She'd had very little experience with the opposite sex. As intrusive and overprotective as her father and brother were, most of her boyfriends were either scared off before things turned serious or she wasn't interested enough to invest in the effort her family would put her through. The closest thing she'd ever had to a boyfriend had been a selfish and demanding oil heir unwilling to compromise in the slightest way. Besides, her exhaustive practice schedule and long daily lessons left very little time for a social life.

It wasn't as if she was some virginal maiden. But her realm of experience was vastly limited. She may have been intimate with a man in the past, but she'd never actually felt close to one. She simply didn't have the necessary skill set to try to decipher a man like Adam.

She just hated that she wanted to try so badly.

Philippe glanced between Adam and Ani, still seated in her chair. "Might I suggest walking along the river to get back? This time of evening, it's quite romantic."

Was it her imagination or had he emphasized the last word unnecessarily? Dropping a small peck on her cheek, he gave Adam a small nod before walking away.

One thing was certain, Adam wouldn't be at all interested in any type of stroll, particularly a romantic one along the Seine. She glanced at the walkway leading to the riverbank with abject longing and sighed. Maybe tomorrow morning she could bring Snowball here and take him on a nice, long walk. Who needed a man when she had her trusted canine companion?

But he surprised her yet again with his next words.

"I could use some fresh air and exercise." He extended his hand. "I say we take Philippe up on his suggestion."

It took a moment for the words to register in her brain, for her to convince herself that she'd actually heard him correctly. Wordlessly, she placed her fingers in his open palm over the table. Still, she couldn't seem to get her legs to work and stand up until Adam gave her hand a small tug.

"What do you say, kitten? Come walk with me."

CHAPTER THREE

"ACTUALLY, I'VE CHANGED my mind."

Adam's announcement as they reached the riverbank had Ani halting in her tracks. She knew it! Whatever had compelled him to suggest going on this stroll with her, he'd up and changed his mind. Nothing like getting a girl's hopes up. He really did have whiplash-inducing mood swings.

She bit down on her frustration and tried to settle the tide of anger threatening to burst through the surface of her calm facade. When was she going to get a chance like this again? She liked to think she'd get another opportunity to come back to Paris. To sit in another café, maybe even with a man. To walk with him as they took in the beautiful sight of Paris in the evening.

But she wanted that experience here and now. Even if the man currently present was only here as a favor to her brother, who was paying him to keep an eye on her.

"Fine," she bit out, turning on her heel to walk back to the hotel.

"Whoa." Adam stopped her with a touch at the small of her back. Even in her ire, she felt the electricity through the thin fabric of her dress.

"Where are you going?" he asked.

"Back to the hotel. You said you changed your mind."

He smiled at her, a twinkle of mischief in his eye. "Just about the walk."

Well, that was something of a relief. She eyed a nearby park bench. He didn't seem the type to sit around and people watch for fun. But what did she really know?

"Hang on a second," he ordered, then stepped a few feet away. She watched as he made a phone call and proceeded to converse in French with whoever was on the other line. When he was done, he came over to her once more.

"Here, let's go." He guided her along, again with the hand at her back just above the waist. The contact was wreaking havoc with her emotions.

"Where are we going?"

"You'll see."

A minute or so later, they approached a docked, glass-covered canopy boat. She could see a number of tables on board topped with white linen cloths and lit candles.

"It occurred to me neither of us really had a chance to have dinner."

She couldn't seem to summon the words as he guided her to the vessel and helped her on board.

"Uh...you arranged for a dinner cruise? Right there on the pathway?"

He shrugged. "I have a few contacts in the city. We can do something else if you're not up for it."

Was he serious? She'd have to be daft to turn this opportunity down. She told him as much.

A tuxedoed crew member greeted them and led them to a table. The glass canopy made for an amazing view and they hadn't even left the dock yet. Ani had to bite back her excitement. This was so unexpected. A girl could get used to such surprises.

Oh, yeah. Despite his tendency to frequently and consistently heighten her emotions, Ani figured she could get used to Adam Steele in all manner of ways.

A sommelier appeared before she'd even had a chance to fully be seated. The woman greeted them with a smile and popped open a chilled bottle of champagne. At Adam's nod, the smiling woman started to pour the bubbly liquid into two tall glass flutes.

Adam lifted his glass as soon as the sommelier walked away. "A toast to your upcoming performance."

"Thank you." Ani clinked her glass to his and took a small sip. The buttery, crisp taste exploded on her tongue. It was exquisite, a burst of flavor filling her mouth and running over her tongue.

Her senses were in overdrive. Watching scene after charming scene as they floated along the river, the taste of the rich champagne and the lure of the man sitting across from her made for a heady mixture of emotion.

Ani watched in awe as the boat passed a group of young adults dancing along the river's edge. The Eiffel Tower stood majestically in the distance, breathtakingly lit up.

"I couldn't have imagined a better way to spend the evening, Adam. I don't know how I'll be able to repay you for this."

He gave her a smile that made her stomach do a little flip. "No need. I'm glad you're enjoying yourself."

She didn't get a chance to respond as yet another server appeared with two salads. Or maybe salad wasn't the right word. On her plate sat a work of art—a romaine leaf topped with perfectly cubed avocado and bright red sliced tomato surrounded by a smattering of exotic-looking herbs laid out in an eye-pleasing design. Ani fought hard to resist the urge to pull out her phone and take a photo. That would look less than sophisticated in such a setting. She didn't want to appear like the awestruck tourist that she was.

The main course was a seared fish fillet topped with a drizzle of zesty plum sauce. It was followed by an airy dessert of fruit-topped macarons that practically melted in her mouth.

"This is perfect," she announced, stabbing a fork into a plump slice of strawberry. "I don't like to eat too heavy before a performance day. This was the ideal meal, light and delicious."

"Glad to hear it."

Ani leaned back to take in the breathtaking view of the riverside as their plates were cleared and the interior lights dimmed even further.

"You speak French," she ventured at last.

He gave a small shrug. "It was my assigned language class in school. Picked it up some more during a couple tours overseas. Then when I bought property out here, it was pretty much immersion learning."

Ani knew she was being silly, but she couldn't help the feeling of inadequacy that washed over her. Adam was worldly, successful and knowledgeable. By contrast, most of her life had been spent honing her musical skills and trying to pick up the pieces of her shattered family after their tragic loss.

"You look like you traveled a thousand miles in your head just now," Adam told her with a small smile.

She hadn't meant to drift off. "I was just admiring the city. It's taking my breath away."

"First time in Paris will have that effect. I take it you haven't been here before."

She shook her head. "No."

"I must say I'm a little surprised. Considering... Never mind."

She knew what he'd been about to say. Her family had certainly had the means. Not only did her father come from money, he'd inherited a successful business and grown it. Of course, there'd been opportunities to travel. She just hadn't wanted to leave home. Not until her father had somehow finished grieving. Only, he never really had.

"I would have loved to," she admitted. "Just didn't ever really get a chance."

Not with a father and older brother to look after. Brant himself had been in no condition to lend any kind of emotional support to their grieving parent. She either had to step up or watch her father withdraw further from the world and life in general.

"Why is that?" Adam probed.

Surprisingly, she didn't find herself annoyed by the question. This wasn't a topic she normally opened up about. But for some reason, it felt natural to do so with Adam. Probably because she'd known him as a child. What other reason could there be?

"My father needed me around," she found herself explaining. "So did Brant. Neither were interested in taking any kind of vacation. Dad sort of immersed himself in his work." And Brant had withdrawn.

"Sounds like you took on a lot at a young age."

"I had to." She sucked in a deep breath. "The thing about having a devoted and loving parent is the unbearable depth of grief that results from their loss." She studied her fingernails. She'd never said as much out loud before. Despite living with those exact thoughts every single day.

Adam was quiet for a long while before he finally spoke. "I guess I wouldn't know."

Ani found herself asking the question she'd wondered about for the past several years, ever since she'd first met him. "How did you come to live with your aunt and uncle?"

Another shrug. "No big mystery. My old man just left one day. And my mother split soon after."

She didn't have the words to respond to that—the concept was so incomprehensible. Despite the unbearable pain, she'd been lucky to have her mom for the short amount of time Ani had been given with her.

A strange yet comfortable silence ensued between them until Adam finally broke it. "Should I order another bottle of champagne?"

"Absolutely not. Not for me, anyway." As tempted as she was by the offer, she did have to perform tomorrow. Bubbly that good was easy to overindulge in. Not to mention, she didn't want to risk too much of a drop in her inhibitions around this man. She had already confided much more than she had ever intended to.

Although, he seemed to have confided as well. She couldn't be too cross with herself. She could chalk it up to two old friends simply catching up. Though her feelings for him were starting to edge out of friendship boundaries.

"In that case, let's go above deck," he suggested. "We're approaching the Eiffel Tower. We can watch it from the outside."

He walked around the table and pulled her chair out. Once more, she felt his hand at the small of her back as he guided her above deck. He had no idea what that intimate touch did to her insides. Probably because he didn't view it as intimate at all. He probably wouldn't give it a second thought. Whereas she felt warmth resonate from his hand and travel all the way down to her toes.

He wasn't usually an impulsive man. In fact, he was characteristically calm and controlled. Every minute of his day was typically planned out. Tonight, he was supposed to have gone back to his hotel room, gone over some more details about the layout of the theater with his crew and then answered some emails. Afterward, he'd planned to work on a bid for an expansion of his firm into the Eastern European market. But then Philippe had mentioned a stroll along the riverbank and Ani's eyes had taken on a wistful look at the suggestion.

Admittedly, he had taken things to a whole other level by arranging for a dinner cruise for the two of them. He couldn't even explain it to himself.

Not that he regretted it. And therein was the real kicker. It was a beautiful night. Paris, as usual, didn't disappoint. He was glad to be out here, watching the sights of this dynamic, historic city with Ani Terrance.

She sighed next to him as they leaned over the railing, watching as the Eiffel Tower approached. "My kids would love to see this. I'm going to try to find a way to fund a trip when I get back."

"They mean a lot to you, don't they? The kids you teach."

Her features softened as she smiled. "They're family. Particularly the girls. Like the sisters I never had. I like to think they view me the same way." She chuckled. "I know that must sound silly. I'm only there to teach them piano. Not for some deep, intense connection."

He instinctively stepped closer to her. The barest brush of his shoulder against her arm. "It doesn't sound silly at all. The people I count as my family aren't blood relatives at all."

"Oh? What about your aunt and uncle?"

Adam felt the familiar churning in his gut at yet another mention of his so-called kin. "I'll always feel grateful to them for taking me in. But we're not particularly close." Aunt Rose and Uncle Stan had been dutiful enough to fulfill their responsibility. But it had been hard to ignore, all those years, their reluctance to have an unwanted teenager thrust into their lives.

Ani didn't press when he said no more. Thankfully.

"Yeah. My 'family,' quote unquote, include the crew back at the hotel, the men I served with, including your brother. A handful of others I've been fortunate enough to have enter into my life," he told her.

She bit her top lip with her lower teeth. "And a girlfriend, I imagine." She'd barely gotten the last word out when her hand flew to her mouth. "I'm sorry. I don't know where that came from. It's really none of my business."

"It's all right."

"I'm just not very good at making conversation."

He felt oddly disappointed in her explanation.

"Well, the answer happens to be that there is no girlfriend. I'm not in one place long enough."

"I see."

"What about you? You never really answered my questions back at the apartment about any men in your life."

She huffed out a small laugh. "I recall you wanting names."

He chuckled at that.

She ducked her head, looked down toward the water. "Are you asking as my bodyguard now? Or would you personally like to know?"

He shrugged. They were in dangerous territory here. He knew he should answer the question the only way that a professional would. But he couldn't seem to stop himself when the right words did not come out of his mouth. "Maybe I'm just making conversation too."

She looked away with a slight smile. "But you're not. You're asking because it's your job."

The truth was, Adam couldn't even be sure anymore. The lines were becoming increasingly blurred. Which was completely unacceptable. He knew all too well the danger of blurring such lines. The risks could be tragic and near deadly. Memories assaulted him before he could push them away. Memories of a deafening explosion, followed by a surreal quiet, then nothing but smoke and fire.

"So, what's your answer then?" he prompted, forcing himself to focus.

She sighed deeply before shaking her head. "No. I have no name to give you. And I'm not much of a social media or online type of girl. I spend way too much time at a different kind of keyboard. So no dating sites. I find myself very single currently."

Currently. "And before? There has to be someone in your past. I'm afraid I have to look at every possibility, Ani."

She shut her eyes. "The only person who even came close was a man named Peter Myer. But he was the one who walked away. Wanted much more than I was willing or ready to commit to."

Adam made a mental note of the name. He would do some research on this Peter later. He already felt an inexplicable, intense dislike for the man. A man he'd never met.

"Peter Myer is a fool," he spat out, before he thought better of it.

She turned to him, gasping in surprise. "Come again?"

No turning back now. "Only a fool would walk away from you, Ani. You're attractive in all manner of ways. I've always thought so," he found himself admitting, simply because he wanted to get it off his chest. Plus, he figured she deserved to hear the truth after all these years. Clearly, the mood and the magic of Paris had gone to his head. "Since we were teens."

She stared at him with her mouth agape. "You what?"

"You had to have suspected."

She guffawed. "No, Adam. I didn't. After all, you looked utterly disgusted every time I tried to talk to you when you came by to visit Brant. You left the pool if I so much as dipped a toe in it. You canceled plans to go to the movies or to a party if Brant agreed to bring me along. In fact, I got the impression you couldn't stand me."

"I tried very hard to have you believe that."

She pulled her hair off her forehead. "But why? Why did you act like you thought I was a pest all those times?"

Adam sighed. He hadn't realized his efforts all those years ago had been quite so successful. A twinge of guilt settled in his chest. "Self-preservation, kitten. I had to save face."

"Save face? I don't understand. What exactly were you thinking?" She seemed genuinely confused.

"Aside from you being the baby sister of one of my closest friends? Or how about the fact that you were way out of my league? The cherished daughter of a prominent Dallas family while I was a castoff nobody wanted. That's what I was thinking."

"You were so much more than that."

He didn't know how to respond to that. A long silence ensued. He'd shocked her. Well, he was a little surprised himself. At no point during the evening had he ever intended to get into all the ways he'd felt for her as a teen.

Time to change the subject. He pointed to the leather clutch she held. "Give me your phone. You want to snap some photos and take some videos to show the kids at the center, don't you?"

Ani gave a visible shake of her head as if to clear it. Then glanced at the scenery behind her. "Yes. I absolutely do."

Adam had just started taking snapshots with the Eiffel Tower behind her when they were approached by another couple.

"We'd be happy to take one of the two of you," the

woman said in perfect English, smiling. "Shame not to get one with you both in it. You're such a lovely couple."

"Oh, we're not—he's just—" Ani stammered. But the woman wasn't really listening as she reached for the phone in Adam's hand.

Adam didn't bother to correct her. He stood next to Ani and smiled for the photo. Before long, all four of them were posing together, the City of Lights a stunning background behind them.

"I might not ever forgive you for this," Moira announced dramatically when Ani made it back to her hotel room. Ani knew her well enough to know she was simply teasing. About what, she couldn't guess.

"I apologize profusely, Moira. But what transgression might I have committed unknowingly?"

"Really? You can't guess?"

Ani simply shrugged. Snowball trotted over and dropped at her feet.

Moira uncurled herself from her seat on the plush leather sofa. A black-and-white movie was playing on the TV, English captions scrolling at the bottom of the screen.

"Aside from a text asking if I'd watch Snowball for the evening, you didn't offer one clue about where you were. Just that you would be walking along the Seine."

"And you wanted more detail than that?"

"Of course," Moira answered, a smile tugging at the corners of her mouth. "Especially since you left with that sexy bodyguard of yours, so I have to assume you two have been together all this time."

Ani kicked her shoes off and headed toward the minibar. She needed a tall, cold bottle of water after all the authentic champagne she'd indulged in. "Again. I apologize, Moira. And thank you for keeping an eye on Snowball for me."

"Anytime. I love that big fluff ball of a dog."

"Still, I owe you."

Moira waved that off. "The only thing you owe me is a detailed account of exactly what the two of you were doing. You were out and about in the city of lovers, after all."

Ani uncapped a large bottle of mineral water and took a long sip before answering. "It wasn't like that. He's been here before and Philippe from the theater suggested we enjoy the walk along the riverbank. There's so much happening there. Everything from dancing to floating cafés to sidewalk performers."

"So is that what you did? Walk along the river? You were gone an awful long time."

Ani swallowed some more water. "At first. Then Adam was nice enough to treat me to a river cruise to sightsee farther along the river."

Moira clapped her hands in front of her face. "Oh, did he now? Tell me everything!"

Ani rubbed a hand across her forehead. "I will. I promise. But can it wait?"

Disappointment washed over Moira's face.

"It's just that I should really go get cleaned up and try to get a good night's sleep before the big day."

Her friend sighed. "I suppose. But right after the performance, you and I are going to sit down while you indulge me in a complete tell-all about your evening."

Ani landed a small peck on her cheek. "It's a deal."

She turned and walked out of the room before Moira could come up with a way to protest the agreement.

In the bathroom, Ani leaned over the sink and studied her face in the wall-to-wall mirror. A large Jacuzzi-style tub of Italian marble called to her, but she did need to get to bed. As it was, she doubted she'd fall asleep anytime soon. Not with the thoughts of the previous few hours running through her head.

She couldn't read too much into the moments she'd just shared with Adam. Aside from their past history, they had nothing in common. And the only thing she should be thinking about right now was her concert tomorrow night.

Still, she'd be lying if she'd said his admission back on the boat didn't make her nearly giddy inside. He'd been attracted to her when they'd been younger. He found her attractive now. The knowledge sent a surge of excitement through her core.

She filled the stainless steel sink, poured a few drops of essential oil in, then soaked both her hands in the warm water. She couldn't risk any inflammation in her finger joints. As much as she'd enjoyed tonight, it probably hadn't been a good idea to stay out.

No one should be distracting her this much. Let alone a man so far out of her reach. Despite his admission, in the end, his words didn't actually change anything. There couldn't be anything real between the two of them. He'd told her earlier he never even stayed in one location long enough to establish any kind of real relationship. Meanwhile, this was her first international trip.

This was not a time in her life to even entertain the notion of any kind of relationship. Her career was finally on the verge of a major milestone. If this mini tour proved profitable for the venues booking her, she could prove herself to the international music community and achieve a level of success most musicians only dreamed of. She'd show that she could drive ticket sales.

And anyway, she had more than her share of overbearing, powerful men in her life. The last thing she needed was a romantic relationship with a man like that. This tour was finally a chance for her to experience some true power and control of her own. She knew her father and brother both loved her dearly and that they meant well, but it was hard not to feel suffocated at times.

Things would be so much different if her mother were alive. The light had gone out of all three of their lives when they'd lost her. Her father had never really summoned a genuine smile after. The sadness never left his eyes.

Therein lay another reason she had no desire to pursue any kind of relationship. She'd seen firsthand and up close how completely shattered her father was after the loss of his wife. Zini Terrance had been taken away from them much too soon. Her father still hadn't recovered. Years of therapy had helped, but the man was a broken shell of the person he'd been previously. Her parents may have shared a love for the ages, but it had resulted in utter tragedy for them both. Ani had vowed as a teen to never leave herself that vulnerable to loss. It simply couldn't be worth the pain.

There was no reason to revisit that vow. Adam Steele was a temporary flash in her life. After this mini tour, she may not even see him again. An ache settled in her chest at the thought, right in the vicinity of her heart.

Ani leaned her forehead against the mirror and tried for a steadying breath.

She'd been woefully unprepared to have Adam Steele reenter her life.

It was barely dawn, but Adam figured he may as well get out of bed. Not like he'd slept much, anyway. A set of dark, almond-shaped eyes had been there to greet him every time he'd so much as closed his eyes. When he did fall asleep, dreams of an angelic face surrounded by fiery red hair had haunted him throughout the night.

Throwing on a pair of shorts and a T-shirt, he made his

way downstairs and out into the street for an early morning run. Hopefully, it would help to clear his head.

Going out with Ani last night had been a mistake. He'd tried to tell himself he'd simply be spending a few hours catching up with an old friend. That it would be a crime to have her miss the beauty of this city her first time here by holing up in her hotel room and practicing piano. But by the time they'd made it back up the elevator, he was thinking of her as much more than a friendly acquaintance from the past.

He had to put an end to that. And fast.

Adam broke into a fast jog as soon as he hit the pavement. Inviting her on that dinner cruise had been reckless and impulsive on his part. He simply should have taken Ani on the scenic route back to their hotel. Hell, he could have even arranged the dinner cruise for her and her friend slash manager instead. In hindsight, that would have been the better plan.

A woman like Ani was off-limits. Completely taboo.

He was older than her, not by a long stretch, but years weren't the only measurement for a life. She was a relative innocent. He'd been a soldier who'd served in some of the most nightmarish, war-torn areas of the world. The ugliness he'd witnessed, the darkness of humanity he'd been privy to, would affect him for the rest of his life. Before that, he'd been an orphaned and unwanted kid who'd repeatedly found himself in trouble.

He'd done well for himself since those younger days. But he'd long ago accepted that he wasn't the type to settle down and commit.

No, he was much better suited to a life of constant change and travel. A life in which he kept the darkness all to himself. Where he could keep his mistakes from hurting anyone else.

Then there was the complication of Ani being the adored baby sister of one of his closest friends. Things didn't get more complicated than that.

Adam set a punishing pace as he made his way down the streets. Around him, Paris was mostly still asleep. A few of the cafés had the lights turned on low, one or two people stirring about inside. He ran by a bakery and the enticing aroma of fresh baked bread had him slowing his stride.

It occurred to him that Ani would never have experienced tasting a fresh-baked baguette straight from a Parisian oven. Maybe he should pick up a loaf for her on the way back. Along with some sweet cream butter. He imagined feeding her a piece the way those couples were feeding each other cake at the café yesterday.

Just. Stop.

Adam ran a few more steps and then stopped to lean against the wall of a fashion boutique. That was it. No more excuses. He had to stop thinking about her. From now on, he'd be nothing more than the man in charge of her security detail. He'd assign April or Tito to take the lead in communicating with the VIP.

That was the way he had to think of Ani from now. Merely another client he'd been hired to serve.

Strictly professional. Even if it meant he had to stay the hell away from her.

Ani awoke to find a text message on her phone.

Please notify me when you're up. We have some details to go over. Also, I have something to give you.

It was from April. Ani had met her on the jet, one of the professionals on Adam's security team. Ani responded to have her come up in twenty minutes after she had a chance to shower.

There was a knock on her door exactly twenty minutes later. Ani opened the door to find April standing in the hallway. She held a large brown bag. A delicious aroma wafted into the room and immediately made Ani's mouth water.

She stepped aside to let the other woman in.

April handed her the bag. "This is for you and your team. Various pastries and a fresh baguette. There's even a treat for the dog. From Adam."

Ani managed to mutter a thank-you through her surprise. A touching warmth spread throughout her chest. He'd thought to get her breakfast.

But why was it April who was delivering it? Adam had mentioned he'd stop by in the morning to brief her about where exactly his men would be positioned during her performance and how she'd be accompanied to and from the stage. Why was April the one here instead?

It should have been a relief. Hadn't she just resolved to herself last night that she had to keep herself guarded as far as he was concerned?

But she couldn't stop wondering about the answer. Though she couldn't bring herself to ask.

CHAPTER FOUR

ADAM OBSERVED THE growing crowd around the theater. A lot of people were here early, as soon as the doors opened. The makeup of the concertgoers surprised him. Elderly groups, several young adults. Even several teens. Ani attracted a very diverse crowd. It had to say something about her talent that her music appealed to such a wide audience.

Something akin to pride blossomed in his chest. Though that was downright silly. He had no right to any such feeling where she was concerned.

He'd avoided her most of the day, aside from a couple of quick, face-to-face checks and text messages. He'd put April in charge of most of the day's responsibilities that involved direct VIP contact.

Far from making him feel better, he'd been miserable and surly, even snapping at his crew more than once.

A buzz sounded in his ear, followed by April's voice. "VIP limo approaching. ETA three mins."

Adam clicked the earpiece. "Cleared for arrival. Side entrance as planned."

"Copy."

Two and a half minutes later, a sleek dark limousine turned around the street corner. Adam scanned the area; the crowd seemed to be contained in front of the box office doors at the front of the theater. A few wanderers here and there paid no mind to the limousine or the two black SUVs that followed. Two of his men were positioned inside, along with the theater's own security crew. April was in the limo with Ani. The performance was due to begin in a couple of hours.

The convoy pulled to a stop at the curb and the limo door opened. April got out first and held the door open for Ani and Moira. Then Ani exited the vehicle, and the sight nearly took his breath away.

She was dressed in a long satin gown the color of the midnight sky over the Mediterranean Sea. Strapless, it exposed her elegant shoulders and long, bare neck. Her hair was done up in a complicated style with delicate ringlets framing her face. She looked like the budding international music star that she was. Someone on the brink of a rich, full life filled with achievement.

Someone he had no business coveting in any way.

He watched as she stepped out onto the curb. Her gaze immediately found him and she gave him a small smile. Yet even from this distance, he could see the confusion clouding her eyes, perhaps wondering why he'd been so unavailable all day. He'd simply been trying to remain at a professional distance. What he should have done all along.

Now, he gave her a nod and an appreciative wink, professionalism be damned. Her smile grew wider. But then April gently nudged her toward the entrance of the building, with Moira trailing closely behind.

He waited a few more moments to ensure nothing or no one suspicious appeared before entering the building himself.

Her dressing room was clearly marked with a gold, glittering star on the door. He could hear voices and the bustle of movement inside. A soundtrack of classical music played in the background. A piano concerto.

He forced himself to walk past and down the hallway without knocking. There was no real need to check on her. April had things well under control. The stage had been secured several times throughout the day. Nothing had been left to chance.

So why did he feel so out of sorts?

An hour and a half went by as the auditorium gradually grew noisier. Adam watched from behind the large red curtain as every seat eventually filled. She'd sold out the house.

Finally, a hush settled over the crowd as the curtains drew apart. The lights flickered twice before dimming. Ani walked slowly onstage to loud applause.

Once again, her gaze made a straight beeline to where he stood off to the side. Even from here, he could sense her nervousness. He gave her what he hoped was a reassuring smile, one she returned with tight lips.

She turned back to the crowd.

"Bonjour!" she began, and then added in flawless French, "I'm so happy to be here tonight. Thank you for inviting me to your enchanting city."

Her audience clapped and cheered in response. With a small wave, she took a seat at the grand piano in the center of the stage. The orchestra section darkened.

She began to play.

The sheer beauty of it stunned Adam where he stood. He'd never particularly been a fan of the classics. But there was no doubt he was witnessing creative magic as Ani played. The notes echoed around him, filling the air with harmony. He realized he was staring at her, slack jawed.

As if she sensed his stare, she looked up and their eyes locked for the briefest moment. Or maybe he'd just imagined it. He forced his attention back to the audience.

Ani had more in her repertoire than just the piano concertos. Throughout the night, she sprinkled her performance with bouncier, more pop-like pieces. A trio of talented background singers accompanied her for those.

The audience loved every moment. He'd never doubted Ani's talent, but he hadn't expected to be completely blown away. Aside from her musical talents, she had an innate ability to connect with her audience, a star quality he wouldn't be able to put into words. Adam didn't know much about creatives, but he knew the combination of appeal and talent that Ani had was a rare gift.

By the time Ani stood up and took her final bow, several audience members were in near tears. He could hardly blame them. Ani announced the orchestra and her singers and took one final bow as the curtains closed. April immediately strode toward her from backstage but Ani was already making her way toward where Adam stood.

She gave him a brilliant smile that had his mouth going dry.

Without so much as a thought, he waved April off. He would take it from here.

"That was something, kitten."

Ani had to resist the urge to throw herself into Adam's arms. She knew she wasn't thinking straight. But some kind of euphoria had come over her sometime during the night. While she'd played, she'd almost had what could be described as an out-of-body experience. It was as if the audience had become an extension of her very being. Now that the show was over, she felt an exhilaration like she'd never experienced before. The looks she'd caught from Adam throughout the night only amplified the endorphins coursing through her body.

She'd done well. The audience seemed impressed. As

did Adam. Hard to tell which pleased her more, as silly as that sounded.

"Thank you," she replied. "I had some churning in my midsection throughout most of it, I have to admit."

She wouldn't tell him the rest. She wouldn't divulge the crutch she'd used as she'd played. Thoughts of the time they'd shared aboard the cruise boat had settled her nerves and boosted her confidence as she'd been up there on that stage.

He'd described her as *attractive in all manner of ways.* She'd replayed those words in her head over and over as she'd played and they'd served to calm her anxiety. Maybe someday she'd let him know the large part he'd played in her successful performance. Right now, it felt too raw to try to explain it. She wasn't sure she could if she tried.

"Butterflies?" Adam asked.

"More like pterodactyls."

He reached a hand toward her before he suddenly dropped it to his side. Had he been about to touch her? "You hid it well," he said. "It looked like you were enjoying yourself out there."

She had to laugh at that; she'd been utterly terrified throughout most of the night. "I was and I wasn't. Let's just say I'm enjoying it now that it's over."

"That's to be expected for the first time. I'm sure the next one will be second nature."

"I'm not so sure about that." Her muscles were still quaking, her stomach still doing somersaults.

"What do you say we get you out of here? So that you can start celebrating," he suggested.

He didn't wait for an answer but clicked on his earpiece to confirm the limo was ready to take them back to the hotel. Then he led her to her dressing room to wrap things up.

She'd done it! She'd gotten through her first real theater performance as a solo act. And it could only be described as a success, Ani thought as she gathered her things. She changed into comfortable capris and a spaghetti strap tank, then slipped on a comfortable pair of flats. She'd deal with the removal of her makeup once she got to the hotel. And then she could finally relax. Maybe Adam might even join her and the rest of her team in some celebratory champagne.

All that mattered was that she'd finally be able to relax and wait for the grip of stage fright to slowly ebb.

Her phone pinged an alert for a text message. The tone told her it was Moira. Ani had half a mind to ignore it. She was more than ready to get back to the hotel and celebrate her little victory.

But knowing her manager, the woman wouldn't be ignored for long. Ani glanced at her screen.

Some early reviews are in already. Emailed them to you. You have to see for yourself!

Ani called up her inbox. And froze where she stood. An icy chill traveled down her spine.

The last email in her queue wasn't from Moira at all. It was another one from her self-described admirer.

You played like an angel tonight. Someday you'll be playing just for me.

She just wanted to get out of here, to have this night be over.

But the crowd had other plans when Ani and Adam made it outside.

His security team cleared a path for them, but Ani was

tussled about and shoved nonetheless. Shouts for auto-graphs, photos and the flash of cameras bombarded her as they slowly made their way to the car. Adam tugged her gently along while she struggled to fake a smile for the crowd.

"We're almost there," Adam reassured. "You okay?" Ani couldn't even be sure how she heard him through the boisterous noise.

"It's a little overwhelming." That was a lie. She was beyond overwhelmed. Even as she scratched out an auto-graph here and there, inside she was a turbulent ocean during a storm. Her performance anxiety was nothing compared to this.

And what about her stalker? What if they were right here? What if he was someone in the crowd, one of the peo-ple fervently trying to reach her? Ani knew it was highly unlikely, but the mere thought of the possibility had her stomach churning.

What seemed like an eternity later, Adam assisted her into the limousine and crawled in beside her. Her stomach clenched with residual anxiety.

Adam took her hand as he signaled for the driver to move. "Hey, you're shaking."

"I just—I guess I wasn't expecting that."

"We'll be back at the hotel in no time. Try not to think about the latest email for now." She'd told Adam about her admirer's last message right away.

Adam continued, "My IT guy back in the States is on it as we speak." He shrugged out of his jacket and draped it over her shoulders. "Here, I know you're not shaking be-cause you're cold. But some warmth will help."

Ani held the tuxedo jacket tight against her. It did help. But his warmth through the fabric was the least of it. The scent of him surrounded her, the effect like a soothing balm on her frazzled nerves.

She uttered a small prayer of thanks that he was the one here with her. As nice as April was, Adam's presence was much more comforting. She should have been better prepared for the paparazzi and the mob of fans. Moira had tried to warn her. But Ani was just so new to all this, focused solely on nailing her performance.

That email had arrived at the worst possible moment—just before she'd had to face a boisterous, reaching mob.

Considering that just a couple weeks ago, Adam wasn't supposed to have even been there tonight, it made for a curious state of affairs. To think, she'd fought her brother and father about having him accompany her on this trip. Now, she couldn't imagine what she would have done without him by her side.

Adam's phone pinged with a text message. He bit out a curse once he'd read it.

"What's the matter?"

"We might have a replay of what happened outside the theater."

"What? Why?"

"April and the others made it back to the hotel already. I'm afraid there's another crowd there waiting for you."

Oh, no. Ani felt the blood rush out of her face and extremities. Her stomach clenched with apprehension. "But why?"

He shrugged. "You put on quite a show. You're probably all over the internet. Music fans everywhere are probably searching who you are and how you came to be here."

Ani rubbed her forehead, her hand shaking.

"Someone must have sent out some kind of social-media alert after your concert."

"I don't think I can face that again," she admitted. "Not so soon."

He squeezed her hand in his large palm and she could have sworn a palpable wave of strength flowed through the contact. When had she gotten so reliant on him?

"In that case, you won't have to. I'll take care of it."

"What? How?"

He tapped a playful finger on her nose and smiled. "We'll just have to take a detour. I know just the place."

Ani was shivering so much in the seat next to him despite the warm car, Adam knew he couldn't take her back to the hotel where a mob of people were waiting for her. She looked downright terrified. Which left him with really one other choice this time of night. He quickly fired off a text to a familiar number.

A response came back almost immediately with an added side note that made Adam laugh out loud. Ani sent him a questioning look.

He leaned over the divider to give the driver a new address, then sent another text alerting his team.

Ani still sat next to him, a virtual bundle of nerves. She was wound up like a tight coil about to snap.

"Try to relax. You won't have to deal with any more crowds tonight."

He could tell she had a lot of pent-up energy that needed to be expunged somehow. He was familiar with the feeling. A sudden burst of adrenaline in response to an unexpected situation always lingered long after the moment had passed. Adam had experienced it often enough as a soldier and many times since.

"Where are we going if not the hotel?" she asked, her voice trembling ever so slightly. Oh, yeah, she really needed some kind of release.

"Somewhere you'll be able to unwind a bit," he told her. "Looks like you could use it."

"I do feel a bit…out of sorts."

"It's understandable. Between your performance and the effect of the waiting crowd, I'm guessing you're still pumped up. We'll make sure to take care of that."

Her eyes clouded over with some kind of emotion he didn't want to speculate on. "What exactly did you have in mind?"

Damn him if he was reading anything too loaded into that question. Absolutely dangerous territory his mind was trying to breach. Ignoring her question, he leaned over and pulled out a frosty bottle of sparkling mineral water from the built-in fridge. "Here, we don't want you dehydrated."

She took it with a grateful smile. "Thanks. It appears you know what I need better than I do."

How could he answer that? He couldn't exactly tell her he felt more in tune with her than anyone else he'd ever worked for. Not even Tonya.

Don't go there.

Adam squashed the useless, painful memories and focused on the matter at hand. Ani could use getting away for an hour or two. He suspected a mundane, normal activity might help her settle her emotions.

One thing was certain: he wasn't going to let anyone get near her as long as he was around.

"So, you never told me where we're going," Ani reminded him after taking a long sip of the mineral water.

"See for yourself," he answered as the car came to a stop. "We're here." He opened her door and helped her out of the car.

Ani looked up in surprise and took in their surroundings. "Where is this place?"

They'd arrived in Le Marais, a favorite spot of his.

"Let's just say this a part of Paris that's a bit off the beaten path. Trendier and younger, so to speak."

The mouthwatering smell of street vendor carts drifted in the air. Adam couldn't tell which of their stomachs was the one that grumbled. "You hungry?"

She ran her tongue around her upper lip and he lost his bearings for a moment. "I could eat, now that you mention it."

"Good. You'll need something in your stomach if we're going to celebrate your performance with champagne later."

He walked her over to a crepe cart where a tattooed young lady with a silver nose ring was waiting on a lone customer. When it was their turn, Adam chose the sausage filling and ordered a strawberry-and-cream filled one for Ani.

"You sent the limo driver away," Ani commented as they sat on the curb eating their snack. A steady flow of people walked by them. Despite the late hour, the shops and eateries around them were full of tourists and locals alike.

He nodded. "Figured it would look conspicuous in this part of town." Plus, he didn't want the poor man to have to wait around until he and Ani were done.

She took another bite and seemed to savor the taste. "Mmm, this is so good."

"Let me taste," he asked without thinking. "It's been a while since I've had a sweet one."

Ani didn't hesitate before offering him her treat. Somehow, they'd reached a level of comfort between them that he hadn't exactly seen coming. It was easy to be around her, easy to talk to her. He could count on one hand all the people he could say that about.

Still, some things were better left unsaid.

Ani seemed to be studying their surroundings. Her gaze

landed on a street musician and stayed there for several beats as she ate. "This is quite the place," she said between bites.

She was right. Le Marais had grown trendier and more popular year after year. It held all the charm of Paris with less of the staunchness of some of the more historic parts. His friend had done well to set up his business in this part of town.

He waited for her to pop the last piece into her mouth before standing. He reached a hand down to help her up. "Let's go."

"Where to now? We aren't leaving, I hope? I kind of like it here."

He shook his head, pleased beyond all sense that she was enjoying herself. "No. We just got here. Let's just say the fun hasn't even started yet, kitten."

Her eyes lit up. "Is that so?" She took his hand and hopped up.

"I just have one question."

"What's that?"

"Do you trust me?"

Ani realized with a jolt the truth of the answer that immediately popped into her head. She did trust him. Implicitly. Without even realizing it, she'd gone from resenting the way he'd been thrust into her life to actually needing him in it. If she examined the reality of her feelings even for a moment, she couldn't imagine being in Paris without Adam Steele by her side.

So she stepped off the curb and followed him without question, trying in vain to ignore the tingling along her skin where his palm met hers.

They soon approached the glass front of what appeared to be some kind of pub. It looked crowded inside and for a moment she hesitated at the door. Crowds didn't really hold a big appeal for her at the moment.

Adam sensed her resistance. "It's okay. You trust me, remember?"

With that, he pushed the door open and tugged her in behind him. Ani released a sigh of relief when a cursory glance confirmed that no one was really paying the new-comers at the door any attention.

A burly, thick-armed man serving drinks stopped in his tracks when he spotted Adam. A wide grin appeared on the other man's face and he reached them in a few long strides.

Adam greeted him in French and the two embraced each other. Adam switched to English to introduce her. "Ani, this is Remy. We served together in the Middle East. He owns this fine establishment."

Remy offered her a dazzling smile and leaned to give her a polite peck on the cheek. He smelled of whiskey and fried food.

"Very nice to meet you."

Adam cleared his throat. "I mentioned we were look-ing for some privacy this evening. To celebrate a special occasion."

Ani gasped and braced herself for Remy to make the assumption Adam's statement must have invoked. It sounded as if they were looking for a quick tryst. She felt her cheeks flame with embarrassment.

But Remy simply gave a brisk nod. "Ah, yes." He pointed up. "The private party room is empty. It's all yours."

"*Merci*, Remy."

The other man smiled, revealing sparkling white teeth and a ridiculously charming smile. "Of course, my friend. I only ask that you see me later so that we may catch up."

They embraced again before Adam led her up a side stairway. The party room Remy referred to consisted of several round tables, another well-stocked bar and a wide-screen TV mounted on the wall. A standard-size billiard table stood at the end of the room.

Adam turned to her. "How's your pool game, kitten?" Without waiting for an answer, he took her by the elbow and led her to the rack of cue sticks.

"Well, this ought to be interesting," Ani declared, choosing one of the shorter sticks.

"Don't tell me you've never played before."

She shook her head. "That's not what I meant." After all, there'd been a table in their family playroom for as long as she could remember. In fact, this was the perfect activity to take her mind off the stress and sheer rush of the past few hours.

Lifting a cube of chalk, she expertly coated the tip of her cue. "I meant it will be interesting to see how well you take it when I defeat you!"

Adam threw his head back and barked out a laugh. "You're on. Ladies first. Go ahead and break."

She leaned over and did so expertly. The balls rolled out across the surface of the table and a solid rolled into the side pocket.

Adam lifted an eyebrow. "I'm impressed."

She sank one more solid, then stood off to the side while he took his turn.

A few minutes later, they were neck and neck, the number of solid balls to stripes at a dead even number.

Ani watched as he geared up for his next shot. This was a different side of Adam. He studied the table with an easy focus. She was used to him being fully alert, constantly surveying his surroundings.

She'd caught a glimpse of it last night during their Seine cruise when he'd let his guard down for a couple of hours. He'd been conversational and forthcoming.

But most of today, up until her performance, he'd pretty much been out of sight.

And now, he was treating her to a lighthearted game of pool because she'd been so frazzled after performing, receiving that unsettling email, then confronting an unruly crowd. Would she ever be able to figure him out? The man was a complete enigma.

She scored a break in the game when Adam missed yet another shot. Ani saw a clear chance of winning. All she needed to do was hit the orange ball on the far side hard enough that it rolled into the green and sank them both.

She angled her cue and thrust it with a hard push and no small amount of force. Inadvertently, in her desire for a strong push, she somehow managed to slam her right hand into the left where it held the cue stick.

A stinging, sharp pain shot up through her wrist and up her arm. "Ouch!" The cue fell out of her hands.

Adam was beside her in an instant, "What happened? Damn it, Ani. If you've hurt your hand—"

She couldn't bear to think about it. The notion that she might have hurt her hand in the midst of a performance tour was beyond what her mind could absorb right now.

"I'll go find you some ice."

Adam ran behind the bar counter and came back with a plastic baggie filled with crushed ice. He placed it gently on the whole of her hand. "I'm so sorry, sweetheart."

"It's my fault. I was being way too competitive. Brant says it's one of my most annoying traits."

Adam shook his head. They stood inches apart. She could smell that alluring, woodsy scent of his that was now so familiar to her. He'd unbuttoned his white silk dress shirt just enough to reveal the tanned V of his upper chest.

And wasn't this one heck of a time to be noticing such things?

"No. I should have thought this through better. Bringing a pianist on tour to play pool…" He cursed again.

"Please don't blame yourself. You know how many times I've played this game without managing to hurt myself?"

"Do you think you've injured it?" he asked, his voice near desperate.

Ani took a deep breath to brace herself before attempting to wiggle her fingers. To her profound relief, the pain seemed to have subsided.

She released a deep sigh. "I think it's okay."

Adam's shoulders slumped with released tension. He rested his forehead against hers. "Thank heavens, kitten. I would have never forgiven myself."

Ani knew she should step back. But all she could think about was how good it felt to have his skin against hers, the warmth of his touch where he held her hand juxtaposed against the stinging cold of the ice. Without giving herself a chance to think, she tilted her chin, angling her mouth so that it was a mere breath away from his. Her heart pounded against her chest so hard she thought she might faint.

Adam sucked in a breath. "Kitten?"

The breathless way he said her nickname sent a thrill down her spine. He was the only one in the world who called her that.

She found herself uttering the thought that had been on her mind since this morning when April had arrived with the bag of pastries. "You were gone most of the day."

I missed you, her mind silently added.

"I had to stay away." His answer was pained, his voice tight.

"Why?"

"Because of what's happening right now."

Electricity hummed over her skin at his admission. He'd

purposely been trying to stay away from her. Did that mean he'd been thinking about her all day, the same way she'd been unable to get him out of her mind? The thought was exhilarating.

"I'm not afraid of what's happening now," she whispered boldly, almost against his mouth.

"You really should be, kitten."

A chill started at the base of her neck and traveled down her spine. She inched ever so slightly closer in spite of his words of warning.

Adam stayed stone still where he stood, the only movement the rise and fall of his chest with each breath he took. Ani knew he was ensuring that she be the one to make the next move. Heaven help her, she knew without a doubt right here and now the truth that her heart had decided long ago, perhaps even back as far as when they were kids.

She wrapped her arms around his neck and touched her lips to his.

CHAPTER FIVE

ADAM WAS HALF-AFRAID she'd step away. More afraid that she wouldn't.

How had they ended up here? Upstairs at his friend's bar in Paris, Ani Terrance was in his arms. And she was kissing him.

He knew he had to take it slow. Everything about Ani screamed inexperienced innocent. But heaven help him, he wasn't made of stone.

When he couldn't stand it any longer, he wound his arms around her waist, pulled her close against him and deepened the kiss. She tasted like home and redemption. Like the sweetest honey. He'd never get enough of her. She felt natural in his arms, like she belonged there, as if she always had.

Her chest rubbed against his and he thought his knees might buckle. She was so soft, her rounded curves enticing him like he was a man starved.

He had to ask her, had to make certain.

"Are you sure about this, kitten? Just say the word, and I'll stop." *Somehow.*

Her response was a low moan before she breathlessly told him, "Yes."

Adam didn't allow himself a chance to think. Cupping her bottom, he hoisted her onto the pool table. Her cry was one of pure sensuality and it drove him to near madness. He kissed her even deeper, fully exploring her mouth.

He stepped between her legs, pulled her even tighter, his palms spread against the small of her back. Then she wrapped her legs around him and he was certain he actually would go insane. She was putting him through the sweetest torture, making him burn with desire. She sighed his name against his lips and it was nearly his undoing.

Anyone could walk up the stairs at any moment and see them this way. Remy might very well decide to check on them. But Adam couldn't bring himself to care.

Nothing and no one else mattered now but the woman in his arms. He'd never wanted anyone so badly, so completely.

It was that very thought that served as a proverbial bucket of ice water poured over his head.

What the hell was he thinking?

The stark reality was that he wasn't thinking at all. He had no business being here with Ani. He should have never brought her here, spent time with her alone. For all he knew, this was still the aftereffects of her performance high. She might not even be thinking clearly. The wisest thing to do after leaving the theater would have been to detour long enough to avoid the crowds back at the hotel.

Deep down he'd known that, even as he'd fired off that text to Remy. He'd brought her here anyway, ignoring the voices of reason in his head. To think he'd sworn that he'd learned from his mistakes.

Though it felt like losing a limb, he forced himself to pull out of the kiss and out of her arms.

The look of confusion combined with desire on her face nearly had him succumbing to his traitorous body once more.

He clenched his fists by his sides instead. He refused

to make the same error in judgment that had led to such tragedy in his past. This time, he may not survive the pain and the guilt.

And Ani deserved so much better.

Ani blinked up in confusion when Adam stepped away. What had happened? Had she missed something? Perhaps he'd received an urgent alert on his phone and she hadn't heard it. But then she noticed the way he was avoiding her eyes. And she realized her mistake.

"We should probably call it a night." He gently took her by the elbow and helped her jump off the table.

"That's it? We're just going to head back to the hotel?"

He shrugged. "Your manager and the others are probably anxious to have you back. And I should go over some things with my team. We can talk about this…" he gestured with a wave "…on the ride back."

She had an idea how that conversation might go. And it mortified her. "Let me guess," she began, adjusting the straps of her bra and tank top. "You're going to say that we both got carried away and things should have never gone so far."

His silence was all the answer she needed.

"We can talk in the cab," he repeated, pulling out his phone.

"I say we don't even bother." She tried to brush past him to walk away but he grabbed her by the upper arm before she got far. For one insane and hopeful moment, she thought maybe he was again going to give in to the attraction so clearly between them.

He quickly nixed that notion.

"You have to understand I have a reputation to uphold. And there are other—"

She held up a hand. She really didn't need to hear any of

this. The fact was he was rejecting her. After she'd practically thrown herself at him. "Honestly, Adam. I'd rather not get into a lengthy discussion."

He gave a quick shake of his head.

She continued, "I can guess what you're going to say. And you'd be right."

"I would?"

"Yes. I agree that we both got carried away by the moment. Being in Paris, a successful first performance, the champagne. You're obviously a very attractive man. It just led to a heady combination and I let myself give in to a whim." Her words were so lighthearted, she almost believed them herself.

"Is that so?"

"Absolutely," she lied.

So predictable. She was certainly consistent when it came to men. And how she would never understand them.

When they reached her hotel room, she was no less frustrated and confused. But she seemed to have put on a convincing act as far as Adam was concerned. He didn't so much as attempt to speak to her on the cab ride back. It looked like he had taken her words at face value. Somehow that made her feel less than triumphant. Rather, she felt hollow.

The feeling hadn't subsided at all seven hours later when she awoke in the predawn hours. Ani pushed her face into her pillow until it was almost too difficult to breathe. This was what happened when she let her guard down. She woke up alone and dejected the next morning, hating herself for falling so easily.

She bit back the sob that threatened to erupt from deep within her chest. She wouldn't cry, damn it. She refused to.

So what if she'd thought this time things would be different. So what if she actually thought that maybe Adam himself might be different. He wasn't.

Peter had pushed and pushed for an intimacy she didn't feel for him. When she'd finally given in, it had been for all the wrong reasons. In an ironic and cruel twist of fate, now that she wanted that kind of intimacy with a man, it was completely out of her reach.

And there was no denying she wanted Adam more than she'd ever longed for anyone.

He clearly regretted kissing her. Well, regardless of what had happened afterward, she had no regrets herself. She'd wanted to kiss Adam, and she had. Damn the consequences. She'd nursed a wounded ego and a bruised heart before. She could do it again.

Snowball trotted out of his bed and jumped onto the mattress next to her. Ani gave the dog a snuggle. At least her pet was here to give her unconditional love. What more did a girl need?

Ani groaned out loud. She did need more in her life. Much more. But it appeared Adam Steele wasn't going to be the one to give it to her.

Her phone pinged with the alert of a text message.

Are you up yet? We need to talk. ASAP

From Moira.

It appeared everyone just wanted to chat with her. Adam last night and now Moira. Ani would guess the latter wanted to talk about the former. Well, she didn't have it in her just yet. Not before a cup of coffee and a long hot shower.

She indulged in a hot, steamy bath instead and had barely stepped both feet out when a knock sounded on her door.

Adam?

Ani knew she was being all sorts of foolish. But the

thought that he might be here to try to clear the air had her heart pounding with anticipation. He couldn't deny his attraction to her so easily in the light of day. For one, he wouldn't be able to use the champagne excuse. Or that she was tired and not thinking clearly so soon after playing for an audience.

Grabbing the thick terry-cloth robe hanging on the doorway, she ran to the outer room to answer the knock.

The person standing on the other side of the door wasn't Adam. It was Moira.

Ani began to apologize. She'd completely forgotten about Moira's text. The only thoughts running through her mind during her luxurious soak had involved a tall, dark and handsome former soldier who insisted on driving her crazy.

Moira didn't look pleased in the least. She held up her tablet. "I'm guessing you haven't been online yet." She stepped into the room without giving Ani a chance to answer and shut the door behind her. "You should probably sit down."

Adam's early-morning run was cut short when he ran by a newspaper stand and caught sight of what looked like a very familiar image. At first, he continued running, convinced he was simply seeing things. But the image stayed with him and bothered him enough that he turned around after about half a block.

Damned if it hadn't been his imagination. Inserting euros into the slot of the kiosk, Adam lifted out a copy of the tabloid. He didn't even need to open it. He and Ani had made the front page.

They stood over the railing of a glass-covered yacht, smiling and gazing into each other's eyes. Their shoulders brushed against one another's.

Heaven help him, the look he was giving her was one of pure besottedness. Had he really been careless enough to wear such emotion on his face?

No wonder the photo editor had chosen this one for the cover.

Piano Star Spends Romantic Evening with Handsome Bodyguard Before She Dazzles Paris with Her Talent.

A quick read of the other captions only fueled his ire, as did the pictures and write-up inside. The woman who'd taken selfies with them aboard the cruise boat had apparently snapped one of the two of them alone when they hadn't been looking. She was quoted as saying that she'd thought Adam and Ani were "just the cutest couple" and had to snap a pic to show her American friends back home that Paris was indeed for lovers.

One of the inside articles was particularly troublesome. They'd interviewed another so-called security professional and had the man's exact quote.

One might wonder if a professional boundary has been crossed. He certainly seems to be guarding her closely.

Adam took a deep breath. He had to get a grip here.

With a baseball cap on backward and mirrored sports sunglasses, he didn't think he would be recognized. He had half a mind to keep going, just continue to run and complete the punishing bout of exercise he'd originally planned. Just pretend the paper in his hand didn't even exist. He certainly needed the exertion to help him vent.

But avoidance wasn't his style. He had some damage control to do.

Ani. What must she be thinking?

He had no one to blame but himself. He was the professional here. She was new to all of this. She was beautiful, talented and charismatic. No wonder the world was already focusing so much attention on her. She'd only had one performance, for heaven's sake.

He had no idea how she might be handling this.

He pulled his phone out just as it started pinging with dozens of alerts and messages. So many people he owed an explanation. But right now, only one held his complete focus. He scrolled through until he found the messages from Ani.

Please call if you're awake.

And another one less than a minute later.

What do we do?

Followed immediately by:

How did this happen?

He typed out a response right away.

Sit tight. I'm on my way. Try not to worry.

His fingers started typing the word kitten before he caught himself.

He would figure out a way around all this.

Though how exactly he was going to do that was a mystery. His very reputation as a professional was on the line here.

Another thought occurred to him that had him swearing

out loud—a passerby gave him a curious look and a wide
berth. Brant and Mr. Terrance would no doubt get wind
of all this if they hadn't seen it already. What exactly was
he going to tell them?

First things first. He had to go make sure Ani was okay.
He called April as he jogged back to the hotel.

"Hey, boss."

"Hey."

"What's up?" April was the consummate professional.
She would never bring up the gossip hanging over his head,
would wait until he mentioned it first.

"Please move up your regularly scheduled morning
meet-up with the VIP. I'd like you to go see her now. I'll
join the meet in a few minutes. We need to go over some
things."

He could have sworn he heard amusement in her voice
when she answered, "I'd say we do."

Adam didn't bother to respond to that. Just waited for
her to hang up.

He was a stone's throw from the hotel when his phone
rang again. April was calling him back. That was not a
good sign.

"Bad news, boss."

A brick lodged itself in the vicinity of his throat. He
could guess what was coming.

"VIP not in quarters. Seems to have left the hotel."

Damn it, Ani.

He hadn't felt the need to place a guard at her door given
the hotel's tight security and the manned elevator lobby on
every floor. He would have to rethink that decision now.

"Did she inform anyone of her whereabouts?"

"Negative."

Adam pinched the bridge of his nose. Of all the foolish
moves. He'd told her to sit tight!

A text came through on his cell just as soon as he'd hung up with April. A message from Ani.

Had to leave. Need air to clear my head.

He called her phone but it went straight to voice mail. He gripped the phone so tight, he thought it might snap in his hand.

He texted her.

Please tell me where you are.

Her response: I don't really know.

He closed his eyes briefly. Did you go left or right out of the hotel when you left? Which exit door did you use?

It seemed to take forever for the floating dots to appear on the screen. But her answer when it finally came through wasn't terribly helpful.

I just need a moment to myself. Please, Adam.

He had an insane urge to throw the phone clear across the street and into the Seine. Yep, he'd really made a royal mess of this one. He was personally involved in an international gossip story, his reputation as a world-renowned bodyguard service provider was sure to be damaged beyond repair, and the VIP in question was now in an unknown location.

Ani sat down on an empty bench overlooking the river and switched her phone off. She couldn't deal with talking to anyone right now. Even Moira had begun to test the limits of her patience.

Not to mention, she didn't want her phone tracked by her ever-resourceful bodyguard.

How had everything gone so horribly out of control? Here she was, trying to make a name for herself as a serious classical musician, and the only thing the world seemed to care about was her love life.

She snorted a humorless laugh. What a joke. She didn't have any kind of love life.

It vexed her that no one seemed to be talking or writing about her performance or her compositions. The primary subject seemed to be those pictures of her and Adam.

It was time to face an undeniable fact: she'd been woefully, naively unprepared for even the slightest hint of celebrity. It was a reality she had to examine closely and make some decisions about. A life of paparazzi ducking and tabloid features wasn't the future she'd planned on.

She reached for the paper-wrapped baguette she'd picked up along the way. The one Adam had had delivered to her the other day had been beyond delicious, melting in her mouth. But she found she didn't quite have an appetite this morning. She didn't bother to unwrap it.

What a sorry state of affairs. Here she was in Paris on a bright, sunny morning sitting on a park bench with freshly made bread. But she couldn't even enjoy it.

A shadow suddenly fell over where she sat. Ani didn't have to look up to guess who it was. "How did you find me?"

He came around the bench and sat down next to her. Even with everything else on her mind, it was hard not to admire the sheer magnetic appeal of the man. Dark stubble covered his square jaw. He was dressed in a tight navy blue T-shirt that accentuated his rock-hard abs. Abs she'd been running her hands over just last night. She had to suck in a breath.

"It's what I do. Part of the job is knowing how to track people down," he answered.

"Makes sense."

"You shouldn't have wandered off, Ani. You're in an unfamiliar city. And what the hell were you thinking, turning off your phone?"

"I made sure I wasn't followed. Well, except by you somehow. But you're exceptional."

"Is that some sort of rebuke?"

She merely shrugged.

Adam blew out a deep sigh. "Jeez, Ani. How am I supposed to protect you if I don't know where you are?"

"I just had to get away, Adam. Surely, you can understand that." She took a deep breath. "April told me that last email was traced to the Dallas area. So I'm not in any danger from my so-called stalker."

"Still, what if you'd been recognized? Like last night?"

She grabbed the baguette and took an inelegant bite right off the end, just for something to do. Quite unladylike, as if that mattered at all right now.

"I'm wearing a wide-brimmed sun hat and large, dark sunglasses," she countered, still chewing yet hardly tasting the bite.

"Did it help?" he asked her. "Getting away on your own?"

"Not really. I'm still trying to figure out why anyone would find me worthy of tabloid fodder. It must have been a slow celebrity-news day."

He turned to her. Despite everything and all the chaos they found themselves in, Ani couldn't help but want him to hold her right now. She wanted to feel his arms around her. She wanted to go back to last night, when he'd lifted her up on that pool table. She'd thought about it all night during her sleepless tossing and turning. He'd crept into her dreams. Only in her mind, the evening had gone completely differently. Adam hadn't pulled out of their embrace abruptly. He hadn't walked away from her.

"You really don't see it, do you?" he asked, pulling her out of her musings. "The tabloids are interested in you because you're alluring and talented. People are drawn to you."

Was that really how he saw her?

Ani shook her head to clear it. She had to focus. They had more pressing matters at the moment. Her inconvenient attraction to this man had to take a spot on the back burner. For now. She wasn't naive enough to think she could ignore it for long. Sooner or later, she was going to have to grapple with her feelings for him.

"That isn't at all what I signed up for," she admitted. "Mysterious emails. Crowds waiting for me outside venues."

"Your life was bound to change, kitten. You had to know that."

She pulled the hat lower on her head, as if she could hide herself from the reality of the world somehow, "I guess I didn't give it enough thought. I was too focused on the opportunity, the chance to share my music with as many people as possible."

"It will take some getting used to."

"If I decide to continue."

His head snapped up. "You can't mean you might want to give it up?"

She shrugged. She wasn't exactly sure what she meant; she just knew she had some thinking to do. "I guess I have some decisions to make."

"We'll figure out who's sending you those emails, Ani. It's just going to take some time. And you've worked so hard to get here."

He didn't need to tell her that. Hours of practices since she'd been a little girl. Sleepless nights spent composing after completing all her regular coursework. And now it was all being overshadowed by useless gossip.

"Maybe I'll just teach. It's not a bad way to make a living."

Adam reached for her hand, gave it a squeeze. It was hard not to think about where those hands had been last night: under her shirt, caressing her body… Heat crept along her skin at the memories.

Stop. Just stop.

"Don't come to any conclusions right now," he said. "You don't want to make any rash decisions."

Ani knew he was right. But the truth of the matter was that she was far more shaken about everything than she wanted to admit.

The only question was, what was she going to do about it?

Adam knew he had about a hundred other things he should be doing about now. There were several proverbial fires to put out. He had a team of professionals still waiting for an explanation and there were plenty of clients he should probably call.

So it made no sense that he was still sitting here on a bench with Ani almost an hour after finding her. As if they were a normal tourist couple sharing a baguette on a beautiful morning in France.

He felt Ani take a deep breath next to him. "Fame and publicity weren't supposed to be that large a part of this tour," she declared, staring off toward the water in the distance. "I haven't even been asked for an interview by a local television station."

"That was before you blew everyone away last night."

Including me, he thought, though he figured that part was better left unsaid.

"Moira's trying to convince me to schedule a press junket either today or tomorrow before we leave. She thinks all this is a *hoot*, to use her word."

He broke off another piece of the bread Ani wordlessly offered him and popped it in his mouth. "I take it you're not a fan of that idea."

"Absolutely not."

"You'll have to let me know ASAP if you change your mind. That kind of event will take a lot of prep."

"I'm not going to change my mind."

"Fair enough."

She chuckled slightly. "Though the kids back at the center would get a kick out of seeing me online."

"You think about those kids a lot, don't you?"

A genuine, affectionate smile spread across her lips. "They're another reason I felt so rattled this morning with all that's happened."

"How so?"

The smile faded. "I can't bear the thought of walking through that center and having a random paparazzi potentially following me. I don't want strangers peering into my life. Digging into my past."

"Is your past so sordid?" he teased. He'd known Brant since they were both kids, and by extension knew she'd led a rather sheltered life.

She gave him a playful shove on the shoulder. "No. Of course not. But there's my mother."

Adam gave himself a mental thwack on the forehead. How could he have failed to consider how the loss of her mother would play into all of this?

"I don't want them so much as mentioning her name. Or how we lost her. My father won't be able to bear it."

A wave of guilt swelled through his core. He should have never let any of this happen, and he vowed he'd find a way to neutralize it somehow. How often in his lifetime could he let a woman down so completely when he was supposed to be protecting her?

"Maybe the interest will die down," he tried to reassure her. Though the comment was nothing more than a small fib. Each tour stop would bring more and more attention to her. She was a phenomenon in the making. He had no doubt of that after watching her from the stage last night and observing the audience reaction.

The real question was, was she ready for any of it? He had the feeling she was stronger than she gave herself credit for.

"Why do I get the feeling you're trying to tell me what I want to hear?" she asked.

"Is it working?"

"Maybe." She smiled at him, sending a silly jolt of pleasure through his chest. The smile slowly faded. "In the end, it's all about the music for me." Ani gave a weary sigh. "What no audience will understand is what the music means to me." Her eyes narrowed, staring off toward the distance before becoming unfocused.

"What's it mean, Ani?"

"It's a connection to my mom. Something we shared, just her and me. I think it's why I was able to handle her loss so much better than Dad or Brant. Why I didn't fall apart the way they did after she was gone."

It explained a lot as to why she was the one left to gather the pieces of her family's broken hearts after the tragedy. "That was hardly fair," he told her. "You were just a child."

She shrugged. "Maybe. But I was lucky to have that piece of her. Every time I began to play, I felt her presence.

My brother and father didn't have anything comparable. I was the lucky one."

She had no idea how selfless she was to see things that way. "You still had a right to grieve. In your own way." He was just beginning to understand how wholly she'd been denied that.

Her gaze found him again, her eyebrows drawn together, as if weighing the full impact of his words.

Adam's phone buzzed in his pocket before either could speak again, pulling them both back to the moment at hand. The damn thing had been going off continually since he'd sat down. He couldn't afford to avoid it much longer.

"You should really get that, you know," Ani prompted, then glanced at her own phone where it rested on her lap. "I'm ignoring mine but I'm guessing it's your team trying to get a hold of you."

Adam nodded. "Along with a slew of others."

"Others?"

"Current and potential clients. Not to mention curious friends and various acquaintances who suddenly seem to have found my number." Interestingly, he hadn't yet gotten any kind of message from Brant. He groaned internally. Not a conversation he was looking forward to.

Ani cupped a hand to her mouth. "Oh, Adam. I'm so sorry."

"What are you apologizing for?"

"For being so selfish. I hadn't even stopped to consider how all of this was affecting you."

Selfish was the last word he would use to describe her. Especially after the conversation they'd just had. He had wondered why she'd been so upset about the gossip sites and the tabloids. Her reaction had seemed disproportionate somehow. But she'd been worried about everyone but herself. Mainly her father and the kids she taught.

"Don't worry about me, Ani. You have enough on your mind."

"But what will you do?"

"Damage control. I can be pretty good at it." Except for that one fateful time when he hadn't been. He fought back the bile that threatened to rise up his throat as the memories assaulted him. The smoke, the screaming. The rancid smell of burned metal. And the utter, useless destruction.

Ani hesitated, then finally stood. "I'm guessing we should get back. Moira's probably ready to panic at my prolonged absence."

Adam nodded and stood as well. He watched as a small toddler ran after a ball toward the water with his frantic mother chasing him. She caught him just in time. The little boy giggled in his mom's arms as she carried him back to their picnic blanket.

Adam glanced toward the shine of the water, the rays of the sun lighting up the surface...then at a couple who held hands as they walked along and chatted animatedly.

Those were the images he needed to hold on to. The ones in his mind would only serve to drive him nearly mad if he let them.

"So, tell me about your team," Ani prompted as they leisurely walked back to the hotel. It was as if they were both trying to avoid the reality that waited for them.

"What would you like to know? I can tell you I only hire the best. They're all former special ops or elite law-enforcement officers."

Ani chewed her lip. There were times like this when Adam was all business. "I don't mean their professional qualifications. Who are they? April mentioned she has a younger sister."

"Yeah, she talks about her all the time. April's putting

her through college. Parents were deadbeats who wanted nothing to do with their girls once they hit the ripe old age of eighteen."

"That's very commendable of her."

"She's a woman of strong character."

They passed a charming patisserie, the rich scent of roasted coffee beans reaching her on an aromatic wave. It occurred to her she hadn't had so much as a hint of caffeine yet this morning. Just went to show how distracted she'd been. Any other day that would have been an unacceptable state of affairs.

Her gaze lingered on the doorway.

Adam must have noticed. "Would you like anything? Another baguette or a breakfast crepe, maybe?"

She shook her head. "I'm not hungry. But I could definitely use a cup of coffee."

He nodded. "Rich and creamy? Or bold and strong?"

"Something in between?"

He ordered for them both when they went into the shop. *Un café simple* for himself and *un café noisette* for her, which he told her was a strong espresso-type coffee with a heap of thick cream. The smiling barista handed them to-go cups in mere moments. They continued their walk.

"What about your other team members?" Ani asked, resuming their conversation. She was trying to keep her mind off everything she needed to think about eventually, all the things she had to figure out about who she was and the kind of life she wanted to ultimately lead. Plus, she was genuinely curious. So far, she'd really only gotten to know April, and not very well.

Not to mention, she needed to take her mind off of what Adam had said to her by the river. Had she really not been given a true chance to grieve her very own mother?

"Let's see," Adam began. "Tito is former navy. He and

his wife welcomed twin girls about two years ago. That was when he decided he was ready for civilian life. So he started working for me. Believe it or not, the hours are better. And I'm a better employer than Uncle Sam in many regards."

She chuckled at that.

"Raj is going to school part-time. Mechanical engineering major through ROTC. He's looking to get his MBA. One of the smartest men I've ever met."

Ani took a sip of her drink as she listened. The savory chicory taste blended smoothly with the heavy cream. So much richer than the *café au lait* she'd been having. She would definitely need to order this again before they were due to leave Paris in a day.

Arriving back in Dallas was going to be a surreal experience. It was almost as if she'd be coming home a completely different person. She'd gone from being an unknown to having her image posted on numerous websites all over the world.

And then there was Adam. She couldn't define what was between them. But she knew for certain she wouldn't be able to stop thinking about him.

Adam continued, "Finally, there's Penelope. But we don't dare call her that. She hates it. Penny just got engaged to her high school sweetheart. She's excited to be moving into a new house once we get back to the States. I'm sure she'll invite you to the wedding. Apparently, it's going to be a huge one. You might not even be the only celebrity there."

The comment served as a reminder of all that she'd been trying to avoid thinking about.

Adam's phone hadn't stopped buzzing and ringing. The latest call had a shadow falling across his face when he looked at the screen. He bit out a sharp curse. The man could swear like…well, a soldier. "I have to take this."

She watched as he stepped away and spoke into the phone. His mouth grew tighter, a muscle in his jaw twitching each time he listened to whoever was on the other end.

When he clicked off the call and reached her side again, she could almost feel the tension radiating off of him. Tension and anger combined.

"Was it that bad?"

"You don't need to worry about it, Ani."

Again with the desire to spare her any upset. She reached for his forearm. "Please, just tell me. It might help to get some of it off your chest."

"I doubt it. But fine. If you really want to know, that was a client who just recently hired us. He wanted to know if he should maybe rethink the contract he signed with Steele Security. If he could trust me with his new young trophy wife to accompany her to visit her family in a particularly dangerous part of Mexico."

"Oh, no."

"The bastard didn't even want to listen when I told him I didn't even particularly do fieldwork. That I would only be leading the team."

"Adam, I'm so sorry. It was no doubt more his insecurity driving that phone call rather than any real concern about you." Not that the knowledge changed anything.

He drained his cup and tossed it in a nearby receptacle.

This was all her fault. He could very well lose business as a result of all this. Adam's reputation and that of his company would still be intact if her brother and father hadn't insisted on hiring him in the first place. The very livelihood of the employees Adam just spoke so fondly of might be in jeopardy as a result. She thought about everything he had just told her about the four who were with them today. And no doubt there were others he employed. What about all their dreams, their plans for the future?

She couldn't bear the thought that they may have to seek alternate employment because of an impulsive decision her family members had made. She hadn't really even needed a security detail. It was just another instance of the men in her life being unreasonable and overprotective.

An idea sneaked into her head. One that might take some of the attention off of the photos from last night. It just might work.

Adam would never go along with it. She had to be brave enough to do this without his knowledge or approval. He would refuse out of concern for her. She would just have to suffer his wrath afterward, if need be.

The local reporters wanted a press junket. That was out of the question. But maybe she would have Moira make a couple of phone calls to clear some things up.

Ani had no doubt Moira would love the script Ani wanted her to say. Her manager did love a good gossip story, after all.

CHAPTER SIX

WELL, IF THIS wasn't a first.

A woman was actually trying to spare his reputation. Adam would have laughed if the situation weren't so damn unfunny.

He rubbed at his forehead and reread the article on the website April had alerted him to a few minutes ago. He sat at the wicker table on the balcony of his hotel room. Though it was still early afternoon, he was having a sweaty bottle of American beer. Some days, a man needed a drink a bit early.

A spokesperson for Ms. Terrance finally returned our calls. She says the two have been friends since childhood and recently decided to take their relationship to the next level. Mr. Steele has been accompanying her on this trip more as a boyfriend than as her hired security. His profession just happens to be an added bonus.

It was actually quite genius. If he was here "more as a boyfriend"—quote, unquote—then he hadn't crossed any kind of line with a client. He took another swig of the ale. Ani's heart was in the right place. She'd done this for him. Still, what the hell had she been thinking?

A knock sounded on his door, so light he'd barely heard it from his seat outside. He knew without a doubt that it was her. He could sense her presence almost before she'd even knocked. And silly as it was, he could swear he could smell her sweet floral scent in the air, even from way out here, despite the breeze.

He didn't bother verbally responding before opening the door.

She'd showered and changed since their walk earlier this morning. In a bright yellow summer dress with spaghetti-thin straps, she had a bright red scarf wrapped around her hair like a headband. The color combination should not have worked at all, especially with her bright red curls. But somehow on her, the look was delectable. In fact, she reminded him of a cupcake, good enough to eat.

Good Lord, snap out of it.

Ani rung her hands, hesitating at the doorway. "On a scale of one to ten, how cross are you?"

He didn't answer but instead turned around and walked back out to the balcony. Ani followed on his heels. He picked up the bottle of beer and took another swig.

"Adam?" She absentmindedly took the bottle out of his hand and drank a quarter of the remaining contents.

"Would you like one?" he asked when she thrust it back into his hand.

She glanced down at the bottle like she hadn't even realized it existed. She was definitely flustered. Well, maybe she should have thought about his possible reaction before she'd gone ahead and made such a decision on her own.

"Goodness, no. It's way too early to be drinking beer," she answered, without the least bit of awareness. "You didn't answer my question. Are you terribly angry?"

"You could have given me a heads-up."

"Would you have gone along with it?"

"Absolutely not."

She tilted her head to the side. "Not that I'm surprised, but why not?"

"There had to have been a better way."

"I couldn't come up with one. This makes sense."

"*You* didn't need to come up with anything. It was my dilemma to fix." He walked over to the railing and leaned with his arms braced against it.

"Well, something had to be done. Look at the client calls you were getting. And the publicity wasn't going to let up. You know that."

Of course, she was right. In fact, the next stop where she was performing could very well be worse.

It was just such a fiasco of a lie. "What about your emailing admirer?" he asked her.

"What about him?"

"News of you being involved with someone else is often the kind of development that would bring a stalker to escalate his efforts. You've gone and upped the ante."

She swallowed. "Maybe. Isn't it just as likely that he may get the hint and move on?"

She had him there. There was no way to be sure. No one case was like another. Infatuated celebrity stalkers didn't often have the same MO aside from the harassment itself. Ani was right. There was a chance her admirer would take this as a sign to move on to someone else.

Still, Adam didn't like the odds. "The point is, you shouldn't have made the decision on your own, Ani. Not without asking me. This isn't some kind of game. Your safety is at stake."

"So was your professional reputation."

She was altruistic to a fault. As if the two risks even compared with one another. Adam didn't know whether to thank her for her foolishness or grab her by the shoulders and try to shake some sense into her.

"It wasn't worth the risk to your personal safety."

"Very small risk."

"That's not your decision to make. Not in this case."

She studied him. "Why? On the surface, nothing's really changed. I still have an unknown person sending me messages, and I'm still under your protection. Why is it that you're so concerned exactly?"

She was much too observant and much too aware. "I'm your bodyguard."

"There's more to it, isn't there?"

Adam felt his fists tighten by his sides. "Let's just say I'd like to avoid making the same damn mistake that cost me everything."

"What mistake?"

Adam braced his hands against the balcony railing. "Just drop it, Ani."

Ani straightened, then pressed her case. "Fine. Suit yourself if you don't want to tell me more. The fact remains that I did what I thought was best. Who knows, there might be paparazzi down there right now." She waved a hand at the street below. "Watching our every move."

Adam didn't think, just turned and stepped over to her, then pulled her up against him. Emotions he thought he'd buried suddenly surged to the surface.

Their lips were less than an inch apart. Ani's skin grew hot under his touch; her cheeks blushed a light pink.

"Then, seeing as the damage is already done, perhaps we should give them a show, kitten."

If this was supposed to be some kind of penance for what she'd done, Ani figured she was a glutton for punishment.

This kiss was nothing like last night in the pub. Then, Adam had been gentle, his lips brushing softly against hers.

This kiss was the opposite of gentle. He crushed his mouth against hers, pulled her tight up against him.

"I don't know why I lose such control with you, kitten," he whispered against her lips. His words sent an electric current down her spine. He wanted her, he was admitting as much.

Right or wrong, she wanted him just as much, if not more.

"I can't seem to stop wanting to touch you," he whispered harshly. "We keep getting in trouble for it."

So he did indeed want her. He just didn't want to want her.

What a sorry state of affairs. Adam was probably cursing the day he'd taken on this assignment. It wasn't as if any of this was planned on her part. She hadn't walked into her father's office that day anticipating any kind of romantic junction in her life. In fact, she was at a point in life where any kind of relationship would be distracting and completely inconvenient.

She had thought she was on the cusp of the career she'd always wanted. Now, her whole idea of success had taken a completely different turn. Did she want the kind of success that came with fame and constant scrutiny?

She had way too much to figure out about herself before she could even consider tying herself to another person. Not to mention, Adam didn't exactly seem the type to settle down or be content with one woman. She'd heard more than a few times from Brant about his steady stream of romantic interests, always spoken with a sense of awe and respect. No, he was definitely more the type that left a trail of broken hearts in his wake. The last thing she needed was a broken heart.

She didn't come from the kind of folks who handled loss well. Or at all, really. Her father was a shell of the man he used to be, paranoid and anxiety-ridden.

So why was she still in Adam's embrace? Why was she kissing him and exploring his mouth with her tongue? Why was she moaning into his lips?

Her foolish heart leaped at what he'd said. He lost control around her. He wasn't ready for any of this either. But he was saying he couldn't help himself. His admission shouldn't have sent such a thrill of feminine pleasure down her spine.

If only she were the type of woman who could be comfortable with a fling. She could be up front with Adam once and for all. Tell him that they should just enjoy each other's company without thought of future ramifications. If only she could go ahead and indulge all the fantasies that had crept into her dreams since he'd come into her life.

The idea of it was oh so tempting.

But she wasn't built that way. She had to stop kissing him. Now.

Abruptly, but with deep reluctance, she made herself break the kiss and step away. Adam looked momentarily confused. He rubbed the back of his hand against his mouth. Then he gave his head a shake as if to clear it. "I'm glad one of us is using their good sense."

"It wasn't easy," she admitted.

"I should never have kissed you like that. I should never have risked where it could have led."

She could only nod. He was right. This was the first time they'd truly been alone together. The room on top of the bar last night had been secluded, but it had still been part of a public place. Anyone could have come up the stairs. Here and now, they could be assured of no inter-

ruptions. And heaven help her, if he'd led her there, she
might very well have fallen into his bed.

He pulled his hair up off his forehead. "You should go."

"I know."

But it took several moments for her body to obey her
brain. Finally, she turned and strode off the balcony and
out of his room before she could change her mind.

Adam made sure to stand stone still until the door shut
behind Ani. Only then did he release the breath he wasn't
aware he'd been holding.

One time. It had taken exactly one time being alone
with her for a few minutes in a hotel room and he'd lost
all control. This was ridiculous. He was a trained military
officer, for heaven's sake. He should be more disciplined
when it came to his desires. No more.

And to ensure it, he decided to make the phone call he'd
been dreading. Without giving himself a chance to hesitate, he pulled out his phone and dialed Brant's number.

He answered right away. "Adam, is everything all right?
Ani?"

Adam was quick to reassure his friend. "Ani's fine. I
just wanted to clear the air about something."

"What's that?"

"What you're seeing and hearing, about Ani and me."

"Yes?"

"I just want you to know it's not what it looks like."

To his surprise, Brant chuckled at the other end of the
line. "Yeah, I figured it was some kind of publicity stunt.
Knowing Moira and all."

"You did?"

"Hey, listen buddy, I'm heading into a rather urgent dinner meeting with some important clients. Can I call you
back in a day or so?"

That was it? That was all Brant had to say about the prospect of Adam potentially hooking up with his younger sister?

"Uh…sure."

"Thanks, man." Brant paused. "Appreciate the heads-up. But you know I trust you." With that, he disconnected.

Adam stared at his phone, somewhat stunned. He had braced himself for a much more uncomfortable conversation.

You know I trust you.

Adam threw the phone onto the mattress and swore. He had to wonder if Brant was a fool.

She desperately needed a good cuddle. There was only one male for the job. Ani curled up into the couch, holding her beloved mutt tight against her. For her reward, she got at least a few dozen wet tongue lashes to her face.

A knock sounded on the suite door and her heart pounded in her chest at the thought it might be Adam. But it was Moira who answered when she called out.

"Hey, I came by a few minutes ago, and you didn't answer your door," Moira announced as she walked past her into the room. "Where were you?"

Ani thought about telling her a small white lie. Moira's eyes seemed to light up with interest any time Ani mentioned Adam. She decided she didn't have the energy to vary from the truth. "I had to see Adam about something."

She was right. Moira wiggled her eyebrows suggestively. "Oh, did you, now?"

Ani released a sigh of frustration and plopped herself back down on the couch. "It's not anything to gush over. I just wanted to see if he'd heard about our leak to the press and how he was handling it."

Moira sat down next to her, knees tucked to her chest. "And how was he handling it?"

Memories of their kiss assaulted her and Ani felt her cheeks flame. "I'm not quite sure."

"Well. That's a good sign. Isn't it?"

Snowball jumped between them and nudged them both aside with his furry behind to make room.

"Again, same answer. I can't quite be sure."

Moira gave the dog a pat on the head. "Ani. What exactly is going on between you two? Every time he's by your side, I can practically see the sparks fly."

"There's nothing going on between us," Ani said, unable to look at her friend. Apparently she had the energy for a fib, after all. But at Moira's huff of disbelief, she had to relent. "Well, there shouldn't be. The truth is, I can't seem to stop thinking about him. And I think he might be attracted to me, too."

There, now it was all out in the open. Not that it made her feel any better.

"Oh, there's no question about that. The man looks at you like he's starving and you're five-star French cuisine."

"Moira."

"No, seriously. He looks at you like he's dying of thirst and you're a fine Bordeaux. Like he's just wandered through a hot desert and you're a frozen vanilla custard." Moira giggled.

"I think I get the picture."

Moira's smile thinned as she turned serious. "So what are you going to do about it?"

"Nothing. Absolutely nothing."

"Huh." Moira tapped her chin, as if contemplating Ani's answer.

"After we leave Paris, I'm going to insist we switch to a different security service. If I even agree to more security, that is. This isn't an extended tour. I just need to get through one more performance and then I'll have a chance to reexamine some things as they pertain to my career."

"Oh, Ani, you can't mean that. You have so much talent. And the audience loved you last night. You were born to do this."

She wasn't so sure about that anymore. And the audience loving her apparently meant they felt entitled to intrude into her personal life. She'd never feel comfortable with that.

"I'm not sure I'm ready for all this, Moira. I need to think."

"You're scared, I get that."

She was right. Now that Moira had come out and said it, Ani had to acknowledge her fear. The whole world was watching her. What if she failed and made a fool of herself? And her growing feelings for Adam only served to complicate the entire matter.

She groaned out loud.

Moira gave her arm a squeeze. "I hate to add to your misery, but we have to talk about all the offers that have come in since you performed. Your limited tour could easily grow to an extended one if you're up for it."

Another groan escaped. She didn't think she was up for adding tour dates in the least. But she'd be giving up the opportunity of a lifetime. Her only mission before she'd gone up on that stage had been to prove to the world that she was good enough. Ironically, now that she'd done so, she was full of self-doubt.

What would her mother have thought? Mom was the one who'd set her down at the piano when she was barely old enough to walk. She'd been Ani's first instructor.

Some of her earliest memories involved sitting on her mother's lap at that piano bench. The instrument itself had seemed gigantic. Ani had found it hard to believe such delicate sounds could come from an object that huge. First Mom would play, and the music sounded magical and otherworldly to Ani's young ears. Then she'd let Ani run her fingers over the smooth, polished keys, encouraging her to press them down herself. She remembered cringing in shock at the sound at first. But Mom had simply laughed that pretty, melodic laugh of hers.

You'll get the hang of it soon enough, love.

Ani felt the sting of tears and pushed the memory away. Even the sweetest of memories could lead to crushing pain.

"Ani, I have to give these people an answer soon," Moira prompted.

Ani nodded and sighed. "I know, I just need to think about it. Just a few days." If only she could take off and go somewhere, to find some isolation and quiet and give herself a chance to breathe.

"Okay, sweetie. I'll hold off for now. And you still have that photo shoot tomorrow. There's no way out of that, it's in the contract."

Ani winced. She'd sort of forgotten about the scheduled photo shoot. Or rather, she hadn't allowed herself to really think about it.

"I know, I'll be ready. But can we talk about something else right now?" She desperately needed to quiet her mind. Why had she never taken up meditation? Or yoga?

"Sure. Anything for you."

Ani's relief was short-lived.

"So about this chemistry that you have with your bodyguard," Moira said. "Let's get back to that."

"Let's not."

"Why don't you just go for it? The man is hot with a capital *H*. If someone who looked like that was interested in me…" Moira smiled wickedly rather than finishing her sentence.

"I can't just 'go for it,'" Ani insisted.

"Why ever not?"

"Even you have to see that the timing is completely off. I'm not at a point in my life where I can handle the emotional pull of any kind of relationship. And he doesn't appear to be the type for heavy involvement, anyway."

"So why does it have to be heavy?" Moira nudged Ani's knee. "Come on. You're in one of the most romantic cities, maybe *the* most romantic, in fact. And there's a gorgeous specimen of a man who wants you. Just go for it."

Moira too closely echoed the thoughts that had been running through Ani's head when she'd been in Adam's arms earlier.

"I'm not one for flings," Ani said, despite the temptation thrumming through her. Except, she hadn't exactly had any deep, meaningful relationships either. Maybe it was just that she wasn't one for relationships in general.

"Wanna know what I think?" Moira asked.

Ani really didn't. Moot point, as Moira didn't wait for an answer.

"I think you're scared of more than just adding tour dates."

CHAPTER SEVEN

ANI WAS HIDING it well. But Adam could sense how nervous she was. The photographer's crew had cordoned off a good twenty-by-twenty square of the eastern side of the Louvre for her photo shoot. Tito, Raj, Penny and April stood guard around the perimeter. Adam was closer to where Ani stood posing.

Of course, they'd gathered a bit of a crowd. Ani had been doing fine until an audience had gradually shown up to watch. She kept glancing nervously at the spectators taking their own pictures.

Come on, kitten. Just a little longer. You're almost done.

"Let's take a little break," the photographer suggested.

Ani's breath of relief was audible from where Adam stood several feet away.

She accepted a bottle of water but made a beeline right to where he was. A heady sense of prideful pleasure filled his chest.

"How am I doing?" she asked.

"You're stunning, Ani." She really was. They'd dressed her in a red satin formal gown, and her fiery red hair hung in loose curls over her elegant shoulders. "You'll have some great publicity images."

"I just want it to be over. I think I'm more nervous posing now than I was actually performing onstage."

She was clearly out of her element. He wasn't about to say it out loud, though. "Won't be much longer. Just listen to the photographer and focus on following his direction. This is almost like a performance, too."

She gave him a wide smile and leaned slightly into his shoulder. "Thanks. That was the perfect thing to say."

He put his arms around her, in a gesture of comfort, and felt her release a deep sigh against his chest.

The rapid-fire click of a camera sounded from where the photographer and Moira stood. Ani jumped back as if struck by an electrical shock. Moira gave them an innocent shrug. Ani rubbed her forehead wearily.

"It's okay. We're supposed to be dating, remember?" Adam reminded her, though he felt less than comfortable himself. A bodyguard wasn't supposed to become part of the foreground.

"Perfect," the photographer called over to them in a thick French accent, "It's how you Americans say…worth a thousand words."

Adam's senses suddenly went on high alert. He took Ani by the arm just as a commotion broke out off to the side.

A man strode toward them with April fast on his heels.

Adam immediately pushed Ani behind him and widened his stance to cover her completely. He braced for a potential physical confrontation. But April apprehended the stranger just in time.

"I just wanted to ask for an autograph," the man protested in thickly accented English. "I was at her concert. Ms. Terrance, you were fabulous that night," he yelled, adding, "I'm a big fan."

Tito approached to take the intruder away. "No autographs. And that's not the way to ask for one," he chided.

Adam allowed himself to relax. What the hell was April thinking, letting someone get past her like that?

She must have read his thoughts. April gave him an apologetic shrug. "Sorry, boss. It won't happen again. You have my word."

"What happened?" he demanded. Ani clung to his back and he reached behind him to give her a reassuring squeeze.

"I have no excuse," April admitted. "Just got distracted when the photographer started taking photos of the two of you together. I repeat, it won't happen again."

Adam gave her a sharp nod as his ire drained away. This was exactly what he meant about staying in the background. He and Ani had been the reason April had been taken off guard. He knew she was better trained than that. And she was right, she didn't have any kind of excuse. But he couldn't ignore the role he himself had played in the breach. This was his responsibility as well as hers. Just as much, if not more. After all, he was in charge. The last thing he needed to be was a distraction.

Right now, he only had one primary concern. He had to keep Ani safe.

He turned to check on her. Her eyes were wide with fear. Her entire body was shaking from head to toe; he could almost hear her teeth chattering.

"I th-thought you might have been right. That maybe the st-stalker had escalated his attempts, after all," she stuttered.

He took her in his arms, held her close. "You're okay, kitten. You're safe." Lifting her chin, he waited until she looked him in the eyes. She'd gone so pale. "We're done here," he barked.

His declaration was met with immediate protests from the photographer and his crew. Adam didn't care. "You have what you need."

Then he lifted Ani in his arms and carried her away.

* * *

"Here, drink." Adam handed Ani a stemless wineglass that she accepted with trembling hands.

She sat on his hotel balcony, the Eiffel Tower looming majestically in the distance, slightly covered in fog. "What is it?"

"Rosé with papaya juice. Just enough wine to take the edge off." He pointed to a half-empty, ice-cold water bottle sitting in front of her on the wicker table. "Straight water doesn't seem to be doing the trick," he added.

"I'm all right, really. In fact, I'm a little embarrassed. My reaction was disproportionate." Who knew she was so much like her brother and father, after all.

"You're still shaking."

"It's mostly residual. Subsiding as we speak." She held a hand up to show him.

"Still, you sure you don't want to see a doctor or something?"

"Heavens, no." At his look of concern, Ani felt warmth spread through her. "Really, I'm fine now. The rational part of my brain knows my emailer is nowhere near Paris. But my nerves are completely on edge."

"That's understandable. Who would blame you?"

"The autograph seeker just took me by surprise. I wasn't expecting anyone to get that close."

"He never should have," he bit out through gritted teeth. "For what it's worth, April feels terrible."

She nodded. "I know. In addition to the in-person apology she gave me once we got back, she's been texting me incessantly to check how I'm doing and to say how sorry she is. Again." Her phone sounded an alert even as she spoke. Sure enough, it was April. How many different ways could the woman come up with to render an apology?

A sudden, disturbing thought occurred to her. "You're

not going to reprimand her in any way, are you?" She would feel terrible if April got into any kind of trouble because of the way Ani had overreacted back at the Louvre.

"No. I have no intention of so much as chastising her. That would make me a hypocrite."

His words stunned her. "What are you talking about?"

He sat down across from her, pulling his chair so close their knees were touching. "April's not the only one who should apologize. I'm so sorry, Ani. I'm even more responsible for what happened than she is."

She reached for his hands where they were braced against his legs, and took them into her own. "The only person responsible is my so-called fan. And me. For the way I reacted."

"You have absolutely no fault in any of this. I was foolish. I repeated the mistake I vowed never to make again."

"What mistake?"

He gave a shake of his head. Whatever mistake he spoke of, it weighed heavily on his soul. "It's not important."

She wanted to argue. The anguish on his face told her exactly how false those words were. Maybe Adam was even denying that truth to himself.

Ani wanted to push for answers but it wasn't her place. She imagined he had seen and been through experiences she couldn't hope to comprehend. He'd been stationed in hellish regions and she knew human nature could be unbearably cruel.

No, she wouldn't push for anything Adam wasn't ready to give. He would share if or when he was ever ready. She could only hope she would be the one he'd turn to.

"Just know that you had absolutely no blame for what happened or for the way it affected you," he insisted.

Ani had to laugh, but there was no real humor behind it. "Well, I suppose we could go in circles all day abdicating each other of responsibility. I, for one, will try to learn from this. Starting with the lesson that I do not need to cower in paranoia every time I'm approached by someone who wants an autograph."

"That's hardly what you did."

"Pretty darn close, I'd say."

He rubbed the inside of her wrist. "Ani, you don't have to do that, you know."

She lifted an eyebrow. "Do what?"

"You don't have to pretend you're not struggling."

She released a deep breath. "You're right. I just wish there was someone I could lean on during all this. Someone like my mom."

She hadn't expected to make the admission. Had barely acknowledged it to herself. So it surprised her that she'd confided in Adam about it.

"I'd say you can talk to me, but I realize it's nowhere near the same as having a trusted parent to rely on."

Ani felt the telltale stinging behind her eyes again. Not a day went by that she didn't think about her mother or the devastation left behind at her loss. But since arriving in Europe, she'd felt an ache that only Mom would have been able to soothe. She swiped at her eyes before the tears could fall.

"I know I'm in a foreign city on the trip of a lifetime," she said, "but what I wouldn't give to be on a beach just soaking in the sun and trying to come to terms with all that's happening in my life right now."

"You have a few more days before you return to the States," Adam pointed out. "I could take you back early if you'd like to be back home."

She shook her head. "No, Dallas would be even more draining. Between my brother and father constantly hovering over me and everything I need to catch up on after being away."

"I see what you mean."

"I think I'll draw the blinds, sit in the dark on the bed and contemplate how I want to move forward in my life. Paris is a wonderful city, but it isn't exactly conducive to quiet pondering."

Adam looked off to the side, appearing to carefully weigh his next words. "I might have another idea."

"Oh, yeah? Consider me intrigued."

He swallowed. "It just so happens I own a place in this part of the world. It's not all that far by plane. Right on the Mediterranean. With a long stretch of sandy beach."

Ani felt her jaw drop. That scenario sounded like pure heaven. The man was full of surprises. "You do?"

He nodded. "Yeah. Ever been to Monaco?"

Adam could count on one hand all the impulsive, spur-of-the-moment decisions he'd made in his life. It was time to add another digit to the count. He hadn't realized he was going to offer to bring Ani here until the words had left his mouth.

He'd ignored the warning cry in his head, telling him all the reasons what he was doing was foolish. And all the ways he would eventually come to regret it.

But he'd seen the turmoil in Ani's eyes after the incident in the square, and all he'd wanted to do was whisk her away from it. Take her somewhere with no crowds to scare her. Somewhere only a trusted few people knew of. He'd only had one goal in mind—to make her feel safe.

For her part, Ani seemed equally surprised to have taken him up on the offer.

Now, as they drove up the winding cliffside to his villa

in a convertible Mercedes, he couldn't bring himself to regret asking her.

"How often do you come out here?" Ani asked, shouting over the roaring wind.

"Not often enough."

Snowball let out a happy little yip in the back seat where he sat in a securely fastened doggy chair.

"But don't worry," he added. "You won't be walking into a dark, dusty, uninhabited house. I have someone I call in when I plan on coming into town. A local woman gets the place ready for me." Thank heavens for her, Adam thought. This time, he'd given poor Jaqueline less than one day's notice. Bless her to the skies, she'd agreed nonetheless. He would have to reward her flexibility handsomely.

"The thought hadn't even occurred to me," Ani shouted with a laugh. She already looked more relaxed and loose than he could recall seeing her since they'd left Dallas International.

It seemed a lifetime ago that they'd left the States. So much had happened since then. If someone had told him that afternoon that he'd be driving to his Monte Carlo estate with the VIP he was guarding, he would have laughed in their face.

But it was worth it just to see the utter relief Ani currently wore on her face.

He could relate. Despite the harrowing ride along jagged cliff edges, Adam always felt the tension slowly leave his muscles whenever he came to Monaco. The fresh sea air and the crystal blue water served as a balm to his soul. This was one of his favorite properties. He had to make more of an effort to get out here.

Though he hadn't seen this trip coming, Adam already felt good about the unexpected detour.

Minutes later, they were driving up the long pathway that led to his gated property. He fired off a text to Jaqueline and the gate slowly slid open. The older woman greeted them at the doorway.

"Mr. Steele. What a lovely surprise it was to hear you'd be coming." She was completely fluent in English, having been educated in Boston as a young woman. Not even a noticeable accent.

She came down the stairs and gave him a motherly peck on the cheek. When Ani approached with Snowball on a leash, the older woman clapped her hands with a grin. She leaned to pet the dog with a stream of French baby talk.

"Jaqueline loves animals," Adam told Ani above the fuss of petting and face licking.

"Snowball tends to make friends quickly."

When Jaqueline finally stood, he introduced the two women. The older woman's eyes lit up mischievously as she studied Ani. Uh-oh. He should have seen this coming. Jaqueline had been very vocal in the past about Adam finding a woman he could bring here more than once. She probably wasn't going to waste any time as soon as she got him alone to hammer him with questions. Also, she'd probably seen some of the online gossip. Jaqueline's hobby was social media.

Adam would have to worry about that later. Right now, he wanted to get them settled. He went back to the car and grabbed both their bags.

"I have a lovely dinner prepared for you when you're both ready," Jaqueline announced, leading them inside.

"Thank you, Jaqueline," Adam replied. "We'll just freshen up and be right down."

He led Ani up the spiral staircase to the second floor. She paused to admire the view of the coastline outside the large panoramic window above the steps. Several luxury boats floated on the water, the sky was a spectacular shade of blue, and the water looked like turquoise jewelry.

"This is breathtaking, Adam. Exactly what I needed."

The statement and her genuine smile pleased him clear to his toes. Without thinking, he dropped their bags and reached out to trail a finger gently down her cheek.

"I hope it serves as the getaway you're looking for, kitten."

She sucked in her bottom lip, and he felt a wanton urge to leave the bags where they were and lift Ani in his arms and carry her like he had the other day in the square. Then he would carry her straight to his suite rather than showing her to the guest room.

Steady there. Ani was here for some much-needed peace and solitude. Not to be seduced.

He leaned down to pick up the bags once more as a disquieting thought occurred to him. "Just one thing."

"What's that?"

"I'm afraid I don't have a piano," he announced, wondering if he should have thought to tell her that. Or if he needed to invest in one as soon as possible.

Anything to keep that smile of contentment on Ani's face.

It hadn't even occurred to her to ask about a piano.

Ani had to take a moment to process that. When was the last time she'd gone so much as forty-eight hours without practicing her craft? What did it mean that the notion didn't scare her in the least? In fact, it felt oddly freeing. Foreign and unfamiliar, but freeing nonetheless.

What was happening to her?

It wasn't like her to accept impromptu invitations to grand estates. And it certainly was uncharacteristic of her to be so blasé about her practice schedule. But somehow, it all felt right. Being here with Adam felt right.

Ani plopped herself down on the king-size bed in the room Adam had led her to. Though "room" was an understatement. The closet alone was the size of her entire bedroom back home.

She'd known he was well-off. But this was a whole other level. Even after these past few days together, she knew so little of the man.

One thing was certain: it was beyond kind of him to bring her here. This would be the mini vacation she was due for, even if it was only for two days. Short but sweet. Hopefully by the end, she'd gain some clarity of mind.

A text message lit up her phone.

Heading down to dinner. No rush. Join me when you're ready.

Good saints above, she'd been so deep in her thoughts that she hadn't realized how much time had passed. Ani glanced in the mirror at the windblown disaster of her hair and her disheveled clothing.

This would not do. She'd unexpectedly found herself in one of the most glamorous parts of the world. And she would make herself presentable for dinner.

Adam would just have to wait. Her stomach growled in protest. So she'd have to get ready fairly quickly.

Another way she'd changed. Ani couldn't recall any time in the past when she would have let her hunger take a back priority to fixing herself up.

By the time she made it downstairs about fifteen minutes later, she had to think she'd made a pretty good effort. She wore a silk summer dress with a flower pattern and butter-soft sandals that she'd bought just for this trip.

Her hair was mostly loose, with a small clip at the base of her neck securing it just enough to keep it off her face.

She walked through the foyer at the bottom of the stairs toward a door that led to a brick patio. Adam had given her a quick verbal layout of the house when he'd shown her to her room.

She found him there sitting at a set table studying a spreadsheet.

"Sorry to keep you waiting."

He looked her up and down. "I'd say it was quite worth the wait."

Ani hoped he didn't see the blush creep up her cheeks as he held out a chair. The night was comfortably warm with just enough of a breeze to feel refreshing. In the distance, the coastline looked like a masterpiece of a painting, majestic and artful.

"This is breathtakingly beautiful, Adam."

"It beats the army barracks."

She chuckled. "Tell me something. Did you happen to win the Texas state lottery at some point and neglect to mention it? I know a soldier's salary didn't allow you to acquire all this."

"You could say that. I've had a good deal of success with various investments. It's akin to winning the lottery. One particular tech start-up opportunity paid extraordinarily well. I invested the profits and the jackpot grew from there. Then I founded Steele Security and invested to make that grow."

He made the statement in a completely nonchalant manner, no hint of pride or boasting. She didn't know much about the stock market, but she knew enough to figure that this much financial success would require much more than luck. Adam clearly had a head for business and the intelligence to make extremely lucrative decisions.

Her curiosity was beyond piqued. "If you don't mind my asking, why are you still so involved with the company?" She motioned around her. "It appears you could sit on your laurels for a bit." He owned a villa on the French Riviera, for heaven's sake.

He shrugged. "I need to stay occupied. Not quite ready to sit on any laurels just yet."

Or he was still trying to prove himself. To whom, Ani could venture a guess. Adam had grown up with an aunt and uncle who'd been kind enough to take him in, but not enough to love him. They'd been ready to tell anyone who would listen that his arrival had put an inconvenient dent in their childless lives.

"You joined the army to get away, didn't you?" she dared to ask, knowing the question was more personal than anything they'd discussed so far.

"Ani, I had nowhere else to go. The day I turned eighteen, my uncle made sure to inform me that his responsibility to me was over."

Again, the statement was completely matter-of-fact, with no discernible emotion. "You don't sound bitter."

"They clothed me and they fed me for years. I had it better than a lot of other orphaned kids."

That was true. They just hadn't loved him. Ani itched to stand and walk over to pull him into her embrace. To try to soothe the unwanted teenage boy he must have been. All those years she'd been crushing on him as a teenager, she'd had no clue the depth of emptiness he must have been enduring.

Jaqueline appeared at that moment with a silver rolling cart. A bottle of red wine sat in the center.

"*Bonjour*, Miss Ani. I hope you're hungry."

Ani patted her midsection. "I'm starving. And that smells heavenly."

Jaqueline nodded. "Grilled fish caught just today. With a light green salad and freshly baked baguette. I've been baking bread all day."

Adam lifted the bottle and started to pour into their goblets. "Would you care for a glass?" he asked Jaqueline.

She waved away the offer. "*Non, merci.* I had a bit of rosé at lunch. No more for me today. Is there anything else I can get for you two?"

Adam leaned over to give her a small peck on the cheek. "You've done enough on such short notice," he told her. "Go on home. We'll take care of the dishes and the cleanup."

"*Au revoir*, then," Jaqueline gave him a grateful smile, waved goodbye to Ani, then turned to leave.

Leaving her alone with the man she was growing increasingly attracted to with each passing minute.

CHAPTER EIGHT

ADAM COULDN'T RECALL the last time he'd had such a pleasurable meal. In fact, he couldn't remember ever taking a full two hours to eat. Though the dinner itself had gone fairly quickly, they'd both simply sat and talked after finishing their food, slowly sipping on the rich merlot. He'd brought Ani here for her sake, but he had to wonder who was doing the other a favor.

"I think that might be the most tired I've ever seen Snowball," Ani said. Their conversation had veered toward the subject of her pet more than once. "He wasn't even interested in the bowl of food I set in his pen, just curled up on the pillow I threw in there and started to snore."

Adam chuckled. "We had a pretty long day of travel." It occurred to him he might be acting as a bad host. Just because he was enjoying himself didn't mean Ani wasn't tired and ready for bed.

"I apologize," he began, hating that he may be right and that Ani was ready to retire for the evening.

"For what?"

"You must be exhausted. I didn't mean to keep you up."

"You're not keeping me up." She took a sip of her wine, then glanced at him from under long, dark lashes. "Actually, I find I don't want this night to end."

Didn't she know what it did to him when she said such

things? He was barely holding on to control as it was. They may be here in a paradise on earth, but the outside reality hadn't changed for either of them. He had no business wanting her, he couldn't offer her what a woman like Ani deserved. He had worldly possessions most men could only dream of. But Ani wasn't the type of woman who would make wealth any kind of consideration when deciding what she wanted from a relationship.

And he knew better than to pine for any kind of relationship himself.

He waited for her to continue, afraid of saying the wrong thing. Or saying exactly what he was feeling.

She finally spoke after sipping some more wine. "I owe Moira a call some time tomorrow. I promised to let her know if I'd come to any conclusions about adding performance dates."

Adam nearly laughed out loud. Talk about flattering himself. She didn't want the night to end because she dreaded the phone call she had to make in the morning. It had nothing to do with him. He shouldn't have been disappointed. In fact, he should have been relieved.

Focus.

"I still don't know what I'm going to tell her," she said, staring off into the distance. The sun was beginning to set, slowly turning the sky from aqua blue to a deep, dark navy.

"Ani, if you're not ready for a career move like that just yet, you have to respect that."

She toyed with the stem of her wineglass. "What if another opportunity like this doesn't come again?"

She really had no idea of the depth of her ability and talent. "You don't give yourself enough credit. I have no doubt the music world will be waiting for you with open arms whenever you're ready."

Ani finally glanced at him, and the turmoil in her eyes

had him aching to reach for her. "What if I'm never ready? What if I'm not cut out for the limelight and the life of a celebrity?"

"Then you should respect that, as well."

"Maybe. I'd have to live with the knowledge that I may have thrown away an opportunity most artists can only dream of."

He couldn't argue with that. *What if* questions always had a way of following one through life. But there was an opposite side to that particular coin. "If you go forward and you're miserable, you'll have the same questions."

She took a small sip of her wine. Adam got the impression she wasn't really tasting it, too deep in thought. There was something else weighing on her mind and impacting her decision about what path to take. The answer came when she spoke again. "I keep thinking about what Mom would think. Music was such a large part of her life. She was my first piano instructor. Some of my earliest memories involve stroking the keys while sitting on her lap."

Ah, so that was the missing piece. He should have known. Ani was afraid of disappointing a parent she'd lost long ago. It appeared they had much more in common than he'd ever known. But the difference was, Ani's mother was a loving and caring nurturer who doted on both her children. He'd heard enough about her from Brant to know that for a fact.

Adam had never experienced such affection. He really had no business trying to give her any advice about the matter, given his total lack of ability to relate. But he wanted desperately to ease some of Ani's turmoil.

"I wonder if I'd be disappointing her if I say no," she continued. "It's silly, I know. But I can't help but believe she'd want me to embrace this chance I've been given."

He reached across the table and took her hand in his. "Ani, I believe more than anything else that she'd want you to be happy."

"I should go check on Snowball," Ani proclaimed, then stood suddenly. She knew she was running from the conversation. But she wasn't ready to confront some of these feelings just yet. And she certainly wasn't used to sharing so much of herself with another person. In fact, it scared her how much she'd just shared with Adam.

She'd never told another soul, not even Brant or her father, the extent of her internal anxiety about letting her mother down when it came to her playing.

Adam slowly nodded. "All right. I'll be right here if you'd like to come back down."

Did she? Earlier she'd told him that she didn't want the night to end. The ocean air, the richly delicious wine and the magnetism of the man sitting across from her was a scene right out of a fairy tale that she wanted to continue forever. But then the conversation had veered in a direction she hadn't been prepared for.

"But I will understand if you don't," Adam added.

No pressure, and she was thankful for it. But part of her wished he would push her just a bit, take some of the decisions out of her hands.

He could ask her to stay with him. See where things might lead. But Adam was too much of a gentleman. That was a good thing, wasn't it?

She mumbled a thank-you before rushing upstairs.

As expected, Snowball was still out cold in the safety of his puppy pen. Too bad. She could have used an attentive ear right about now.

You just fled from the one person you've ever felt comfortable confiding in.

She had her reasons. She was just having trouble articulating what they were. Part of the issue was that Adam himself was so closed off, holding himself at a distance. Despite having known him most of her life, she didn't actually *know* him. Not even the most basic details of his background. Years ago, she'd asked Brant how Adam had come to live with his aunt and uncle, but her brother had shut her down, telling her it was none of her business and to stay out of his friend's business. Then he'd given her a serious noogie.

Ani dropped down on the bed and released a deep sigh. It bothered her more than she cared to admit that Adam wasn't ready to divulge anything real about himself to her. While she'd grown to trust him implicitly. The dichotomy made her feel lacking, inadequate. Shouldn't he trust her a little bit, too, at this point?

One thing was certain—she wasn't going to find out anything holed up in this room. Bouncing upright, she freshened up in the bathroom and went back downstairs.

Adam was in the kitchen, elbow deep in suds, washing dishes. His back to her, he had his shirt sleeves rolled up and a kitchen towel draped over his left shoulder. Ani's heart did a flip in her chest. It had never occurred to her how sexy she would find a man in the middle of a household chore.

Not just any man. Adam Steele.

She figured she would probably find him sexy doing most anything.

She walked over and removed the towel from his shoulder. "I'll dry."

"How's the bunny rabbit?" he asked with a sideways glance as she lifted the first plate off the rack.

"Ha ha. My *dog* is resting comfortably, thank you very much."

"Glad to hear it."

"I suppose any dog you ever get would be much fiercer. The size of a small car, perhaps?"

"At least."

"I would expect nothing less."

Adam chuckled. "I worked with a canine unit for a while in the army. A German shepherd. He was trained to sniff out explosives."

Finally, a small tidbit of information about his past. As innocuous as it was, it was *something*. She'd take it.

"What happened to him?"

He shrugged, dipped another plate into the suds, then wiped it with a thick sponge. "Reassigned. He wasn't actually my dog."

"Do you miss him?"

He snorted. "About all I miss from those days." He dropped the last plate onto the rack a little too forcefully. "Brant was the one who gave you Snowball, wasn't he?"

"Yes, he rescued him from a local pound about three years ago when he was just a few weeks old. Just a tiny puppy."

"Brant was worried about you. Mentioned you were going through a tough time."

"I'd just been dumped. My on-and-off boyfriend of about a year decided our relationship needed to remain in the off status."

"What happened?"

She took the cutting knife he'd just cleaned, and dried it off with the towel before placing it on the counter. "The usual. He felt we'd grown apart. He said I never had any time for him, between my constant practice schedule and my volunteer work at the center."

"Brant told me he never liked him. He was obviously a blind and selfish fool."

Ani stilled in front of the counter. So she'd been a topic of discussion between Adam and Brant. The notion sent a hum over her skin. "Oh?"

"I asked about you from time to time."

"I see," she responded, taking a fork he'd just washed.

"You know, small talk during those long, boring patrols."

It appeared an opportunity had presented itself. Ani took the chance it offered. "You know, it just so happens I asked him about you as well."

Adam paused ever so slightly. "Is that so?"

"Yeah. Brant told me to mind my own business."

He reached into the sink to remove the plug and drain it. Several beats passed and he hadn't said anything in response to her comment. Ani concluded he wasn't going to when he turned to face her, leaning his hip against the counter.

"That's because Brant's a good friend. One who can be trusted to keep confidences that shouldn't be told."

She wasn't surprised by that answer, but she was sorely disappointed. She opened her mouth to speak but couldn't come up with anything to say. He tilted her chin with the tip of his finger.

"Good night, kitten. I'll see you in the morning."

Ani had Snowball out in the grassy area by Adam's infinity pool when she noticed him coming up the stone steps. Dressed in sports shorts and a T-shirt that accentuated all the contours of his muscles, and judging by the sheen of sweat over his tanned skin, he'd clearly been out for a run.

"You're up," he said when he spotted her. He reached down to give the dog an affectionate pat.

"I slept longer than I usually do," she answered. She wouldn't share that she'd only overslept because she'd had so much trouble drifting off once she got into bed. Her mind had been busy all night with thoughts of the man who stood before her. Snippets of their conversation over dinner, the way she'd felt in his arms when he'd carried her out of the square. The feel of his lips against hers when he'd kissed her on the hotel balcony. She'd tossed and turned until the light of dawn had crept through her window.

"Probably the fresh sea air."

"Right," she replied simply. "You've obviously been up for a while."

He wiped away the sweat on his chin with his forearm. "Went for a quick run along the beach. Go ahead and grab some breakfast. Jaqueline stopped by with some pastries earlier. Cheese-filled croissants."

"That sounds heavenly." But what she could really use was caffeine.

Adam must have read her thoughts. "And there's a carafe full of freshly brewed American coffee. I always keep some on hand."

"Perfect."

He gave her a wink and a smile that had her stomach doing a small dive. "I'll be back after a quick shower."

True to his word, Ani had barely had a chance to pour her coffee and grab a croissant when he ran back down to join her at an outdoor patio table. His hair was still dripping wet, and he'd barely bothered to comb it. The result was a disheveled, tousled look that she found ridiculously sexy.

He was wearing swim trunks.

"Did you pack a suit?" he asked as he sat with his own mug of coffee. "You did say you wanted some time on a beach. If not, we can pick one up from one of the boutiques."

"I have a suit. And spending time on the beach sounds like exactly what the doctor ordered." Also, it would give her an excuse to delay calling Moira.

"Eat your breakfast, then go throw your suit on. I'll play fetch with your pet rabbit."

Ani bit back her laugh. "Please don't call him that," she said with mock outrage. "He can hear you."

Twenty minutes later, Adam proved true to his word. Snowball was panting heavily and refusing to retrieve a stick Adam had just thrown.

"Looks like this fella could use a midmorning nap," she said. "I'll take him up to my room and get him settled."

He wiggled his eyebrows. "I'll be waiting."

Ani was on her way back downstairs when the front door opened into the foyer. Jaqueline stepped inside, carrying paper bags of various sizes. The enticing aroma of fresh bread suddenly filled the air.

Ani strode over to her. "Here, let me help with some of those."

"Merci," the other woman replied, handing her some of the bags. "I thought I'd get started on lunch."

The French certainly knew how to eat, Ani mused. At this rate, she'd have to shop for new clothes upon her return to Dallas.

Jaqueline suddenly stopped and scrutinized her face. Had she left a smudge of sunscreen unblended? Ani rubbed at her check.

"Forgive me for staring, dear," Jaqueline said with a warm smile. "I'm just so glad Adam has brought someone here finally. Usually, when he visits, he takes a morning run and then holes up in his study for the rest of the day just working."

Ani wasn't sure what to say to that. In fact, the unexpected conversation was throwing her off balance.

Jaqueline continued, "I'm glad he's finally found someone to distract him from all that work he does."

It appeared she had come to all sorts of conclusions about the two of them.

Ani finally found her tongue. "Oh, it's not like that. I just had a tough couple of days and he brought me here to unwind. We're not, like, together in that way."

But what exactly were they? There was no denying the attraction between them. Nor the way he'd seemed just as affected by their kisses as she was.

Jaqueline ignored her. "You know, the last time he brought a woman here, it didn't go so well. She ended up leaving in a huff. You probably know of her. That model that does the perfume ads."

"Oh?" was all Ani could muster. Adam had dated a famous perfume model. She'd been here at this very villa with him. "Were they very serious?" She couldn't help but ask.

"I think so." Jaqueline awkwardly squeezed her arm in reassurance while still clutching a bag. "But don't worry, he seems to be having more fun with you. He's smiling more."

Ani felt her heart sink and she nearly dropped the parcel she was holding. Of course she'd known that Adam must have been involved romantically with other women. But hearing he might have been serious with someone triggered a tightening in the pit of her stomach. A well-known perfume model, no less.

"How long ago was this?" She had to ask, a glutton for punishment.

She didn't get an answer.

Instead, Adam loudly cleared his throat behind them.

When she turned and saw the expression on his face, Ani lost her grip on the bag. It landed on the floor with a thud.

CHAPTER NINE

THE WALK DOWN the rocky path toward the beach was thick with tension. On the one hand, Ani could see why Adam might be cross. She had been caught gossiping about him with the woman who served as his housekeeper. On the other hand, what was the big deal? So much for relaxing with some sun and sand by the water.

The sight that greeted her when they reached the bottom nearly took her breath away. It was the bluest water she'd ever seen. Majestic yachts floated in the distance. The cliffside was dotted with buildings and structures built right into the mountain. She paused to admire the view. Adam kept right on walking.

That was it. She'd had enough of the grumpy silent treatment. Catching up, she grabbed his elbow and made him turn around to face her.

"Is there a problem?" He wanted to know.

"You tell me."

"If you had a question, you should have asked me. Not Jaqueline."

It was hard to read his eyes behind the mirrored glasses. But his tone was all too clear.

"For the record," Ani said, "Jaqueline started the conversation. And yes, I should have come to you with any questions that arose from it. But I don't see why you're so irate about the whole thing."

"Don't you?"

"Let me ask you, would you have told me anything about your past if I'd asked you?"

"It depends on what you wanted to know."

Ani crossed her arms in front of her chest. "That's a tad hypocritical, don't you think?"

It was the wrong word. A muscle twitched along his jawline. He pulled his arm free. "Care to explain what you mean by that?"

She wasn't going to do this. There was absolutely no need for this conversation. She'd thought perhaps they were growing close. That maybe he was growing to care for her a bit. But she'd been wrong. Because here he was, nearly livid at the possibility that she might have learned a thing or two about him.

"Never mind," she bit out. "This is pointless."

After tomorrow, this whole sad state of affairs would be over and they could both go their separate ways. If she did decide on going on the additional tour dates, she would have to find another security service. She'd have to look for a bodyguard with a better disposition, for one.

She ran past him toward the water. Her skin was burning hot with irritation. Stripping off her summer dress, she made straight for the ocean and dove in when she'd gone far enough out. The saltwater felt cool and soothing. To her surprise, Adam was standing less than a foot in front of her when she resurfaced. Shirtless and wet from the chest down.

How had he gotten here so fast? She'd had a good twenty feet on him at one point. He'd even had time to rid himself of his shirt and sunglasses.

"You didn't answer my question," he pointed out.

Oh, yes. He was perturbed that she had called his actions hypocritical. It was her turn to get angry. Out of pure frustration, she hooked her leg around the back of his knee and pushed against his chest with all her might.

It must have been shock, because Adam went down with a resounding splash into the water.

She came this close to laughing. Until he shot up out of the water to glare at her. "Feel better?" he demanded.

"I could ask you the same question. Clearly, you needed to cool off a bit."

"Looks like someone schooled you in some self-defense moves." He wiped down his face with the palm of his hand.

"Just what the teenage boys at the center showed me."

"You learned well."

She sat back, allowing herself to float. "That makes me realize something I hadn't thought about before."

"What's that?"

"You've been derelict in your duty. Shouldn't you have been teaching me some self-defense moves yourself?"

He narrowed his eyes in question. "What?"

"Most movies and books involving bodyguards have at least one scene where the woman is soundly yet cautiously manhandled while the so-called protector shows her how to defend herself."

"Is that so?"

She nodded. "I shouldn't have to tell you this."

He gave her such a casual shrug her instincts went on high alert. "It's not too late. I could start right now."

She squinted at him, not liking the sound of his voice at all. "What did you have in mind?"

"Every time you manage to take me down again, you can ask me a question."

Ha! As if she trusted him to really reveal anything.

He continued as if he'd read her mind. "I promise to answer whatever the question is. Fully and truthfully."

She was intrigued despite herself. Darned if she'd show it, however. "Maybe I'm not that interested any longer," she threw out.

"Maybe you're a liar."

That did it. She did want to topple him over again. But she wouldn't have the advantage of surprise this time.

"I don't want to hurt you, Adam."

For the first time since he walked in on her and Jaqueline in the foyer, she saw the hint of a smile on his face. "Feel free to try, kitten."

"Fine." She stood up in the soft sand.

Trying the same maneuver again, she went to hook her foot behind his knee. He stepped away before she could so much as reach him.

He smirked at her.

Making the perfect fist, she got ready to aim for his side. Not really to hurt him, just to throw him off balance so she could trip him into the water. He grabbed her wrist before she could make contact.

A fake-out. It was her only hope. She threw her hands up in the air as if completely frustrated. Not that she wasn't. "Fine, you win. I'm going back onto the shore."

Pretending to stride by, she bent over and lunged her shoulder toward him instead. He barely moved.

"Oh, kitten. I was hoping you could do better than that."

"Yeah, well, so was I."

Was it her imagination, or was that actual amusement she saw in his eyes? At her expense!

He rubbed his chin. "Perhaps you're right. Maybe I should show you some basic jujitsu moves."

"Jaja what now?"

He actually laughed. "Here. I know you're dying to see

me fall in again. A freebie." He reached for her stealthily, without warning. "But you're coming with me."

Before she knew what he intended, he launched himself backward into the water, pulling her on top of him.

What had he been thinking?

Ani landed on his chest, his arms around her midriff. He still held her as they broke the surface of the water a second later. And now he could hardly think at all. She'd thrown her arms around his neck at some point. Now they stood, their faces an inch apart, skin against wet skin.

"That was uncalled for." Her breath was thick when she spoke. "You owe me an apology."

He wasn't sure if they were speaking of the stunt he just pulled or what had happened between them back at the house. He decided he didn't care. It was hard to care about anything but the feel of her when she was in his arms like this. "I'm sorry," he whispered.

"Me, too," she said, surprising him. "I'm sorry, Adam."

"What exactly are *you* apologizing for, kitten?"

"For upsetting you earlier."

Adam swallowed. At the time, he'd been beyond annoyed. Now he felt like a heel for the way the scene had played out. He just wasn't used to talking about himself. He didn't want to think about his past, let alone have it be a topic of discussion.

"And I'm sorry for this," she said on a breathless whisper, just before touching her lips to his.

The blood pounded in his veins. Her hesitant, gentle kiss threw the last gates of his resolve wide open. He pulled her tighter against him, plunged deeper into her mouth. Her arms grew tighter around his neck. Hooking his hands at the backs of her thighs, he lifted her to wrap her legs around his waist.

Time seemed to stand still; he couldn't get enough of her. Every nerve ending in his body was burning with desire. He had no idea how long he stood there in the water, holding her and tasting her. Finally, a small cry of sanity cut though his desire-fogged brain. He somehow managed to break the kiss.

"We need to stop, kitten. Or I'm likely to carry you out behind one of the cliffs and…" He knew better than to put into words all the things he was thinking.

She blinked up at him. The heat in her eyes nearly had his knees buckling beneath him.

He doubted the depth of her desire could match his own. Reluctantly, he disentangled their bodies, though he felt the ache of the loss clear to his bones.

Ani gave her head a shake.

By the time they made it back to shore, Adam almost had his breathing back under control. Almost.

"Guess we should have thought to bring towels," she muttered as she pulled her dress over her wet body. The fabric clung to her curves and Adam nearly groaned out loud.

"I thought we'd walk along the sand for a while," he answered. "I wasn't really expecting to go for a swim quite so soon."

"Well, I wasn't expecting any of that." She plopped down on the ground, shifting her legs underneath her.

Adam dropped down next to her. "That makes two of us. Though I guess I should have been better prepared."

"What's that mean?" Picking up a handful of sand, she let the grains slowly sift through her fingers.

"It means we're from two different worlds." He looked off toward the horizon. "You asked in Paris how I came to live with my aunt and uncle. Would you like to know the full story?"

"Of course. All I ever heard was just rumors that can't all be true because many of them contradicted each other. You were a bit of a novelty. Everyone talked about you."

He grunted a humorless laugh. "The reality wasn't novel at all. My old man took off and my mom chased after him. He left because he didn't want the burden of a family. And she chose him over me, her son. Last I heard, he sobered up and cleaned himself up. They have a whole other family. They still wanted nothing to do with me. Until learning about my wealth, that is… Now I hear from them all the time."

"I take it you ignore them."

He shrugged. "I ignore my parents, yes, but I have a younger brother and sister. They're actually pretty cute." Was that a hint of pride she heard in his voice? "I make sure they're taken care of."

"Taken care of how?"

"I send them a monthly stipend. I have a PI check in regularly to make sure the money is being spent where it should be and not on party expenses for two people who only ever thought of me as unwanted."

"Adam, I'm so sorry. I wish I'd known."

The pitying tone of her voice was exactly why she hadn't known all this time. Why he hadn't spoken of it with anyone but Brant, who'd been decent enough to keep it to himself all these years.

"Would it have made a difference if you had known?" he asked.

She looked at him then, her beautiful dark eyes wide with understanding. "It would have to me. All those times, I felt so out of place whenever you and Brant hung out together. So unwanted."

"I'm genuinely sorry about that. I was a thoughtless heel back then to make you feel that way."

He'd tried so hard to hide his feelings for her as a way to protect himself. She'd been so far out of his league. Just as she was now. He may be proficient in a few languages and enjoy a professional success few could dream of, but most of that had been pure luck. Ani had been born into a well-known and respected family and she was on her way to worldwide success. He simply didn't measure up.

He couldn't say any of that out loud. He'd tried so hard when they were kids to get Ani to believe he found her annoying, that he didn't want her around. The exact opposite had been true. And it had scared him to death.

Judging by the way he was feeling now, he'd been right to be scared.

Ani followed Adam as they walked back up the pathway that led to the house, both still dripping wet. She didn't know what to make of him. He seemed determined to push her away the moment they got too close.

"I think we should head to the casino this evening," Adam announced, pulling her out of her thoughts with a completely unexpected suggestion. "I'm sure Jaqueline would be happy to sit with Snowball. She seems to be quite fond of him. How's your blackjack game?"

"Nonexistent. I don't even know how to play."

"We'll have you rolling dice then, that's simple enough to learn."

If this was Adam's attempt to distract her from their earlier conversation, she wasn't sure it was going to work.

"I think we could both use a night out," he added. "What do you say?"

"I don't know if I have anything appropriate to wear. I didn't pack any of my formal attire that I brought along for the performances."

They'd reached the patio outside his villa. "There's a

gown or two that should be hanging—" He caught himself just in time.

"I take it the perfume model left a few items behind in her hasty departure?"

To his credit, he looked properly chagrined.

Doubtful the woman's discards would fit Ani, anyway. She was probably tall and statuesque with ample curves in all the right places.

"I never got around to asking Jaqueline to clear them out. We can stop at one of the boutiques later today," Adam said. "Pick something up for you."

She shrugged. "I suppose that would work."

He paused, then took her by the hand. "Listen, Ani. The model wasn't anyone I was ever serious with."

"Oh?" She wasn't quite sure what else to say. He'd surprised her.

He nodded. "I was at a point in my life when I needed a distraction with no strings attached. She fit the bill."

"I see."

"I got the impression she needed a distraction as well. But I didn't bother to ask. And she didn't ask me either."

Ani could only remain silent as he went on. "We had some fun together while it lasted. But she's not someone I even often think of."

With that, he pulled away and turned to walk into the house. Leaving Ani with one question on her mind. Who was the woman from his past Adam *did* think about?

The first boutique they visited, Ani managed to find the perfect dress: a strapless velvet gown in a midnight burgundy. Now, back at Adam's estate, she studied the end result in the floor-length mirror of her closet. The color shouldn't have worked with her bright red hair but somehow it flattered her, if she did say so herself. Adam hadn't seen it on her yet. She wondered if he would like it as well.

The man was a complete enigma. She knew he wanted her; the way he kissed her left no doubt. But he always held something back. And he'd blown her mind with all the things he'd revealed today. Still, she couldn't help but feel there was another piece of the puzzle missing when it came to understanding who he was behind the successful soldier turned billionaire business tycoon.

She turned to study her reflection from behind. She'd never been to any kind of casino before, let alone one known all over the world and featured in countless movies. But she figured she'd be passable.

It had taken her a while to warm to the idea, but she was growing more and more excited for the evening ahead with each passing minute. Tonight was going to be an opportunity to escape reality and ignore all the concerns that had been pulling at her these past few days. From anxiety about her career to the demands from Moira and others at the label, to the pressure of appeasing her family…and then there was Adam.

As far as he was concerned, she would just have to pretend. She'd let him take her by the elbow and walk her into an exclusive casino as if they were a real couple with a real future.

She much preferred that fictional scenario to the uncertainty she seemed to be facing in every aspect of her life.

CHAPTER TEN

SHE WAS LOSING a good amount of his money, Adam thought as he watched Ani throw another bad roll. Yet another stack of her chips was swept away by the dealer. It was worth it to see the genuine smile on her face. She was thoroughly enjoying herself. Considering the limited time they had before they each returned to reality, he was happy to see her letting loose a little. But her stack had most definitely dwindled in a shockingly short amount of time.

He would have to go get her more. After this next round, though, he was going to have to cut her off. She was just so bad at this and luck didn't seem to be on her side tonight. He happened to be a wealthy man but there were countless other entities he would rather donate his funds to rather than one of the richest casinos in the world.

Besides, she might have better luck at one of the slots. It certainly couldn't be worse.

He returned with another silver bucket full of chips only to find Ani had left the craps table. He spotted her over at the wide curved mahogany bar.

She was talking to a man. A handsome man in an expertly cut tuxedo.

Adam felt his fingers tighten around the rim of the bucket. Silly, really—he had no claim to her. She had every right to speak with any man in here. It made no sense that he wanted to body slam the man into the bar and wipe that charming smirk off his face.

He approached just as he heard Ani decline a drink offer. "Adam! There you are. This is Martin. He works for the Opéra de Monte-Carlo. It's part of the casino. Martin, this is my friend, Adam."

Adam knew he hadn't imagined the way Martin's smile had grown wider and Ani's use of the term *friend*.

The two men exchanged pleasantries in a mixture of both English and French. Adam held up the bucket full of chips toward Ani. "I got you more."

She tilted her head and smiled. "I decided to quit. Turns out I'm not very good at the craps table."

"We'll have you try the slots then." He gently took her by the elbow and led her away.

Ani stumbled but ultimately followed him, offering an apologetic wave at Martin. The other lifted his eyebrows as they walked away.

"Well, that was rude," she admonished when they were out of earshot.

"So was the way he kept ogling your cleavage."

Ani gasped with outrage. "He was doing no such thing! I'll have you know, he offered to introduce me to some of the orchestra players once he learned I'm a pianist."

"I'll bet he did."

She paused as they reached the row of slot machines. Beeps and whistles sounded the air around them.

"What's that supposed to mean?"

"Did he even give you any kind of proof?"

"Proof?"

Adam dropped several chips into the slot and pulled the arm lever. Nothing. "Let me get this straight—he found out you're a professional pianist and told you he just happens to work at the casino's opera house?"

She lifted her chin. "That's right. And you were incredibly rude to him." She reached inside her clutch purse. "And as far as proof, here's his card."

Adam squinted in the dim lighting to study it. Looked real, all right. "Huh."

She didn't respond, just grabbed the bucket out of his hands and stormed over to another machine.

Adam rubbed his forehead. Damn it. He'd just acted like an uncultured brute, dragging his woman away from a male who'd shown her interest.

His woman?

He refused to analyze that thought. Sighing, he walked over to where Ani was playing three machines at once, inserting the maximum amount of chips in each one. She really was a bad gambler. One machine registered a handful of coins in return.

"You must really take me for a fool," she said without looking at him, her gaze focused on the flashing lights of the slot she was playing.

"That's not true. It just seemed too much of a coincidence. And regardless of who he is, he was definitely ogling your cleavage." He hadn't imagined that part.

"Humph" was her only response.

Moments later, she turned the empty bucket upside down. "I appear to be out of chips."

"That took very little time. Would you like a drink?"

"Yes, I would like a drink and some air. I'll be outside."

Adam returned to the bar and ordered a bottle of champagne with two flutes. He could use a drink or two himself.

He found her by the lit fountain in front of the entrance. A rare, limited-issue Bentley pulled through the circular driveway before he could cross over to her.

When he did hand Ani a filled flute, she looked less than pleased with him. Her next question confirmed it.

"That was quite embarrassing, Adam. Why did you behave that way in there? With Martin?"

He didn't really have an answer. Not a satisfactory one, anyway. He would have to tell her the truth—to admit that he'd been jealous.

"I mentioned his ogling, did I not?" He took a long swig of the champagne. The highest quality this side of the Mediterranean, but he wasn't really tasting it. "I didn't like the way he was looking at you."

She turned to face him. "Well, that's something. Because it really bothered me the way some of those women in there were looking at you."

That was unexpected. "Huh."

She drained her glass in one impressive shot, then took the bottle from him to pour some more into her empty glass. "Maybe we need to figure this out, Adam."

"What's that?"

"Exactly what's happening between us."

Damned if I know, kitten.

Adam had whispered those words about three hours ago into her ear in answer to her loaded question. Only, it wasn't any kind of real answer.

Then he'd slowly lifted her chin and brushed his lips over hers ever so slightly.

Now, as she lay in bed with her window wide open, listening to the soft sounds of the night, she could almost feel herself back by the fountain in front of the Casino de Monte-Carlo. The taste of his lips still lingered on hers.

Like last night, she wasn't getting a wink of sleep. Insomnia had never particularly plagued her, but since arriving in Europe, she couldn't quite seem to get her mind to shut off when her head hit the pillow. It didn't help that

Snowball was snoring in tempo, right by her head on top of the extra pillow.

But she mostly blamed Adam. Nearly all of her mind ramblings involved him in one way or another.

The moon cast a small glow of light about the room. A glance at the hanging wall clock told her it was 3:00 a.m. She may as well get some fresh air.

When she made it outside to the brick patio, she was surprised to find herself not alone. Adam was swimming laps along the length of the infinity pool.

With half a mind to turn around, she realized he'd somehow sensed her there and was looking right at her. She moved to the pool deck.

Adam swam to the edge where she stood above him. "Did I wake you?"

"No. I couldn't sleep." She crouched down to get closer to his eye level. "You either, huh?"

He brushed the hair off his face. The moonlight added a navy sheen to his wet, black hair. The way he had his arms braced on the edge of the pool accentuated the toned muscles of his chest and arms. Ani's fingers itched to touch him.

"Not uncommon. A lot of things keep me up at night."

The statement was so loaded and heavy, Ani longed to comfort him somehow. She had to remember he'd been an army officer deployed overseas. His nightmares were likely real memories of awful scenes he'd witnessed. She thought of all the times she would catch Brant staring off into space as one shudder after another rocked her brother's solid frame. He never wanted to talk about the terrors that caused it.

What horrors the two of them must have seen.

"A middle-of-the-night swim can do wonders to soothe the weary soul," Adam added.

"Is that so?"

"Most definitely. You should try it. Go grab your suit." His gaze fell to her bare thighs, then traveled up. "Or you could just jump in as you are."

Ani resisted the urge to cross her arms over her breasts. She should have grabbed some type of cover. The satin sleep set she wore was thin and flimsy and left very little to the imagination, especially around the vicinity of her chest. But it wasn't as if she'd expected to run into Adam at three in the morning.

What she ought to do was bid him good-night and rush back to her room.

But it did feel nice out here. The night was balmy with just a hint of a breeze. And they only had one more full night here. She didn't want to leave just yet.

"I think I'll just soak my feet."

She stood and walked over to the concrete steps that led into the pool, going as far as the third step, then sitting on the side edge. Adam swam over to join her at that end.

"Do you want to talk about it?" she asked when he reached her. He was perilously close to her left leg. She could feel the warmth of his skin against her knee. "What keeps you up at night, I mean?"

He rubbed his eyes. "Trust me, you don't want to hear about it."

"That doesn't mean I can't. My shoulders can bear more weight than you might think, Adam. I can lend you one. Or both."

Okay, it was a lame thing to say. But she meant it. Whatever else was happening between them, she liked to think they'd gotten close enough as individuals to trust and confide in each other.

He rested his arms on the wall, and his elbow touched her thigh. "I don't think I'd know where to start, kitten."

She'd apologized to him earlier about prying, but she found herself on the brink of doing it again nevertheless. She chewed on her bottom lip until it ached, concerned about his potential reaction to the question she was about to ask. "You could start by answering a question for me."

"What's that?"

"Why'd you really bring me here?"

"You've been wondering about that, have you?"

"Yes," she admitted. "You had to know I would. You said something back in Paris about not wanting to repeat a past mistake."

"I shouldn't have said that," he said through gritted teeth. "It's history that should stay well in the past."

"History has a way of creeping into the present. Like when it keeps you awake at night."

His shoulders dropped. "You're right."

She sucked in a deep breath for the courage. She had to continue now that she'd started this. "Tell me, Adam."

Adam squeezed his eyes shut, the pain etched into his features visible even in the soft light.

Ani would have done anything to ease the pain emanating from him. If only she knew what that might be. "What mistake were you referring to?" she asked quietly.

Even under the water, she could sense Adam's entire body clench with tension. The anguish practically vibrated off him.

"The one where the woman I wanted to marry almost lost her life because of me."

The air around them seemed to still completely. Whatever had happened with this woman, Adam was carrying a palatable amount of guilt about it.

Despite the myriad of questions hammering in her brain, Ani remained unmoving and silent, giving Adam the full choice of how and if he wanted to continue.

"We were in a small province to secure the perimeter after enemy troops had fallen back. Troops who were defeated, but they still left their hidden traps and weapons behind them."

Ani swallowed past a painful lump that had formed at the base of her throat.

"A journalist for an Atlanta-based news agency and her cameraman were granted authorization to embed with our infantry," he continued, staring off into the distance. "She came often over the span of a few months to cover the story. We grew close."

Ani didn't need him to paint a picture. She could see where this was going.

"I was the officer in charge the last day we went out. She joined us to file a report and have her cameraman film."

"What happened?"

"She wasn't supposed to be there. I'd told her no at first. Something didn't feel right. There'd been rumors of renewed hostile activity. But I let her convince me ultimately because of our personal relationship. She wanted her story. I relented because she talked me into it. Because she told me I was holding her back. Just like my—"

He didn't finish his sentence but Ani could guess what he'd been about to say. His mother had walked out on him, no doubt accusing him of holding her back from the life she wanted to lead. One without a child weighing her down.

Adam sucked in a deep breath and rubbed his forehead before continuing. "We were traveling in an armored vehicle. I let her open the hatch just enough for her cameraman to take a quick photo. That's precisely the moment we hit the improvised explosive."

"Oh, Adam."

"She was critically injured, as was the cameraman. The

surgical team at the military hospital on-site was able to save her but she suffered permanent injuries and scars. Luckily she's made a full recovery, though it was a long road."

"What else?" Ani prompted.

"I went to see her as soon as I got permission, ready to drop on one knee. Had the ring and everything."

Ani fought back the stinging in her eyes. The thought of Adam being ready to commit to someone else caused a sharp pain around the area of her heart. Still, she had to ask her next question. She had to know. "What happened?"

"Tried walking into her room but was stopped by a wall of family and friends. She refused to see me."

Ani couldn't hide her gasp of surprise.

Adam went on, "I can't blame her for wanting nothing to do with me." He pushed himself off the wall and back into the water. "But all that mattered was that she was going to be okay. I walked away and never contacted her again. Heard a few years later that she married her high school sweetheart and became an elementary school teacher."

He made his way back to the bottom step and began to climb out of the pool. Ani's hands were trembling as she reached for a towel tossed over the railing. She stood and handed it to him. They stood face-to-face, the height difference mitigated as she remained on the top while he was two steps below.

"Adam, you can't blame yourself for what happened," she insisted, knowing full well he would pay her words no heed.

He took the towel from her, his fingers brushing hers. "Thank you for that, kitten. But I know what I did and all the ways I fell short in my responsibility."

Ani wanted to stomp her foot in protest. He'd been blaming herself all these years for something he couldn't have controlled. "I'm glad your reporter is okay," she said instead. "I'm glad she recovered fully. I'm sure she was hurt and scared and had her reasons for not wanting to see you. Reasons I guess I wouldn't understand."

"What's that mean?" he asked on a low whisper.

Ani swallowed through a throat that had suddenly gone dry. "It means I can't understand how any woman could just let you go."

Adam lifted an eyebrow. Rather than pull his hand back from where he'd reached for the towel, he grasped her wrist instead and pulled her closer. "You have to be careful about saying such things to me, kitten. Words like that might have consequences."

As if daring him, she stepped even closer, feeling the length of him against the thin satin of her top. Her body immediately responded through the fabric.

Adam noticed.

"Maybe I'm ready for consequences," she whispered breathlessly, hardly recognizing her own voice.

Still he made no move. She would have to take matters into her own hands. She wanted him and she was tired of waiting.

Thrusting her hand into his hair, she pulled his face to hers and claimed his mouth. She'd never been so bold with a man, so achy to have him kiss her and hold her.

Adam might not have made the first move, but his reaction was immediate and fierce. Lifting her by the backs of her legs, he hoisted her up and took her to the closest lounge cot.

Ani could hardly breathe. He was gentle, attentive. Completely in tune with her at every moment. Her skin burned everywhere he touched her, everywhere he kissed her. She'd been dreaming of this, imagining the way he would feel when he loved her. But nothing could have prepared her for the reality of it.

By the time he carried her upstairs and into his bed, she was nearly delirious with pleasure and need.

The consequences Adam had warned her of continued well past dawn.

It felt like déjà vu. Ani had awoken to an empty bed.

As disappointed as she was not to have Adam's warm body to snuggle into, she knew he was an early morning runner. She'd immediately gotten Snowball from her room and was with him on the grassy patch of yard with him now as she watched Adam jog up the stone pathway.

Just like yesterday. Only her world was so much different now. Adam Steele had made love to her. Her body reacted in response to the thought.

Judging by the sweaty look of him, he hadn't taken it easy on his run. Where did the man get such energy? Especially considering he'd been swimming in the middle of the night, and then not to mention all their shared activities afterward. A blush crept down her cheeks clear to her neck.

He stopped several feet in front of her. Snowball let out a small whimper. He'd noticed it, too—no pat on the head for her dog this morning. In fact, Adam's entire being stood rigid and tense. He wasn't quite meeting her eyes.

This did not bode well.

"Will you be ready to leave in a couple of hours?" he asked, without so much as a good morning.

Ani's heart sank. She refused to believe the worst just yet, but she was certainly beginning to suspect it. She nodded. "Not much to pack, after all."

He crossed his arms in front of his chest. Everything about him was closed off, resistant. "Good. That's good.

We'll get you back to Paris to rejoin your team and the security detail. Then we can head to Brussels with plenty of time leftover."

Snowball went to rub against his ankle, begging to be acknowledged.

Same here, buddy.

Adam glanced down as if finally noticing the dog for the first time. Finally, he bent to give him a playful rub along his fur. When he straightened, he finally did meet her gaze. But his eyes held no warmth, and zero of the passion he'd shown himself to be capable of last night.

She knew she was being too silent, but for the life of her she couldn't come up with a thing to say. Also, she feared the risk of sobbing out loud and uncontrollably if she so much as opened her mouth. So she stood there, dumbstruck.

She could almost see the proverbial curtain he'd pulled between them. Why couldn't the man understand what was so clear to her? Up until now, she hadn't even realized she'd been missing having love or passion in her life. Now that she'd experienced it, she didn't think she could bear to lose it. To lose Adam.

"He must have missed you last night." Adam pointed to the dog.

Finally, an acknowledgment of what had happened between them. Ani cleared her throat before attempting to speak. "I don't think he noticed I was gone. Found him still curled up and snoring soundly when I got back."

He shoved his hair off his forehead, glanced out toward the ocean. "Good. That's good."

Ani tried to cling to some semblance of hope. It was a good sign, after all, that he'd been worried about her dog. But his next words threw cold water on that. "Look, Ani. I know we need to talk about all this. But I figure we should just focus on getting ready for the return to Paris right now. We can talk as we fly back."

What was there to talk about? Ani knew better than to ask. There was no reason to discuss what they'd shared last night unless he regretted it.

"I'm gonna go shower. I'll meet you up front when you're ready. The jet's waiting at the airport."

Ani felt the burn of tears behind her eyes and watched his back as he went into the house.

Looked like she'd be adding another discarded gown to Adam's guest closet.

Adam turned the hot water on as high as it would go and stepped into the shower stall. He'd already punished himself with a particularly harsh run and now he would punish himself with a near-scalding shower.

He'd been a selfish bastard for so much as touching Ani.

She was brightness and light and positivity. Whereas all he'd ever known was darkness throughout his life. He had no business risking that any of that darkness would touch her in any way. He should have stayed the hell away from her.

She'd paid him a compliment and he'd basically turned into a pile of desire and longing. And he'd lost control altogether when she'd pulled his mouth to hers and kissed him as hard as she had. Even now, his body reacted to the memory of that kiss in ways that had him groaning in need and frustration. Maybe a cold shower would have been a better option. He had to stop thinking about Ani Terrance in any way that wasn't strictly professional.

He'd been entrusted to protect her and look what he'd done instead.

Oh, and there was that whole thing about never being able to look Brant in the eye again. He would have to come clean with his friend. Couldn't risk the other man finding out some other way. And he'd just have to brace himself for Brant's inevitable right hook that Adam wouldn't return nor so much as duck. He deserved no less.

He cursed out loud and punched the tile wall hard enough that his knuckles throbbed. What a complete mess.

Even if it took the self-restraint of a million monks, he absolutely could not touch her again. In fact, after her performance in Brussels, he would get her safely back to the States and then he would bid her goodbye. Raj and April could take over any remaining security needs for Ms. Terrance, including tracking down the sender of the blasted emails that had started this whole strange turn of events.

But first, he had to get her back to Paris. On a private plane, just the two of them. Mostly alone in the cabin.

One thing was certain: their flight back to France was bound to be a memorable one.

Ani wanted to forget everything about this return flight. With Adam working diligently on his laptop, she'd been feigning sleep in order to avoid talking to him. But that was getting old. And she knew she wasn't going to fool him much longer.

There was no point in having the discussion Adam was looking to have. Other than to make him feel better. It would make her feel considerably worse, if that was possible. She didn't need to hear about how it had all been a mistake. How one thing had led to another and how he should have exercised more constraint.

She stole a glance at him now through her partially shuttered eyelids. Even now, the sight of him tugged at her heart. What she wouldn't give to approach him, settle herself in his lap and ask for the comfort and solace she knew he could provide. If he'd only let himself.

But he wasn't ready to do that. He'd pulled himself away and shut himself off so completely, she knew it in no uncertain terms. Ani felt the sting of tears under her eyelids. This was exactly what she had meant to avoid. This feeling of loss and aching emptiness. She'd let herself fall for him when she had no business doing so. He wasn't ready to let anyone in; he was carrying too much of a burden. One he'd placed on his own shoulders and refused to put down.

She didn't think she had what it would take to reach him. She was too broken herself. Too confused about the reality she suddenly found herself in. Monaco had been a magical escape, a fantasy she couldn't hope to ever return to. Fantasies weren't real. Life didn't work that way.

Hers didn't, in any case. The gaping hole in her core left by the loss of her mother was proof of that. The magical time she'd spent with Adam had only been temporary, a brief respite. So she'd just continue to sit here and pretend to sleep until they reached the staunch, cold reality that awaited them back in Paris.

Except Snowball completely blew her cover. He suddenly jumped from his curled position on her lap and gave her a kiss that was overly wet even by his standards. Ani startled. Her eyes flew open.

Adam noticed immediately. "You're awake."

"Snowball seems to have wanted it that way."

"So I saw. He even jumps like a bunny," he teased, but Ani couldn't quite bring herself to smile and Adam's tight one seemed less than genuine.

"Can I get you anything?" he asked.

"Some water would be nice."

He got one from the bar and tossed it to her.

"Listen, Ani—"

But she cut him off, feigning a nonchalance she didn't

feel even as her heart continued to shatter in her chest. "I know what you're going to say."

"You do, huh?"

"I can guess. But I'd like to say something first."

His lips tightened before he responded, "Go ahead."

Now that she'd started, Ani wasn't sure how exactly she wanted to continue. "You're an incredible, accomplished man, Adam. I wish you could see that the way I do." She bit her lip before continuing, "I believe with all my heart that the woman you once wanted to marry has forgiven you. She's clearly moved on. Maybe it's time you allowed yourself to do the same."

He blew out a long breath. When he spoke, he didn't acknowledge anything she'd just said. It didn't surprise her. "Ani, I never meant for things to become this complicated."

Ani tried to breathe through the hollow churn of disappointment in her gut. Adam wasn't even going to broach the possibility of forgiving himself. And she wasn't sure how else to push. Or even if she should.

"I know. I just need to get past this next performance. Then we can address all the ways we're so wrong for each other and why we should go our separate ways."

He studied her features. "How'd your call with Moira go?"

Touché. Adam's question was his not-so-subtle way of pointing out that she was doing her own avoidance of sorts. They both knew Ani had never made that call.

She looked out the window, hoping he'd get the hint. This conversation was over before it had started. For now, at least.

CHAPTER ELEVEN

PERFORMING THIS TIME felt different.

Ani took the stage at the Forest National arena near Brussels and bowed before sitting in front of the piano and addressing the audience. She definitely felt less nervous than she had in Paris. After all, she'd done this once before and had triumphed.

Adam stood to the side of the stage, speaking into his earpiece and surveying the audience. He looked devastatingly handsome in the navy, Italian-cut suit. He turned to her and gave her a small wink before she walked out to play, making her heart lurch in her chest. He'd stayed away from her since they'd returned from Monte Carlo. April and Raj had taken over most of her detail.

Much to her dismay, she'd cried about that both nights until she fell asleep. She missed him. Somehow, when she hadn't been paying attention, she'd gone and fallen genuinely in love with her childhood crush. Or maybe she'd been in love with him all along. Whereas Adam had been avoiding an attraction to her all those years ago, she'd already started giving him her heart. There was no doubt now that it belonged to him fully and probably always would.

And wasn't this a fine time to be thinking about her foolishness when it came to Adam Steele?

Ani focused on the keys and began her first number.

The next two hours seemed to go by in a flash and before she knew it, she was taking her encore bow. April whisked her off the stage as soon as the curtain closed. Adam was nowhere to be seen. Just as well. He'd made his decision and Ani wasn't one to grovel.

Somehow, someway, she would get over the hurt of losing him. No doubt it would take time. Years, perhaps.

Once she reached the backstage dressing room, she shut the door behind her and leaned against it. Moira's knock came within seconds, but Ani chose to ignore it. She just needed some time to breathe.

It was over. She'd fulfilled her contractual commitments and her shows had been a notable success judging from the standing ovation out there.

But one thing was certain: she wasn't ready to make this a full-time career. She simply didn't want this kind of lifestyle. She liked having a home base and being able to volunteer her time where she was needed. She was going to have to turn down offers to continue touring. Moira would be disappointed, but this was Ani's life and she had to do what was right for her.

She hoped her mother would agree if she were here.

Her life plan was still an uncharted mystery, but at least she knew what she didn't want. As for what she did want... She thought of Adam once more and her heart fluttered in her chest despite herself. It had hurt just to look at him standing offstage. What she wanted most appeared to be out of her reach.

Adam forced himself to stay away from Ani's door. Her last performance was over. Which meant that in less than two days, his contractual obligation to protect her would also be complete.

Along the same lines, his IT guy had informed him that they were narrowing in on the server location where the mysterious emails had been sent. Pretty soon, they'd have a solid identity and neutralize any kind of threat. She'd have no need for him once that happened.

Judging by her performance just now and after the one in Paris, Ani was certain to have the whole world at her feet with her talent as a musician.

There'd be no holding her back.

The knock came again about an hour later. Ani gave in with resignation and went to answer the door. She had to let Moira in sometime.

But it was April on the other side of the door. "Hey."

"Hey. Come on in."

April strode into the room and pulled a bouquet of flowers from behind her back. "This is from all of us on your security detail to congratulate you. Way to knock 'em dead. In Paris, too."

Ani took the arrangement and inhaled the wonderful aroma, beyond touched at the gesture.

"And the boss says to tell ya 'good job.'"

Ani stilled in the process of putting the flowers in a tall glass of water. "Oh, he did, did he? Did he happen to mention why he won't come down here and tell me himself?"

April bounced on her heels. "Uh... I dunno. I don't really ask him questions of that nature."

Ani released her outrage on a sigh. "Sorry, April. He and I haven't exactly been communicating. Guess he wants to keep it that way."

April scratched the back of her head. "It's probably not my place to say, and I have no idea what's going on between you two. But for what it's worth, he seems pretty miserable."

Well, that was some small source of satisfaction.

"Also, for what it's worth, the flowers were his idea."

Rather than placating her, April's statement had the opposite effect. Of all the nerve! He couldn't come down here to congratulate her and he'd sent someone else to deliver the flowers he'd thought to get. As if they hadn't been as intimate as two people could be just two short nights ago.

Ani felt her blood pressure rise by several units. "I see. Is he still in the building?"

April nodded. "We don't leave until you're ready to."

Ani pointed to April's earpiece. "Could you radio him and ask him to come to my dressing room, please? Tell him it's urgent."

When Adam arrived less than five minutes later, Ani had only grown more steamed.

"You summoned?" he asked.

"Only because it didn't occur to you to come on your own."

April was smart enough to make a hasty exit as soon as they began their snarky exchange.

"Was there something you needed?" Adam asked as April shut the door behind her.

"Yes. I need to know why you've been avoiding me."

She also needed to stop noticing how devilishly handsome he looked. He'd taken off the suit jacket and rolled up his sleeves. The top three buttons of his shirt were undone and revealed enough of his chest that she remembered running her hands over and kissing that exact spot. She shook her head.

"I haven't been avoiding you," he protested.

"You didn't even bring me the flowers you bought yourself."

He crossed his arms in front of his chest and widened his feet, apparently ready to do battle. Well, so was she.

"You said on the plane ride that you'd rather not talk,"

he said. "I guess I was supposed to know you changed your mind about that."

"You were supposed to ask, Adam."

"Fine. I'll ask. Do you want to talk?"

If Ani was holding anything, she would have been tempted to throw it at him. "Yes, let's talk," she said, angry. "Go ahead and tell me how this thing between us will never work. That we're too different and you have no room in your life right now for any kind of relationship."

He lifted an eyebrow at her.

"I'm right, aren't I?" she pressed. "All that is pretty much what you intended to say."

"You are," he admitted. "That doesn't make any of it less true."

Why was she pursuing this? Why was she even going down this path, knowing full well it was only going to lead to further heartbreak? It was all so pointless. She didn't have what it would take to reach him.

Still, the words continued to flow out of her mouth. Deep down, some deeply seated need within her wanted to try. "You were abandoned by your mother, then made a mistake with a woman you were in love with. A mistake that you can't get over. And it's making you turn your back on what could be a really good thing." She clenched her fists by her sides. "Just because you're scared to move forward and try for happiness."

"Do we really want to talk about who's scared, Ani?"

The thick, heavy tone of his voice sent alarm bells ringing in her head.

"I could go ahead and tell you what I think," he offered.

She flung out her arms, palms up. "By all means."

"You spent the whole time in Monaco avoiding talking to Moira. You're on the precipice of this opportunity that most artists can only dream of. And you can't figure out how to proceed. Why are you so afraid of making a decision and then just sticking to it?"

How could he ask her such a thing? "Not everyone is cut out to live a public life. Can you blame me for grappling with that?"

"Of course not. So accept that about yourself and say no."

He couldn't understand. He had no idea how it felt to lose the woman who had started her on the journey to becoming a musician. In addition to being her parent, her mother had been a source of support and nurturing and teaching. A true mentor. "It's not as easy as you seem to think. I had to consider what my mother would say. She was my first instructor. If it wasn't for her, I wouldn't even be a musician."

"And now her absence is a convenient excuse."

The blood drained from her face. "What?"

"An excuse to stay precisely where you are without ever having to decide."

Ani wanted to believe she hadn't heard him correctly. But the ringing in her ears hadn't muddled his words. He'd been loud and clear.

She could throw it in his face how wrong he was, that she *had* decided in fact. And that she was figuring out how to tell Moira about her rejection of the offers.

There was no point. He saw her as a spoiled and coddled child unable to steer her own life.

"Get out, Adam."

He cursed and reached for her, the regret clear in his dark eyes. "Ani, I didn't mean—"

She held a hand up before he could continue, and stepped out of his reach. "Please. Just leave."

As if he needed any more confirmation that he could be an insufferable bastard. He'd gone over and over the whole scene with Ani as he'd tossed and turned all night. He would take it back if he could.

Adam waited until the morning to try to set things right with her. He'd been completely out of line and lashed out. All because she'd spoken the truth. And he hadn't been able to take it. For a hardened soldier who'd seen more than his share of travesty, he hadn't been able to cope when the woman he'd cared for his entire life had held a mirror up to him and asked him to face his past.

He would tell her all that as soon as he saw her.

Hopefully, the hours of sleep had taken some of the edge off her anger. Not that he deserved any kind of leeway. He'd been way out of line. And he needed to tell her that.

No one answered when he knocked on her hotel suite door.

He walked down two doors to Moira's room. Maybe they were having breakfast together.

But Moira was alone when she answered. Unless you counted Snowball, who ran over to him barking, then rubbed against his ankle. Adam crouched down to give him a quick pet but he rolled over onto his back and kicked his leg up in the air.

He was particularly needy this morning. Adam proceeded with an obligatory belly rub. Moira was glaring at him when he straightened.

"Where is she?" he asked. "I'm in charge of her security. I need to know."

He could have sworn Moira sneered before answering. "She's not here. She left."

A heavy weight settled over his shoulders. "Left? Where to?"

"Took a commercial flight back to the States last night. Asked me to watch Snowball and bring him back with us so she wouldn't have to crate him on the plane."

Adam felt his gut tighten. He'd driven her away. Another strike on his already tarnished existence. "She's not supposed to travel anywhere without Steele Security officers."

Moira leaned over and picked up the dog, who proceeded to lick her without pause. "She didn't. April took her."

Was he the only one Ani had kept in the dark about her plans to leave? Adam swore out loud and called up April's number on his phone. Moira stood watching from the doorway with both derision and unhidden interest.

April answered on the first ring. "Hey, boss. What took you so long to call?"

"Care to tell me what's going on?"

He could practically see her characteristic shrug through the phone. "Simple. She wanted to leave. Told me you'd have a 'tantrum'—her word—if she traveled to the airport without security, so I took her. And with all due respect, you can fire me if you want. But us girls gotta stick together."

Adam rubbed his forehead where the beginning of a pounding headache was starting to set in. "I wished you'd told me, April."

"She asked me not to. And I like Ani."

Yeah, so did he. And he'd blown it with her. He knew there couldn't be a future between them, but it was tearing him to shreds inside that she would hate him now for the foreseeable future. And she had every right to.

"So are you gonna?" April asked through the tinny speaker.

"Am I going to what?"

"Fire me?"

"No, April. I'm not going to fire you."

Her sigh of relief was audible through the call. She thanked him profusely before hanging up.

Not that he was due any gratitude.

"She wanted to get home to work on some audition

pieces. That's what she said, anyway." The hint of blame was clear in Moira's voice. She would be right. This was his fault. Adam could guess why Ani wanted to get home a day early: to avoid him.

Moira put the dog down midlick. He scrambled away and jumped up on the couch, whimpering as if he was missing something.

Yeah, I miss her too, pal.

The first part of Moira's comment registered in his brain. "What audition pieces?"

"She's looking to audition for some orchestra positions throughout the States. Maybe even in Europe. That way she can still be a performing musician but she doesn't have to tour or deal with publicity headaches. She said she got the suggestion from someone she met in Monte Carlo at some casino you took her to."

The theater manager she met at the bar that night. And he'd accused her of being naive for believing the man.

Adam wanted to punch a wall. He'd accused her of being afraid to move forward. The reality was that not only had she moved forward, she'd figured out a path without compromising anything of herself or squandering her great talent. She hadn't even bothered to set him straight because he simply wasn't worth it. Not after the unforgivable words he'd spewed at her.

"Anyway," Moira went on, "I'm glad you're not going to fire April."

He could only nod. Of course he wasn't going to fire her. The only person who deserved any kind of punishment in all this was himself. And losing Ani so completely, without any hope of winning her back, would feel like a penance for the rest of his days.

CHAPTER TWELVE

Adam wasn't looking forward to this meeting, even less than the one he'd agreed to over two weeks ago when he'd gone to see Brant and Mr. Terrance. So much could change in a matter of days. And so much could stay exactly the same. The same receptionist was seated at the outer desk when Adam made it to the top floor. Like the last time, she motioned him in.

Brant stood up from his desk and came over to give him a big bear hug when Adam entered his office. Probably the last hug he'd receive from his oldest and closest friend. Yet another painful personal loss he would have to endure. And he had no one but himself to blame.

Adam had to accept that things would be different between them after this conversation.

Brant motioned for him to sit in the chair opposite his own.

"So Ani's performances were both a huge success, it sounds like," Brant began, dropping down into his own seat.

"They were. Everything went smoothly."

"I got your message about tracing those suspicious emails," his friend said. "Nice work figuring it out."

Adam nodded. "Turns out they were sent to her from one of her music students. He meant no harm. Just figured she might find it flattering to have a secret admirer. The poor kid didn't exactly think it through."

"I guess not."

"The counselors at the center made sure to speak with him about the inappropriateness of his actions. He feels terrible."

Adam had sent the same message to Ani to notify her of the discovery his investigation had unearthed. She hadn't responded.

"The kid's got some impressive technical skills," Adam continued. "Hacked into the youth center's Wi-Fi to access their contact list. It's how he obtained Ani's updated email address."

"Well, leave it to my sister," Brant said. "Not only has she forgiven him, she convinced the center not to pursue any kind of charges. And she personally took the kid to sign him up for a local coding class."

Adam wasn't surprised in the least. That sounded like the woman he'd fallen for. The woman he'd foolishly managed to lose.

"I'm just glad it's all over," Brant added. "But better safe than sorry. Especially when it comes to loved ones."

"Some things are too precious to risk," he agreed, well aware of the irony of his words.

"So tell me about Ani's concerts," Brant prompted. "I was really hoping to fly to Europe to catch one, but this merger has hit one snag after another. The timing just wasn't right. Dad and I both felt terrible about missing the chance to see her."

"She blew both audiences away."

Brant's grin grew wider. "That's my sis."

"She's something else."

"She really is. And I hear you took her to spend some

time at your villa in Monaco. That was above and beyond, man."

Adam shifted in his seat. "We should probably talk about that."

"Yeah?"

"The truth is, Ani and I became close during the Monaco visit."

"Close?"

"Real close. I'm not sure how else to put it."

Brant crossed his ankle over his knee. "I see."

Adam cleared his throat. "So, just give me some warning. So that I can brace for the blow. That's all I ask."

Brant squinted his eyes. "What in the devil's name are you talking about?"

"When you land the first punch. I just want to be prepared."

"You think I'm going to punch you? Why would I want to do that?"

"Because of what I just told you. That Ani and I—"

Brant jumped up before Adam could continue. "Whoa, whoa. I don't need to hear the details, brother."

Adam ducked his head. This conversation was even more awkward than he'd feared.

"Just fair warning, though," Brant said.

"What's that?"

"I reserve the right to change my mind about that punch if it turns out you've taken advantage of her in any way. Buddy or not."

Brant's statement was no less than what he'd expected. Still, Adam felt a brush of ire rustle up his spine. "She's been taken advantage of, all right. Probably her whole life."

Brant stiffened where he stood. "What's that supposed to mean?"

"You really don't see it, do you? Nor does your dad, I bet. Neither of you ever have."

"See what?" Brant demanded.

"Everything Ani's been to you both since the loss of your mom. How strong she's been. How she's held you up. Both of you. You both would have fallen apart without her. You've been blind to all her sacrifices."

Brant's eyes narrowed to ominous slits. "I don't need you to extol the virtues of my sister. I know all she's done for us. Been to us."

"Do you really, Brant?"

A hint of color rose on the other man's cheeks. Someone who didn't know him as well as Adam might not have noticed. But there was no doubt Brant was angry.

Despite that, Adam continued, "Ani happens to be strong and resilient and caring. And she deserved more from her father and brother than to have to bear the burden of trying to dull your pain, on top of struggling with her own."

Several beats passed in the most uncomfortable silence he and Brant had ever experienced between them. And that was saying a lot.

Finally, Brant blew out a loud breath. "You're right. My sister is one of the most generous people I know. If it wasn't for her, my dad and I would have been even more of a mess after we lost Mom. She was the rock we both leaned on. She took care of everything. Even as young as she was and with how much she was grieving herself. It's past time we acknowledged that. Though we'll never be able to make it up to her."

Adam tilted his head in agreement. "She deserves to be happy."

"Sounds like you really care for her."

Adam had been coming to terms with that fact since she

had left Brussels without him. He'd never felt such emptiness, or been so damn lonely, as he'd been after Moira had told him Ani was gone.

The only sound conclusion was that he not only cared for Ani, he'd fallen in love with her. He couldn't even say when. Perhaps he'd loved her since they were both kids and she insisted on trailing him and Brant until one of them told her to scram.

Adam looked Brant straight in the eye before he answered, "I always have. And I always will."

Brant nodded once. "Then why are you in here fighting on her behalf when you could be out there fighting *for* her?"

Adam leaned over, bracing his arms on his knees. "I think I may have blown it with her."

"You have a tendency to do that, don't you, bro?"

Just like that, the awkwardness between them dissipated like mist in the air. His friend had never been afraid to tell it like it was. It was a quality Adam both admired and dreaded being on the receiving end of.

"And if I know you," Brant continued, "you're probably wracking your brain for what to do about it when the answer is so very obvious."

At Adam's blank stare, Brant threw his arms up in the air. It was a gesture reminiscent of his sister's. "Just go see her, man. Sounds like you both could use some clearing of the air."

Brant was right. Regardless of where it would lead, apologizing to her face-to-face was the least Adam could do. But ultimately, it was her call to make. "I'll try. If she agrees to give me the time of day, that is."

"She'll give you a chance. If you deserve it," Brant declared.

That was the question, wasn't it? Whether Adam deserved her at all.

He had to find out. Even if it meant he might never recover once he learned the answer. He was about to shut the door behind him when Brant's final comment gave him pause.

"You deserve to be happy, too, Adam."

Adam paused in the act of ringing Ani's doorbell. The faint piano music he could hear coming through her door had him straining to hear. The piece was unfamiliar to his ears. She hadn't performed this one in Paris nor Brussels. He would have remembered. It was stunning.

The tempo was upbeat, yet somehow a sadness resounded through the musical notes. Even without lyrics, the song spoke of desire. Of loss and pain.

Or maybe he was a fanciful clod who'd gone and lost his heart and now he was hearing poetry everywhere.

He wasn't sure how long he stood there. He just knew he couldn't interrupt her, had to hear the melody to its conclusion.

When Ani stopped playing, he inhaled a fortifying breath and rang her bell.

He heard shuffling on the other side. Yet the door didn't open. She must have seen him through the peephole but wasn't responding.

Served him right. He shouldn't have come unannounced. He felt his hope deflate like a punctured balloon. She was going to ignore him.

He opened his mouth to try to reason with her through the door, but couldn't seem to find the right words. All the lines he'd rehearsed back at home seemed inadequate now. He braced both hands on opposite sides of the doorway and resigned himself to the facts—this time, the damage he'd caused was irreparable. And he would have to live with that.

He turned around to leave.

Ani stood frozen in front of her door, torn as to what to do. She longed to see Adam, to talk to him. She longed to be in his arms again.

But her emotions were still too raw, and she had a piece to finish if she was going to be ready for this first audition.

Still, she'd missed him so much. Hadn't been able to stop thinking about him since arriving back home. He'd texted and left voice mails but she hadn't had the fortitude to try to answer. And now he was here in person.

She watched through the peephole as he stood there, simply waiting. Even through the distorted view, her breath caught at how handsome he was.

She flung the door open before she could change her mind, catching him just as he was turning to leave.

"You didn't try very hard," she said with as steady a voice as she could muster. "Only rang the doorbell once."

He flashed that charming smile of his she'd missed so much. He was dressed casually in khakis and a soft white V-neck. Dark stubble covered his strong jawline. She itched to reach out and run her fingertips over it.

"I was going to come back with a bouquet," he said. "Flowers convinced you to see me last time."

She looked upward as if contemplating his statement. "Though that didn't end too well, did it?" she countered.

"Touché. Can I come in?"

She stepped aside and nearly reached out to touch him as he walked past her into the living room. The familiar scent of his aftershave brought forth memories of Paris and Monaco and all that they'd shared.

He walked over to her grand piano in the corner of the

room. Trailed a finger along the keyboard. "That was an extraordinary piece you were playing when I arrived."

"I've been working on it all week. It's starting to come around."

"You wrote that?"

She nodded. "I did." Little did he know, he'd played a major part in the process. Ani had thought of him while creating the stanzas. She'd poured all the anguish, the longing, the loss she'd felt since leaving Brussels into the music.

"You're unbelievable, Ani. I don't know anything about music, but what I heard had me mesmerized outside your door."

She could only thank him. For several moments, they both simply stood in silence. Unspoken words hung heavily in the air between them. Ani wasn't going to budge. This was all on him.

"What's the name of the piece?" he finally asked.

Ani took a deep breath before responding. "Monaco Moonlight."

His eyes darkened when he heard her answer. He glanced from her to the music sheet. When he finally spoke, his voice was thick with raw emotion. "Ani, I've been such a blind idiot."

She crossed her arms in front of her chest. A desperate attempt to keep from rushing into his arms the way she so badly wanted to. She'd missed him so much. But he'd broken her heart that night in Brussels. In so many pieces. She was still in the process of trying to mend it. "You won't get any argument from me on that front."

"I was a fool to say the things I did. I was only protecting myself."

"Your duty was to protect me." Instead, he'd shattered her.

He visibly cringed. "I know. If you let me, I'll never forfeit that duty again. I promise."

"You pushed me away, Adam."

"I know, kitten. The truth is, I need protecting, too."

That was a bit of an unexpected curve. "You do?"

He reached for her, but Ani wasn't ready to accept the hand he offered. Not just yet. She stayed firm where she was, though every cell in her body cried out to go to him, to hell with the consequences.

"Ani, please save me from myself. Say you'll forgive me."

She felt the last bricks of her wall crumble, slowly but surely. She was fooling herself to think she could deny what she felt for him, that she'd ever be able to get over him in this lifetime. How did she have any recourse but to forgive him?

"I guess I don't have a choice," she said on a sigh with mock resignation.

"Yeah?"

She shook her head seriously. "It appears you've somehow managed to become my muse. I'll have to keep you around. In the interest of my professional growth."

He reached her in one quick stride, then lifted her in his arms. Ani felt her whole body shudder with desire at being held by him again.

He trailed a line of soft kisses along her neck. "I can think of all sorts of ways to inspire you, kitten."

EPILOGUE

"IT'S MUCH WINDIER up here than I would have thought." Ani adjusted the tie holding her hair back, but it was no match for the wind. Several strands escaped again and whipped about her face.

"We are pretty high up." Adam stated the obvious.

"I can't believe we didn't come up here that first trip to Paris."

Ani glanced down at the breathtaking scene from the viewing deck of the Eiffel Tower. The stunning image would stay with her forever. The city lights framed by the majestic river could have been a painting hanging in a museum.

Adam took her in his arms from behind and rested his chin atop her head. He'd surprised her with a weeklong trip to France, followed by several days at his Monaco villa. Almost a replay of their first time here without any of the angst.

All to celebrate her latest successful audition. Ani hadn't quite decided if she would take the freelance opportunity with the Boston Pops Orchestra. The thought of leaving her beloved Dallas still had her torn.

The good news was, Adam had vowed to follow her wherever she wanted to go. And as long as he was by her side, she was home.

She snuggled tighter up against him. She wouldn't have thought it was possible to fall more in love with him over the past year, yet somehow she had.

Even after all this time, her heart still fluttered in her chest whenever he walked into a room. They stood there for several moments, enjoying the view and the night. She didn't think she'd ever felt this content.

Finally, Adam turned her around to face him. "So, I was thinking next time you go to Boston that I should come with you."

"I'd like that very much." She was planning to visit at least a couple more times before making her final decision.

"In fact, I think you should have your own personal bodyguard when you go."

She smiled at him with all the love filling her heart. "A girl can't be too careful."

"Exactly," he agreed and reached into his jacket pocket. Ani lost her breath when she saw the object he pulled out.

A small velvet box. He opened it to reveal a sparkling tear-shaped diamond ring on a tricolor gold band.

Ani clasped a shaky hand to her mouth. "Adam, it's lovely."

He took her hand in his, dropped a kiss to the inside of her wrist. "Anikita Terrance, you've been my top VIP for as long as I can remember. Would you please do me the honor of becoming my wife?"

Her whole body vibrated with pure happiness. She didn't think it was possible to feel this much joy. Throwing her arms around his neck, she finally managed to make her mouth work enough to give him an answer.

"*Oui, mon amour!* Yes!"

* * * * *

HER MOTHERHOOD
WISH

TARA TAYLOR QUINN

For Rachel, again and again.
This is my heart letting yours know how special
you are and how much you matter.

Chapter One

The day started like any other. Thirty-six-year-old Woodrow Alexander—Wood to anyone who expected him to answer—rolled out from under the sheet and into a pair of lightweight pajama pants. He timed his movements in perfect tandem with Retro, his six-year-old blonde female Lab, who jumped off her side of the mattress, stretched and rounded the bed.

Retro, short for Retrospect, stood guard at the opened door to the bath attached to their quarters while Wood used the toilet. Then, side by side, the two of them left their suite and traipsed down the hall toward the kitchen, avoiding the living area and the closed door on the far side of it leading into the home's other master suite. Elaina needed her sleep.

While Wood started the coffee maker, brewing a ten-cup pot of the dark Colombian blend he and his ex-wife both preferred, Retrospect let herself out the doggy door and into the yard beyond. Wood had put in the kiva fireplace at the pool that Elaina had wanted while they'd still been married. He'd built the outdoor kitchen space off to the left of that. Planted rosebushes. Built his workshop shed in the far back corner. And then, also to her specifications, he had left the rest of the yard natural. Some grass grew. He kept that mowed, but the rest of the space stood home to a lot of trees in random places, with roots that stuck up out of the hardened ground. He'd offered to clean it up for her. She'd said she liked it rugged.

He liked her happy.

By the time Retro was back indoors, he had food in her bowl and, his first mug of coffee in hand, padded barefoot back down the hall, past two closed doors, two offices—his and hers—glancing into the guest bedroom with attached bath that came after, and finally reaching his suite at the end of the hall.

Leaving his door cracked for Retro's reentrance after her breakfast and another trip outside, Wood got in the shower. Shaved—Elaina had told Wood once, when she'd still been gloriously happy married to Peter, that he should try leaving a bit of whisker roughage on his face. He didn't like the result. It itched. And then, dried and standing in front of the mirror, he ran a comb through his short but bushy blond hair. Thick curls had looked far better on Peter, his younger brother, than they did atop Wood's rounder face.

Once dressed, Wood sat in the worn green armchair that had once been his father's—a chair that was in his room partially because it matched nothing else in the house—and laced up his work boots before clipping his utility knife to his belt, dropping a couple of carpenter pencils into his shirt pocket and heading back out to the kitchen.

Retro hadn't made it back into his room. Which meant the dog had followed Elaina back into her suite to watch over her as she showered that June Thursday morning. The golden Lab always slept with Wood, but the rest of the time she chose randomly which of the two of them to hang with.

Frying some bacon and mixing pancake batter, Wood got out bologna and bread to slap together a couple of sandwiches for lunch, adding bread to the running grocery list they kept on the fridge. Elaina's toast plate was already in the dishwasher, her yogurt cup in the trash, but he knew she'd had both with her coffee while he'd showered. She always did. Every morning. Same thing. They had a system that allowed them to live separately while still occupying the same building.

He was just sitting down to eat when Retro bounded out from Elaina's quarters, followed closely by the dark-haired beauty his brother had married. And then he had.

"I'm doing a double rotation today, so don't worry if you don't see my car," she said, her satchel already on her shoulder over the white doctor's lab coat and light blue scrubs she wore pretty much every day. Swallowing a big bite of syrupy pancake, Wood nodded. Told her he'd take care of the communal grocery list.

"Be safe," she said, her keys already in hand as she headed for the door.

"What about your lunch?"

She kept her soft-sided cooler in the freezer. Loaded it every morning on her way out the door, either choosing leftovers or more yogurt and fruit. Which was about the only time he ever really saw her. When they'd divorced, neither had wanted to move, and she'd been unable to take on the cost of a house alone, so he'd built a small entryway and installed an outside door to the far side of Elaina's suite, allowing her to come and go without interrupting him.

Or without him knowing her every move.

"I'm buying lunch today."

For years he'd suggested she do so. For years she'd refused to spend the money. *His* money, back then.

Now, in her second-to-last year of her residency as a nuclear radiologist, she was earning a pretty decent salary. Things were changing.

"Be safe, Wood," she said again, her hand on the door.

"Be safe," he said in return.

Their mantra. It was like they couldn't leave each other's presence without the words spilling out of them. A direct result of the grief they shared.

Breakfast done, he rinsed his dishes, took a couple of seconds to give Retro a bit of a rubdown, then grabbed his lunch and headed out. He didn't have far to go. Less than five miles to the luxury apartment complex going up not far from the new Oceanfront Medical complex. Still, it didn't look good if the framing-crew supervisor showed up to the job late.

He was a mile out, and twenty minutes early, when his phone rang. Someone calling off for the day, most likely. He glanced at the number showing up on his dash. Not one he recognized. All of his guys would show up in his contact list by name. As would his boss, the general contractor on the project. He let the call go to voice mail.

One unknown caller starting out with "Mr. Alexander? This is the police…" was the only scary call he ever planned to answer in his lifetime. His phone dinged to indicate he had received a new message.

He waited until his truck was parked along the back of the temporary fence marking the crew parking lot before listening to the voice mail. The Parent Portal—a fertility clinic that, while located right there in little Marie Cove, was making a name for itself—needed him to call.

Stupidly, relief swept through him. Elaina was okay. He had no one else to lose. Figuring the call had something to do with Peter, who'd done much of his gynecological residency at the clinic, he dialed, sat back and watched as one truck and then, a few seconds later, another slowed and pulled onto the lot. His men. Hand-chosen by him. Arriving for another day of sweating it out under California's June sunshine as they nailed the thousands of two-by-fours and four-by-sixes to frame the current project.

"Mr. Alexander? This is Christine Elliott, managing director of the Parent Portal…"

The woman didn't bother with hello. Had apparently recognized him on her caller ID. He'd had no idea the number she'd left had been to her private phone. He'd been expecting to speak with a receptionist.

"Thank you for calling back so expediently," she said. "I'll be as brief as possible."

She'd said it was important. Figured they were going to honor his brother posthumously for all of the volunteer hours he'd put in, beyond residency requirements, when the clinic had just been getting up and running. He'd let Elaina know and have her call the clinic. It was her the clinic would need to speak with.

The fourth truck pulled in. Two more and he'd be set for the day. He still hadn't said a word. The woman just continued talking.

"I have a request for contact, and the matter is urgent…"

He'd been watching a couple of workers get out of their trucks… One punched the other on the shoulder and laughed. Brothers. Wood's gut lurched.

"A request for contact?" He wasn't sure he'd heard her right.

"From your sperm recipient…"

Turning away so that the parking lot was no longer in view, he shook his head. "What now?"

"Your sperm donation was used four months ago, Mr. Alexander, and fertilization was successful. The recipient is currently four months pregnant and needs to speak with you."

His sperm. It took a few seconds for him to even figure out what she was talking about. To remember years back—when his brother had first started at the clinic. They'd needed sperm donors, and Peter had hit Wood up. Always willing to help his younger brother, to support him, Wood had been fine with the donation—not so much with the pounds of paperwork he'd had to fill out. Most particularly when it came to education and occupation.

"I quit high school when my mom died so that I could go to work and support my brother," he said now, as much to himself as to the managing whatever she was. "No one was ever going to choose me as her donor."

He had to make that clear. So she could find the guy she really needed. And then it occurred to him. "Unless…are you looking for Peter?" Surely she knew his brother was gone? Peter had no longer been working at the clinic—had, in fact, been out with Elaina, celebrating having just received his medical license and the practice he'd just joined, when their car had been hit head-on by a drunk driver…

Still, it seemed like everyone in Marie Cove had heard about the crash. Particularly in the medical community.

"No, we're beyond careful with our record keeping, and the frozen sperm was most definitely that of Woodrow Alexander, not Peter. Although, I have to say, I was so incredibly sorry to hear about your brother's death. I was at the funeral…"

Wood wouldn't have known her from Adam. And couldn't say half of who was there. He'd been too busy dealing with Elaina's grief—and pain—as he'd kept a hand on her wheelchair at all times and prayed that nothing happened to her until he could deliver her safely back to the hospital, which she should never have left in the first place. His own despair… Well, Wood had handled that in private. Over time. With more than a few bottles of whiskey. Until, more than a year later, he'd thrown out the last one, half-full, and never touched the stuff again.

"I'm still having a hard time believing someone would choose a high school dropout for her sperm donor when she has doctors to choose from," he said, bringing himself—and her—back to the present.

"Your family's health history is excellent, you're

a tall and blue-eyed blond, and your essay was…remarkable," Christine said.

He'd forgotten about the essay—an exposition of why he was donating sperm. Sort of remembered writing about his brother. He'd been so proud of him—like Peter had been his son, rather than just the runt that had been three years younger than him and always tagging along.

"Blue-eyed blonds are chosen more than any other combination," Christine said softly, almost as though she knew Wood needed a minute to catch up.

"So, you're telling me I've got biological kids walking around someplace?" He'd really given it little thought. Had been certain that Peter wasn't seeing him for who he really was when he'd been certain that Wood's sperm would be recipient-worthy.

"Not yet. It's only been used this one time."

Deflating before he'd even really begun to inflate, Wood tapped the steering wheel. That made more sense.

"So…who is this woman who chose a dropout over a doctor?" he asked, feeling kind of bad for the kid of such a choice maker.

"Her name is Cassie Thompson. She's given me permission to give you her direct number. I can also have her call you, or the two of you can have a supervised meeting here at the clinic, if you'd prefer."

There was no fourth option—opting out. That was part of what made the Parent Portal so unique, as he recalled. Donors and recipients both reserved the right to have contact with the other if ever a need or desire arose. The clinic acknowledged that sperm was more than just biology. That human needs and emotions could come to play at some point—hence the contact requirement. It was all tied up in a nice legal bundle, which had been a part of the mound of paperwork he'd been required to get through in the process of doing his little brother a favor.

"Can I ask why she wants to meet me?" He'd gone over every page of the contract he'd signed. Understood every word before he'd signed it. And then promptly dismissed the details as irrelevant.

"That's for her to disclose." Christine sounded more formal now. "I can only tell you that it's a matter of some urgency."

"You're sure she's pregnant."

"Yes."

"And that the baby is mine."

"Biologically formed from your sperm, yes."

Right. Right. He got the designation. He might be less schooled than a lot of people, but he was not a stupid man.

"Then please give her my number," he said. And then added. "But please tell her to call between six and ten tonight, if that's possible. After five, at any rate."

No way was he having a conversation about his

sperm at work. Nor was he going to miss a day of it. He hadn't, ever, and wasn't going to start.

But that didn't stop him from thinking about the damned situation all day long. He might not vividly recall everything he'd documented in that file of his, but he knew for certain he'd been completely honest. That was how he rolled.

So, what, had she missed the education part? The career page? Was she hoping to find out he'd made more of himself in the time since he'd allowed his little fish to be frozen?

Maybe she just wanted to get a firsthand, in-person peek at what her kid could turn out to look like.

Yeah, and that didn't sound like an urgent matter.

More likely the woman was having second thoughts now that she was really pregnant. Though what she thought he could do about that, he didn't know.

Nah, no one would spend all that money, put herself through the insemination process, just to change her mind.

As the afternoon wore on, he wondered what she looked like. Who she was.

Wondered if she'd be anywhere near the strong but still gentle and loving mother who'd given birth to him and Peter. Raising two headstrong boys on her own after their father died of a heart attack when Wood was five.

By quitting time, he'd run out of distractions. She'd be calling soon about an urgent matter. And he hoped to God it wasn't to tell him that there was something wrong with her baby.

That his sperm had given her a less-than-healthy child.

Because he had no idea how to fix something like that.

Chapter Two

She had a tiny baby bump. Her sonogram included a video with gray shadows of moving arms and legs. Two healthy heartbeats. Hers and the baby's.

She'd only told the key players in her life—the partners in her law firm, her mom and stepdad, some friends—that she was pregnant.

Cassie Thompson was going to have a baby. She was not going to let one dark spot on a piece of film control her life. Or stop her life. It might change her existence, but, as with anything, she'd deal with change as it happened.

She'd known something was wrong. The look on the ultrasound technician's face had changed from smiling and happy to neutral, her voice changing after the celebratory words as they found the heartbeat. Her morphing tone, which became more professional as she pointed out other body parts, had been telling. The woman had seen something on that screen and hadn't been at liberty to verbalize what it might represent.

Okay, so there'd been a few minutes the day before, after the ultrasound, when she'd first heard the doctor tell her that there was a shadow on the baby's brain, indicating a possible blood abnormality, that Cassie had fallen apart. Then panicked. But she'd gotten a hold of herself. Called back to ask questions. And then spent the night as a single, capable, in-control thirty-four-year-old corporate lawyer would—researching every piece of writing on fetal blood disorders she could find so that she had every base covered. Taking a break or two to hug the teddy bear she'd purchased in celebration on her way home from the clinic the day she'd been inseminated. And to cry.

By morning she'd been cried out, at least temporarily, and had a list of things to do. Doctors to call, specialists in neonatal hematology, tests to request. All of that went beyond the amniocentesis her doctor had already scheduled for that next week *and* calling Christine Elliott at an ungodly hour to arrange to contact her sperm donor. She'd once heard the woman say she'd been in her office since six in the morning, had taken a chance, would have left a message, but got lucky and spoke with the director on her first try. The stars were aligning.

By five that first Thursday afternoon in June, on her way from work to the home she owned in a gated community on a small private stretch of the beach just outside Marie Cove city limits, she was regressing back to the day before, the moments when she'd spoken with the doctor. She needed to be taking charge. Doing something productive.

When bad things happened, when times were hard, you got up out of bed just like every other day and went about your work. You just kept going. Doing. Working. The rest would work itself out, or not, just the same. Her daddy had never said those words to her, maybe hadn't had the wherewithal to put it just like that, but his steady, reliable actions had shown her. When Cassie's mother had told him she was leaving him, he'd blinked. And gone to work.

Cassie had been four at the time, but she still remembered that.

The day her mother had remarried—a finance broker with a successful career—Cassie had begged a family friend to leave the second the ceremony was over so she could get to her father, with whom she'd be staying during the honeymoon. She'd been eight and worried sick about him. She'd found him in his yard, building a shed. And she'd spent the rest of that weekend building right there with him. Prob-

ably getting in his way more than anything, she'd realized years later, but at the time, he'd made her feel
as though she was a huge help.

She hoped, in some fashion, she had been.

Her sperm donor, A203B4, had a name now.
Woodrow Alexander. He'd said she could call anytime after five. Five-oh-three was after five.

She glanced at the screen on her dash, at the button on her steering wheel that she could push to command the car's system to make the call.

He'd requested that she wait until after six.

An hour wasn't going to make a difference to
her baby's future. Unless she went crazy with stress
waiting for that hour to pass. Woodrow Alexander
was her only real possible strength in the event of
worst-case scenario. She just needed to know that
he was on board and then she'd be fine.

Five-oh-four. Her thumb was over the call command button. Just as she was passing the car wash.
Pulling her blue Jaguar onto the lot, she put money
into the machine and followed the instructions to
join the queue being propelled through the automatic
washing tunnel. Watched as the pink, blue and white
spirals of soap filled the windshield. Baby colors. A
sign. Smelled the bubblegum smell. Kids loved that
scent. Watched as the powerful dryer forced bub-
bles of water off the newly waxed, shiny metallic-
blue hood of her car. And then pulled into one of the
many vacant vacuum slots.

Thursday evenings at dinnertime apparently weren't big car wash times. She hadn't known that, but she was thankful because it meant she got to use the vacuum from her slot and the one at the empty stall beside her, allowing her to clean the entire interior of her car twice as easily.

If six o'clock hadn't rolled around, she'd probably have sucked up rocks from the parking lot next, but the time had ticked by. She had a call to make.

Retro—so named because in retrospect Wood probably should have checked with Elaina before buying a dog on their wedding day—trotted up to Wood, Frisbee in her mouth, and dropped it at his feet.

"Good girl," he said. And then, as he bent to pick up the disc, "Stay." The Lab stood there, her big brown eyes intent on him as Wood wound up and threw as hard as he could, sending the disc sailing through the trees to the far back of their property. Retro continued to stand there, on alert, until Wood smiled and said, "Fetch." Retro took off, finding her prey. She'd succeed and bring it back again, too. For as long as Wood would throw it for her. Some nights they were out there for an hour or more. The dog needed exercise, and Wood, well, he liked working with the dog.

She'd brought youth, new life, into a grieving home the day he'd stood before a judge at the courthouse in jeans and a button down shirt while Elaina, also in jeans, cried a little beside him and took him as her husband in place of the man they'd both lost.

His phone rang before Retro made it to her target. Pulling the cell from his shirt pocket, he recognized the number and answered immediately.

"Mr. Alexander, I'm sorry to bother you—"

"My name's Wood," he interrupted, for no good reason other than that she sounded tense and he needed to put her at ease.

"Okay, Wood, thank you for agreeing to speak with me—"

"Signed documents said I had to." He broke in a second time, going for light conversation when he knew the phone call was anything but. He didn't need her gratitude. And didn't want to hear that his sperm was inadequate, that it had created an unhealthy baby. Didn't want to know that he'd inadvertently caused her distress. Caused some kid even worse than that. Possibly.

But why else would she need to speak urgently? That meant there was a problem. He'd known it all day. And still didn't want to hear how bad it was. He couldn't take back his deposit.

She couldn't sue him. That was in the contract, too—he'd reread every word as soon as he'd gotten home. But he'd help her financially if he was in any way responsible for her incurring extra expenses. He'd already made that decision. His savings had taken a hit during the three years Elaina had been finishing medical school, but he'd had several years before that to build them...

"Yes, well, thank you for agreeing to speak with me so quickly," she amended after a short pause. "I won't keep you. I'm just covering all bases and need to know if you'd be willing to donate bone marrow if it's needed..."

"Of course," he responded immediately. And then stood there, holding his phone, looking at the blue disc on the ground at his feet, at the dog looking up at him, not sure what donating bone marrow entailed. And was afraid that since he'd already given her what she needed, she'd just hang up. "Wait. What's going on?" he asked.

"Probably nothing. But, just in case..."

He wasn't getting it. "You're calling just on the off shot that someday your child might get sick and need my bone marrow?" That was taking worrying to an extreme. Surely...

"No." Her breath was all he heard on the line for a moment. Unsteady breaths. "I had an ultra-sound yesterday. The doctor said that they found a darker, shadowed spot in the baby's brain that indi-cates some kind of blood abnormality. They have no idea what it is yet. And, in fact, the doctor said that there are times when the dark spot is an anomaly. That it will just disappear. But it's something they have to check out."

"So…it's possible there's nothing wrong at all." Damn, that was good news. Real good news. Could be nothing.

"Yes."

"Okay, then, sure," he said. "If you ever need my bone marrow, of course I'd donate," he told her. "Who wouldn't, to save a kid's life?"

A kid. *His* kid. Not really. But biologically. He'd never taken that donation seriously. Not from the very beginning. He'd tried to tell Peter that adding Wood's sample to sperm collection was a waste of time. All of Peter's doctor friends had been donating.

He'd pretty much forgotten about it. Had certainly never considered that there could be a kid walking around town that looked like him. That had his DNA. That could need his bone marrow to save his life.

"Okay, well, thank you!" Her tone was completely different now. Lighter. "Just thank you. I hope I never need to call you again, but you have no idea how much it means to me to know that this base is covered…"

She really was going to hang up. "Wait," he said for the second time in their brief conversation. He wasn't ready just to be done. He was going to have a kid in the world. Felt like he had to do something about that. Be responsible somehow for the child, more than just an outside chance of becoming a bone-marrow donor. "I'd, uh… Can I know more, please?" he asked.

"About a bone marrow transplant? What it would require of you? I'm not a medical expert, but from what I read last night, it could be quite painful. I'm not going to lie to you about it. It's not a pleasant procedure, from what I understand..."

"Not about bone marrow," he said, uncomfortable with Retro standing there staring so intently. He picked up the disc, lobbed it sloppily and rolled his eyes when it landed in the pool. She'd get it as soon as he released her. And then he'd have to deal with a wet dog. "I'd like to know more." About the baby. About her. "I'm assuming there will be more tests done?" Abnormalities always seemed to lead to them.

"An amniocentesis next week."

She had a whole week to wait. That wouldn't be easy.

Hopefully she wasn't going to be doing it alone. "Are you married?"

"No. Are you? I'm sorry, I should have asked. Your wife should certainly be consulted, since we're talking about an intrusive medical procedure..."

About to tell her that Elaina didn't really play into decisions like this one, he checked himself, threw the Frisbee, let Retro go and admitted, "I'm divorced. But..." If he needed someone to be there after the procedure, to care for him... "We still share a residence," he told her. "She has her space, with her own entrance, and I have mine. She could be around if it came to me needing someone present after the procedure." To drive him home. Whatever.

He heard the splash as Retro went in. Felt the cold spray as she came back to him, dropping her prize and shaking herself off.

"Would you like time to speak with her, then, before you give a definitive answer?" Her tone had become more guarded.

He'd meant to relieve Cassie, let her know he had all bases covered—not send new alarm in her direction.

"No. She's at work. And I don't need her buy-in, although I'll tell her about it, of course." Wanting to give her everything he had that could possibly help, he added, "She's a resident at Oceanfront," he continued. "Nuclear radiology. She knows pretty much everybody there and will be fully supportive if there's any issue…"

As would Peter have been. "My brother was in medicine, too," he added, so unlike himself, as though he was trying to get good credit for himself on his brother's merit. "Obstetrics and gynecology," he added, because it was somewhat pertinent to the current conversation, in that they were talking about an unborn child.

And because Peter had been the reason he'd donated sperm in the first place. Wood threw the disc all the way to the back of the yard again. There was wet fur to dry.

"Was in medicine? He's not anymore?"

"He was killed in a car accident just over five years ago."

"Oh my God. I'm so sorry. No, wait. Was it that accident with the drunk driver going the wrong way on the exit ramp? A doctor was killed…"

And the drunk driver had been an underage teen who'd pretty much gotten away with murder. The case had been in local news for more than two years afterward.

"Yes." There was nothing else to say about it. He didn't need or want her sympathy. He wanted… "What did your doctor tell you? What's her opinion?" He knew all medical professionals had them, knew that most of them were trustworthy and often right.

"She said she can't tell anything from the ultrasound other than that there's an abnormality in the video. It could be that the baby's anemic. It could be…leukemia…"

His hand dropped to Retro's head. Stayed there a moment before he bent to pick up the disc the Lab had just returned.

"Did she give you percentages on how often a test result that looks like yours comes back as leukemia?" He needed facts. Held himself stiffly. Couldn't let fear, worry, get in the way.

"She said there's a good chance it isn't." The woman's voice was soft. He wanted to go to her. Make things better, but had no idea where she was.

Who she was, other than a name. "And that there's also a chance that it is."

In other words, the doctor really didn't know at that point. He knew the lingo.

"There are other blood conditions, things that have to do with Rh negative and positive mixtures, but that possibility was ruled out before insemination."

Cassie Thompson was just a voice on the phone. It wasn't enough. Not when a woman carrying his sperm was in distress.

"Do you have family there with you? Support?" he asked, throwing the disc again.

"I haven't told anyone yet," she said, a bit hesitantly. "I don't want to until I know more about what's going on. I'm struggling enough with my own worry without having to take on everyone else's."

He got that. Completely. Though he had to point out, "They might be able to help you, to ease the burden a bit…" He'd never really been able to see a way for that to work for him, but he'd seen it in others. Elaina, for one. She'd said many times, told other people, too, that Wood being there for her after the accident had saved her life, said that, without the physical security and emotional support he'd provided, she wouldn't have made it. He'd only done what family did.

"It makes me feel weak when people worry about me," she said.

He'd never thought of it that way, but he got exactly what she was saying. And then said, "So how about if you and I meet for lunch or something? I know what's going on, but I'd be more like an extension of the medical team—not someone whose feelings you'd need to worry about."

He felt a bit stupid when he heard his words. "I'm not coming on to you," he blurted out, sure he'd quickly made matters worse. "Seriously," he said, looking for a way to reassure her and coming up blank. "I just... I'd like to do something to help... offer what support I can. And it makes sense, just in case things don't turn out how we'd like and you need my bone marrow, that we've actually met before we get into all that. I could have Elaina call you if you'd like. To vouch for me."

"Maybe we could all three go to lunch?"

Maybe. She'd be interested. And was family. Sister-in-law, wife for a minute, ex-wife and now? He didn't know what. Family that he loved in a non-romantic way. Still, he'd rather meet Cassie himself first, though he had no logical reason for the preference. "I can ask, but she's in her third year of a four-year residency and doesn't have a lot of free time."

"But you do."

"I work a day job," he reminded her, in case she'd forgotten the file she'd have read four months before. Or thought that he'd changed careers in the six years since he'd answered those questions. "My hours are boringly predictable."

"I'd actually like to meet you," she said, giving him a feeling of pleasure. "As long as you're sure that it's just a meeting between sperm donor and recipient."

"You want me to have Elaina call you?" He was being completely sincere.

"Is that too nuts?"

Hell, he didn't know.

Not in today's world, it probably wasn't.

"I'm sorry," Cassie said before he could make arrangements for the call. "I'm a lawyer. I like everything tied up neatly so there are no surprises..."

Hence calling her donor the second she thought she could possibly need his bone marrow. He was getting it.

"And yet...life has a way of giving them to you anyway," he said softly. In the form of an abnormal ultrasound, in this case. Then added, "The offer for lunch is there if you want it. No pressure." He'd rather not involve Elaina at that point, but he would if Cassie needed him to.

"What about Saturday?"

Retro was back. Had been for a while. Wood was done throwing. "Give me a time and place and I'll be there," he said. She named a diner not far from the clinic. Independently owned, the place was bright and airy and known for putting on great brunches. He'd been there a time or two.

"How will I know you?" he asked, refusing to

delve into reasons why he didn't want Elaina to know yet what was going on. This baby thing…it was his. Not a part of familial obligations or Peter's memory, either.

"I'll text you a selfie," she said. "And could you text me one of you, too?"

"Yeah, sure," he told her, feeling relieved all of a sudden at her agreement to let him help. He quickly checked himself. Meeting this woman, whose baby had a potential health problem that could stem from him, was not a cause for feeling good about life.

But if he could help her…

That made perfect sense.

Chapter Three

Cassie wasn't opposed to falling in love, getting married and living happily ever after. Or living in the trenches with someone and fighting life's battles together. It just hadn't happened for her. She couldn't force love. But she *could* create a family of her own.

She'd explained it all to her mom and stepdad first. Then her friends, and finally, the other lawyers in the firm. All without qualms. She couldn't sit around and expect others to make her happy. Finding her own joy, building a happy life, was her responsibility, and she was on it.

Yet, Saturday morning, when she got out of the shower and had to choose what to wear to lunch with her tiny family's sperm donor, she was in a quandary. Defensive. Like she had to justify being a single woman having a baby on her own. Afraid he wouldn't agree with her reasoning to create a one-parent household. Or that he'd find her lacking somehow in her inability to find a spouse.

Ludicrous. All of it.

He'd texted his photo to her the night before. She'd seen the message come through with a photo but hadn't opened it. She didn't need it until she got to the restaurant.

She'd decided to wait to text him a photo of herself until she was dressed for the day, thinking he'd be better able to recognize her if he knew what she'd be wearing. Not that color was an issue. Her wardrobe was all black and white, with an occasional hint of red thrown in. Jeans, business suits, shorts, leggings, swimwear, solids, striped and plaid—all black and white.

Maybe she just didn't want to give him a lot of time to find fault with her before he even met her. She wasn't a great beauty, most particularly by California standards. She had the stereotypical blond hair and blue eyes, but her features were strong, not soft. Angular. Like the rest of her. At five eleven, there was nothing petite about her. And while her body had grown taller than the average woman, her boobs hadn't followed suit. They weren't big. And she didn't giggle. Ever.

But she could soften her edges.

Decision made.

The black-and-white tie-dyed sundress with tiny sleeve caps covering her bony shoulders came off its hanger, and black flip-flops completed the ensemble.

She always wore eyeliner so that people could see that she had eyes there above those cheekbones. And she always wore earrings, too, to detract from the angular jawbone just beneath them, and that morning she particularly liked the look of three crystal and onyx drops, placing one dangling decoration and two smaller studs in the three piercings going up each ear.

Her hair, which she regarded as her best feature, she left long and straight, its silky weight helping to distract from her shoulders. Deciding, with one last look in the mirror, that she'd done the best she could, she took the selfie and quickly texted it, feeling self-conscious. Which zapped some of her usual confidence.

And allowed worry to intrude. What if the amniocentesis showed something? What if there really was something wrong with her tiny little baby?

Hot and then cold, she felt like lying down. Canceling lunch.

After getting into the car, she regained her senses. Her looks didn't matter. Him liking her didn't matter—as long as she didn't turn him off so badly he reneged on his promise to donate bone marrow to her baby should the need arise.

More importantly, unless the need arose, there was no need. She could worry all week, borrow trouble, and then the test could come out just fine and she'd have wasted a whole week of enjoying this very special time in her life. She'd have lost a week of happiness.

And while she wasn't a raving beauty, she knew she was a likable person. Always had more invitations to do things than she had time to accept. Or wanted to accept.

Soon, she approached the diner's spread-out parking lot. Avoiding the front spots because they were too hard to back out of with all of the cars coming and going, Cassie drove around back. After she put her car in Park, her gaze went immediately for the ocean off in the distance. The water helped her to keep her mind on the very real power that life had to sustain itself. On the fact that miracles happened every single day.

And then, pulling out her phone, she touched the text messaging app button, scrolled and touched again, bringing up Woodrow Alexander's picture. And almost dropped the phone.

The man was…not what she'd expected. Not only was he true California gorgeous, with those vivid blue eyes and thick blond hair, but his features… They must belong to a standout movie-star hunk. Way out of her league—or the league of anyone she'd ever been lucky enough to attract. Certainly more

handsome than any father her child might have come
by naturally.

She felt the sudden need to cover up the feelings
she couldn't allow to bubble up. The fear that seemed
to be so dangerously close to the surface. She was
looking into the face of the man who had fathered
her child. The man whose genes her baby carried.

And she was finding everything about him wonderful. Even the slight wrinkles at the corners of his
eyes that seemed to speak of the things he'd seen.
And the wisdom gained from them.

Those eyes... They surprised her the most. His
gaze was straight on. Even from a selfie. And seemed
to be filled with a command to see things for what
they were.

Whatever the hell that meant.

She had to get out. Walk to the door of the restaurant. Face the fact that the only reason she was
there, meeting Woodrow Alexander, was because
her baby might be terminally ill. As though meeting the real-life man made the dark shadow horribly
real. A true threat.

And then a funny thing happened. As she stared
into those eyes gazing up at her from her phone, she
felt as if he'd read her mind and was telling her that
she was a strong, capable woman who'd get through
whatever was to come. One who knew better than
to allow panic to take over what could be good moments in her life.

More likely, it was just her better self, saving her.

Dropping her phone into its proper slot in the big black designer shoulder bag she took everywhere, she deposited her keys into their own pocket and opened the door of her Jag, stood up and froze. Standing there, not two feet away, watching her—how long had he been standing there?—was the man in the photo. His gaze, sharp and yet filled with something that reminded her of her own strength, could have been staring out at her from her phone.

"Wood?" She tried a smile. Managed a tremulous half grin. Walked toward him, with her hand held out. It took her a minute to look off to the side of him, to see if he'd come alone. The spot was unoccupied, and she had no reason to be glad for that.

Other than that the meeting was hard enough without having to do it twofold. Compassion was all fine and good—until it was directed at her over something she was powerless to control. Because sometimes she was more her mother's daughter than her father's.

"Cassie." He didn't ask, as she had. Her name on his lips seemed mere confirmation. He didn't smile, either. Didn't even seem to try. Smart man. Why pretend?

Used to meeting the men in her life eye to eye, she had to crick her neck to look up at him, but she did so naturally, drawn by that expression in his gaze.

As though it was familiar to her. And yet, it wasn't. At all.

This man looked like no one in her life. Ever. The whole moment took on a surreal relevance that she was pretty sure was going to go down in the book of life memories she'd never forget.

In shorts, a polo shirt and tennis shoes, he could have been any number of beautiful California men. There was no particular confidence about him. No arrogance. Just an air of acceptance of what drew her to him in a way she couldn't deny.

"Thank you for meeting with me," she said as her hand briefly touched his and then let go. They turned toward the restaurant door.

"I'm the one who invited you," he pointed out, and she did smile then.

And suddenly had her appetite back.

A good thing, since she was eating for two.

Wood ordered a burger. He didn't eat out a lot. And at home usually ate healthier dinners in deference to the grocery choices he made for his housemate's sake. True, in the past few months, Elaina had no longer needed his financial support, but neither did it make sense throwing money away on two sets of meals.

Cassie had a chef salad—full size, not the discounted lunch version. He liked that she wasn't shy about her appetite and reminded himself that she'd have no reason to be. She wasn't out to impress him. Just to meet him.

A man who happened to be the father of her baby.

Technically.

Giving himself a mental shake as he watched her talk to the waitress, he allowed that the situation was a bit confusing. A kind of battle of wills between emotion and mind. His heart racing ahead on one track—attached to his child, family, in trouble. And his mind knowing that the child wasn't his. He knew that mind had to win this one.

And that his mind would. Extricating his emotions from situations so that he could do what must be done was one of his greatest talents.

"I have questions," he said when the woman taking their order was finally satisfied that she had their choices correct down to bottled water, not tap, and sugar-free ranch dressing for Cassie's salad. "If you'd rather not answer, just say so. It won't hurt my feelings."

Because this was a mind thing only for him. A supportive role. The only kind he really knew how to do well.

And something he actually liked to do, too. Helping others had just rewards.

"I actually have questions, too," she told him, smiling in a way that made him more aware of the natural beauty of her features. "A lot of them."

He'd give her whatever she needed as long as it was at his disposal to share.

"But you go first," she told him and then, elbows on the table of the booth they shared, clasped her hands together, looking at him expectantly. Like she was prepared for some kind of interview.

Odd, since she was the one who'd chosen him.

In a manner of speaking.

He started out with the basics. Was reminded that she was a lawyer. Doctors and lawyers: his life seemed to be anchored with them.

And, lately, with confusion, too. Why would a woman of her intelligence choose an uneducated man to be the father of her child?

He'd get to that. Later.

She owned her home in a neighborhood he'd helped build, not that he told her that. A neighborhood still above his price range, but one he'd set his sights on. Assuming Cassie's baby didn't need his savings.

The home he and Elaina currently shared had always just been a temporary landing place. Until she finished med school and residency. He'd built some equity there, though, which would allow him to put down a nice sum on his next home.

When she—and he—were both ready to move on. In the meantime, there was comfort in sameness, comfort in watching over Elaina until she wanted to stand alone. Comfort in family.

"Did you grow up in Marie Cove?" he asked. He and Peter had been raised in a sleepy little burg east of LA, but when Peter had been offered a residency in Marie Cove, he and Elaina had talked Wood into moving to town with them. They'd been together for a few years at that point. He'd had his own small place by the beach those first few years. Until the accident had changed everything.

She shook her head. "Not officially. I was born in San Diego but went through all twelve grades of school in Mission Viejo," she said, naming a somewhat affluent town between Marie Cove and LA.

"Are your parents still there?" A man of his thirty-six years really shouldn't be so fascinated by those who'd raised the people he was spending time with. But there you had it. Family was fascinating. Especially when you didn't have much of it.

"My mom and stepdad are."

"What about your dad?"

"He died when I was sixteen," she said. "Killed by a suicide bomber when he was deployed overseas."

Her manner, as she spoke, was matter-of-fact. She looked him in the eye. Didn't tear up. And yet Wood understood that look as though it had been coming from him, not to him. Just because a person was able to compartmentalize didn't mean that they didn't feel.

He just hadn't met a lot of people who seemed to be as good at it as she was. As he was, as well.

Or he was so far out of his element that he was building castles in the sky over her. Something he hadn't done since before his own father had died of a heart attack. He'd been five. Peter, two. And Wood's castle building had abruptly ended.

"Did you see him much when he was home?" he asked, though he sensed that she'd have been more comfortable if he'd moved on.

"Yeah. All the time. Any time he was home. Mom let me stay with him for as long and as often as he could keep me."

"Was he still in San Diego? What about when you were in school?"

She shook her head. "He bought a small place here in Marie Cove shortly after their divorce. To be close enough to Mission Viejo to be able to get me to and from school."

"Did he remarry?"

Why so many questions about the guy, he didn't know. It just seemed important, somehow, that he understand this part of her. The father in her life.

"Nope. I think Mom was the love of his life."

"But he wasn't hers," he surmised aloud. "She didn't take to military life?" he was just guessing. But it sounded as if the two had remained on a friendly enough basis that they didn't need parenting laws to dictate their time with their child.

She shook her head and then glanced away. It was the first time she'd felt closed off to him since he'd taken her hand in the parking lot. Odd, since they were complete strangers.

Odder still that the sudden lack bothered him as much as it did.

The woman was pregnant with his child. He'd noticed a little swell beneath her dress as she'd gotten out of her car—of course, it could just be the natural curve of any woman's belly, but...

She looked back at him then and shot all thought from his mind when she said, "It wasn't the navy so much that caused their problems. My father...was not quite a slow learner, but close," she said, speaking hesitantly as though choosing her words carefully. "He graduated from high school a year late and did well enough to make it as an enlisted man in the navy. He was educable. He just didn't put a lot of two and two together on his own. Not in a book-learning sense. But because of that, I think, he had a way of understanding the things that really matter. He lived a simple life, and yet, most of the lessons I learned, the ones that serve me in the hardest times, I learned from him." Her gaze had softened so much Wood almost got lost in it.

It took a second for her words to register, but when they did, they hit him like the swing of a two-by-four hanging from a crane. Had she just told him why she'd chosen him, an uneducated man, as her donor?

Because she'd so admired her own father?

He'd been planning to ask why. Mentally crossed

that one right off his list. He did not want to hear that he'd been chosen because he was uneducated.

And because he had no immediate response, he sat there silent.

"He and my mom hooked up after her parents were killed in a boating accident. He was nineteen and she was eighteen, both working at a '50s diner in San Diego. My dad was a huge comfort to her. She says even now that she doubts she'd have made it through that time without him."

That reminded Wood of Elaina's words about him...

Cassie's soft smile struck Wood. Another one of those stand-out moments that he'd probably not forget, and yet one that had no context in his unemotional mindset.

"It was the summer after they'd both graduated from high school. He'd already enlisted, and she was due to start college in the fall. Her parents had just died a few weeks before, and one night they went together to a party on the beach and just kind of started hanging out after that. They slept together before he left for boot camp. And when he came back and was being deployed, they got married. I think she truly thought they had a shot at making it work. Dad loved her so much, was so good to her. She knew he was going to make a great father someday. All things she also still says today.

"But as soon as she started college, they grew

apart. He was gone a lot, and when he was home, he couldn't relate to most of what was captivating her. Didn't know a lot about the business world or stock markets or marketing. But just a few months after they were married, Mom found out she was pregnant. By the time I was a year old, I think I was the only thing they had in common. When Mom graduated, with a great job offer in Mission Viejo, and he didn't understand why she couldn't just take the lesser job she'd been offered in San Diego, she knew that if she didn't leave then, they'd end up hating each other. They were always kind to each other, respectful of each other... Mom and Richard, my stepdad, were both at his funeral."

His biggest fear had just come to life in the form of two people he'd never met. Had Cassie's dad's lack of education, of potential, been at least partially responsible for the failure of his marriage?

He didn't like Cassie's story. At all. A man had loved his family with all of his heart, and it hadn't been enough.

And yet...to have a woman like Cassie there, adoring him, looking up to him in her own way... Maybe her father hadn't been all that unlucky after all.

Some people just had to take what was given to them. To see the gifts where they were.

That was intelligence in the way that mattered most.

"I'm an average learner," he blurted, against his

better judgment. "I'm not well educated, but I have the mental capacity to be."

She blinked. Sat back. "Okay."

"Just in case you think your kid is going to get genes like your dad's from me. He isn't. Or she isn't."

And he was doing a fantastic job of proving so.

"I...didn't think anything of the kind." Her frown drew more attention to those eyes of hers. They were mysterious, set so majestically in that striking bone structure. And then she shook her head. "Why would you..." Her voice trailed off, leaving him to fix his mess.

"I've been struggling to understand why a woman would choose a man with less than a high school education to father her child when there were doctors and lawyers to choose from for the same exact cost." He looked her straight in the eye. He wasn't ashamed of who he was. Of the choices he'd made. But he didn't kid himself, either. A lack of education hurt a man's potential in some ways.

Women ways, for one. His capacity to earn was potentially less.

Cassie leaned toward him. Opened her mouth to speak just as their waitress arrived at their table, requiring Cassie to sit upright so her oversize bowl of salad could be placed in front of her. Wood would have forgone lunch to hear whatever it was she'd been about to say.

He put the lettuce and tomato beside his burger in

the burger where they belonged. Squirted ketchup for his fries, feeling uncomfortable and a little pissed at himself, as he sat there exposed in a way he'd never been before.

And why? The woman was a stranger to him.

"It was your essay."

He glanced up at her words, found her watching him, her salad sitting untouched with a small ceramic carafe of dressing beside it.

"I saw your level of education, of course, and probably because of my dad didn't put a whole lot of stock in the lack of formal schooling. I made my choice based on your essay."

He'd reread it the other night. He'd been honest about his reason for donating—because his brother had asked him to, and supporting Peter's efforts was important to him.

"You wrote about family," she said. "About the gift that comes from having someone who is a part of you, who will always be a part of you, in this life and beyond."

Yeah, he had, but only because he had to fill the word count required, not because that was his reason for donating sperm. He'd been talking about why he'd felt it important to be there for his brother. Why he'd been willing to donate a part of himself just because Peter had asked him to.

"You quit school your senior year to go to work so

that you could keep him with you after your mother died," she said.

It was a fact that supported his thesis statement. He'd needed the word count.

"That's why I chose you," she said. "I believe that character is, in part, genetic. And I know that, for me at least, character is far more important than being a doctor or a lawyer."

With that she picked up the dressing, poured a generous amount all over her salad, picked up her fork and started eating.

Wood wisely followed suit.

Chapter Four

Cassie could tell she'd offended Wood. Made him feel stupid. Because she'd barreled ahead, uncharacteristically talking about her folks, wanting him to know who she was, what she came from, wanting him to like her, she'd completely spaced on his own lack of education. But even then, there was a difference between Wood and her dad. Her father had needed help, and extra time, getting through high school. Wood had chosen to quit to raise his brother.

She didn't think less of either of them. She hoped he got that. Would have pressed the point home, except that she didn't want to risk making the situation worse by drawing more attention to it.

She didn't want to make him feel bad. To the contrary. He was the genetic other half of her baby. Sitting right there across from her.

She hadn't expected his mere presence to affect her like it was doing. To draw her in, man to woman.

He picked up his burger and started eating. Chewing. Swallowing. "Do you have any other questions for me?" she asked.

He hesitated, holding his burger, but not raising it for another bite. "I do, actually," he told her. "Probably not my business, but I'm curious… Why did you choose to go this route, with insemination, rather than a more traditional choice? Not that I think tradition is always the best or right way, but in a case like… You're going through it all alone…"

Raising a child alone, she translated. Without a father figure. She'd worried about the lack of influence of a steady man in her child's life.

"I'm not against marriage, if that's what you're thinking." She picked around her salad with her fork. Found a piece of hard-boiled egg and stabbed.

He finally took a bite, still watching her. Lifted his napkin to his mouth and dropped it back to his lap. He was neat and tidy, she'd hand him that, from the clean shave to the straight corners on the collar of his shirt.

"To be honest, I always thought I'd grow up, fall in love and get married. I never saw myself living alone. Or doing this alone." Oh God. Now she was sounding pitiful, and she didn't feel that way. At all.

"I've just never been consumed with a need or desire to be with one person over another. And I couldn't risk doing to anyone what my mom had to do to my dad. If I'm not compelled to be with a particular person before marriage, I darn sure won't be after that first glow wears off."

He nodded, swallowed and, meeting her gaze, said, "I know exactly how you feel."

"You do." Not a question. If the man thought she needed to be humored...

"I do," he reiterated. "Completely."

"You were married."

He stilled. Watching her, he said nothing. Maybe wishing he could take back his words. Or hoping she hadn't drawn the conclusion she had.

Oh Lord. Leave it up to her to inadvertently choose and then need to contact a sperm donor who hadn't at one time been head over heels in love with his wife.

Their whole meeting was oddly...odd. Her rambling on about her parents. Him...saying things he probably hadn't meant to say. It was like they had started talking and forgotten who they were talking to—virtual strangers.

Except for the baby they had in common. One that might be in a fight for its life.

Might be. Her baby could be just fine. Or could just be anemic.

She thought of Wood's original question. Why she'd chosen to be inseminated.

"I'm thirty-four," she suddenly said, somewhat inanely. She was just so damned...not herself around him. Felt more...vulnerable.

Having spent her adult life open to dating, but never finding a man who captivated her, she didn't know what to do with that.

"It might sound trite, but biological clocks really do tick. Chances for birth defects increase with a woman's age, and statistically, that means that I run more risk after I turn thirty-five. I left it as late as I could, factoring in the probability of having to go through the process more than once." She shrugged. "I got lucky there. It took first time."

But there she was, still facing a possible birth defect.

Dropping his burger to his plate, he met her gaze, holding on as though he was holding her up somehow, as though with a mere look he could infuse her body with strength. Which was ludicrous.

And yet...happening.

"What day is the test scheduled for?"

Yep. There they were. Putting it right out there where she had to face the possibilities—and deal with the panic that hit her every time.

"Wednesday."

"What time?"

"Eight." She'd taken the earliest appointment. So she could still make it to her office for a full day's work.

And so she didn't have to deal with a full day of anxiety and lack of focus leading up to it.

"I can take you, if you'd like. Since none of your support system is aware that it's happening."

"I'm sure you have to work."

"I do have doctor appointments of my own now and then," he told her. "My crew will be okay if I'm a couple of hours late. They're good guys."

He seemed to want to take her to the appointment that she was dreading more than any other she'd ever been through.

"What do you do for a living?" she asked when she couldn't make herself tell him that she'd be fine on her own. He'd said "a day job." She couldn't remember exactly what. And she really would be fine on her own.

She would be. She just needed a minute.

"I'm still in construction."

His profile had said so. "Framing, right?"

He picked up his half-eaten burger. "Yes."

He waited. She didn't know what to do. Well, she did. She had to tell him she'd be fine on her own. She just wasn't doing it.

"I understand if you'd rather go alone." His words reached out to her. Softly enveloping her.

"The thing is... I'd actually rather not. I just don't know how it's okay for you to go with me."

He shrugged. And grinned, of all things. "It's a medical test to determine whether or not you need my bone marrow," he said, making it sound so simple.

It wasn't simple. None of this was.

The intensity of his gaze told her he knew that.

As she waffled, he continued to hold her gaze tenderly. Until she relaxed again. Or gave in.

"Okay, then, I would appreciate the company," she said. "I really don't want to tell anyone about this until I know more. But… I'm… It would be easier not to sit there alone."

She could. There was no doubt in her mind about that.

"It's just two people sitting there waiting for a test," he said. "Seriously."

He was right.

She knew he was right.

"So…this is kind of weird, isn't it?" she asked.

"A little."

But they were okay.

And that mattered.

"So what do you do as a corporate lawyer?" Lunch was almost through, and Wood wasn't ready to get on with his day—or to leave Cassie to hers.

"A lot of contract reading," she said with a chuckle. "But really, all kinds of things. I have several clients myself, and the firm has some that we share. We advise on everything from criminal complaints against a corporation, civil complaints—usually meaning lawsuits—deal negotiations and anything else that comes up."

"So you go to court."

"On occasion. Mostly I'm in meetings. Researching. And doing a hell of a lot of contract reading," she repeated with a self-deprecatory grin. Like she was downplaying the high-powered importance of her job.

"Don't do that," he said.

"Do what?"

"Undermine what you do."

"I…wasn't…"

All he did was look at her, and she dropped her gaze. Signaling that he was right.

She looked at him. Sighed. "I don't know what it is about you… I'm just not myself. I'm constantly afraid of offending you and I don't even know why."

Her honesty put him at ease, endeared her to him a bit.

"I live with a nuclear radiology resident," he told her. "She was a med student before that. And when Peter was in med school, he talked nonstop about his classes and the things he was learning every step of the way. I can handle conversation involving higher learning."

She shook her head. "It's not that. And if you have such an issue with your lack of education, then why don't you just go back to school?"

"I don't have an issue with it." Normally, never.

"Then why do you keep trying to make an issue of it between us?"

He wished he knew. Shook his head. "This situation is a first for me, I'll give you that," he told her. All that mattered was them getting through this together. Making sure that the baby she was carrying made it into the world in good health, or got healthy as soon as possible if it didn't. And yet…for the first time in his life, he wanted to be more than he was. And he had no idea why.

Pushing her nearly empty salad bowl aside, she put her forearms on the table, leaning toward him a bit. "You could always take the GED," she told him.

"Done," he said, adding, "I wasn't going to be able to advance without a diploma equivalency." But other than the requisite contractor licensing he'd needed to obtain to do his job, he'd never sought out any other education. Although he had time. Plenty of it.

And financial means now, too. He just wasn't interested in being a thirty-six-year-old college student now. Or a thirty-year-old one, either, several years ago. Peter had completely understood. Elaina didn't really seem to. She didn't push him, but the comments she sometimes made, the questions she asked…

Their waitress had just slipped the bill onto the table as she passed; the staff was hovering to turn their table.

Cassie reached for the bill. He took ownership of

it before she could touch it. He'd issued the lunch invitation and was already pulling out his credit card. But he wasn't ready to pay yet.

"Do you know the sex of the baby?" He'd meant to segue into the question a bit better. Justifying a reason why he'd need to know. Had kind of hoped she might give him some indication without him having to ask.

She shook her head. "A lot of times they can tell with the first ultrasound, but he or she wasn't cooperating," she said, sitting back. For the first time he saw her reach for her stomach. Put her hand there. And hoped she was feeling okay.

Not sure what to do about it if she wasn't.

"The amnio will tell us that, for sure," she said.

"So that's something to look forward to from the test results."

She smiled at him. Nodded. And, because of that hand on her stomach, he somehow had to ask, "Have you had much morning sickness?"

"Nope." Another smile. "Until now, this whole experience has been a breeze."

He mentioned a movie he'd seen where the heroine was going through a first-time pregnancy and had everything go wrong, in terms of preparation, but with a picture perfect pregnancy and healthy baby. It was a comedy. She'd seen it, too. Somehow a half hour passed as they discussed TV shows, moving on to crime procedurals. Wood enjoyed hearing her take on those that involved lawyers. Hearing her talk about white-collar crime from a technical perspective was better than any movie, as far as he was concerned.

The conversation led into a discussion of their work hours. She asked about his current project. He told her a bit. Nothing specific. Not a whole lot of interesting conversation about hammering boards together. Or overseeing others doing so. He liked the work, though. Liked the math involved. Like solving puzzles every single day. She smiled when he mentioned that, asked if he ever played games on his phone. Pulled hers out to show him a couple of her favorites. One of which he had on his phone, as well.

They had to go. He knew it. But wasn't satisfied. She was strong and beautiful and…pregnant with his child and bearing worry about that all alone. He wanted to do more for her.

"Listen, if you ever have anything you need done at your house…I'm happy to help," he said. He'd done all that needed doing at his place. Or all that he had any interest in doing. "You want a light moved, or a ceiling fan put in…maybe some help putting together baby furniture… My tools travel…"

"I might take you up on that." She was smiling again, her tone easy and relaxed, and he was glad.

And then his phone rang. *Elaina.* Cassie must have seen her picture come up on his caller ID. She glanced at his phone and immediately looked away, the smile fading from her face.

"Excuse me, I have to take this," he said. They always took each other's calls or called back as soon as possible.

As Elaina let him know that she was off earlier than planned and would stop at the big box store for the toilet paper and other household items they needed, Wood watched Cassie pull her bag onto her lap, getting her keys out.

"Are you at home?" Elaina's question took him by surprise. They didn't generally check up on each other.

"No," he said.

"I was just going to ask you to check the cupboard for body wash," she said. "I think I took the last one."

"You did." He'd noticed it gone when he'd needed a new box of tissues. And was concerned that if he didn't get off soon, Cassie would be gone before he did.

"Are you gone for the day?"

A fair question. Any other day he'd have thought nothing of it.

"No. I'm at lunch," he said.

And glanced over to see Cassie watching him. Like she could somehow see that he hadn't been enough for the woman on the other end of the line. He hadn't been romantically interested in her, where he could have been, and he hadn't been enough to attract her interest, either. Not in that way.

Elaina was asking if he wanted to do dinner. Another perfectly normal question between them. He agreed. And rang off.

"Your ex-wife?" Cassie asked, scooting to the edge of the booth, her bag on her shoulder.

"Yes."

"Everything okay?"

He stood as she did, pulling cash for the bill out of his pocket and leaving it on the table as he grabbed his credit card. "Fine," he told her, the truth loud and clear in his voice as he followed her out.

She continued to be friendly as they walked back to their vehicles. His truck was just beyond her car, so he stopped as she split from him.

"Thanks for lunch," she said, turning at the driver's door to look back at him, standing just off the rear bumper.

"What time do you want me to pick you up on Wednesday?"

She hesitated, and he waited for her to tell him she'd changed her mind and would go alone. "I'd really like to be there, Cassie," he said softly. But the decision was hers.

She nodded. Connected gazes with him for a second, and then said, "Seven-thirty in the morning would be great. I need to get there early for prep time…" She waited only long enough for him to nod and then was in her vehicle with the door shut, reaching for the safety belt.

He'd been dismissed. Or felt as though he had. And didn't blame her. Or Elaina, either.

Didn't blame anyone.

He just didn't like how things had changed between them the second Elaina's call came through. And wondered how much of the change had really happened and how much he'd read into the situation.

He knew Elaina thought he should make more of himself...it didn't mean she was right. Or that Cassie, another highly educated woman, would agree with her. It also didn't mean that if he'd gone to college, become some high-powered real estate magnate or developer, that their marriage would have worked.

His brother had been the love of her life. He'd known that going in.

And the knowing didn't keep feelings of failure from his doorstep. Because maybe...if he'd been more, different somehow... Elaina could have fallen for him, too. Or at least found him attractive. In a husbandly kind of way.

He hadn't gone into the marriage expecting that kind of attraction, and yet, somewhere along the way, he'd begun to doubt himself when it didn't happen.

Shaking his head, he started his truck, attempting to rid himself of the malarkey.

He was who he was.

And that was going to be enough.

Chapter Five

Things might be fine for Wood. They weren't fine for Cassie. Sitting there with Wood, talking about movies and jobs and games on their phones…she'd forgotten that he was just a medical part of her insemination process. For a second or two, she'd even forgotten that she was pregnant. She'd been a woman enjoying a meal alone with a man.

A man she found incredibly attractive. A man whose gaze could settle the fears and doubts pushing up from inside her.

A man who'd paid for her lunch.

Kind of like a date.

And therein lay her problem. For a second there,

she'd felt like she was on a date. Wished it had been a date. For a second...

And then his ex-wife had called. Bringing reality crashing back down around her. He hadn't asked her out on a date. He'd asked her to lunch to discuss their situation. He had his own life.

Still shared a residence with his ex-wife. Still took her calls and...

And she had her own life, too.

Ten minutes after she arrived back home, she was out on the private beach she shared with several neighbors, in a maternity swimsuit, reclining with a towel, a book, a thermos of water and her phone. There were a few others out, on both sides of her. Close enough that she could hear voices. Not so close she could make out what they were saying.

With the sun warming her skin while the light breeze caressed it, she was tempted to lie back, close her eyes and nap.

A great plan, except that she wasn't a napper. Closed eyes during the day were viewed as an invitation to her mind to begin to spin. She opened her book, a novel that had been on the *New York Times* bestseller list the year she was born. Something to do with a woman who traveled the world while different parts of herself raged war inside her. And there was a man, too. She'd probably fall in love with him.

Cassie was pretty certain the hero of this book

would ask the heroine on a date the first time they met. Even if she was carrying his baby.

All she'd wanted to do was have a family of her own. Not entangle herself in other people's lives.

Wood was being sweet, but he owed her nothing. She couldn't let him feel like he did. He was obviously a decent man. One who took responsibility very seriously. To the point that he was still sharing a home with his ex-wife.

Because he was still in love with her?

Maybe. And even if he wasn't, he clearly felt responsible for her. The speed with which he'd answered her call, the look on his face as he'd glanced at Cassie, had made that much obvious.

Wood was in her life because she'd chosen his sperm. And called him. He was there only to try to prevent his child from serious health issues, if reason arose.

He wasn't the father of her child.

It wasn't fair to him, or to herself, if she didn't keep that fact straight from the start.

Their situation…it couldn't help but be emotional, with a baby's life possibly in the balance. And as such, any other feelings they might feel when they were together were only growing out of that one thing they had in common. The one thing that had brought them together.

It would be completely wrong for her to think

it was anything else. To confuse need, or compassion, for love.

As her mom had done with her dad.

She picked up her phone. She wasn't going to call Wood. Seemed too familiar. Didn't like the feel of a text, either, since it seemed private and hidden, just between the two of them.

She didn't have his email. Or his address, not that that mattered. If she mailed a letter on Monday, it was probable that he'd get it on Tuesday, but there was no guarantee; she had to reach him before Wednesday morning, when he'd otherwise show up at her house at seven thirty and she'd be too glad to see him and too on edge about the amniocentesis to send him away.

I've changed my mind about Wednesday. I need to do this alone.

As she typed out the text, she had to hold her phone in the shade of her body and pull her sunglasses down her nose to reread her message. Satisfied, she hit Send.

Opened her book.

And pretended that she didn't feel like a soul lost out at sea.

Elaina had suggested that she and Wood drive up the coast for dinner. It was Saturday night, and neither of them had been out for a while. A comedian Elaina and Peter had introduced him to was performing at a little dinner theater they'd frequented many times, and Wood accepted the invitation, ready for a few minutes of respite from the intensity trying to rage inside him. His libido and emotions warring against facts.

In a short green fitted dress with high heels to match, his ex-wife was a beauty without even trying. Male heads always turned when he walked in a room with her. He had no idea if she ever noticed that.

And had never asked himself why the attention hadn't ever made him jealous. Even when they'd been married, he'd never felt like she was his woman. Or his partner—not just in a sexual sense, but in a companion sense. They'd been friends, family, just not...partners

Because he'd known better. Elaina was his brother's wife. He'd never loved her in that way.

That night he'd managed to get a table for two close to the stage by paying a hefty sum for it. Dinner, a bourbon pork that was one of their favorites, was superb. She was nursing her one glass of wine and he'd almost finished his second beer as she glanced over at him, brows raised, and he smiled. He'd hung his jacket over the back of his chair, had already unbuttoned the top button of his shirt, and still he was warm. How guys wore suits all day long every day he could never understand. Elaina liked him in them, and so he owned one.

On the drive home, the tension that he'd been trying to ignore all night rose to critical level. It eased as he thought about waiting until the next day to talk to her. It wasn't like Wednesday would happen overnight. He had three more days.

Cassie was alone every second that passed. Dealing with her worry, keeping her secret, alone. She'd changed her mind about letting him go with her to the appointment. He'd sensed that was coming. She'd been like a different woman after Elaina's call. Still kind and pleasant. Just…different. He'd felt the loss—and sensed that she was feeling it, too. She'd wanted him to go with her. There'd been no mistaking that.

"You awake?" His voice broke into what should have been a relaxing, comfortable silence.

Elaina lifted her head. "Yeah." And then, "You ready to tell me what's on your mind?"

Gaze leaving the largely vacant freeway briefly, he glanced at her. He knew her well. And she knew him well, too.

"I had a call yesterday morning… Do you remember when Peter first started his residency at the Parent Portal?"

"Of course. We had to move to Marie Cove because of it. You said you got a call," she continued.

"Was it a job offer? Back in LA? Is someone offering you a chance at full contracting?"

He had his contractor's license. Could be in business for himself. Bidding jobs, hiring crews like his, along with plumbers and electricians and drywallers. She wanted that for him.

He liked being free to be available at home whenever he was needed. Liked not having a job that required his first loyalty. And the rest… He already picked his own crew. Bid his jobs. Ran them. He just did it all for whatever contractor hired him…

"No…the call wasn't for a job. It was from the Parent Portal."

She leaned forward. He heard the movement. Could see her turned toward him, briefly highlighted and shadowed by the headlights that sped past in the opposite direction across the median.

"Something to do with Peter?" she asked, her voice softer, hoarse. She'd told him once that she missed his brother every second of every day.

Wood could relate. He was pretty sure that not a day had gone by since his little brother's death that he didn't think of him at least once.

"Indirectly," he told her. "Peter asked me to donate sperm to the clinic," he said, just needing it done now. If she showed shock, surprise even, that someone had picked his sample over others', so what? Didn't change any of the facts. "He was hitting up everyone he could," he added.

"I remember," she told him. "He donated, too. We talked about it…" He heard her intake of breath as she broke off. And then she said, "Is that what this is about? Someone used Peter's sperm? His baby is out there and the family is seeking contact?"

Something like that. But not quite. "Someone used my sperm," he told her. "And the woman was seeking contact."

He glanced her way and then back, sparing himself whatever surprise she might be showing. Didn't hear an intake of breath, even.

"Was that your lunch today?" she asked him, sounding more curious than anything.

"Yes."

She was facing forward now, no longer even pretending relaxation. Her eyes wide-open, she stared out the windshield. Her hands were clasped together over her stomach, but that telltale rubbing back and forth of one thumb up and down the other gave her away every time.

"What did she want? Is the child in some kind of danger?"

"She's only four months pregnant. And yes, the fetus could be compromised. She'll know more next week. Worst-case scenario, she might need my bone marrow."

Elaina's head turned toward him then. "You told her you'd donate, right?"

"Yes."

"Good. Wow. How horrible for her. I'm assuming it's blood related?"

He answered her questions. Cassie's age, which she'd told him over lunch. The fact that it was her first child. What he knew about what was seen on the ultrasound. Mostly just confirmation of what she was guessing was going on. And as he reached their exit and slowed the truck, he listened as she told him in more detail what a bone marrow transplant would involve for him, the donor, and for the baby, too. Describing tests and time frames. Procedures. The wait to see if the transplant was a success. Percentages of chances of success.

She was still discussing the situation as he pulled into the garage, and as they walked into their house together.

Elaina went down on her knees to greet Retro, who came running in through the doggy door. Taking her head in both hands, rubbing her and bending to bury her face in the dog's neck for a hug. "Did you get any sense of what kind of support system she has?" she asked, her face even with Retro's as they both looked up at him.

Their gazes were a spotlight, the family spotlight, on him, and there he stood. Trying to find his place.

"A solid one," he said. Repeated almost verbatim what Cassie had told him about her friends and family. Her law partners.

"Good," Elaina said. "She's going to need it. Long

term, if the situation requires it, but right now, too, as she makes her way through the initial adjustment…"

"There might not be an adjustment," he had to point out. "The baby could be just fine."

"She's had the scare, Wood. She's known real fear," she said. "That doesn't just disappear with a healthy diagnosis."

Good point. One he filed right there on top with everything else that had just taken over his list of important matters.

"You feel responsible for her," Elaina said next, standing to face him.

"Of course I do." He started to feel defensive, and shook his head, meeting Elaina's open brown gaze. "I feel strongly about doing what I can," he admitted to her. "My genes could be responsible…"

"It's not thought to be hereditary, but leukemia is a genetic disease," she affirmed. "Still… I worry about you, Wood." She looked him right in the eye. "Your whole life…you take on others' problems, to the detriment of having a life of your own—after your dad died…then giving up your football career for Peter when your mom died. And taking me in when Peter did…"

"What would you have had me do? Turn my back on them? Or you?" He'd thought she'd known him better than that. Understood him better. He'd done what he had because he'd wanted to, as well as needed to.

"No, of course not. It's just…"

"It's my biological child. I can't turn my back on it."

"Of course not. I'm not suggesting you do. At all. I'm just… Be careful, okay?"

Don't expect too much to come of it, Wood translated. Don't expect too much of Cassie. As he had of Elaina.

He'd never forget the night he'd tried to kiss her, thinking they might become a real husband and wife, trying to give her the option of a full life again, and seen the horrified expression on her face when she'd realized what he was doing.

Horrified for him, that was.

She'd been sorry. So sorry. Had cried for him.

All in all, she'd taken the actual rejection much harder than he had. He'd been told no before. Had been ready to shrug it all off. Hadn't really even been feeling it all that much himself, but had been willing to try to build more…

Until she'd felt sorry for him. That was what had rankled. Not the fact that he hadn't had sex that night.

"Believe me, I'm in this for the child," he told her now. "The mother is out of my league."

"I don't like it when you talk that way about yourself." And yet, he noticed that she didn't deny his assertion.

"I offered to take her to the procedure on Wednesday." He told her about Cassie's decision not to tell her loved ones about the worrisome prognosis until she knew more.

He stood there, letting her study him, not sure what she'd find.

And then she nodded. "You're always the guy with the strongest shoulders. I do love that about you, in spite of what I just said about you having a life of your own."

He smiled at her. She saw him as he was. That's what family did.

"Would you do me a favor, then?"

"Sure, what?"

"Would you call Cassie? Let her know that I'm a good guy who's only trying to help where he can? She's...an independent sort, and while I get the idea that she wants me around, she won't let herself accept help."

"I'll call her if she wants me to, Wood, of course, but ultimately the choice is all hers. You know that."

He did. Completely.

"And don't forget, I'm here for you, too," Elaina added. "I get that this can't be easy. Feeling responsible like you do. But you have to know that things like this... We try to find scientific explanations, but in the end...a sick baby...sometimes it's just fate..."

He knew she was right.

And hoped to God the baby he'd helped make wasn't sick.

Chapter Six

Cassie didn't sleep well. Chamomile tea helped—she got some rest, but not a lot. Up early Sunday morning, she put on black spandex running shorts with a white T-shirt and went for a walk on the beach. A group of her college friends was coming to town later that morning for brunch at a five-star restaurant set up on stilts overlooking the ocean. Any of them that could make it met once a month, taking turns driving to each other's towns—all within an hour or so from LA.

She'd announced her pregnancy at the last one, and everyone had been incredibly supportive. Of the twelve of them, she numbered five unmarried.

Two were divorced. One had been living with her lover for almost a decade. The other was completely career driven and just not interested in marriage. They'd all made it to the May brunch, and every single one of the eleven had had tears in her eyes as they'd hugged her.

That morning, for the first time ever, Cassie didn't want to go to the brunch. Until she knew more, she just couldn't fathom the idea of eleven friends hovering over her, needing to help, with her not knowing how to let them. And until there was known reason to worry, she wasn't going to make the situation bigger than it might be.

Okay, she wasn't telling anyone besides Wood, because then it would feel more real. It might just be one of those things…a shadow on a film that indicated no more than that.

She had to keep telling herself that. Focusing on the chance that the coming test might show nothing wrong with her baby was her only way to calm the panic. To survive the waiting. Inaction didn't sit well with her. If the results didn't come back good, there'd be plenty of time for worrying.

The sand cool beneath her feet, she walked as far north as she could, ending at a rocky inlet that rose into cliff side. Most of Marie Cove was set several hundred feet above sea level, making it less attractive for tourists wanting beachside vacations. She had her portion of the mile-long beach to herself and, down by the water, walked in ankle-deep, standing there as the waves moved in, splashing her up to her calves, and then rolled back out again.

Her father had once told her that the waves were like life. They might come in and bring stuff—good or bad—and then they went away again. Nothing was always, he'd said. Not the good, but not the bad, either.

Looking down, she couldn't see what that particular wave had just brought in. The rising sun was still low on the horizon, but glinting off the water. What she did know was that this moment in her life would pass. She'd handle what was to come, and there would be good waves ahead.

Didn't make the prospect of brunch with eleven friends who knew her well any easier to manage. Not when she felt so incredibly alone, small and frightened. The only thing stopping her from canceling was the fact that everyone was driving to Marie Cove, since it was her turn to host.

When her phone vibrated against her butt, signifying a new text message, Cassie pulled it from the pocket of her shorts, hoping her friends were canceling. One at a time? All eleven of them?

More likely one of them couldn't make it…

Wood.

She'd waited the rest of the afternoon and evening on Saturday, expecting a return message from him.

When he'd failed to respond, she'd been unreasonably disappointed. Not because she feared he'd come anyway—she'd somehow known he wouldn't—but because he hadn't tried to change her mind.

Still standing up to her ankles in water, she touched the text icon and then his name.

I told Elaina about our situation. May I give her your number so she can call you?

Not necessary, she responded instantly.

Just want you to know you aren't in this alone. My biology is partly responsible, and as one human being to another, I care.

Tears came to her eyes at his response. Such a stupid, uncalled-for thing. Tears.

If you won't take her call, will you at least let me take you on Wednesday?

With a couple of steps, she was out of the water, sand caking around her feet, typing on her phone with shaking fingers. She didn't stop to think. Just typed.

Yes. Thank you.

Phone in hand, she walked quickly back down the beach and then up to her yard, heading straight for the shower. She had a brunch to get to.

And suddenly she wasn't dreading it as much anymore.

Sitting at the kitchen table alone Monday night, Wood cut into the chicken thigh he'd grilled, took a bite, enjoyed it, cut the next one and handed it down to Retro, who took it gently and chewed before she swallowed. Had she wolfed it down, she wouldn't get any more. Manners were important.

Elaina had called to say she wouldn't be home until late. That was happening more and more. Wood was pretty sure she was seeing someone. When he'd asked her about it, she'd told him there was no one important to her. He didn't believe her. And he also hurt for her.

Would she ever believe that loving another man didn't mean she'd loved Peter less?

After dinner he took Retro for a run and then met a couple of guys from work, both job supervisors, for a beer at an upscale club they liked to frequent. Socializing was good. It wasn't long before they'd been joined by four beautiful women, all of whom were entertaining and looking for fun. But, though he enjoyed the occasional flirtation, he wasn't in the mood. And wasn't into the loud music, either.

Leaving his second beer unfinished, he headed out, restless, yet not ready to get in his truck and go home. Feeling unsettled didn't sit well with him. He was the fix-it guy, not the one with something that needed fixing.

Marie Cove's Main Street was a bustling, well-lit four-lane road filled on both sides with restaurants, clubs and shops that could rival anything in Beverly Hills. He walked among people, all of whom had probable destinations, not even sure where he was headed.

He and Elaina needed to move on—and out—from their complicated situation, even though it was platonic. He'd known for months. Had been prepared for a while, but having her absent so much in non-work hours, maybe getting closer to that time when she was ready to end living arrangements that had grown comfortable, could explain his unease.

Yet it didn't. Truth was, he preferred nights out alone to sitting at home with the love of his brother's life shut away in her suite. Though he'd never been romantically in love with Elaina, it bugged the hell out of Wood that he had been unable to make her happy. And maybe bothered him some that until she was gone, he couldn't have more than casual, no-strings-attached relationships with anyone else.

A group of women, early- to midthirties, professional looking, passed, sounding to him as though they were all talking at once. They seemed to all hear each other. He'd never understood that. In the next second, he wondered about the older couple, mid-sixties maybe, both in shorts and nice shirts, holding hands as they passed him. On their way to a late dinner? Or on vacation?

People surrounded him. One or two alone, like him, most in groups or couples. It was the way of life. He didn't begrudge them. Or envy them, either. He just couldn't find his peace that night.

It wasn't until the third group of women passed, and he found himself studying them, that he admitted to himself he was looking for one woman in particular. One who wouldn't have been at a club, drinking or dancing. But might be out to dinner. Or in one of the fancy bars where lawyers met important clients to discuss business. He couldn't just happen to run into her unless he was out and about.

What did it say about him, a thirty-six-year-old guy who'd spend his evening wandering aimlessly just to catch sight of a woman he couldn't get off his mind? Probably that he was pathetic. He didn't much care what anyone thought of him, though. Cassie might be with clients. Or friends. For all he knew, her parents drove down every Monday for a visit. But no matter whom she was with that particular Monday night, he sensed she must be feeling more alone than she'd probably ever been. Alone with her fear. Her worry. Her battle not to give in to either.

He wanted her to know that she truly wasn't alone. That he had a stake in the outcome of the upcoming test. That he cared about that outcome. And not just because of his bone marrow.

What he really wanted to do was call her.

He didn't want to scare her off again.

Up one side of Main and down the other, he wrestled with himself. Walked off some tension. Let the voices and bustling and sights around him distract him a bit. And still he wasn't ready to head home.

Retro would be ready for bed. Wondering where he was. Lying beside his dog in the dark, or with the TV on, or sitting up reading didn't appeal to him. His mind, in its current state, would linger places it shouldn't be.

An hour and a half after he'd left the club, Wood stopped in at a small, more quaint than ritzy, place across the street from his truck. Sat on a stool at the bar, ordered a beer on draft and pulled out his phone.

Hey, he typed. Hit Send. Dropped the phone on the bar next to his glass. Sipped and tried to let go of this absurd pressure to connect with someone he barely knew.

She was alone and pregnant. The child was biologically half his. He couldn't quite wrap his mind around it. The baby wasn't *really* his. At all. And yet…it was half him. His seed. His genes. It could look like him, maybe even dislike grape jelly as much as he did.

His nerves tensed when his phone vibrated against the wood of the bar top.

Hey.

Leaving his phone where it lay, he read her reply as it popped up on the screen.

Took another sip of beer. Watched the bartender

mix a scotch sour. Heard a woman flirt with the two older guys at the end of the bar.

And, of course, he eventually, after a good two minutes, picked up his phone.

How you doing?

The phone had barely left his hand before her response came back.

Okay.

Not "good." Or "fine." Just "okay."

Two things came to mind. She had to be worried. And she was talking to him.

What did you have for dinner?

Innocuous. But keeping her company. If she wanted it. If not, she wouldn't answer.

Taco salad. You?

Grilled chicken with camp potatoes

The kind you make in foil on the grill? she replied.

Yeah. He was surprised she'd known that.

My dad used to make them.

Right. An uneducated man, like Wood. But that was not the reason she'd chosen his sperm. So why did he keep coming back to it?

He wanted to think he had no concerns about his intelligence. Knew full well his mental capabilities.

And yet, when he viewed himself as he figured the world saw him, he had to wonder why he'd made the choice not to further his education when he'd finally been in a position to do so.

He needed to get over himself. So he told her about Retro, the Lab who'd shared his dinner. Found out that she didn't have any pets but had thought about getting a cat, because they were self-sufficient if left alone for long periods of time. And then that she'd had a dog as a kid, a Corgi, but that it died when she was in high school.

She'd had a busy day at work. And had six meetings the following day, as well. She was more of a night person than early morning but was still up by dawn most days.

She liked milk chocolate, but not dark. Steak but not roast. And took her coffee black.

You at home? He'd run out of food questions.

Yes. You?

No. Downtown. He named the place.

You are not texting me while you're out to dinner.

Nope. Just sitting at the bar having a beer.

Alone?

Yeah. Alone in a bar, texting her. Like she was the
only thing on his mind.

Oh. Her reply was short.

Yeah. He felt a need to explain. To say more. But
didn't. Would make things too complicated.

Figuring he'd effectively ended the conversation
by not responding to her last text, he was surprised
when his phone vibrated again.

Do you like peanut butter?

Yeah, why?

I'm making cookies. I'll package some up for you. A
thank-you for Wednesday.

She was making him cookies. Thinking about him.

Wood was still grinning about that as he lay in
bed an hour later, listening to Retro snore beside him.

Chapter Seven

She was not helpless. She was not out of control. She hadn't felt the baby move yet, but that didn't mean anything was wrong. She wasn't even five months pregnant. Wasn't supposed to be feeling movement yet.

There was a healthy heartbeat on the sonogram.

And she had bone marrow lined up if they needed it.

But what if…

Just as her head started to run away with her for the zillionth time Tuesday night, Cassie's text notification sounded.

Wood again.

Asking her if she'd ever gone skydiving.

She hadn't. He had. Said that while it seemed

scary at first, once you took the training, it was mostly just a matter of trusting the process. She'd never been up in a hot air balloon, either. He'd flown them for a time, to earn extra money. He'd never been on a commercial train. She had once, in Europe, an overnight trip from Paris to Barcelona. He'd never been in-line skating. She used to do twenty-mile skates to let off tension during law school.

As soon as she answered one question, he came back with another. She knew what he was doing. Distracting her from the fear that she wouldn't admit to. How he just seemed to know how to help, she couldn't explain, but didn't question, either.

Cassie was smart enough to accept kindness where it was offered.

For the sake of her baby.

Maybe she'd ask Wood to be the baby's godfather. Down the road. If things went well. It was something to think about, anyway.

Or maybe everything would be fine and they'd go their separate ways and these days out of time would fade into distant memory, transporting them back to strangers who passed on the street without saying hello.

The thought made her sad. And she didn't think that these excruciating hours that seemed to crawl at the pace of years would ever become distant memory to her. No matter what happened, she was never going to forget. Or take life for granted again, either.

She was up before dawn on Wednesday morning. She'd taken the day off work, after all. The doctor's office had told her she might have some cramping. She'd also been told she could resume normal activity immediately following the procedure, but she couldn't be sure she'd have the proper focus her clients deserved that day. Thought maybe she'd spend the afternoon lying on the beach. At the moment, the thought of the sun's warmth brought comfort.

By six thirty she was pacing. Wanting to call her mother. But refrained when she imagined the worry she'd hear in her voice. She had to get through the procedure first. To be able to tell everyone that everything went fine, the placenta wasn't damaged in any way. And they had a healthy...boy or girl?

Her friends had asked her at brunch on Sunday what she was hoping for; a son or a daughter. She'd told them all she wanted was a healthy baby. There must have been something in her voice as she'd answered, because no one pushed her after that.

No one had asked questions, either, which had been a blessing.

She buzzed Wood in at the gate when he typed in her code and was waiting outside by the time his truck pulled up, a bag of homemade cookies in her hand. In black jeans and a polo shirt, he jumped out, opening her door for her—a completely unnecessary but compassionate gesture—and closed it behind her once she was inside.

She watched him as he walked, not meaning to notice that he was the hottest guy she'd ever known, but aware anyway. The square of his shoulders, their breadth, the bulge of muscle in his arms, the way his chest tapered to that completely flat midsection... She couldn't see any lower than that, and as her gaze moved back up toward that thick and curly blond hair, and the strength in his features, she caught him looking back at her.

Checking up on her, she was sure. And she flushed with shame as she realized she'd been lusting over a man who was only there because her baby might need his help.

She'd been feeling that way because at the moment, she'd do about anything to keep her mind off what was coming. She wouldn't know anything right away, of course. She was aware of that. But just to know that the amniocentesis was done, that the baby was unharmed by the test, would be a relief.

While she sat, mostly frozen, beside him, Wood talked about the weather during the ten-minute drive to the doctor's office complex across from the hospital. Innocuous conversation that required nothing of her, and yet provided a tiny bit of distraction at the same time. Kept her somewhat grounded in the world around her, and not completely consumed by the one inside her.

Checking in and filling out the requisite paperwork didn't take nearly as long as she'd expected, leaving too much time to sit and wait for her name to be called in a room that was mostly deserted, since she'd taken the first appointment of the day.

But before panic set in, Wood started talking about boys and girls, baseball bats and hair ribbons, building scenarios with each—not necessarily gender-related ones, either. At one point her daughter grew up to be the youngest baseball player to beat Babe Ruth's home run record.

And then he started talking about names. Not really asking her if she'd decided on any, just throwing them out there. Partnering them with her last name. He didn't ask for any responses, but engaged with any comments she made. Mostly, she could just sit and breathe, finding her calm spot, and focus on his voice, if not his words.

The procedure itself wasn't as much of a big deal as she'd expected—maybe because her expectations had had such critical results attached to them. The test could show something horrible, so the procedure had taken on that menace in her mind. It wasn't completely pain-free, but the discomfort was minimal and things went quickly, perfectly; soon, she was back out with Wood, postprocedure information in mind, ready to go.

"You want to get something to eat?" Wood's unexpected invitation tempted her.

Now that the test was done, she was feeling kind of hungry. And kept replaying the expressions on the doctor's face, too, as the procedure was performed, as though the obstetrician could somehow read test results when Cassie knew darn well that the fluid had to be allowed to grow things in a lab before anyone would know anything. Being alone, lying on the beach, or on the couch, sounded about as appealing as standing in a blizzard in shorts.

"Don't you have to get to work?"

"I told them not to expect me until after lunch."

She didn't feel much like eating anymore. Or driving, either. What if she cramped? Or started to bleed? But there was someplace she really wanted to go. With her natural inclination pushing her to politely decline—accepting help on a personal level didn't come easily—she hesitated. He was there. He knew her current hell. He was the only one in her world who understood.

And it wasn't right to take advantage of his kindness. Or make it more than it was. Neither did she want him hanging out at her house, watching her. He'd said he was off until lunch.

"I'm not hungry, but would you mind if we made one stop on the way home?"

"I don't mind. Where do you want to go?"

"The cemetery."

The shocked look he immediately gave her almost made her smile.

"No, I'm not preparing for the worst," she told him laconically. "I just… Whenever I have a big decision to make or need to remind myself that everything will work itself out one way or another, I visit my father's grave…"

There was only one cemetery in Marie Cove, and Wood headed the truck in that direction. He asked her about the test, if it had hurt, if she'd liked the technician. He didn't ask if she'd gotten a sense that the technician had noticed anything.

"They said it'll be three days, at a minimum, before we know anything. Could be as much as a week."

He glanced her way. Nodded and signaled a turn. "Then that's all we need to deal with at the moment. Those days."

He was right, of course. And she was thankful he was there.

Once they reached the cemetery, she directed him to the gravel drive that led to her father's tombstone, and then, slowly on foot, took him to the half-rotted bench that sat directly opposite it. It tilted to the side as she gingerly lowered herself, but then steadied.

"I have no idea who put this here, or for what purpose," she said as she held the splintery bench with both hands beside her thighs. "But I've always thought of it as a throne with mystical powers. It's peaceful here. And if I close my eyes, I can hear my father's voice."

She closed her eyes as she said the words, but, as aware of Wood as she was, didn't completely leave the world behind as she usually did. Still, the peace was there. For a long moment she soaked it all in. The silence. The peace. Wood's presence.

It seemed right somehow, that she be there at that time, after a procedure that would tell her the fate of her baby, in presence of both her father—and the father of her child. Seeking sustenance from both.

As parents. Nothing less. Nothing more.

She didn't hear him move but wasn't surprised, when she opened her eyes, to find him standing right beside her, looking toward her father's grave.

"My dad had a way of getting to the meat of the matter," she said softly.

"What would he be saying to you right now?"

"To let go of them things I can't make no difference to," she said, quoting the man she still adored. "And to remember that I've got what it takes to handle whatever comes."

The last wasn't quite a quote. But close enough.

"I know these things," she told Wood, looking up at him. The sun was behind her, warming her neck, illuminating his face. "But sometimes I can only feel them when I come here."

"It's just you and him here," he told her. "Like it used to be when he was alive—just you and him at home, during the times you were with him."

"And now you," she said aloud. His face changed as their eyes met, and she couldn't look away. It wasn't right, this intense emotional connection she seemed to be developing with a man who was only there because her baby might be sick, but the words were there, between them, bonding them, and she couldn't take them back.

Wood spent most of his free time over the next three days out in his workshop, with Retro lying on her bed in the corner by the open door.

He'd made a grilled chicken salad for dinner Friday night and, keeping the last of Cassie's homemade cookies for himself at home, had run a good-size portion of the salad up to Elaina, who was working a double shift at the hospital. She'd thanked him profusely.

And he'd avoided the patient floors, not wanting to think about illness. About things that went inexplicably wrong with the human body.

He hadn't talked about that tiny little human being growing inside a woman he barely knew—not with Elaina, not with anyone—but he was thinking about it constantly. Needing to know that the baby was okay.

Not for him, but just *because*.

Each night he'd texted Cassie. Innocuous stuff. Sports one night. She liked basketball because it was fast-paced. Baseball bored her because it wasn't. He liked them both, and told her so. Football, she could take or leave—but she knew all the teams and many of the best-known players from ten years before, because her dad had watched every game and so she'd shared that experience with him.

He found out she'd played tennis in high school and college. He hadn't told her he'd quarterbacked his high school football team. Or that he'd been scouted, after his junior year, by a decent California university. That door had closed when he'd quit school, but it wasn't like he'd been guaranteed a spot anywhere. Only that his stats had attracted some attention. His and a lot of other guys'. He'd given up a lot, but didn't regret the choices he'd made. Maybe he'd questioned fate a time or two, but no response had been forthcoming and he'd let it go.

On Friday he was waiting until later to text, figuring, with Saturday being the third day, she'd be more on edge. Late at night was usually the hardest time when dealing with life's challenges. He didn't have to be up Saturday and had a topic of discussion already picked out: old television commercials, which ones she remembered. For some reason they stuck with him, but he'd done some research, too. Had a list ready on his laptop. Planned to give her a word or two and see if she could guess the product. Or remember the jingle.

Like the Clara and Wendy's "Where's the beef?" ads from the year he was born. The original ad hadn't run for that long, but the fame of it lived on. He sanded, preparing for a second coat of a protective mostly colorless varnish on his latest project, thinking about his plans. Feeling good about them.

And heard his phone signal a text.

Message from doctor. Scheduled appointment tomorrow at ten to discuss results.

Sander in hand, he stood there, suspended. Read the text a second time. Put the sander down.

Any indications of what they are? His big thumbs didn't type fast enough for him.

Just a message from a call service, haven't talked to anyone yet. I chose to make the appointment and hear in person. Because I'll have questions and it's best to have those answers immediately available...

She's scared, he translated mentally. Putting off the news for one more night. Putting herself in hell, was more like it. But he understood, too. If the news was bad, living with it all night without finding out how bad, knowing percentages and next steps, would be excruciating.

But if it was good...

I'd like to take you to the appointment.

Let her argue with him, or worry about how she couldn't let herself rely on him, to take her mind off matters of so much greater importance. She was less than ten minutes away if she was at home. He wanted to go to her. Just to sit there, if nothing else. He didn't kid himself that he had some magic, proven cure for real or potential tragedy. But he understood the benefit of having another presence nearby so that the world didn't completely close in on you.

Thank you.

    So…that was a yes? Just like that?
    What time? he typed.

9:30.

For a ten o'clock appointment, just a few minutes away.

I'll be there.

He set the phone down. Picked up the sander while he awaited her response. Wanted to get the last coat of varnish on so that it would have time to dry before morning. Wanted to focus on what he could affect. To control the emotions that would overtake him if he gave them the slightest chance. He needed to maintain control so that he could help her.

At nine he finished sanding. And had heard nothing more from Cassie.

By ten, he'd finished the last coat of varnish and was headed back to the house, Retro by his side and phone in hand. He started the conversation about commercials with an easy quote: "Plop, plop, fizz, fizz…"

She responded immediately, finishing the line.

By 2:00 a.m., he was out of commercials. And moved on to old sitcoms.

He should be tired. Saying good-night. Getting a few hours' sleep. But he didn't.

Cassie was still awake. And so he'd type all night, if that's what it took.

In a matter of days, the woman had become a part of his life.

Chapter Eight

In a black-and-white flowered T-shirt dress that clearly showed her little baby bump, Cassie smiled at Wood as he held his truck door for her Saturday morning. Right on time.

She'd worn three pairs of flip-flop-shaped earrings in each ear, one silver with black flowers, one white with silver flowers and one black with white trim. She was ready to collect important information, and that was all. Dealing with whatever she heard would come later. Just get the information and go. Then deal with it.

She had her plan. You couldn't deal until you knew. So she couldn't have a plan for dealing until she knew what she had to deal with. Collect the information. Go. Deal.

Deal. Deal. Deal.

She could and she would.

Wood had climbed in beside her. Was starting the truck. Feeling closer to him, she chatted about the beautiful blue sky, the balmy warmth and a possible walk on the beach that afternoon as he pulled from her driveway.

And then she drew a blank. All of the things she'd been telling herself all morning, the easy conversational tidbits she had to offer, just flew out of her mind. By the time she saw her house again, or had a chance to walk on the beach, she'd know if her baby had a chance at a life. Or not much of one.

Collect. She just had to collect for now.

The wealth of love she felt for the little one she hadn't even yet felt move was unfathomable. It was seemingly impossible, except that she *was* feeling it—the love, and the fear attached to that. She'd never known such a debilitating, freeze-your-brain panic.

Everything might be fine. She was not going to borrow trouble. She was only going to get information that she wanted to have.

"Do you remember the episode of *Friends* when Danny DeVito showed up as the stripper at Phoebe's wedding shower?" She heard Wood speak. Turned and looked at him. Had to concentrate on a replay of his words to know what he was talking about. A television show they'd spoken about.

For a moment she couldn't remember who Danny DeVito was. And then had a flash of him on another old sitcom. Something about New York taxicabs. He'd been a mean boss. A really short and somewhat plump little man. And then, "Yeah, I kind of do," she said.

"If the character Danny DeVito played had ever asked anyone if he'd make it as a stripper, he'd most likely have been told no," he said.

Well, duh… He'd been cast in that role on that show because of the ridiculousness of the fit.

"But the character got to do it," Wood continued. "And he was pretty good at the dancing part of it.

"And what about the fact that Ross's wife left him? He thought his life was over," Wood added. "But if she hadn't, then he wouldn't have been free to get together with the love of his life. And after ten excruciating years, they finally end up together."

Wood had just pulled in to the doctor's office. And she was still breathing calmly. She glanced at him, a thank-you on the tip of her tongue, and he said, "You never know."

"You never know what?"

"You just never know. Things can look like one thing today, but they could be entirely different down the road."

And the waves…they brought in some bad stuff, but they brought good, too.

"Nothing is an absolute certainty," Wood said, glancing over at her.

And she knew what he was telling her. Even if the news was bad, she had to believe that good could come of it. She had to have hope.

The man was right.

And good for her.

Which made it so hard to remember that he was there because he was her sperm donor. Not her partner.

Rather than an examining room, Cassie was shown into a doctor's office. She'd opted to go with an obstetrician from the Parent Portal, but that morning's appointment was at the doctor's private office by the hospital. The same facility where she'd had her amniocentesis. She sat in the chair across from the desk as instructed and watched as Dr. Osborne, whom she'd only actually met twice, closed the door and took her seat behind the desk.

Keeping her distance. A professional distance. Cassie understood the unspoken need to establish roles. It was a tactic she'd used herself when she'd had unpleasant legal information to deliver to a client.

Bracing herself as best she could, she thought about waves. A short, plump stripper. And a different man wearing black shorts and a white polo shirt, sitting just feet beyond that door, his elbows on his thighs, hands clasped in the air between his knees. She thought of thick, curly blond hair and blue eyes. Those deep cerulean eyes that could also be her baby's.

And ten minutes later, as she walked through the door from the hallway to the waiting room, all she saw were those deep blue eyes, their gaze seeking her own, as though he'd know all just from that glance.

She blinked, her mouth starting to tremble, and he stood, coming toward her.

Wood was beside her, not touching her, just there, and she nodded, at what she didn't know, and headed toward the door. There was no paperwork to sign. She already had her next appointment scheduled. It was time to go. So she went.

He stayed beside her all the way to the truck. Opened her door for her, closed it behind her. Climbed in beside her and sat there holding his keys. He didn't ask. Just sat there. Watching her.

And in that moment, Cassie fell a little bit in love—a feeling she knew, under the circumstances, she couldn't trust.

God knew, he didn't want to push. The morning, his association with Cassie, wasn't about him. But if he had to wait much longer to find out the fate of the baby he'd fathered, he was going to need to pound a hammer against some rock.

His heart thudded as she looked over at him and he saw the tears in her eyes, and all worry stopped. Just as it had when his mother died. When Peter died. And Elaina almost did. His job was to be there. To take care of those about whom he cared. It was what he was good at.

But…he didn't know what to do now.

"It's not leukemia." He barely heard the words before the strongest woman he figured he'd ever met broke down into sobs. Like, literally broke down. Her head fell, her shoulders rolled in and her body jerked with the violence of the emotions racking through her.

Pushing up the console in between them, he moved over and rubbed her back, handing her a tissue, waiting for the initial emotion to pass before attempting to find out more. And when it did, when she straightened, dark eyeliner in streaks around her eyes and down her cheeks, he gently wiped the darkness away.

"Oh my God, I'm so sorry." Sounding breathless, Cassie glanced at him, eyes red and cheeks blotched. "I don't know what happened there. I just… I thought I could handle anything, but…holding it all in… I don't know. Maybe I've never cared so much, but…"

"Cassie." He'd moved back over to his seat.

"Yes?"

"What are we handling?"

She stared at him. And he heard his words in instant replay. *We.*

It wasn't leukemia. She didn't need his bone marrow. Technically, he was out.

And he wanted more. She could choose to give it. Or not.

"Fetal anemia."

With those two words, an answer to a non–sperm donor question, everything changed between them. Her baby might need a blood transfusion, but since they'd found the condition early enough, could treat it, the baby had a normal life expectancy. Cassie no longer needed her sperm donor. But did she want a friend?

Once she started talking, Cassie couldn't seem to stop. Sitting in Wood's truck, words just poured out of her.

"The anemia is mild at this point," she said, still wrapping her mind around the fact that her baby wasn't dying, didn't have a terminal disease. But her child still had a medical issue. "There are several known causes, the most common of which is blood type incompatibility, but we know we don't have that, as your blood type was checked against mine before insemination."

His blood. Hers. Together inside her. The realization brought a warmth…and strange bit of calm… to an unreal day.

"Which is why they didn't immediately think of anemia. It's possible my blood and the baby's commingled…" She went to describe something she didn't fully understand, in the words the doctor had used. And then realized he didn't need her plebeian explanations. "I'm sure Elaina can explain it all to you better than I can," she said.

And then stopped talking. He'd never, for one second, given her reason to believe he wanted more from her.

But her…she was starting to fantasize about the man. To want more. She was the one in the wrong.

"I'd like to hear it from you." Wood broke into her thoughts. "While I'm only a donor, the reality is that that child is a product of my body. I'm finding that knowledge to carry some weight, paperwork aside. I know I have no rights to parent the child, but the law can't stop me from caring."

Something told her she should discount that point. Couldn't find an argument. A lawyer, used to proving sides, and she couldn't find an argument.

"That being established, I'd like to be kept abreast of this information."

His request was fair. She was the one who'd contacted him. Who'd drawn him into this. Staring out the windshield of the still parked truck, she told herself she could draw clear lines and stay on her side of them.

"Fetal anemia can be fatal, but only if it's not

tended to," she continued. "For right now, I'm just to watch my diet, and there'll be a change in my vitamins to compensate for the baby's lack of iron. I'll have to be monitored closely. They can watch things through ultrasound to begin with, judging blood flow from shadows. If things continue to get worse, they'll do another amnio. Since they don't know what's causing the anemia, they can't really predict how this is going to go."

"Worst-case scenario?"

She didn't want to go there, but found herself able as she looked into his concerned gaze. The man was a well of strength like none other. He just took it on. Made it look easy.

"In-utero blood transfusion."

"I didn't know they could do such things."

"I didn't, either, until today. Apparently it's done like the amnio, with ultrasound assistance, except the needle goes directly to the baby." She shuddered. "I'm going to put that one out of my mind."

"Good idea. They've caught it early, and that's always better than not."

She nodded. Wanted to believe that there was no real danger. Had been hoping so hard to hear that the test would show nothing wrong with her baby at all. That the ultrasound shadow had been just that... a shadow.

But her baby didn't have a terminal blood disease. That was the bottom line. Elation flooded through her again, a muscle-weakening euphoria that brought on another threat of tears as the reality started to sink in. There was a slight complication, but her baby was healthy overall. With a normal life prognosis.

She was really going to have a baby! A child of her own to live with, raise and love.

"If a transfusion *is* needed, my blood is available," Wood said, his hand on the keys.

She nodded again. Filled with conflicting emotions and gratitude and something deeper, too, as she looked at him.

Aware of an if-only that was dangerous at best.

If only they were a couple, not just the mother and father of the child she carried. They'd be kissing, touching, spending the day together, celebrating the day's good news and sharing the tad bit of worry, as only parents could. Others would love her baby. She had no doubt about that. Love it fiercely. But not with the special bonding love of a parent.

Almost as though he could read her mind, Wood glanced away. Put his hand on the key in the ignition. But didn't turn on the vehicle. "So…is it a boy or a girl?"

She'd been keeping the news to herself. Trying to keep herself in check. He was the donor, not the father. Shouldn't the baby's family be the first to know?

And the presence of him, the warmth, the touch of his fingers on her cheeks, the look in his eyes, the willingness to stay up most of the night texting with her about old television shows, his awareness of struggles she was keeping deeply hidden inside her…

Was he hoping for one or the other? Did it make a difference to him?

She truly hadn't cared about the sex of the baby. And yet…knowing made her love that little body growing inside her even more. Made the relationship that much more solid. *Real.*

He wasn't there for a relationship. With either of them.

He'd started the engine. Accepting her silence without argument. Or even persuasion.

"It's a boy," she said as he put the truck in gear. "I'm going to name him Alan, after my father."

She didn't know what to think when Wood backed up and pulled out of the lot without saying a word.

Chapter Nine

"Have you got a couple of minutes? I have something to show you." Wood kept his gaze on the road as he made the request, not allowing himself to so much as look in her direction as he digested the news she'd just given him. He was going to have a son.

Only biologically.

In that initial moment, the idea was killing him.

He'd debated for a minute or two, following through on the plan he'd concocted Wednesday after he'd dropped her off at home. Might have changed his mind, donated the bench he'd made. Only the fact that he'd already delivered his offering to its intended location earlier that morning, a location she'd certainly be visiting probably that weekend, prompted him to ask the question.

"Of course," she said, and he allowed himself to live with the anticipation of her pleasure during the short drive—attempting to shut out all else.

He was going to have a son in the world, but not in his life. He'd done a favor for Peter.

Like the night before Peter had married Elaina. He'd asked for Wood's promise that, if anything ever happened to him, Wood would look after his wife.

He'd made the promise. Because he'd been protecting his brother, tending to his needs, his entire life. But he'd have asked Elaina to marry him even if he hadn't told Peter he'd take care of her. She had no real family of her own. No insurance without Peter's job providing it. The other driver had been underinsured and had no money.

And there was Elaina's future. They hadn't even been sure she'd walk again.

She'd put her own career plans on hold to work two full time jobs to put Peter through medical school.

She'd never, ever even pretended to be in love with Wood. Yet he'd given his life over to her. Had been willing to make a real marriage for them.

Because a real marriage was what he wanted?

But not without the kind of love that went with it?

He turned in to the cemetery. So much for tuning out what was bothering him…

"The cemetery?" Cassie asked, sitting forward to peer out around them. "What do you have to show me here?"

He'd gone up the private drive leading to her father's grave, and she was out of the truck before he'd even turned off the motor. Running toward the bench across from her father's headstone.

"Oh my gosh, Wood! It's…" Bending, she ran her fingers over the project he'd sanded and varnished the night before. And then she sat, eyes brimming with tears as she looked up at him. "Where did you get this? It's beautiful! Exquisite, really." She looked from him to the cherrywood bench. "I can't believe you did this."

He let her talk. Smiling in spite of his self-admonition not to make too much out of her gratitude. It was about her vigil with her father, her safe place, not about him.

"Come…" She patted the two-seater bench. "Sit with me."

Reluctantly, he did as she asked, all the while reminding himself of the boundaries he had to maintain. For so many reasons. And truly enjoyed sitting there with her, even if just for a few seconds.

As he'd purchased wood, measured, cut, hammered and glued, he'd pictured her sitting on the finished product. He hadn't allowed himself to imagine using the bench with her, though. An occasion where the two of them would visit her father together.

"I just love it, Wood." She was looking at him, and the emotion in her gaze…it swooped deep inside him. Finding a home there. "I just…" She frowned. "You don't think they'll take it away, do you? The cemetery people? I'm technically only allowed to put things on his actual gravesite."

"I got permission before I brought it over," he told her. "It's bolted down, and I wanted to make certain that was okay." He'd checked other specifications, as well. As a contractor he knew all about permits, property rights and liabilities.

She teared up again but blinked away the moisture before it fell. "I just don't even know how to thank you, Wood. It had to have cost a fortune. I have no idea where you even found something so perfect."

He'd expected her to be pleased. But not to sound so beholden. "It wasn't expensive," he said quickly before she could read more into the gesture than he'd intended. "I've got less than twenty bucks in it," he continued.

"You found something like this at a garage sale? I can't believe it. It's perfect. And looks brand-new. Who would part with a bench of this quality for twenty dollars?"

"I made it, Cassie." He should've just told her from the beginning. Wasn't sure why he hadn't. Those hours he'd spent in his workshop, thinking of her, had been private. Between him and the wood with which he'd worked. "Seriously, it's no big deal. Just a hobby…"

"You made this?" Eyebrows raised, she looked from the bench back up to him. "And you think this is just a hobby? Good Lord, Wood, you could open a shop. Make a fortune. This is…"

He shook his head. "I don't want to open a shop," he told her. Elaina had had the same reaction the first time she'd seen his work. Peter had still been alive then, and making a big deal out of Wood's bedroom set. He'd been proud of Wood's talent. But he'd also understood that it was a stress relief for his brother. Something he enjoyed. To make it into a business would take away what he got most out of woodworking.

She studied him for a moment, and he turned away, in over his head. For a man used to being completely comfortable in his own skin, he found the current challenge to be somewhat overwhelming. And yet he had no desire to get himself out of it. To the contrary: the more he was with Cassie, the more he wanted to stay.

And not just because of the small bump becoming visible on her silhouette. Not just because of the baby. As his glance had fallen away from hers, it had landed on that bump. He shouldn't be looking. Shouldn't be seeing more than was there.

She needed him right then. He fulfilled a need in a very stressful emotional time. Didn't mean he had enough going for him to hold her longer than the moment.

It wasn't even right or appropriate for him to be thinking of her that way.

"I've known you such a short time, and yet… you've become a friend, Wood. In some ways, a close friend."

. He nodded. Glad for that.

"You always seem to know just what I need, or to have a way to make the worry sting less…"

He tuned in, was all. She did, too, not that he was going to tell her that.

"I feel like I'm doing something wrong here," she continued slowly, looking at him, not at her father's grave. "You're doing so much for me, a virtual stranger. Willing to put yourself through medical procedures. Keeping track of the baby's health. And I… I'm just emotionally overwhelmed, I guess. I've loved having you in my life this past week…so much…and I feel like I'm doing something wrong, caring about you like I do."

She cared about him. Just because they'd shared a tough secret that week. Because he'd helped her get through a hard time in her life when no one else knew she was going through it.

He cared, too. But knew better than to tell her so. Because he didn't believe it was anything that would last. He would not let her become another Elaina in his life.

He knew the world saw him as lacking. He'd seen the looks on others' faces when he admitted he'd never graduated from high school. There was no way a guy like him could challenge a woman like Cassie for the long haul.

And yet, it was women like Cassie, smart, strong, hard-working women, who most attracted him. He wasn't a butt or breast man. It had never been about the looks to him, so much as it had been the person.

He'd expected to show her the bench and then take her home. To talk about the baby some. Maybe hear how her dad would have loved having a grandson. Or a granddaughter, if the results had gone that way.

"Elaina thought I should open a furniture shop, too, to sell the stuff I make," he told her. As though she'd understand the things he wasn't saying. "She went on and on about it the first time she was in my workshop. And still mentions it now and then." Elaina was always wanting him to reach higher. Not for the money, necessarily, but so that he could make a name for himself.

He liked the name he had.

When he finally glanced Cassie's way, he caught her staring at him.

More explanations battled for expression. He fought back. The more he wanted to tell Cassie, the more he knew he shouldn't. Because to do so would cross a line he couldn't afford to cross. He might not fully comprehend it all, but he didn't doubt his instincts.

"It's one of the reasons our marriage didn't work."

His arms started to itch, like they did when he wanted out of wherever he was.

He didn't want to leave. Or to take her home and then part.

"Another is that we married in a time of extreme emotion, extreme need, and that didn't end up translating into romantic love."

Her mouth hung open.

He'd said too much. Or not enough. He couldn't tell which. "I'm sorry."

"I'm not shocked, Wood, if that's what you're thinking," she finally said, facing the grave now, not him. "And I don't want you to be sorry. I just don't know what to say."

Or probably why he'd said what he had to *her*.

"And since the divorce?" she asked. "Obviously you date."

He shrugged. Uncomfortable in a new way. "Casually. Elaina gets on me because she says I go for women in need and then get used. But other than with her, I've gone in with my eyes open, enjoyed some time and haven't been hurt when it's done. I've spent my whole life caring for others. It's what I'm good at. But if that means that, ultimately, I live my life alone, I'm okay with that. It's nice to be alone sometimes." To not have to worry about anyone. He didn't say the words aloud. They made him sound selfish.

And maybe, in some ways, he was.

"Do you ever think about having a family of your own?"

He supposed the question was fair. "I think I'd be a good father." He'd known how to provide for Peter. How to help his brother over the hurdles of teenage troubles in a way that had strengthened Peter, not weakened him.

"I think you're a good man, Woodrow Alexander." Cassie's voice had softened. As had the look in her eyes. It was like she was touching him with gentle, featherlight caresses. He wanted to close his eyes and savor the feeling, but he knew that to do so would break the spell.

He closed his eyes, anyway. He had to break away from Cassie or become a man he didn't want to be, one who wanted what he couldn't have.

"We should get going," he told her but didn't stand immediately.

"I'm not going to fall for you, Wood, and then realize that it was only the emotional upheaval of pregnancy and the scare for my baby's life that made me feel that way.

"I promise you," she continued. "I'm aware of the dangers, and I won't let that happen. I'm only looking for whatever friendship you want to offer. And would be honored to return the same."

He met her gaze, searching for any sign of weakness in her, and found none.

"I find you incredibly attractive," he told her.

"I'm attracted to you, too. But I won't take a chance on you and then, when our world's right, change my mind."

He smiled, rubbed her cheek with his thumb. "I can't take that chance, either. Not with you. I very much want to be your friend, though."

She smiled then, too. "So...we're okay?"

He shook his head, frowned. "When *weren't* we okay?"

"Are we okay to be in touch? Or is this it? I won't see you again after today?"

"You want the truth?"

"Of course."

Feeling as though they'd already bared their souls to each other, he didn't see much point in holding back now. "I feel a bond with you. And with that child you're carrying. Any chance I have to be in his life, tomorrow, next week and forever, I will accept with full responsibility and caring."

"He doesn't have a father," Cassie said, then sucked in on her lips, as though biting them.

He waited.

"I can't make any promises, Wood, but part of the reason I went to the Parent Portal was because I recognize that some people yearn to know where they came from. Look at the huge interest in familial DNA searches these days." She shook her head, glanced away and then back. "I take full responsibility for this baby, but I won't ever deny him the chance to know his father. If his father wants to know him."

The sun exploded inside him. Burning him. Giving him the most acute pleasure. And hurting, too. "His father *definitely* wants to know him," he said, knowing that with those words he'd just changed his life.

That there'd be complications and struggles and challenges beyond what he could see.

But he couldn't take the words back. Didn't even want to try.

Chapter Ten

"I clearly have no idea what I'm doing." Cassie sat with her mom Sunday afternoon in chairs they'd brought out to the beach. As soon as she'd called to let her mother know about the week she'd had, the scare, and the better than not outcome, Susan Anderson had insisted on driving down from Mission Viejo, leaving her husband, Richard, at home to handle business there.

Sipping from an insulated water bottle, Cassie lodged the rubber-lidded metal container in the sand beside her and stretched her legs out. The chair was only a few inches above the ground and made it easy for her to get comfortable.

Physically.

Emotionally she was completely the opposite.

"You always know what you're doing," her mother said, hands folded across the black spandex of the one-piece suit that showed her fifty-six-year-old slimness off to perfection. Cassie hoped to have a body half as nice as her mom's when she got to be that age.

"You always have," Susan continued, her gaze blocked by the dark-lensed sunglasses she wore. But Cassie could pretty much see her expression anyway. Susan was not a warm, fuzzy woman—until it came to her only child. Cassie had never found her mother lacking in compassion, nurturing and support. "I remember one time when you were three or four. You were only allowed an hour a day of television, and then it had to be only material made exclusively for toddlers and young children. But one night you turned on a rather intense police procedural and were sitting in the living room watching it. I saw what you were doing but was more curious about why than I was ready to stop you. You kept looking behind you and then would turn the volume up louder. Eventually your dad came out of his den, where he went at night to watch his shows while I gave you a bath and read to you. He took the remote and turned off the television, reminding you gently that you'd already had your hour for the day and that those shows weren't good for you."

Cassie listened, not at all sure where this was going, but fascinated, just the same. Her mom rarely talked about the years she'd been married to Alan Thompson. Never when Richard was around, which was pretty much always.

"You nodded, and when he sat down, you climbed up into his lap, wrapped your arms around him and just sat there."

She had no memory of the moment her mother was retelling, but she could remember sitting on her dad's lap many times during her growing-up years. She'd always felt so safe and secure in his arms. Except when he'd been hugging her goodbye to go on deployment. She'd hated those times.

"I asked you later why you turned on the TV when you knew you weren't allowed to do so, though I'd already figured it out…"

Cassie waited. Trying to remember her little-girl self, to remember how she'd felt or what she might have said. Her guess was she'd wanted to know what her father was watching. Or to watch it with him.

"You said that you thought Daddy was lonely and so you were making our room more like his so he'd come out and be with us."

Oh.

Tearing up, she glanced at her mother. Wishing so hard she could remember having said that.

"Why haven't you ever told me this before?"

Susan shrugged, shaking her head. "I'd honestly

forgotten it. Just…hearing you talk about this man, Wood, the way you're worrying about him being in your baby's life, but not being able to be a real father to him…it just reminded me…"

Silence descended, except for the sounds of a few of her distant neighbors out enjoying their stretch of the little private beach. Cassie had told her mother pretty much everything about Wood, other than her very private feelings for him. As soon as she'd heard herself tell the man he could be in her baby's life, she'd known that she'd opened a door that could have painful and perhaps catastrophic consequences.

"It's not like Wood has indicated, in any way, that he'd like us to even go on a date, but I have a feeling that if I allowed it, Wood would marry me because of the baby," she said aloud. "In the moment, even knowing him as short a time as I have, the idea is tempting, but then life would settle down, and who knows what we'd find together? If anything. I can't be responsible for breaking up another marriage…"

"Another?" Susan took off her sunglasses and stared at Cassie. "What marriage did you break up? And why don't I know about it?"

"I broke up you and Dad," she said, looking her mother right in the eye. "You don't think I know that?"

"Whatever gave you that idea?"

"I heard you arguing, Mom, though I don't have specific memories of the words you said." She could remember the fights, though. The anger in her mother's voice. And the sadness in her dad's. "I asked Dad about it once when I was in high school. And he told me that it had been his fault, but it wasn't really. He said that when it was just the two of you, you working all the time was fine, especially with him being away. But that once I'd come around, he wanted me to have the kind of home life he'd never had. He wanted you to be a stay-at-home mom. He didn't want me in daycare, or being raised by non–family members."

"That's true," Susan said, nodding but still frowning. "But that wasn't why we broke up, sweetie. We broke up because while we got along, we weren't happy together. We were too different. Wanted different things, not just with you but with a lot of things. I wanted to be successful. To have a nice home with a pool, beautiful landscaping and a kiva fireplace out back. He wanted a cottage with grass in the yard."

As she listened to her mother talk, Cassie smiled to herself. Her mother had just pretty much described Cassie's home—both parts. Her cottage-style home had some grass in the front yard and she didn't have the pool, but she had the beach. And the landscaping. She was the best of both of her parents.

Her Alan deserved that. To be able to access the best of both of his parents.

"So…why did the two of you get married in the

first place?" she asked softly, a question she'd been carrying around for about as long as she could remember. And had never asked her dad because she'd been afraid the answer would hurt him too much.

"Because I was pregnant with you."

"What!" Sitting forward, mouth hanging open, she stared back at her mother. "I was born a year after your wedding."

Susan shook her head. "Your father didn't want you to ever think you weren't wanted, or were a mistake, so we fudged the date of our anniversary."

"You're kidding me." She said the words. Needed them to be true so her world didn't tilt so far off its axis, but she was reading the real truth in Susan's gaze.

"As you know, we met at work the summer my folks died and our first date was at a beach bonfire," Susan was saying. "We'd both just graduated, and he was on his way to boot camp, just like we told you. He was different from any guy I'd ever known. Sensitive. And extremely good-looking. He was in great shape. I was trying to forget my father's death, and he sensed that I wasn't in the same frame of mind as the rest of the kids that night. He just seemed to know. One thing led to another and..."

"...you didn't use protection?"

"He didn't have any and I...was a virgin, actually. I know, hard to believe, in this day and age, that a woman would make it all the way through school without having sex, but, like you, I graduated high school early, and I've always been very focused." Susan chuckled, and Cassie smiled, too. She'd inherited a good bit of that professional mind-set.

"I'd never even considered having sex that night," Susan continued softly, looking out at the ocean, sounding almost...nostalgic. "But I felt so much better, just being with him. I drank some wine. And..." Susan shrugged. "My life changed irrevocably that night, but I wasn't sorry," she said, still looking at Cassie. "I tell you that with complete and utter honesty. I have never regretted having you. Or knowing your father, for that matter. I regret hurting him, more than you'll probably ever know. But I'm also convinced that my divorcing him hurt less in the long run than if I'd stayed. At least we were able to remain friends."

She'd never really thought of them that way— her parents as friends. Adults with their own relationship. Had figured they remained kind and polite to each other because they shared her. But maybe there'd been more than that... Maybe she'd have seen more if he'd still been alive after she graduated high school.

"My point in all this was not to talk about your father. Or me. But to tell you to trust your heart, Cass. You've always managed to find a way to accomplish what you need to accomplish—even at three or four years old and hurting for your lonely daddy. You knowingly broke the rules, something you pretty much never did, you know, to accomplish what you felt needed to be accomplished. Think about it…you were a toddler, and yet you somehow knew not to come to me with that particular problem. You knew you had to find a way to take care of it. And you did." Susan smiled, her eyes a bit misty, but she didn't hide them behind her glasses as she might ordinarily have done. "I can't believe I'd forgotten about that night. It defines you, Cass. It's the you I've always known and loved."

Cassie didn't know about all that. "I snuck out with Drake and had sex," she blurted out, naming the boyfriend from her senior year of high school. "We drank beer a few times, too."

Nodding, Susan continued to smile. "I know."

Frowning again, Cassie sat back, wondering if she should just go back to bed and start the day over. See if it would run a more normal course. "You knew?"

"Of course I knew. You left a condom wrapper in the back pocket of your jeans. And threw away a beer bottle in your bathroom trash. You wanted me to know. And that's why I worked hard to find a way to keep the two of you on my radar any time you were together after that."

She didn't purposely do either of those things. But she couldn't believe she'd been that careless, either. So unlike her.

"Like I said," Susan said, putting her glasses back

on, "you always know what you're doing, Cass. You just might not always be honest with yourself about that."

Okay, say she went with that…

"So what am I doing with Wood?"

This time when Susan removed her dark lenses, her expression was completely serious. "I have no idea. But I know that you're doing what you need to do, and that you'll make it right, somehow."

"So you think it's wrong?"

"No! Absolutely not. What do you think this whole conversation has been about? Trust yourself, Cassie. I mean that—whatever happens, you'll make it right. You'll do what you need to do to be the caring, considerate decent person you are. And you'll do all you can to help those around you be as happy as they can be, too."

She needed to believe that.

Wanted to believe it. But didn't always see herself that way. Shouldn't she have fallen in love by now, had a family the traditional way, if she was such a good person?

"You've never done anything in a traditional way," her mother said, leaning her head back against the seat and burying her manicured toes in the sand. "Of course, your father and I didn't give you a traditional upbringing, but even with the choice to have a baby… you wanted to fall in love, to marry, but you didn't settle for less when that didn't happen. Instead, you found a different way to have the family you need and want."

Yeah, she was good with the insemination choice. It was just…

"What if he's the one?" The question escaped, emitting a dark cloud of emotion inside and outside Cassie. Her stomach clenched, and she rubbed the tiny baby bump, knowing that she had to keep calm. For Alan's sake.

Alan. Her son. Who didn't have leukemia. Thank God. A thousand times over.

"What if, down the road, when life settles, we still feel the same way about each other? What if he really is the guy I've been looking for my entire life?"

"How can he be? He's already made up his mind. Even though he says he's attracted to you, and he's attentive, he's not going to trust that it could be anything more than that. He's already closed his heart to the possibility. I'm guessing he was irrevocably changed by his failed marriage. And in fairness to him, he's probably right to do so. You're far more like his ex-wife than not." Susan's words didn't hold even a hint of hope.

And she knew why she'd broached the subject with her mother.

She'd needed to hear the truth.

And she just had.

Chapter Eleven

Wood told Elaina the results of Cassie's amniocentesis Sunday evening. He listened to every word of her medical translation of them, focusing completely, asking questions. He needed to know all scenarios, possibilities and outcomes, suspected causes and lifetime prognosis. Basically, there was little threat to life because the condition had been identified early on, and likely prognosis was normal birth, healthy baby.

Elaina did say that Cassie and the baby would be monitored closely. The pregnancy would likely be designated high risk, simply because of the monitoring, but that there was little cause for worry.

Wood was worried anyway. That was unusual for

him, even if he was not just a sperm donor, because he tended to be the strength others leaned on. Even when his mother died, he'd spent little time on his own grief, thinking instead of how it was affecting his brother and what he could do to smooth Peter's way. When Peter had died, his mind had been consumed with thoughts of Elaina—assessing her needs, taking care of all he could.

Much like he was thinking of Cassie, he realized. Constantly.

But that tiny life growing inside her... He had no idea how to help it. No concept of a "sit and wait," hands-off regimen. Which left him uneasy. Unsure of himself.

The feelings were new, and not at all welcome, filling his mind with questions that had no answers, as opposed to actions he could take.

Added to the confusion was the new role he had—the no-name, no-definition role. He would be a welcome figure in the life of his biological child. What did that mean?

Confusion kept him from contacting Cassie the rest of the weekend. He needed some space—and figured she might want distance, too—while he sorted out how he handled the drastic turn his life was taking, while, on the surface, it didn't change at all.

It wasn't like he was preparing for a new baby. For his first child. He had no obligations and no rights to be a provider. There were no announcements to make to his coworkers, no upcoming additions to his insurance plan, no medical arrangements to make for the birth.

There wasn't even the need to clear his schedule. It wasn't like he'd have a seat in the delivery room. Or be present for a single middle-of-the-night feeding.

And yet…he cared more about Cassie and her baby than he'd cared for anything in his life.

He caught a couple of guys looking oddly at him at work on Monday. Like he had some kind of vicarious pregnancy glow or something. The idea amused him. He went with it, until Gerald, his next in command, mentioned that he'd groused at a couple of guys, asking if something was wrong.

"Just some personal business," he told the man he'd been working with for more than a decade. "Not even bad business, just trying to figure out the best way to handle it," he added. Lying wasn't his style. But neither was baring his soul.

"Financial stuff," Gerald said. They were standing together on site, on a two-minute, drain-a-water-bottle break, watching as their crew measured, cut, squared and nailed. "I'm telling you, man, you need to hire someone to handle that for you. I got it in the beginning, when you were just dabbling, but now…"

Gerald knew he'd had some luck with investments. In the beginning, Wood had talked about it. Because the amounts he'd risked had been small and he'd never expected his activities to amount to anything. Over the years, he'd been more quiet about it. Gerald had no idea how much luck Wood had managed to gain for himself. Nor would he.

He didn't want anyone treating him any differently. Money couldn't buy what mattered most. And it could go as easily as it came.

Pulling some bills out of his wallet, Wood handed them to Gerald. "Take the guys out for a beer after work," he said. "With my apologies."

Gerald stared at the money like it was covered with vomit. "Why ain't you doing it?"

"I've got to figure this thing out," he said. "Plan to work on it as soon as we're out of here," he added, tossing his empty water bottle into the dumpster and getting back to work. He generally moved around to different jobs on the crew, working beside his guys, and had chosen to run a nail gun that day.

It wasn't like his jobs were the only ones out there, and he liked his crew as it was. Although, from what he'd been told, the guys liked his way of doing things—assembly-line style—as much as he liked having them on his team.

The conversation with Gerald was a warning to him that he couldn't spend another day in a quandary as he had the previous one and a half. He had to be *doing* something. An active life was a healthy life.

A mind left to wander tended to get lost.

Both sayings his mother had often repeated—and had made into wall art that had hung above the

kitchen table when he and Peter were young. Those
pieces of painted wood were old, faded and peeling
now, but they were still hanging in his work shed,
nailed to the inside of the door.

It was thinking of the workshop that gave him
the idea. Barely waiting until his crew had left for
the day—he made a habit of sitting in his truck and
watching as they left the site—Wood texted Cassie.
For the first time since he'd dropped her off on Saturday, he was feeling energized. Confident. More like
himself.

Do you have a crib yet?

No. The text came back almost immediately. Two
picked out. Couldn't decide.

May I make one for him?

Him. Alan. His son. Biologically speaking. And
biologically speaking, he wanted to make that boy
a crib in the worst way.

You don't need to do that.

She hadn't said no. He read significance in that.
I need to— He deleted. Typed again. I want to.
Hit Send.

I would love it!

He grinned. Really big. And then typed.

Are you free anytime this week to go with me to pick out wood? And finish?

It had been so long since he'd had a major project to do. Something other than fiddling and house and yard maintenance. Lord knew Retro hadn't made any use of the doghouse he'd built.

I'm free tonight. The text came back.

Well, didn't that work out just fine. He was free, too.

It would have made more sense for Cassie to meet Wood at the home improvement store out by the freeway, rather than having him pick her up. She'd had the thought as she was waiting for him. Too late to change the plans.

Put her lack of forethought down to the fact that she'd been distracted when they'd made the arrangements.

She'd still been at work when he'd texted and had another couple of hours of work to do to prepare for a client meeting in the morning. Work she'd planned to do over the weekend but hadn't completed because of her mother's impromptu visit.

The time with Susan had been good, though. Great, actually. She'd taken her mother to the cemetery, to show her the bench Wood had built and delivered. Instead of just the quick visit she'd envisioned, Susan had taken a seat and talked to her for over an hour—offering details about her life she never had before.

Like the night Cassie had been born. Susan had told her daughter she'd had a picture-perfect pregnancy. Had gone into labor a day before her due date. She was slowly dilating. And then her blood pressure had soared. She'd been scared to death, but Cassie's father had been right there, holding her hand, telling her over and over again that everything was going to be okay. That things always worked out as they were meant to work out.

Cassie thought of the waves, rolling in, receding out. Bringing good and bad.

There were other stories, too. All good ones. A family vacation they'd taken to Disneyland. Alan had been like a kid with a kid, and Susan remembered feeling like a child herself for that short time.

And any time Alan was in town, he had dinner ready every night when she got home from work. Had always insisted on doing the dishes, too.

Her mom had actually cried a little, wishing things had been different for all of them. But Cassie figured they'd worked out as they'd been meant to. It was like Susan had said the day before. If she'd stayed, she and Alan would most likely not have remained friends. They'd have been bitter housemates at best. And Cassie would have grown up with all that tension instead of with two households full of love.

And if Cassie, in her current state of flux, started something with Wood, she could end up just like her mother. Accidentally hurting a good man with whom she had little in common except the child she carried, then having to live with that knowledge, and the regrets it brought, for the rest of her life.

As she waited for Wood's truck outside her law office, she started to feel a little better about their situation. She wasn't psychic. Couldn't see into the future, but she had a feeling that all would resolve itself. As long as she listened to her heart and to her conscience. As long as she didn't grasp for something she only wanted in the moment.

Climbing up into Wood's truck was beginning to feel like habit. She knew the exact height of the running board, where the handle was that she could grasp and exactly how the seat felt against her legs and back. She knew the musky, masculine smell.

He, on the other hand…had clearly come straight from work and was the quintessential stereotypical male fantasy model in construction gear. All he needed was a hard hat and a bare chest and…

The hard hat was on the seat beside him.

Which left her imagining that chest…

"Is something wrong?" he asked, waiting as she fumbled with the seat belt before he drove away.

"What? No!" She'd left her satchel in her car. Had only the cross-body clutch she wore into stores when she shopped. Nothing she could bury herself in, looking for something, anything, as a means of hiding her embarrassment.

"I'm sorry, I should have gone home and changed after work. I probably smell like sawdust. Or I'm wearing it." With a glance in the rearview mirror, he brushed off the top of his head.

Nothing fell.

"You look wonderful. A little too good," she added. If things were going to work between them for the long term, they had to be honest with each other. And with themselves.

"What's that mean?" He glanced her way, but she was pretty sure there was a bit of a smug smile on his face.

Woodrow Alexander being smug? That was a new one for her.

Dangerous for her. She couldn't be pleasing him. Not in that way.

"I just…this is…you, me, the baby…it's all new territory, you know?"

Pulling to a standstill at a four-way stop, he looked over at her, his expression serious. But open, too. "I do know," he said. "Have you changed your mind? About me being involved?"

Did he want her to? Disappointment crashed through her. And then dissipated. Because she pushed it away. "No. But I keep the door open for you to walk out at any time. You have no responsibility or obligation here."

It was his turn to speak. And he did. Not saying a word.

Cassie spent the rest of the short trip to the store reminding herself of the waves.

Pulling into a spot far back in the lot, Wood put the truck in Park and turned to Cassie as she unbuckled her belt and reached for the door handle.

"Can we talk?" he asked. He'd had no intention of doing so. But she'd broached the subject, which meant she could have spent a weekend similar to his. He had to do all he could to put her mind at rest.

With a look of concern framing her beautiful features, she gave him her full attention.

"You're right," he said. "This thing that we're doing ." He had no other words to describe them. "…it's brand-new territory. Odd territory," he added. "I know it's not going to be easy, but, first and foremost, you can rest assured that I will never be walking out that door. Open or closed. I'm in, unless you tell me to go."

She smiled, glanced out her window for a second, and he suspected he'd seen a sheen of tears in her eyes—suspected that she didn't want him to see them.

They were still there when she glanced back at him. "I want you in, Wood," she said. "I don't ever see myself telling you to go. How could I deny my son the chance to know such a good man? Most particularly when he is flesh of your flesh?"

The old-fashioned phrase reached out to him. Into him.

"You've only known me for a little over a week," he had to point out.

"Eleven days," she shot back. She was counting. And not counting down, ready for him to be gone. "I'm a good judge of character," she said. "In my job, I have to be. Not that he probably ever knew it, or knew I noticed, but my father used to always watch people, listen to them, before he opened up to them. He'd get their measure by things other than words. He taught me that. In eleven days, your actions have shown me that my son would be missing a vital piece of himself if he didn't know you."

Those complications he'd known were coming… one had just flown right out of his heart and into the world. Their little world. And now they had to deal with it.

"I think what we need is some kind of definition," he said. "Not one designated by any sense of normal, or what other people think…but one that works for us…" Lord knew none of his other relationships had been traditional. Normal. Not since his father had died. He'd learned from them, too. "If we know, going in, what our expectations are going to be, then this will work, too."

This thing with Cassie had to work. There just

wasn't any other option. There was a boy coming who would benefit from knowing him.

She'd just hooked him and reeled him in for life.

Whether they got hurt or not, there was absolutely no turning back.

Chapter Twelve

She had to trust herself to do the right thing. Right for her baby. Right for her. Right for Wood. Or maybe she should focus on doing what was the best for all of them. Which road would lead to the most happiness for the most people?

The guidelines between right and wrong were more clear cut when she was doing her job. But in life…when there were so many parameters, so many different societal mores and lifestyles and views of the world…what was right for some was wrong for others. It was like her mom said—she had to rely on her inner self. Live her life, and let others have theirs.

Which all sounded great, and a little lofty, but how did that translate into reality?

Before she could come up with any kind of parameters to describe who they might become, Wood suggested that they go inside and focus on the crib first. She'd practically run beside him, getting into the store. For the first time since she could remember, she was at a total loss. This wasn't just about her, or about someone else's life. It wasn't just about being a part-time daughter to her father and tending to him when she could. It was about other lives, ones that were now permanently attached to hers, and her choices were going to affect all of them. For the rest of her life.

How did you control something to make certain that you didn't screw it up?

"Maple is a viable choice, as is this birch here," Wood was saying. He'd mentioned owning both a jointer and a planer—tools, she knew. "Pine is good, too, but a more basic option, in my opinion. Cherry's a great choice, if you like the color," he said. And then added, "But you can have pretty much any color you'd like. I can dye it. We have several non-toxic options, depending on what kind of top coat you'd want…"

And she'd thought crib plans would be less overwhelming.

"Maybe it'll help if you decide what kind of style and design you want first," Wood said as she stood there, looking at the array of choices, her mind a complete blank.

He opened the folder he'd grabbed from the back seat of the truck, moving close to her so that she could look at it with him, and started pointing out various cribs, from a Shaker style to the traditional granny style that had been around for decades. There were plain, square legged and barred, those with fancy scrollwork, and some that fell in between the two.

She looked at them all as he showed them to her. Listened as he talked. But all she could think about was how good it felt to be so close to him. And how manly he smelled. None of the expensive cologne or aftershave she was bombarded with all day at work— from the partners and the clients—but just a fresh, clean, sexy smell that was driving her nuts.

Even the deep tone of his voice reverberated through her, touching her intimately.

"I need some direction here." The words got through her distraction to sit heavily upon her.

Yeah, she needed direction, too. And had no idea where to source it.

"It's your gift to your…to the child your donation helped create." She stumbled a bit over the words. But quickly continued before either of them could make note of what she'd almost said. "I think you should make the choices." Yes, she liked the idea. More and more as she thought about it. "Make whatever crib you want, with whatever wood you want, in whatever color you want," she told him, not only feeling good about turning the project fully over to Wood, but actually satisfied that she'd made the best decision.

One down…several major ones to go.

Eager to begin his new project in ways he'd never have imagined, Wood wanted to do some research before making choices. He knew about the different kinds of materials he could use, but he wanted to familiarize himself with more history when it came to crib making. This wasn't going to be just any crib. It was going to hold and nurture his…the child that his donation had created.

Finally, he had a job to do. Someone to be. The crib maker.

He had a purpose in this infant's life.

The strength of satisfaction that thought brought—that gave him pause.

And yet, with Elaina in her residency, earning her own money, Retro having learned more tricks than she'd ever use, their house fully maintained and his crew at work running smoothly, with more jobs lined up after they finished the current one, life had become more about routine than actually living. The only excitement in his life had come from his investments, and because money wasn't the most important thing to him, even those had begun to pall. He'd mastered that challenge to his satisfaction.

But it was more than just having something to do. He finally had a purpose where his son was concerned. A job.

He was part of the process now.

Just the idea of it had him antsy in his seat as he drove silently, leaving Cassie to whatever thoughts she was having. She'd been distracted from before they'd entered the store and hadn't come out of it yet. While he wanted to know what she was thinking, he recognized the inappropriateness of querying her on it. Her life, her business, was hers.

He was in charge of Alan's crib. Peter was probably grinning down at him from his presumably blessed place in the sky.

Because his brother would know, as Wood did, that his son would be sleeping in the best crib a guy could make.

And it hit him. Alan Peter. Peter Alan.

He liked the name.

But he hadn't suggested it.

He was just the crib maker.

Pulling into the parking lot, Wood stopped by Cassie's car. He'd already suggested dinner before they'd left the store. She'd regretfully declined, saying she had to work. The regret had been stated, but also, he thought, discernible. She'd have liked to accept his invitation.

He liked that.

And hoped her distraction was due to whatever case awaited her. Not to the conversation they'd sort of had before going into the store.

"Back to what we were talking about earlier," she started, not reaching for the door handle that would release her from the truck.

He wasn't surprised she seemed to have read his mind. They were surfing along the same wavelengths at the moment.

"I'm thinking it would be good if we both wrote down a list of what we'd like to see happen in the future," she said. "A list of expectations, like you mentioned."

He hadn't mentioned a list. And, at the moment, wished he'd kept his mouth shut in general, now that he had a job to do.

"Because you're right, we do need some kind of definition," she continued. "Boundaries, at least."

He nodded. Boundaries. A good word. Denoting safety. Something he could adhere to that would prevent disaster. "You make the list," he told her. "I'll abide by it."

"How can you say that when you have no idea what will be on it?"

He shrugged. "You say you know me. Well, I figure I know you, too, and I'm confident that whatever you ask will be appropriate. Now get your beautiful butt out of my truck so I can focus on crib building."

"I need more, Wood," her gaze had darkened.

He stared at her.

"I need you to make a list, too. Your life…it plays a key part in all of this, and I can't speak for you. Or to it. I don't want to be blindsided down the road. More importantly, I won't allow my son to be."

She had a point.

"I meant what I said about wanting Alan to have a chance to know you," she said. "I talked about it with my mom this weekend… I took her to the cemetery, and we actually sat together on the beach after that, had the best talk we've ever had about my dad…"

Damn. The woman had a way of making him feel good.

"My father added so much to my life. And now that I've met you and see what a great guy you are and know that you want to know Alan, how could I deny my son the opportunity to have that kind of opportunity, as well? Mom came to the same conclusion even before I expressed my thoughts aloud."

Funny how a parent's approval still had the ability to add validation when he'd been without any since he was seventeen. Not that he was seeking permission for anything. Just…added perspective, from one who'd been around a few decades longer than he had, was nice.

"And we have to figure in, at least in the moment, that I'm finding myself really, really attracted to you," Cassie added, with added tension in her voice. In the tightness of her lips.

Figure in? You didn't figure that in. You ignored it. Moved on.

"You talked about that with your mother, too?" he asked, to buy himself time, even knowing that no amount of it was going to be enough.

"No." He liked how she was looking him right in the eye. And was getting turned on by it, too, which was a problem.

"I'm hoping it's just proximity," she continued. "And a product of you being my rock during the toughest week of my life. And pregnancy hormones. I'm in the fourth month, and from what I hear, some women tend to get horny—"

She broke off, and he felt a bit tight beneath his zipper. Growing uncomfortably tight.

"And I'm particularly easy on the eyes where the ladies are concerned," he pointed out with a grin, hoping to defuse the moment. But he managed to turn the air between them in the car so thick he could hardly draw in a complete breath as he met her gaze.

His words faded as their gazes locked, hers seeming to darken, and the next move had to be a kiss. It was destined, with a moment like that.

He stopped himself from tilting toward her, though. Because some things mattered a hell of a lot more than sex.

"We just have to make certain nothing happens," she said slowly, looking toward his mouth.

"You're right," he said the words with more force than he'd intended. "I've already determined that it can't happen on my end, either. Not now, at any rate. Not anytime soon," he continued, telling himself as much as her. "Sex between us would only complicate an already complicated situation."

He was pretty sure there'd been a flash of disappointment showing before she blinked. Nodded. Tried to give him what was probably meant to be a relieved smile. And then she asked, "Just out of curiosity, can I ask…is there something…unattractive about me?"

Confusion flooded him.

So.,,what…she'd been hoping he'd say yes?

He needed to open his fly and relieve some of the pressure. But he dealt with the pain instead.

The woman's mixed messages were wreaking havoc on his night. Crib making was definitely the better alternative.

"I only have casual relationships so I don't risk hurting anyone." He said the first thing that came to mind.

"Not that I'm suggesting we do this, at all, to the contrary, but what you just said, is that true?"

"It is. I'm very clear from the beginning."

"But…why? You could still have a family, Wood.

You'd make such a great husband, great father..."
The compassion in her tone caught his gut.

"You can tell all that from knowing me eleven days?"

She didn't answer. Just looked at him. Waiting.

She'd given him her honesty.

"I'm a fixer. I see someone in need, and I feel a need to do what I can to make it better. And apparently I'm content to settle for gratitude instead of the deeper, lasting emotion that makes for a successful relationship."

No, that wasn't quite right. Maybe partly, but... "I need to help where I can," he said. "To tend to those in my sphere. To whatever feels like family connection to me. It's just who I am. But at the same time, I'm tired of settling for nothing more than that. Maybe I'm tired of running scared at the thought of losing any more. I lost my dad, then my mom, then Peter..."

Speaking the truth lifted a weight from him, even as it denied him what he wanted most at the moment. He looked at her. "As far as I'm concerned, every single thing about you is attractive. Inside and out. I want you in a way I don't remember ever wanting a woman. And that makes me even more certain that I won't sleep with you. You need me right now. But in the future, when you have a healthy baby and are ready to move on... I need to be able to still be there for you. And for Alan. I guess what I'm trying to say is that I can't take a chance on being your second best."

"What if…in the future…we still feel this way?"

She was making this more difficult than he'd ever imagined. He wanted her so badly; maybe because she was pregnant with his child, but he really didn't think so. At least not foremost. The woman had been twisting him in knots from her first phone call.

He shook his head.

He knew himself.

"If we keep that door open, we both know where it will lead. Sooner rather than later."

Her eyes darkened again. He'd bet his had, too, if they really did such things.

They were so close, their gazes locked.

The kiss needed to happen. Right then. Right there. He knew it. She had to know it, too. She licked her lips. He hid a wince of pain. He was stronger than anything his penis could do to him.

She was the one who looked away first. But it had been close.

"So…you make your list, and I'll make mine?" she asked, reaching for the door handle.

The expectations. Now translated to mean boundaries. Fences and cages and walls that would protect those they loved.

He nodded. Vigorously.

Chapter Thirteen

Cassie was completely consumed with a case that next week. A privately held nonprofit she'd brought as a client to the firm was facing employee issues, and if she didn't find a way to get the situation handled immediately, it could have catastrophic consequences.

Through all of the internal and external investigations, Cassie believed that the organization's executive director had done nothing wrong, but that a disgruntled worker was making untrue accusations. Her job was to give the best legal advice to protect her client, not to determine guilt, but for her own sake, she had to know.

She worked long days and into the night, researching case law and reading social media accounts on both sides, building reasonable doubt while she looked for something more substantial. She did her best to keep her brain occupied during every waking hour.

Giving herself time to take a break from her personal life.

The irony in going from no personal life to having so much of one she needed a break was not lost on her.

And every night, after she'd readied for bed, she allowed herself to read whatever texts Wood had sent that day. He'd sent photos of his final three crib design choices. For two nights they discussed various pros and cons. She liked the idea of having a crib that could convert to a toddler bed, so that took out one choice. He mentioned making a dresser, crib and changing table, and when she sent back excited emojis, that took away the second of the three choices, leaving only one.

Then he'd moved on to finishes and colors. By the end of the week, she'd ordered a complete nursery, including glider rocker and bookcase in a maple wood with natural finishing. She'd decided to add color to the nursery in wall decor, sheets, rocker cushions and changing pads.

She insisted on paying for all supplies, but stopped

short of offering him money for labor when he started to sound put out and said they'd work it out later.

Each night he asked how she was feeling. She said fine. And he told her to have a good night. She wished him the same. Neither of them mentioned the lists they were supposed to be composing. Or anything else about either of their lives.

Maybe they didn't need the lists. Maybe they'd found a plan that worked for them: texting at night so they both knew the other had made it through another day. And sharing nothing about their individual personal lives. When she had news to tell him about Alan, she'd do so. And once the baby was born, then there'd be a lot to say about him. But for the now, all was good.

Except that she missed him like crazy. Which made her crazy. She'd known the man a couple of weeks and was mourning his absence like he'd been her best friend for life. Wishing she could talk over her current client's situation with him, because she so badly wanted to hear his take on the situation, brought her up short.

She trusted Wood that much. Valued his opinion that much.

And at night, she'd go to sleep and end up naked with him, finally seeing his manliness intimately, to touch him, only to wake up alone in bed with a longing she couldn't assuage.

She had no idea how any of that changed anything in her life. But she knew it did.

Wood told Elaina about the nursery project. He'd be spending most of his waking nonworking hours in his workshop.

He'd also told her that Cassie had indicated that he'd have some sort of relationship with the boy. She'd touched his face, sympathy shining from her eyes. But "Be careful" was all she'd said.

He wished he could assure her his eyes were wide-open. That he wasn't going to get hurt, which she seemed certain was already a done deal.

Just because Elaina hadn't been able to love him like that didn't mean Cassie couldn't.

The thought was beneath him. Feeling sorry for himself. Finding unfair fault with Elaina. And building castles where Cassie was concerned. Nonproductive.

Shame washed through him, and he pushed a little too hard on his planer. Lost a board that had cost him over twenty bucks. Not a good way to start a Saturday.

Picking up another piece, he steadied himself, focused on the task at hand. Worked hard for an hour, took a water break, and his mind wandered to a place it had spent much time, unsuccessfully, that week. His list.

So far, there was nothing on it. He wasn't even sure

what he wanted to put on it. In a perfect world, he and Cassie would be in love and she'd be having his son.

He didn't even know for sure if that kind of love even existed outside movies and novels.

He was no more in love with his ex-wife than she'd ever been in love with him. And who knew if Peter and Elaina's love would have withstood the stresses and challenges of time? He liked to think it would have, but...

The world wasn't ever going to be perfect. Not his. Not anyone's.

He wanted to raise his son. Wanted to be involved in every aspect of that brand-new life.

Too late for conception.

And going forward?

He couldn't figure out how the future would look. But was absolutely certain that as long as he had the chance, he had to be as much a figure in Alan's life as Cassie would allow.

Alan's mother. What did it say about him that his favorite part of life right now was climbing into bed at night and texting the woman who was carrying his child?

Couldn't be good.

He'd been back to work for a couple of hours or so when Retro stood up from her bed and ran outside with her tail wagging. Glancing up, Wood saw Elaina walking toward the shed, a basket in her hand.

Standing straight, he left the crib frame he'd been working on and moved toward the doorway, watching her.

"What's up?" he asked. Maybe she'd done the closets first. Was on her way out, stopping to tell him her changed schedule. It was one of their understandings…they generally let the other know their plans.

"I brought lunch," she said, and he stepped back as she entered the shed. "I figured you'd get involved and forget to eat."

He'd been known to skip lunch on occasion when he was deep into a project. But not because he forgot. The choice to ignore the meal in favor of another half hour of doing something he loved was a conscious one.

With the basket hanging over one arm, she reached with the other to pull a TV tray out of the rack of four of them. Grabbing it from her, he set it up.

She'd made tuna melt sandwiches for him. And brought herself out a plastic bowl filled with greens with a generous scoop of tuna on top.

She asked to see the nursery plans, studied them as she ate, asking questions.

"I'd add shelves on the changing table instead of these two drawers," she said, pointing to an area on the rough picture he'd drawn. "You can get those square storage baskets to fit, and it would be much easier to pull out one of those to reach for something in a pinch than to have to move and yank out a drawer. You know, if you have one hand on the baby on top..."

He studied the drawing. Agreed with her completely.

"And maybe instead of this two-inch solid piece around the top of the table, put in the same spindle design you're using on the crib. That way you'd still have that little bit of barrier, but the baby could turn his head and see out.

"And I'd do the same for the cradle. I know a lot of them have solid sides, but would you want to lie in such a small, closed-in space and only be able to see the ceiling?"

He wouldn't. And liked her suggestions.

"I was thinking maybe we should set up a meeting between you and Cassie," he said. "Just so you know each other..."

He was a guy who needed his family together, apparently—and Elaina was family.

She chewed. Grabbed a couple of grapes, popped them into her mouth.

"I'd rather not." She glanced up at him, and he recognized the sympathy in her eyes. Hated it there. "When Alan's born, I'll be right there any time I'm invited. The best aunt ever."

He heard the "but" she didn't say before she continued.

"I know you feel a need to be involved right now, with the baby's health issues, and I support any decisions you make, but..." There it was. He waited.

"I don't want to watch you get hurt."

"And you're so certain I would be?" He heard the anger in his tone, even if she didn't. "You really think there's no way a woman like Cassie would go for me, don't you?"

The accusation was too clear to miss. The shock on her face was clear, too, as she stood. "Why would you say such a thing?" Her mouth hung open.

He didn't take the words back, even knowing they hadn't been fair, that he'd hurt her. Maybe if Elaina hadn't always been constantly trying to push him to make more of himself, he wouldn't feel as though he wasn't good enough.

She turned to go, leaving the mess of their not-quite-finished lunch sitting on the tray. At the door, she half turned, looking him right in the eye.

"For the record, if anything, I think she's not good enough for you, Wood, and I've never even met her. I don't know that you'll find a woman that I think is deserving of you. I also know that you give everything you are to family who needs you, to your own detriment, to the point of not having a life of your own, including marrying me. It breaks my heart to think of you doing it again because a stranger chose to use a donation Peter talked you into giving. You've given up enough of your life for your brother."

With tears in her eyes, she left the barn.

And he let her go.

* * *

Cassie spent Saturday evening in a private conference room, eating a catered dinner with the executive director of the charitable organization Safe!

By the time she got home that night, she still didn't know what course the board of Safe! would take, but she knew that she'd done all she could to guide them toward a successful outcome. And that she'd follow through for them, no matter which of her options they chose.

And she hadn't heard from Wood all day. While she never answered until night, he generally sent a text or two that would be waiting for her when she climbed into bed. Or lounged on the couch before bed.

A text or two that she knew were there…carried with her…and looked forward to reading.

She took her time getting out of her suit and into the nightshirt she slept in. Brushing her teeth. And her hair, too, though she didn't normally do that before bed. She went to get a fresh bottle of water. Checked the doors again, though she knew they were locked. Stopped in her office to glance at the mail that had come. Mail she'd already gone through.

Eventually, she made it back to her room. Climbed under the covers, sitting up with pillows propped behind her. And picked up the phone she'd left plugged in on her nightstand. And felt her spirits drop as she saw that no text messages had come through.

She'd given him extra time. Why hadn't he reached out?

Had something happened? How would she know if it had? It wasn't like they were on each other's in-case-of-emergency call lists.

Maybe they should be. If something happened to her and they needed Wood's blood to save Alan's life, she had to set up a family trust…name him legally as…*something*. Her legal brain clicked in, and she tried to bring back everything she'd ever heard or read about estate law. It hadn't been her area of interest.

She knew a couple of people she could call, though. But ten o'clock on a Saturday night wasn't the time.

Should she text Wood just to make sure he was okay?

Shaking her head, she grabbed the remote. Clicked to turn on an old sitcom. And then switched to another old show, one that centered around cops and lawyers. Something she could get lost in…

The jolt came out of nowhere. Not sharp, but definitely strong. And completely unexpected. She'd been feeling little movements, kind of bubble-like, on and off for most of the week. She hadn't been certain they were the baby. Had hoped.

But this… She waited, heart pounding, to see

what would happen next. If the baby had just kicked, would he kick again?

Or was something wrong?

Did anemia lead to other things? Was her baby in distress? If the pregnancy were progressing normally, she might not have wondered, but...

That worrying week had taken a toll. Could something be wrong?

Picking up her phone, she searched the internet. Landed on a reputable hospital website. Spent forty-five minutes reading everything she could find about signs of miscarriage, fetal blood disorder symptoms and a side piece about preventing diaper rash. There'd been no other movement in her stomach, no cramping or even a hint of needing to use the restroom, though once she thought about it, she did kind of have to pee.

So she did. Checked for spotting. There was none. And climbed back into bed. Picked up her phone and typed, "What does it feel like when your baby kicks?"

Twenty minutes of reading later, she was smiling. Wishing the sensation would come again. With a hand on her growing belly, she said, "You just do whatever you have to do to make yourself comfortable, Mama's baby Alan. Move around as much as you like. Four months and one week can seem like a long time. Oh...and if you wouldn't mind...could you please kick a lot? Just so I know you're okay in there?"

He'd kicked.

She'd felt her first real evidence that he was alive. Their first son-to-Mama communication.

Picking up her phone again, she opened her messenger app.

The baby kicked for the first time tonight. Just keeping you informed.

And then, turning out the light, she lay down and let the television talk her to sleep.

Chapter Fourteen

Wood was out in the shed, gluing and nailing the last of the crib frame, when Cassie's text came through.

He read it once. Continued to work. Read it again. Worked some more.

Kept picturing Cassie's belly bump with his hand on top of it. Imagined her smooth, soft skin. And couldn't come up with any idea of what that kick would feel like to him. He'd never felt a baby kick on the outside, let alone from inside a sac of fluid, through layers of protective fat and skin. And maybe he never would—feel it from the outside.

But he wanted to.

Just as he'd been antsy to text her all night. But Elaina's words were still rankling. Still demanding he make sense of them.

His idea, that she thought herself too good for him, had hurt her badly. Not that he'd ever made the exact claim, but his comment to her had been laced with a resentment that had been building inside him for too long.

The idea that he'd been harboring a wrong assumption all these years still hung there. Suspended.

As though awaiting trial. More evidence.

Something.

As the night had grown late, and he was starting to bother himself with how much Cassie was on his mind, he'd determined that it was probably best that he go one night without checking in on her. One night.

She'd gotten along fine without him her entire life. One night wasn't going to make a difference to anyone but him. And he needed to do without her or risk messing up his entire life. And her and Alan's lives, too.

And so it went for much of the night. By the time he fell into bed a couple of hours before dawn, he'd completed four spindles. Had no answers. And hadn't texted Cassie back.

Wood mowed the lawn first thing Sunday morning. He played with Retro for over an hour after that, working on having her sit and stay until Wood gave the command to let her go find the ball he'd thrown.

He talked to the dog about Alan, though. For a good part of the morning. And when Retro finally tired of playing, sitting in front of Wood, her tongue hanging out, Wood slowed down, too. Met the dog's gaze and realized that he just needed to do what Retro did. What Wood had always done. Tend to his people. Period. Retro didn't question herself. Didn't worry about what could come.

Wood was making too much out of everything. Elaina. Cassie. The baby. They were all in his life at the moment, which meant that he would be there for them. He couldn't predict the future. Couldn't control it, either, God knew. But he could trust himself to deal with it.

He was a smart man. A strong man. He'd never failed his family before. Never not met his obligations. Even at seventeen, he'd come through. There was no reason for him to doubt himself now.

Peace settled within him as he went in to shower.

He was planning to spend the day in his workshop. With perhaps a side trip to the beach. Some of the guys on his crew were having a family cookout and sand volleyball tournament later that afternoon, and he figured he'd put in an appearance. He'd put up the money for the hamburgers and hot dogs.

But first…after dressing in shorts, a T-shirt and flip-flops, he grabbed his phone off his nightstand.

Opened the text message app. Clicked on Cassie. And hit Call.

"Wood? Are you okay?" She'd picked up on the first ring. He heard tension in her voice.

"Yeah," he told her. "Sorry I didn't get back to you sooner." About to make some blow-off excuse for the fact that he hadn't returned her text the night before, he saw Retro sitting there, staring at him. "You have any interest in meeting my dog?" he asked, ideas coming to him as he stood there. "We could take her for a walk along the ocean path..." Several miles of pathed path, converted railroad track, accessible only from private beach access.

"I'd love the exercise," she said, sounding better already, and he pushed back the twinge of guilt that came with her improved disposition. Guilt for not having contacted her sooner.

Guilt for the sudden adrenaline surging through him. Something he'd never felt at the prospect of spending an afternoon with anyone.

He shook that off. Asked her how soon she could be ready. And offered to come get her. The day seemed just about perfect when she agreed to have him collect her.

It had been a long time since Cassie had had a dog of her own, but after about fifteen minutes in the company of Wood and Retro, she wanted one. It wasn't a practical idea. Not with working full-time and a baby on the way. But someday…

Alan would need a dog. She felt sure of it.

Riding in Wood's truck felt…comfortable. Normal. Even with the dog nosing greetings at her behind the ear from the back seat. She laughed out loud and shushed Wood as he started to discipline the dog. "I'm fine," she said. "She's just being friendly."

And she was—as friendly and kind as her master. They walked for half an hour, mostly talking about Retro and her training. And the balmy late June weather they were enjoying. It had rained a couple of days during the week, for a few hours each day, but that Sunday afternoon graced them with beautiful blue skies and sunshine. In black biker shorts, which easily accommodated her growing belly, and a thigh-length white cotton top and tennis shoes, Cassie felt the week's tension fall away.

And then, with Retro walking more calmly on the leash beside him, Wood said, "I'm sorry I didn't text last night. I made a conscious choice not to, and I regret that choice."

He made a conscious choice? That weight she'd just shed started to set upon her again.

"You need to do what you need to do, Wood," she said at once. "And you have no reason to apologize or feel in any bad way about that. This baby…having him, creating him, even, was my choice. You owe us nothing. To the contrary, we owe you everything. Your generous donation allowed Alan to come into existence, allowed me to have the family I've always wanted…"

He walked steadily as she unloaded feelings that had been building since they'd found out that Alan was going to be okay.

There was silence between them for a few seconds after she stopped talking. People passed them, a few bikes, a pair of senior citizen in-line skaters. Families sat on the beach in the distance as the path led downhill from cliff side to shoreline.

"I purposely didn't text because I don't want to insinuate myself into your life more fully than you'd like and thought that perhaps I might be doing so."

The boundaries he'd talked about. She hadn't even started a list.

"I'd tell you if you were," she said.

"I wish I could be sure of that."

Pulling him off the path, though, at the moment, there was no one else close to them in either direction, she looked him straight in the eye. "If you're sure of nothing else, be sure of that, Wood. I'm not a woman who's afraid to speak up. If you were trespassing in my space more than I wanted, or in any way that made me uncomfortable, you'd know about it."

He stared into her eyes. She let him see everything that was there.

"Case in point, my unease regarding your taking any responsibility or feeling any obligation here."

He nodded. And when he grinned, it was like the sun had just become twice as brilliant. Blinding her.

"I want you in my life," she added. "And not just because of Alan. I like you, Woodrow Alexander."

"I like you, too."

She needed to hug him. So started walking again instead.

He'd made up his mind. He was doing nothing wrong. And he wasn't going to.

As long as he was honest with Cassie, and himself, they'd find a way through whatever complications arose. When they arose.

"What would you think about having dinner once a week?" he asked as a sedate Retro walked beside Cassie on their way back. Twice, Wood had noticed the Lab turn and gently lick Cassie's hand.

Cassie glanced at him. "Really?"

"Yeah. I eat alone an average of seven out of seven nights a week," he said. "I was thinking it would be a way for us to get to know each other better. For Alan's sake."

At least in big part for the baby's sake, or he wouldn't have asked.

"I'd love to have dinner on a regular basis," she said, and her obvious pleasure made him smile. He'd been doing that a lot that afternoon. Way more than usual. Something about her brought out a happy in him that he didn't feel all that often. "I'd still like to exchange nightly texts, though, if that's not a problem for you," she added.

Yep. Life was much better when you just let it flow. "Believe me, it's not a problem."

"I just like knowing that you're okay," she told him. "I know that's ridiculous. I've lived thirty-four years without knowing a thing about you, and suddenly, I relax better at night knowing you're out there and all right."

Her words almost stopped him in his tracks. He had to consciously prevent himself from asking her to repeat them.

It was a basic concept in his life, his own bottom line—he needed to know the ones he cared about were all right.

When you'd lost a loved one…more than one…

She'd just told him she cared about him—like one who cared for their family.

"Ditto" was all he said.

But once again, his world had just changed.

They were almost at the truck, another quarter mile or so, and Cassie didn't want to go back without clarity. She didn't have a list. Couldn't put boundaries around them. But she also didn't want to screw up what might be the best adult relationship she'd ever had.

Certainly one that was seeming to mean more to

her than any other, excluding her parents. Far different from her parents. Closer, in some ways.

She needed more. And didn't know how to establish that in a way that didn't ruin things between them. She kept reminding herself she'd only known him a matter of weeks.

Her heart didn't seem to get the point.

"So...you felt him move last night?" Wood asked, his hands in his pockets as they walked. No chance her fingers could bump into his. But she bumped her arm to his. And managed to hold the contact as they walked.

"Yeah, I think so. I'm pretty much certain that's what it was. Based on what I read on the internet."

"But it hasn't happened since?"

"No. And from what I've read, that's common, too. At first."

"What was it like?"

She glanced over the foot and a half or so that had been separating them the entire walk—purposefully, she was sure—and liked the warm curiosity in his vivid blue eyes.

"Like something's pushing at you from the inside out," she said. "I know that sounds obvious, but...it was strong enough that it took my breath away. Not from the force, but from the shock of it."

"Did it hurt?"

She shook her head. "Not at all. It was kind of like a soft rubber ball, or something, just bouncing once off the inside of my skin." Not quite, but it was as close as she could come.

He asked about morning sickness again. So far she'd had none. And, hard as it was to believe, she didn't want to talk about her pregnancy at the moment. And have the conversation take up her last moments with him.

Retro saw another dog, watched intently, but didn't miss her stride. Cassie handed over the leash anyway, just in case, and felt a sweet warmth pass through her as her fingers brushed Wood's.

He'd shown her a picture of the crib frame he'd already completed while they'd been stopped at a light on the way to the beach. And talked to her about Elaina's suggestions for design changes. Something perverse had made her want to reject them outright, and when she'd recognized the feelings of jealousy, she'd reeled herself in. Thought about the changes and approved every one of them. Even relaxed enough to feel gratitude toward the other woman for suggesting them.

"I've given a lot of thought to your request for clear boundaries." She felt like she blurted the words. As they neared the parking lot, the path grew more populated. A family of five on bikes. Couples walking hand in hand. A group of teenage girls, scantily dressed, talking loud and giggling.

"And?" Wood didn't seem to notice the cacophony

going on around them. She resented its intrusion but was grateful for its protection, too.

"I need a better understanding of what you're envisioning." The words were a cop-out. She didn't want to impose boundaries. Or wasn't ready to define them. What if she inadvertently shut out something that she didn't even know was there yet?

Or turned her back on something because she couldn't see it?

As a toddler on a tricycle almost ran into Retro, Wood veered them off the path and down toward a stretch of beach. Up the hill, on the cliff side, his truck sat waiting for them, ready to end the outing. She could see it there.

"I have someplace else to be in about an hour," Wood said, telling her, she was sure, that he was putting off the conversation that had to happen.

Because it would end what had only just begun?

He'd assured her he was always going to be around. Because of Alan. But a lot of people raised kids without really even speaking to each other.

"It's a cookout on a private stretch of beach not far from here, actually. Retro and I are going to be heading there as soon as we drop you off."

"Okay." She really didn't need a blow-by-blow accounting.

"I'm the host," he continued, stopping in the sand to look up at her. She met Retro's gaze. The dog sat and was staring at her as though she knew something was coming.

"It's for my crew and their families."

She got it. He had plans…

"I can't take you," he said, his voice changing, and she finally looked up at him. At the short, bushy blond hair, the smoothly shaved skin, those eyes that showed her so much more than his words said.

She read regret there. And she was starting to understand.

"Because they'd think we're an item."

"Yes."

"You don't want people to see us together."

Regret surged through her, now, too. Something else they shared.

"We can't be an item," he said. "That's my boundary." He was still holding her gaze, his face just so incredibly beautiful to her. More than handsome… he was it. The man to her woman.

"We can't be a couple."

She'd known that.

And a flower in her soul wilted.

"And I can't have casual sex with you."

His honesty broke through to places in her heart no one had ever been before.

"I don't think I'd find sex with you casual, either," she said, needing so badly to kiss him even as she said the words, but knowing just as strongly that she wouldn't.

"Other than that, I have no boundaries." In that split second, everything changed. Instead of doors closing, it felt like Wood had just opened them. Wide.

"So…we're friends."

"I can see you being the best friend I've ever had."

"Yeah, me, too," she said. Smiling. Retro moved, nudging against Wood's thigh, and hers. As if to say she wanted to be included in their relationship, too.

To give them her blessing.

Or to stop them from doing something they'd both regret. Like stepping half a foot closer and actually touching.

"And as for Alan…as I said, I want you involved, Wood, if you want to be. I'm not saying that your opinion will reign supreme or anything. I always have the final say because the ultimate responsibility is all mine, but I want you to weigh in on any major decisions. If you want to be consulted."

"Always. Anything. Major, just big or really small…"

She had more to say…tried to keep her mouth shut…but couldn't. "I'm thinking about telling him from the outset that you're his father," she said. "In today's world, with so many different lifestyles, we can help him understand that while you aren't part of our family, you are family to him."

When moisture filled his eyes, she knew she'd done the right thing in telling him. But also in making the choice.

"He'll have to know that my word is law," she told him, not wanting to give him the wrong idea. "I can't give up any custodial rights, just as you won't have any monetary responsibility," she told him. "I still plan to have 'sperm donor' on his birth certificate under the designation for 'father'…"

She could see him struggling to remain serious. To give her words the respect they deserved, but she rejoiced when he cut off her stipulations with a hearty laugh. Loud enough that a group several feet away turned and glanced in their direction.

"Did you hear that, Retro? I'm going to be a father…"

Simple words. Boisterous laughter. Playful chatter with a dog.

And, Cassie knew, those moments had just been embedded on her heart forever.

Chapter Fifteen

Two and a half weeks later, when Cassie went for another ultrasound, a check specifically to keep an eye on the shadow that had originally alerted doctors to Alan's iron deficiency, Wood was there. During their nightly texts, she'd been more and more open with him about her anxiety regarding her baby's health. Telling him every time she had a thought that there might be something not quite right. He'd become quite adept at looking up pregnancy symptoms simply to relieve her fears. She'd acknowledged, multiple times, that she knew she was just reacting to a stressor caused by the original scare.

And Wood saw that his role in the pregnancy,

along with building the nursery furniture, was to keep Cassie from falling into a pit from which she couldn't escape. He liked understanding his definition in her life. And set out to be great at it.

So when she'd asked if he wanted to accompany her to the ultrasound, he'd accepted without thought. He'd already taken her to two appointments. Would happily be her driver to all of them.

As usual, she'd scheduled the first appointment of the day, and he spent the ride over telling her about the rocking chair he was building. The crib was done. He'd opted to build the rocker second, partially because it was going to be the second most critical piece of the ensemble, but because it was going to be the most challenging, as well—not that he told her that.

"You look like you've grown since Monday," he told her that second Wednesday morning in July as they waited for her to be called. True to their agreement, they'd been meeting for dinner once a week— on Monday evenings right after work.

In black dress pants and a white-and-black knit top with a short black jacket, she was sitting upright with her hands resting on the mound of her stomach. Proprietarily, he decided. She wasn't huge yet, by any means, but he could definitely tell that she was pregnant.

"It feels like I have," she told him, turning her

head to give him a small grin. Her lips had a slight tremble. She was nervous.

Understandable, considering the last ultrasound she'd had had given her cause for great worry.

He grabbed her hand. Gave it a squeeze. "It's going fine," he said. And then realized what he'd just done, that he was sitting there holding hands with Cassie. There was nothing sexual in the contact. He'd been one hundred percent focused on offering comfort. And yet he knew he'd crossed a line.

They hadn't outlined any further boundaries since that walk on the beach, but there was one very clear unspoken one between them. They didn't touch again.

Ever.

Before he could drop her hand or try to slide his away without either of them noticing, the door opened and her name was called. She stood, taking his hand with her.

"Is it okay if the father comes with me?" she asked the nurse standing there waiting for her.

"Of course!"

Wait. What! Wood's job was sitting in the waiting room, watching as other women filed in, doing what the room was for. Waiting.

But he was no fool. Cassie wanted him with her. She was giving him the chance to see proof of his son's life on film. A word of warning might have been nice, but then, it also might have messed things up—making more of the moment than it was. He stood, she dropped his hand and he followed her through the door.

She hadn't planned on asking him in to the actual ultrasound. She might regret the invitation at a later time. But as Cassie removed her jacket, climbed up onto the table and lay back as instructed, she felt like she could breathe because Wood was there. The technician had already been in the room, waiting for them, and already had jelly and the portable camera ready as she instructed Cassie to raise her top and lower her pants enough to expose the full round-ness of her belly.

Knowing that Wood was seeing her naked skin for the first time distracted her so much she jerked when she felt the first chill of cold from the jelly on her stomach.

"You can stand over here," the technician said, looking at Wood and pointing to a place just off from Cassie's shoulder on the other side of the table. "That gives you a good view of the screen." She continued talking as she moved the camera around in the gel, almost like stirring batter in a bowl.

In another second or two, Cassie's uterus, contain-ing Alan, would show on the screen. If she stared at it, she wouldn't see Wood right there on the other side of her, watching her distended belly button stick-ing up in the air.

She looked at Wood. In the jeans and T-shirt she knew he wore to work, his attention was fully on the screen opposite the bed, not even looking at her belly.

And then he did—glance at her naked stomach, and then up to her face. Their gazes met. He seemed to be talking to her. Telling her everything was going to be just fine.

He couldn't possibly know that. She didn't know it.

But she took another breath. An easier one.

"Okay, let's see what we can find," the technician said, and Cassie prepared for the professional silence she'd encountered during the first ultrasound—when the technician saw something but couldn't legally give her opinion.

Wood glanced at the screen and then back at her, and the intimacy of the moment wrapped her in a private cocoon for a second or two.

He'd told her he'd never seen an ultrasound before. She liked being his first.

"There he is." The technician's tone still held flowers and light.

"Here are his arms…and his legs…"

The camera moved on her stomach. She listened. And watched Wood's face as she caught his first glance of the child she'd created. There was little expression, just focus, and then he looked at her. His expression was completely new to her…awe and caring and shock, too. Emotion poured over her, welled up within her. She swallowed back tears.

And continued to watch his face. She couldn't look at the screen.

"And…here's his heartbeat…" the technician said in a singsong tone. The sound of the baby's heart came into the room…more rapid than an adult pulse, but she'd known it would be. Counted the beats. Listened for regularity. Found it.

And smiled when Wood glanced down at her again.

In some ways she wanted the moment to last forever. At the same time, she couldn't wait to have the test done. To get back to work and have everything be normal.

To know that Alan was progressing normally. She should hear later that day, given the circumstances. A radiologist would be reading the film, charting to the doctor, within the hour, in case the situation was growing more critical.

"I'm aware that you can't divulge any medical information or advice, other than that which you've already explained." Wood's voice broke into her thoughts. "But could you show me where the shadow was that alerted doctors to an iron deficiency?"

She stared at him. What was he doing?

The camera moved around on her stomach. "Right here." The technician moved. Cassie heard the rustle of the woman's purple scrubs, saw movement out of the corner of her eye. She stared at Wood's face, but it was in its stoic place.

What was he seeing?

If it was bad, she wanted to be upright, dressed—feeling strong, not vulnerable, when she heard about it. She wanted to be mobile and able to take action.

The technician mentioned taking some pictures, and then she was handing Cassie a warm cloth to remove the jelly from her stomach. Telling her they were all done and she was free to go.

She went through the motions. A little embarrassed now as she pulled up her waistband, covering the small bit of hair that had been showing from down below. And shoved her shirt down over her belly. Her hands were shaking as she reached for her jacket. The door closed behind the technician.

"There was nothing there." Wood's words fell into the room.

"What?" Jacket half on, half off, she looked over at him.

"I saw no shadow on the screen where she indicated. Nothing. It was just a light gray mass, like the rest of the area."

Her face started to pucker. She could feel it. Tried to contain it. "No shadow?" she asked. "Really?"

Head tilted, he seemed to wrap her in understanding. In love. "No shadow," he said.

Watching her diet and the added iron were working?

Without thought, she moved toward him. Wrapped her arms around his middle and started to cry.

Wood was still at work that afternoon, up on a piece of scaffolding, when Cassie texted that he was right. The doctor had confirmed her ultrasound was clear of shadows. Until she had a second amniocentesis, scheduled in two weeks, they wouldn't know for sure how much Alan's red blood cell count had come up, but for the moment, the doctor was optimistic that the baby was completely normal.

He almost fell off the portable metal rafter.

Gerald, who was doing an inspection with him, reached a hand out. "You okay, man? Bad news? Is it Elaina?"

"No," he said. "Not Elaina, and not bad news." His son was healthy! Or at least optimistically considered so. That was not his news to share.

There wasn't really anything stopping him. Cassie was planning to tell Alan that Wood was his father. He was going to have an official role in the boy's life.

He'd told Elaina. She'd been openly pleased for him.

What he didn't share with Elaina was the incredible moments he'd experienced in the ultrasound room that morning. Not even the fact that he'd been in the room. The moments were precious—and they were *his*. Not open to speculation or judgment. Not to be turned into concern on his behalf.

The hug he and Cassie had shared, the feel of her protruding belly pressing tightly up against him— that he put firmly in its place of a time out of time. She hadn't been hugging him. She'd just needed a hug. Anybody would have done.

It had been…heady, though. He wanted more. Badly.

And he skipped right on past that thought every time it surfaced.

He wasn't going to let Alan down. Or Cassie or himself, either.

He almost told Cassie so when they texted later that night. Because they were telling each other more and more of their everyday thoughts. But he opted not to make a big deal out of what had to remain nothing.

He'd made it to thirty-six years without a major screwup. He was not going to start playing with fire.

Which was what he did tell Cassie the following Monday when they were discussing where to meet for dinner. They'd already settled on a small diner outside town, not because they had anything to hide, but because neither of them wanted the complications of answering to anyone they knew that they might run into. Her parents knew about him. Elaina knew about her. Beyond that, they just wanted to get through the pregnancy before bringing any more complications into their lives.

Before other people and their opinions unwittingly created obstacles they didn't yet have to face. One step at a time, they'd decided somewhere along the way. A mixture of what Wood knew and Cassie had learned from her father.

He'd just been home to shower, change and feed Retro and was on his way back out to his truck when Cassie called. She told him she'd had a rough day with a client and didn't want to have to sit in a busy restaurant waiting on others to serve her.

She wanted to go home. Heat up the cabbage rolls she'd made the day before and relax out on the beach—with him. He felt the same—strongly.

The strength of his desire was what had him telling her he couldn't play with fire. He couldn't sit with her on her private beach. If they were going to have dinner, it had to be at the restaurant. She hadn't said another word, other than telling him that she'd see him at the restaurant in a few.

He told himself not to make trouble. To trust himself. But as he pulled into the parking lot and saw her at the door of the restaurant, reaching to open it, her loose black shirt only partially hiding the shape of the belly growing larger with his son, he wasn't sure how much of himself he could trust.

Cassie's blond ponytail was tight to her head, as though it didn't dare let a piece slip loose. Her white pants looked crisp and clean, in spite of the fact that he knew she'd just come from work. And those unique, angular features...he knew them. Intimately. As though they were a part of him. Partly his.

He made it inside just as she was being seated and followed her to a quiet booth in a back corner. No restroom or service station nearby. Just quiet.

"Wow, this was lucky," he said, sliding in across from her. Assessing as she settled across from him. "As close to being at home as we can get." She looked tired.

And radiant.

"I asked for this booth," she said, giving him a smirk. And reigniting intimate ideas of dinner on a blanket on the beach. From a bag in his truck. Her car.

Anyplace they could be alone together without entering each other's homes.

A hotel room. Or anywhere but there.

Cassie told Wood what she could about her case. She'd spent the day trying to convince the Safe! board of directors that they could keep on its executive director.

They talked about the furniture he was building. He'd taken to sending her pictures every night, showing her his progress.

"What?" he asked her as she sat with her glass of iced purified water with lemon and listened to him talk about a design he wanted to engrave in the crib and cradle panels and then follow with matching design in each drawer face.

"I just can't believe how lucky I am that out of all the files I looked at, I chose you," she said, too tired to keep her mouth completely shut. "Seriously, this baby is going to be so much more loved than I ever imagined, and I was conjuring up enough to keep him satiated for a lifetime."

"Maybe I'm the lucky one." His quiet, serious response surprised her.

"How can you say that? I've upended your life. Forever. Any plans you had to have a traditional family life are just gone…"

"I'm here by choice."

"I know." She hesitated and then decided to finally say something that had been on her mind. "But the type of man you are… You really had no choice. You're *you*, Wood. There's no way you could in good conscience walk away from any child created through your actions, let alone your genes, if you were given the choice. Sometimes I think I was wrong to give you that choice. I put you in an untenable situation."

The look of dismay that crossed his face was gone almost immediately. And engraved on her heart, too. "There is no way, ever, anywhere, that me having access to my son would be a bad thing. You've given me what's probably going to be the greatest gift of my life, Cassie. As tough as this is, I'm happier now than I can ever remember being. I wake up in the morning eager for the day. Even when things go wrong, they don't bother me as much…"

She smiled. And teared up a little. "I feel the same way," she said. And not just because of Alan, though the baby was a huge part of it, too.

They'd ordered, a chicken salad for her and spaghetti for him, but still had no food. She didn't have much of an appetite at the moment, either.

"Besides," Wood said after a silence. "My life hasn't been traditional since the day my father died. And my marriage most certainly wasn't."

It was the first time he'd sounded at all…dissatisfied…with his situation with Elaina and she was too tired to politely let it go.

"Why did you marry her?" she asked, jealousy prompting her need to know. To understand why, even after their divorce, Wood and his ex-wife lived together.

Was she in love with Wood? She couldn't be, could she?

They'd never even kissed.

But when she'd hugged him, he'd hugged her back, and she'd never wanted him to let her go. Not just for the immediate comfort he'd offered, but because he was Wood. And when she was with him, she felt things no man had ever made her feel before.

Made her feel like he was the one she'd been waiting for.

He'd been playing with his straw wrapper. And then pulling his straw in and out of his nearly empty glass of tea. She'd made him uncomfortable.

Crossed one of those invisible lines.

Hopefully he'd come up with a way to save them from the current precipice. One or the other of them always did.

Together they were stronger than their individual selves.

"Elaina was Peter's wife first."

Cassie's jerk of surprise knocked over her glass of water.

The cold liquid spreading between them was nothing compared to the spear he'd just put through her heart.

The man had actually married his brother's wife. She'd heard about a Bible story growing up and read a few historical romance novels as a college student where men did that. But in real life? Wood was *that* guy.

And she got what he'd been trying to tell her all along. The way he tended to her, was right there doing all the right things, making her feel understood and cared for…that wasn't about her in particular. It was just Wood.

He'd married his brother's wife. And even when the relationship had ended, he'd still provided a home. Support.

Because that was Wood.

And if she slept with him out of an overflowing of emotion, acute attraction, yes, but…she couldn't be sure some of her feelings weren't an overabundance of hormones, or deep caring because the man was her child's other biological component…and if she slept with him and then later discovered that what she'd felt hadn't been more than the sum of all that, that she wasn't in love with him on a partner level—he wouldn't walk away.

He'd be right there. For Alan. And for her.

In a way, he'd be like her father—alone, kind of sad, incomplete, a part-time dad.

No matter how much he might be hurting, he'd never walk away. Find a new life for himself. He'd stay the course. Be her friend. And a great father to Alan.

Because that was Wood.

And unless she wanted to carry a lifetime of regret, unless she was willing to be the woman who trapped him, there was no way she could give in to the feelings for him growing inside her.

And no way she could believe any feelings he had for her were real love, either.

Chapter Sixteen

Wood stayed at dinner far longer than he'd planned. Their food arrived, they ate some it, the plates were removed, he paid the bill, and he and Cassie sat there, sharing memories of their childhoods. Which moved into conversation about raising a son with awareness instead of privilege as much as possible. About helicopter and lawnmower parenting—hovering over your child too much, and just plain mowing down everything in his path.

And they talked about siblings. Because her childhood had lacked them. And his entire life had been shaped by having one.

Which led him to think about Alan. And how great it was to have a brother. To *be* a brother.

"If you remain single, do you see yourself having more children?" he asked, in spite of the time pressing at his back. He wasn't going to make it to the workshop that night.

Her brow creased, and a shadow blew over her expression. "I have no idea," she said. "Growing up an only child with three parents, I always told myself I'd have at least two kids, because not having a sibling is so hard, but now..." She shrugged. "I turned out okay. And I've got great memories from a mostly happy childhood. And right now... I just pray that Alan thrives, is born healthy and that I can give him a happy life."

He nodded, saddened that her dreams could have to change but knowing that life seldom worked out as one perceived it should.

"I feel a lot more empowered to give him that happy life now that I know you're going to be a part of it. Not just that he'll know his father, but that his father is you..."

He needed to reach for her hand. To lean across the table and kiss her. And, of course, he could do neither of those things. He wanted to offer up his sperm if she ever did decide to have another child.

"We should probably get going," Cassie said while he was still rejecting the responses he wanted to make to her comment, trying to find one that would be acceptable. She pulled her satchel up onto the table. Retrieved her keys. "I've still got work to do tonight."

It was almost eleven. Standing, he pulled his

keys out of his pocket and followed her out the door. Walked her to her car. Couldn't just let her leave.

"You've given me the greatest gift I've ever had," he told her as they stood beside her door, face-to-face, looking at each other. Not touching, because they couldn't. "And if I had a choice of all the women I've ever known to be the mother of my son, it would still be you."

Her smile was tremulous, her eyes glistening beneath the parking lot security lights. When her arms reached out for him again, as they had Wednesday after the ultrasound, he stepped into them. Wrapped his arms around her. Took a deep breath, memorizing. Brushed his lips against her temple.

And let go.

Wood was barely in his truck when his phone rang. He clicked answer before the caller ID number popped up on his dash screen, grinning. Cassie, being Cassie, was probably now going to apologize for the hug.

"Hey," he answered, his voice soft and filled with the emotion that overtook him any time she was around. Or he thought of her.

An emotion he wasn't willing to analyze.

"Wood?" *Elaina.* She sounded upset.

Instantly changing gears, his chest tight with concern, he said, "Yeah, what's wrong? Where are you?" He'd head in that direction immediately.

"I'm at home. I just…when I got home and you weren't here, and there wasn't a note… I just got worried. You're okay?"

He understood the panic. Immediately. "I'm fine," he said. "Just let time get away from me. I'm on my way home now."

The pause that followed his words made him feel like a heel. They always left notes. Always. And while he no longer needed their contact to be that all-consuming, and didn't think it was good for her, either, he should communicate the change, not just leave her hanging.

He should have let her know he'd be out. Such a simple thing. One he'd always done without thought.

And he'd forgotten.

"It's okay," Elaina said, then, her tone kind. And healthier sounding. "Seriously. Don't feel like you have to come home on my account. I'm actually sorry I called. I just…you're always here…and I thought…"

He'd been in an accident. It happened. Without warning. She'd lost her parents that way. And then Peter. He'd lost, too.

Having family, loving them in all their guises, wasn't easy. Accepting their issues, dealing with their challenges, was sometimes frustrating, sometimes extremely difficult and yet, ultimately, what mattered to him most.

And things still needed to change. He had to talk to her.

"I was already on my way home when you called, El. I'll be there in less than five. You want to share a nightcap before bed?"

They used to do it a lot. Hadn't in a couple of years. Not since the divorce.

"No way. Don't you dare come home on my account. I'm… Just forget I called…"

"El!" he said abruptly, sure she was going to hang up. "I'm serious, I'm almost turning onto our street. I was on my way home. And I'm in need of a drink. You're welcome to join me."

"I'd like that. It's been a long night," she said with a weary sigh. "We lost a patient during a procedure…"

Those words blew his plan to have that talk he needed to have with her that night.

As she described what she legally could of her evening, he listened to every word. Caring. Forgiving her the panic for his lack of a note. And feeling like crap because he wished his life was different. Wished it was Cassie he was going home to. Wished he'd met her before she'd decided to have a family, that he'd dated her, married her, and that the child she was carrying had been conceived by choice from both of them.

"Cass? Do you intend to take the full twelve weeks coming to you for maternity leave?" Troy, the most senior of the partners in her firm, asked as he stopped by Cassie's desk on Thursday of that next week.

Looking away from the case file she'd been reading on her computer screen, Cassie wondered why Troy was asking. She adored him, purely professionally, of course, but also knew that he didn't spend his brainpower on the day-to-day running of the firm he'd started nearly forty years before.

"I haven't decided yet," she told him. If Alan was born healthy, she only planned four to six weeks off work. She needed to keep herself fully invested in the firm's cases or lose some of her position among the other lawyers there. It wasn't discrimination, it was just fact. But beyond that...she needed to work to feel secure. As her family's sole support, she couldn't let herself yearn for the life of a stay-at-home mom. Was pretty sure she'd go nuts if she had it.

And if Alan wasn't born healthy...

"I've got a case that could use your brand of expertise," Troy said, coming more fully into the room. "But it's sensitive, the client is skittish, and it won't be good to change up his lead counsel midstream. Shouldn't be much to do in December and January, but next spring things will really ramp up. I could keep you apprised and ready to roll if you think you'd be back by February."

"I'll be back," she said. And was grinning when she was once again alone in her office. She'd just been given the professional compliment of her career. Troy had given her a very brief rundown of the assignment. The potential merger involved, among others, two parties who'd been through a rancorous divorce, but it would serve all of the companies by bringing them together to give them the market power they needed to survive. Just the thought of it energized her.

Alan *had* to be born healthy. And this was a sign that he would be, she told herself. Because she had to get back to work soon after he was born. The partners had already allowed that she could work from home as much as possible as her due date grew close, and then after maternity leave. And she had interviews set up that next week for a live-in nanny. It would all work out. Was all working out.

But the professional honor didn't make it into the texts she shared with Wood that night. The opportunity she'd been given, her choice to accept and her need to plan accordingly, were all on her as a single parent.

She told him that, for now, she'd had the outcome she'd sought for the nonprofit case, though. The executive director still had her job.

Alan had woken her up three times in the night, playing football, she'd decided. And she was suddenly ravenous at the oddest times during the day— all of which she'd also shared with him.

He continued to send nightly photos of the nursery furniture progress and shared an anecdote or two about his workday. Usually something someone had said. And once when someone hadn't shown up for work and they'd found out he'd been in a car accident.

She felt his pain on that one. Told him so.

He'd shrugged off her concern, saying he was fine.

The following Monday night, when they met for dinner, they'd both been on guard, she figured, based on the fact that both of them had avoided meaningful looks and intimate topics. She told him about the upcoming amniocentesis, scheduled for that Wednesday, possibly the last if everything checked out okay, and he offered to take her as usual. She accepted the offer. As usual.

And when they parted that night, a quick hour after they'd come together with a couple of hours' daylight left ahead of them, they'd hugged, also mutually, like near strangers.

But they'd hugged.

They had an unusual relationship. One that they'd both accepted as permanent.

And they were making it work.

But she wasn't as happy as she'd been when they'd been talking about their feelings. And agreeing to be friends.

Two weeks went by. Amnio results came back good. He'd stayed in the waiting room during the test and had dropped Cassie back off at work immediately after.

He saw her for dinner once a week. Usually on Monday, but she'd had to reschedule for Tuesday once. They texted every night, a way, she'd mentioned a few times, to know that they were each okay. He worked on the furniture. Elaina was out more. Dating, he hoped. It was okay for him to think of living his life alone, but he didn't want it for her.

She had too much to give. Not that he could affect her choice one way or another.

Mostly life was stagnant, and while normally that would be a good thing for him, he was no longer satisfied with just having no catastrophes with which to deal. For a week or two there, when he and Cassie had been making their plans, possibility, and a new-to-him happiness, had abounded. But instead of them flourishing, he felt…stagnated. Elaina, who knew him so well, called him on his dissatisfaction one night the last week in July.

"Are you mad at me?"

They were at dinner downtown on a Wednesday night. Her suggestion. She'd been excited about a new chef she'd heard about at work. And while the food was as good as promised, he'd have been just as happy at home, his shed waiting for him when the dishes were done.

"Of course I'm not mad at you," he told her. "I'm just not used to us getting dressed up and going out during the week," he added, hearing the lameness of his response even before he uttered it.

"It's not just tonight," she said, raising her glass of wine for a sip. "You've seemed...not yourself lately. You frown more. And aren't as relaxed when you're sitting down."

He had no idea what she was talking about until she said, "Even now, look at you...sitting upright, as though you're on trial or something. It was the same when I saw you on the couch last week. It's not like you used to slouch, but you have this way of laying yourself out in a chair like it's as comfortable as a bed..."

Trying to relax in the chair as though that would make everything go away, he told her, "I'm not at all upset with you. I'm preoccupied with the nursery furniture, though. I took on a lot with only five months to complete it all..." He took a breath to continue explaining himself, not at all sure where he was going or when he'd stop.

"You're falling in love with her," she said.

He didn't know if he was or not.

But seeing the look on her face, the compassion, something inside him gave loose. "Tell me something, El..."

"Of course, anything."

She was all the family he had left.

"When you agreed to marry me...for that first little bit...when emotions were running so high and we were both still reeling from everything…you felt things for me, didn't you? You really believed our marriage would work. And, for a few months there, you thought we'd find our happily-ever-after."

He looked her straight in the eye. Needing her honesty. No matter what it might be.

No matter that his brother had been the love of her life. No matter that she might, in some ways, think he was beneath her—or not—for a while there…

She didn't look away. Didn't speak, either.

And he considered that maybe her honest answer was that she'd never felt that way about him. That she was afraid to tell him, thinking it might hurt his feelings.

For a second there, he hoped.

And then she nodded. "I hoped," she said.

But it hadn't happened.

He didn't voice the next question. Did she honestly believe that it wouldn't happen on Cassie's part, either? That the feelings he was getting from her were based on all of the other strong emotions she was feeling at the moment, with her life changing so drastically, with the hormones, and with the baby's health in question, just as Elaina's had been residual from the shock and grief of losing Peter? And her own physical rehabilitation after the accident?

"Just promise me something?" she asked.

He would if he could.

"Don't talk yourself into falling for the mother because of the baby."

He nodded.

"And don't lose sight of the fact that she's going through a lot right now."

She'd pretty much answered the question he hadn't voiced. With another nod, he signaled for their check.

Chapter Seventeen

Cassie was just settling into bed that last Wednesday night in July, a second pillow behind her now that the weight in her belly was starting to expect more from her back, when a text came through. Wood had already texted, earlier in the evening, just to ask about her day. A normal check-in kind of thing. And as usual, she hadn't answered, savoring her moments with him at bedtime. Saving her response until then so that she could have those moments.

Expecting to open the text and see the night's furniture photo, she frowned. He hadn't sent a photo. He'd sent a question instead.

Are you upset about something?

What on earth?

No. Why?

She put her finger to her mouth. Didn't bite at the nail—that was gross and a habit she'd broken long ago—but she did nip at the skin. Waiting. Then turned on the TV, called up a feel-good ancient sitcom on her streaming service. Set the volume low.

Rubbed her belly, wondering if she could somehow wake up Alan, just to reassure herself that he was fine. He'd been a bit quiet for a couple of days. Moving. Just not as much as he sometimes did.

You feel more distant. Maybe I am It's unsettling.

Oh. Well. Scooching a little bit farther down in bed, she snuggled the covers to her breast and looked at the phone screen. Blinking. Staring.

Not sure where to start. Or stop.

But sure of the problem.

The bond between them had clearly become one.

So they had to deal with it.

And maybe communicating via text message was the best way...

I am being extra careful.

Yes. That was good. Maybe that would do it. So many reasons to be careful. No need to dissect the situation.

Careful how? Of what? Why?

She sat up a little bit. Ran her fingers through her hair, ended up with a couple of blond strands in her hand. Shedding extra hair was a pregnancy side effect, she'd learned, and a product of stress. Either way, the woman who trimmed the dead ends off her hair every six months wasn't the least bit worried about it.

Her phone binged Wood's dedicated message tone.

You there?

She'd already seen the words. She'd been staring at the screen when they'd come through.

Yes. Just trying to figure out what to say.

This whole relationship with him was so hard. And worth any amount of work.

I'm going crazy needing to get naked with you. I think about it all the time. But I need you in my life. She deleted that last line. Typed again. I want you in my life. Alan needs you. And so I'm being careful not to screw things up.

She reread. Hit Send.

And nothing happened. The phone went completely silent. Tempted to do what he'd done to her and ask if he was there, she decided not to. She trusted him to choose his own reaction. And trusted herself to follow his lead.

Apologies ahead of time for the crudeness. I have a hard-on that is causing physical distress. Carrying one around has become more common these days. It's the price I'm paying, that I'll gladly pay for the rest of my life, to know my son. And to have you in my life.

The insecure hormonal being that had taken over her body wanted to play coy and ask what he meant. That person who wasn't acting like the Cassie she knew wanted confirmation that he was talking about her. That she'd put him in his current state of physical distress.

Cassie wasn't giving in to emotions that weren't valid. She had enough real-life drama to deal with.

The lawyer in me wants to tell you I'm sorry. The woman in me is over here beaming.

She turned off the television to read the text messages.

So that's it? That's all that's been going on here? That's why you've changed?

She hadn't realized he'd noticed. And was ready to cry happy tears because he had. And cared. But he was acting like her constant desire to jump his bones was a small thing.

Yes.

She'd never had a one-night stand in her life. And didn't want one.

Nor was she going to risk trapping him.

He was taking too long to respond.

I've typed six responses and deleted them all. I'm relieved as hell. And realize we have a situation. I currently have no workable solution.

She smiled. Curled her toes and slid back down until her head was on the pillow, one hand holding her phone, the other cradling her belly.

I feel better, anyway. She hit Send.

Me too

His response was followed by a heart emoji.

She started to cry. Happy tears. He'd just sent her love.

* * *

The next Monday evening, Wood pulled into the parking lot of Cassie's law firm. She'd asked him to meet her at her office for dinner, instead of at a restaurant. She hadn't said why. He supposed she was working late. And that she'd either have ordered in dinner or they'd eat out of vending machines. Either was fine with him.

They'd texted every night since that fateful conversation. Neither of them had mentioned the subject for which they had no solution. But she was no longer being distant with him, and that seemed to make his world right again. At least in the moment. He needed more from her. A whole lot more. Physically and otherwise—physically, more and more—but knew that to rush things could blow the rest of their lives. And any chance he'd have to share his son's life.

She'd told him that the receptionist would be gone when he arrived, but that he could push a buzzer and someone would come let him in. At the time, the plan had seemed fine. He was completely amenable. He wanted to see her.

Then he entered the heavy glass door of a building he'd only ever seen finished from the outside. He'd showered after work, but his shorts and flip-flops definitely felt out of place in the marbled plushness awaiting him. When he'd been picturing vending machines, she'd obviously been telling him fine dining.

At least in terms of setting. So *him* to go for the vending machine version.

He'd been about to turn around and leave, text her, maybe with an excuse to be late or a request for a switch to Tuesday for dinner, when she came out into the lobby through a smaller door off to his left.

In a black dress, matching jacket and black heels with white polka-dot bows on the top, she fit right in with the place. Her long hair was down, flowing around her shoulders, and he could hardly breathe.

"I was watching for you," she said, smiling like she was glad to see him—and like she didn't find one single thing wrong with his appearance. She pointed to a security camera he hadn't yet noticed.

"Come on back," she told him, and because she was happy he was there, because he wanted to spend what time with her he could, he followed her.

Cassie couldn't remember a time when she'd been so unsure of herself. Everything was ready. Including the fact that she knew two of the partners were working late that night, both with evening client appointments, and would be in the office long after Wood was gone. They both knew he was going to be there. They knew she was hosting a small dinner, using the kitchen in the firm to keep the food warm.

They would both assume he was a client. She hadn't said he wasn't.

Nervous and excited for no explicable reason, she

led him to her office door. It wasn't her house, but it was still home to her. She was going to have Wood in her personal space, and that felt so good.

And scary, too. The desire she felt for him was palpable—combustible. So much so that she feared if she even so much as touched his hand, the tight rein she had on herself would explode and they'd both get burned. Sex wasn't going to solve anything for them. To the contrary, it would only complicate a vulnerable, precious situation.

"Here we are," she said, opening the door. The firm's offices were cleaned professionally once a week. She'd cleaned again, anyway, that afternoon. Dusting behind things. Dusting books. Getting a smudge off the windows that had a lovely ocean view. Straightening the knickknacks on her desk—a framed photo of her and her father, taken at his house in front of the Christmas tree they'd decorated together when she was fourteen. A colorful flower pot she'd picked up in Italy. A carved wooden angel a client had given her.

She knew she wasn't going to look anything but pregnant, but she'd worn the dress that showed off her legs best, and had been walking around in her favorite pair of high-heeled shoes all day in spite of the added weight she was carrying.

"This isn't a seduction," she said as soon as he was in the room, afraid to look at his face, to see what his reaction would be. He needed to fit in, to be comfortable in her world. Not to have sex with a randy pregnant woman.

Sex clouded things and they couldn't afford any more lack of clarity. Her father never fit in her mother's world, and they'd all gotten along just fine. She'd grown up well loved. Well taught. Happy. And still alone.

"I'm not locking the door, and I've let the lawyers working late tonight know that I'm available if they need anything. We can be walked in on at any time." She blurted, in case he thought she was coming on too strong with the dress. And the intimacy.

He stood there, barely in the door, looking around, and she couldn't tell what he was thinking. Wasn't even sure he was going to stay.

"I have some papers for you to look over," she blurted. "Legal papers."

His face turned toward her, his expression easy— and inaccessible. "So we're not eating?" His head motioned to the table over by the window. Bearing glasses with ice, water and little lemon slices floating on top.

"I made cabbage rolls again yesterday," she said. "It's what I do when I'm working out a problem in my mind. Cook, I mean, in general, not just cabbage rolls…"

"What papers did you have for me to look at?"

Okay, so she should have given him some warning. She'd just landed on the idea the day before, when she'd been cooking, in an attempt to find some clarity on their situation. More than anything, she'd needed to have him in her space. Legitimately in her life.

And knowing that there was a fine line between him playing a part in her world, or being completely out of it.

She was tired of feeling like they were something scandalous.

Lustful, unsatisfied illegitimate friends who'd met over a medical procedure. He looked uncomfortable.

"I'm sorry," she said, standing there with her hands clasped below her pregnant belly.

"For what?"

"You can go. And we'll be fine."

Shaking his head, he stepped closer to her. Still with that foot of distance between them, but closer than he'd been. Close enough that she could smell that he'd showered recently. And see the shine of light in his eyes. "I have no desire to leave," he told her. "I'm just…kind of pleased," he told her. "This is nice. Completely unexpected. And…smart, too. You've thought of everything."

She'd tried. "I hope you like beef and rice cabbage rolls."

"I do."

His hands were in his pockets, pulling his shorts taut. That was the only reason she noticed the bulge there.

"I thought we should talk, really talk. And in

order to do that effectively, we needed privacy. And no waitstaff watching us and stopping by to see that we were okay."

He nodded. Still watching her. Her body was heating up by the second. She could only imagine the man's effectiveness when he was actually trying to turn on a woman.

It seemed like he broke a spell when he turned his head toward her desk. "I'm a bit confused about the paperwork you want to go over, though," he said.

"You don't have to agree to anything or sign anything," she told him, suddenly worried that he'd feel ambushed when, in fact, she was trying to gift him. "Not if you don't want to. I just…" She shrugged.

He nodded, walked toward her desk, took a seat in one of the chairs she'd dusted, and for a second there she was jealous of the leather that got to touch his backside.

This wasn't going well. Not at all as planned. And she'd given it so much effort.

Where was her poise? Her talent for taking control of a situation and putting everyone at ease? She'd never been in her office and not had it.

The paperwork was supposed to come at the end of the evening. Preferably with a newly determined resolution for their issue. You didn't sign deals before you'd worked out the terms. She knew this. And had blurted it right out there anyway.

The man definitely kept her hot and flustered around him.

Moving behind her desk would give her confidence, or so she thought. Standing there, looking at him sitting where many of her clients, paralegals, peers and partners had sat over the years, she had a sudden vision of him taunting her until she brushed everything from her desk to the floor, climbed on top of it and asked him to join her.

So, yeah, probably the paperwork would be best. Out of order and all. Yanking on the top drawer handle, she pulled out the folder she'd prepared that afternoon.

Opened it.

"I've laid out terms for after Alan's born," she said in the most professional voice she could muster. "This is just my version, meant to be a starting place for us. I figured you could read them and then if you'd like to proceed, offer any changes, we can discuss and then I'll have the final papers drawn up for both of us to sign."

She sounded like a prosecutor. Not a mediator.

Not good.

Thinking about the cabbage rolls warming in the kitchen down the hall, the salad in the refrigerator, wondering if dinner would be ruined before it began, she slid the folder across the desk. Sat down to wait.

Wood didn't move. "I'll sign," he said.

"But…"

"Whatever it is…if you're asking, finding it important, want it, whatever, I agree. Legally, he's all yours. I've never intended to take any of that from you. If you need it, I'll sign."

"Wood, not that I'm your lawyer, but as your friend who's a lawyer, I need to advise you not to do that. In the first, and most basic, place, you shouldn't ever, ever, ever sign anything without fully reading the document first. And second, I could be asking you for child support in here."

A lot of women would—given that he wanted to be acknowledged as Alan's father.

She was getting more agitated by the second. Needing to kiss his infuriating mouth so it would quit saying things that were throwing her off course.

Wood sat forward. "What you don't seem to get is that I'm okay with whatever it is you need, Cassie. I'll make it work. Because being the boy's father means that much to me."

She teared up. Another first for that chair. That room. He took the folder.

"But if it means that much to you, I'll read every word."

She nodded. Good. "It does." Maybe now she could get back on track.

"I just have one request."

"Of course, what?"

"Can we please eat dinner first? I knocked half

my sandwich off a scaffolding at lunch, and I'm starving."

And they could talk about other things over dinner.

If he didn't want to be a full father to her child, she still had some time to enjoy his company.

And his sexy body across from her, in the privacy of her office.

Chapter Eighteen

"This table is as nice as any you'd get at the finest restaurants in the city," Wood said, putting his napkin across one knee as he sat down opposite Cassie.

He'd offered to help her bring in dinner from the kitchen, but when she'd said she could handle it, he didn't press. Chances were she wouldn't want her associates to see him—in shorts, not the business attire of a client—serving up a meal together with her as though they were in their own home.

As she'd returned, everything neatly on the trolley she'd rolled in, he understood that she really hadn't needed him.

"The view is one of the reasons I chose this office," she told him then, removing the covers from their dishes.

He looked from the magnificent view of the sun setting over the ocean to the steaming food on his plate. And knew an intimate thrill even from that. He was about to taste her cooking.

To have a meal she'd prepared specifically for him.

What kind of a sap was he turning into?

And why?

"You entertain here often?" he asked after he'd consumed half the food on his plate in total silence. The food was that good. He really was starving.

And he couldn't say the things that were on his mind. Like how perfect her plan had turned out to be. How beautiful she looked sitting across from him. And how much he wished he had that view every meal, every day.

It wasn't fair to her. Or to himself.

"This is a first," she said, in answer to his question. "Sharing a meal with someone here. In this room. I eat lunch here most days that I don't have an appointment, but there's a room down the hall where we generally have working meals with clients. It's a conference room, but it is always stocked with napkins, silverware, condiments, glasses and an assortment of drinks."

One point stuck. He was a first for her. He liked that.

"So..." She spoke the one word, fork suspended,

in a voice that made him look at her. And then she just sat there.

"What?"

"I've come up with some potential plans for dealing with our sexual attraction to each other."

The bite going down got stuck. Wood swallowed a second time. Coughed. Took a sip of water. And then said, "I'm listening." Like a guy watching a train wreck as it happened. Fascinated and filled with dread.

"One. We continue to talk about it, take the mystery out of it, treat it like the rain. It's natural, serves a purpose, and yet, we don't want to get caught in it...recognizing the signs when they come for what they are, knowing they'll pass and continuing on in spite of them."

Initially, he liked the theory. But... "Sometimes rain comes without warning, and people get caught in it."

Sucking in her lower lip—creating a *downpour* for him—she nodded. "Right," she said. "So, number two. We find other lovers pronto."

He shook his head. "You're six months pregnant. Probably not a lot of guys, at least not any that you'd want to be with, are going to be open to casual sex with you right now." At least he hoped to God not. "And I'm not into being with one woman while imagining she's someone else."

He was fairly certain that any sex he tried to

have right then would feature Cassie whether she was present or not.

"Number three. We do it once. Just get it out of our systems. No foreplay. No extraneous touching or exploring. No looking into each other's eyes…"

His penis favored that one in big measure. *Huge* measure. "I thought you said this wasn't a seduction." He was desperate to maintain control.

"It's not."

"Yet you look like you're on a date."

She didn't even blink as she met his gaze. "I'm twenty-six and a half weeks pregnant," she said. "I feel like a tub. Kind of hard to discuss sexual attraction in any legitimate way feeling that way."

He had no basis with which to argue that one.

But… "I can't speak for you, Cassie, but there's no way once would be enough for me. No matter how much you try to strip it down."

He wanted to strip her down. Right then. Right there. In front of a sunset that would grace the entire world within a day.

"So, four. We each take accountability and responsibility for our own needs, tending to them privately, alone."

He came a little as she said the words. And then his body started to relax. He wasn't going to get any. "I'll be thinking about you," he told her, looking her straight in the eye.

"I'll be thinking about you, too."

* * *

Wood read the paperwork while Cassie was clearing up dinner. It would have been good if he'd found her work distasteful. Overkill. Invasive.

"So?"

He took a second to form words that didn't send them into another tailspin. To form cohesive, father-like thoughts as he reeled with the unbelievable gift she was giving him. The honor.

And the responsibility. Would he be good enough at fatherhood to be worthy of her offer? "You want to name me on the birth certificate. To give me legal visitation rights. And to name me as his guardian in the event anything happens to you." He still couldn't believe what he'd just read.

"No custodial rights," she said, perhaps thinking she sounded stern. He wanted to lay her down on the couch with him and kiss them both crazy. "And no financial support, either," she said. "Not for anything. I'm willing to listen to your opinion on all major issues, to give you a chance to have one, but all final decisions are mine, just like I said before. And put in there. I need to be the only one supporting him. You can't be the nice guy that comes around and buys him everything he wants. All purchases, even birthday and Christmas presents, have to go through me."

He'd read all of the legalese. Twice. Understood it all, too. It wasn't his first contract. By far.

"And, as you see there, I release you, and anyone else who could at any point in the future be petitioning on Alan's behalf, from ever coming after you for child support. That statement is mandatory if you're to be named on the birth certificate, because legally, your name there makes you open to that obligation."

He nodded. Was just...speechless. Could hardly believe what he was reading. And had no idea how to proceed. She was making dreams come true he hadn't even known he'd had.

"It's just... I need 'us,' our relationship, to have a legal definition. In writing. Before we end up doing something stupid and trying to make it into something it might not be."

She was confusing him. Partially because he was reeling with the whole new life she'd just handed him in the form of official documents. Couldn't get much more legitimate than that.

"I don't think I'm following you."

"You and I. We're...or rather, I, am...we can't... You have a history of becoming what those in your family need you to be, regardless of your personal feelings. And I...grew up feeling torn up inside, all the time, because I knew my father was hurting and alone. He married my mother because she was pregnant and she married him, I'm sure, in part because she was so vulnerable having just lost her father. You married Elaina to take care of her when your brother died. People do things in the heat of intense emotion, and it doesn't work. I can't take a chance that we're going to fall into that same trap. And someone ends up like my dad, lonely, alone, hurting for the rest of

his or her life. Or like you and Elaina, divorced, but
still sharing a house." She shook her head. "This...
feeling...or whatever is between us... I don't trust
it because there's no way for us to know if we're
caught up in the intense emotions of the baby and
him—maybe not being well, just like my mom and
dad and you and Elaina..."

Some of the elation he'd been feeling faded...but
not much. Not in that moment. She made perfect
sense. Was saying what he'd already figured out on
his own. And she was still inviting him into her life,
into his son's life, permanently.

He read the paperwork again, key sentences, just
to make sure he was getting it right.

He didn't like the money part but didn't worry all
that much, either. A simple phone call, making Alan
the sole beneficiary to his financial portfolio, with
Cassie as executor, would take care of that.

"I've done all the talking," Cassie broke the silence.

"I'm listening. Reading."

"So, give me your input."

"Give me a pen. And a notary—I'm assuming
one of the lawyers you mentioned still being here
is licensed."

"Why would you say that?"

"Because I know you." He grinned. "You're always prepared."

She started to smile and then sat up straighter in
the armchair across from him. He wanted to tell her

that he could see up her dress, but he didn't want her to put her legs together. They were making room to accommodate her belly. And he was allowing himself the view. A crumb from the dessert he couldn't taste.

When he glanced over, he saw her watching him look, and he wondered if she'd known all along. He'd caught her staring at his fly, too, earlier. Probably not smart. But nothing he was going to deny them, either.

"I'm serious, Wood," she said then, her hand on her rounded stomach again. So many nights he'd imagined touching that bump. Feeling his baby inside her. "Let's talk about the agreement. Is there anything that makes you uncomfortable?"

"Of course there is."

"Okay, so what is it? Let's talk about it."

He shook his head. "There's no need. I don't like that I can't help you both out financially," he said. "I can afford it. I want to do it. But I understand why you need it to be this way. I actually agree with it. I just wish things were different. They aren't, and I'm ready to sign. I want to sign, Cassie. I want to be locked in."

"You're sure?" Her head tilted as she studied him.

"I'm sure."

"I'll add a clause that offers you a forty-eight-hour right to rescind, for any reason," she said.

He wasn't rescinding anything. "Do what you have to do."

She grinned. Nodded. He nodded back.

Picking up her cell phone from the arm of the chair where she'd laid it when she sat down, she pushed one button.

"Marilyn? You can come in now," she said. And then to Wood, "My paralegal. I asked her to stop by on her way home from dinner with her husband, unless she heard from me not to bother."

He broke into a full-out smile. Glad as hell she was as thorough as she was. He was a signature away from being a father.

And being legally linked to his son and to Cassie for the rest of his life.

Cassie called her mother as soon as she got home that night. She didn't change. Didn't even kick off her shoes. Sitting on her sofa, she just dialed. Susan was a night person and Richard wasn't, so she figured they could have a private conversation. And she needed one. Telling her mother about dinner with Wood, leaving out the bit about their physical situation and the sexual solution they'd chosen together, she did tell her mother about the binding legal agreement they'd signed, and finished with, "I'm excited, like I just got married, and all he did was sign a joint parenting agreement," she said. "Do you think that could mean that I have real feelings for him? Beyond the pregnancy and hormones and all that?"

A short silence followed her words, and Cassie waited, half holding her breath.

"I don't have that answer." Susan's disappointing response took a while in coming.

"What I do know is this…" Cassie sat upright, fully focused as her mother continued, "It's not a mistake, sweetie. I can't tell you why it's happening this way for you. I can only tell you that things happen for reasons. And that how you handle the seemingly impossible is what defines you."

"I can't sleep with him."

"I'm not saying that."

"I know. *I* am. I can't take a chance with a man's life. Wood isn't the type of guy who'd move on if it didn't work out. He'd stick around and continue to be a great dad to Alan, and our friendship would be ruined. Or at least stilted. Like you and Dad were. How do I know I'm not just feeling so strongly toward him because of what he's doing for me? And because I really want a traditional family? And maybe even a second child?"

"I feel like I'm failing you, sweetie, but I just don't have that answer."

"So what do I do?"

"What would your father say? He was about the wisest man I ever knew when it came to dealing with the problems life left on the doorstep."

"He'd say to be grateful for what I have." Alan. Wood's friendship for life. A career she loved. The support of family and friends…

"Sounds right to me."

Chapter Nineteen

Wood waited for Elaina to get home that night. He needed to tell her about the agreement he'd signed with Cassie. In the first place, Alan was officially a part of their family. In the second, he had nothing to hide.

And in the third, he felt like celebrating.

He was going to tell his men at work the next day, too.

And probably anyone else with whom he happened to come in contact who'd listen to him babble about it.

Elaina didn't pull in until after midnight, had unsavory-looking marks staining her scrubs and exhaustion all over her face. She smiled when she saw him by the door leading into the kitchen. Gave him a wave as she entered her suite from her own door, and that was that.

His news was too huge for him to accept an exhausted reaction. Too huge to put on her when she'd obviously had a long hard day and just needed to rest.

Elaina would approve. He already knew that. Not that he needed her approval. He just needed his friend—and ex-wife—to know. It didn't seem real until she—his only family—knew.

That thought in mind, when the crew broke for lunch the next day, he grabbed his bagged sandwich and ate it in his truck on the way to the hospital. He didn't visit Elaina often at work, but he knew which floor to go to, whom to see to find out where she was. Maybe it would have been better if he'd waited, rather than appearing in dusty jeans and a sweaty T-shirt at his sister-in-law's place of employment, but there was no guarantee she'd be home that night. If something happened to him, she needed to know he'd changed his trust papers, giving everything to Alan, not her.

Like she'd care. Elaina had never been interested in his money. His support, yes, but not the cash flow.

He just needed her to see his right to his son in writing. To know it existed. It was that important to him. Too important for a phone call.

As it happened, she was in the cafeteria, so his interruption had been well timed.

He saw her almost immediately. Headed in her direction, folder in hand, and thought a better plan might have been to save his lunch and eat with her. It took another second or two before he realized that the laugh he'd just heard roll across the room had come from her—and the deeper mirth from her companion.

The sound of her laughter surprised him. Was almost unfamiliar sounding. He couldn't remember the last time he'd heard her laugh like that.

Then it hit him that Elaina wasn't alone. Nor was she sitting across from an associate. She was seated right next to the guy—taller than her, in a white doctor's coat—and their shoulders were touching, their backs to him. Elaina turned to look at the guy and then jerked back.

She'd obviously caught a glimpse of Wood in her peripheral vision, because she jumped up. Her brow creased in concern, she hurried the few steps it took to get to him.

"Wood? Why are you here? Is everything okay?"

"Fine," he told her. "Everything's fine." He looked toward the other guy, only saw the left side of the back of his head and ear. Curious as hell, he wanted to check the guy out, but he wasn't going to make more of it than it was. Or freak her out.

Elaina took his hand, pulled him around a pillar. "Don't make a big deal of this," she said. "He's new to town, an internist I met on a case a couple of months ago. We have lunch together sometimes."

Her hand was trembling. She cared about this other doctor more than she wanted him to know. More than she could admit to herself, he guessed.

He remembered back to the beginning of the summer, Elaina saying she was going to buy lunch at work. Hoped to God this guy was the reason why. That he was managing to find a way into Elaina's heart.

"Does he know about Peter?"

"Who around here doesn't?"

"Yes, but did you tell him?"

That was the key. Elaina never talked about Peter to anyone but him, as far as Wood knew.

When she nodded, he smiled.

"You like the guy."

"I think he's funny," she said. "He's entertaining. And that's it."

And had to be wondering why in the hell his lunch companion had just deserted him so suddenly. He hadn't turned around to find out. Not yet, anyway.

Wood had to go. He wasn't going to mess this up. Not by scaring the guy off. Or pushing Elaina.

"Okay, well, I just came to show you this," he said, holding out the folder. "It's an agreement I signed last night with Cassie. I have another copy at home. I'm just… I wanted you to see it. To know." He smiled, telling himself there was no reason for him to feel the least bit sad, or like he was no longer needed. He and Elaina would always be family.

Telling her to enjoy her lunch, sincerely meaning the words, he left.

And thought about the son he was going to have.

Life happened as it was meant to. And it was good.

Now that the agreement was signed, Cassie had a whole list of things coming to her to talk to Wood about. She hit him with the first one by text message Tuesday night. He'd sent her a picture of the cradle he'd sanded that night in preparation for the first coat of varnish. With her air conditioner on, blowing out the humid August heat, she laid against a series of throw pillows on the couch in nothing but her sleeveless cotton nightgown, her belly serving as a holding table for her phone.

Do you want to be present when he's born?

The question had seemed pertinent when it had hit her earlier in the day. Seeing it typed out, not so much so. Yes, a father witnessing the birth of his son was accepted and even miraculous to some. But not when the parents weren't a couple.

Already typing to rescind the offer, she stopped when his response came through.

Yes.

She could have sworn her belly moved at the response. Alan had been more active for the past week or so, kicking at random times throughout the day—and night—but there's no way the boy could have read his father's response and have had a reaction to it.

He could be feeling the clenching in her lower parts, though. Reacting to that.

There's a one-day class available through the Parent Portal for women in their third trimester and their coaches. I was going to have a friend drive up from San Diego to go with me, but if you'd like to be there, I'll tell her she doesn't need to come up.

It was asking a lot more than just a background identity in her son's life. Maybe too much for him. If he said no, she'd have a boundary she wouldn't cross again.

Or so she told herself while she practically held her breath waiting for his response.

Sitting up, she put down her phone. What was she doing here? Creating some kind of fantasy where she and Wood were the parents she'd always dreamed her child would have?

Because that wasn't this. At all. And she had to make certain she knew that.

Give me date and time.

Was that a yes? Attending a parenting class wasn't something that you just did if the time worked out.

They're offered on a regular basis. 8:30–3:30, various days. I plan to do a Saturday. Goes over third trimester, what to expect in the last stages and then labor and birth.

They cost seventy-five dollars, too, but she was covering that part, no matter who went with her.

Pick a Saturday and let me know when to pick you up.

Well, now wasn't he assuming a lot?

He'd taken her to all three of her major tests—of course they wouldn't suddenly start meeting at the clinic.

I'd prefer to be asked if I'd like you to pick me up. She hit Send, in spite of the fact that she knew full well she was being cantankerous.

Noted.

It wasn't his fault she'd chosen a sperm donor who was so nice she was becoming addicted to him. Most definitely wasn't his fault that she was alone, making all the plans, the decisions. The choice had been fully, consciously hers. And what she still wanted.

Just…

Nothing.

It was time to count her blessings and remember all of the things for which she had to be grateful.

And she added a new one.

She was grateful that there was still a possibility that she'd meet a man who moved her as much as Wood did without all the other emotional baggage in the way.

Wood was just finishing dinner Wednesday night—meat loaf and asparagus—when Elaina came through the door of her suite into the kitchen.

"I thought you were going out with friends tonight," he said. "I would have knocked and let you know there was extra…"

"I already ate," she told him. "We met early for appetizers, and I didn't want to stay and drink. I was thinking maybe you and I could watch a movie or something."

He had furniture waiting to be built.

And this was Elaina, probably in an emotional flux because her new relationship, if it was one, was now known to him. Making it that much more real.

He'd told her, and himself, many, many times over the years, as he'd told his brother on his deathbed, that he'd always be there for Elaina. And so he did his dishes and put leftovers in containers for her, while she changed into sweat shorts and a T-shirt, her long, dark hair loose around her shoulders. She poured herself a glass of tea, offered him one and put a bag of microwave popcorn in while he chose the movie. If life were carefully choreographed, it could look like a normal night in a normal home.

Instead of a space in Nowheresville being used as a hideout from all that life had to offer. And dish out.

A space he'd created for her to hide out.

And him?

He didn't see himself beating a path to Cassie's doorstep...begging her to give them a chance. Assuring her they could make it work.

He opened the streaming service, and she chose a thriller drama neither of them had seen. And fifteen minutes into the movie, he knew something was up. Elaina wasn't eating her popcorn. Hadn't touched it since she set the bag on the coffee table. She wasn't drinking her tea. And she wasn't watching the movie.

"Why did you really want to spend the evening with me?" he asked. He knew her well.

And to her credit, she didn't try to convince him she was really into movie watching. "It's...things are changing. I knew we'd both move on at some point. Hoped it would be once I was making enough money to get a place, and I am now. But..."

Was she getting ready to tell him she was moving out? "But what?"

"I just... I'm afraid that you know that the time's getting closer, and that it's pushing you into something. I just...can't bear the thought of you being hurt again, Wood. I'd feel so much better if you were dating someone. Hanging out with a woman who just liked you for you, not someone who needs something from you."

That feeling she always seemed to raise in him, the one where he wasn't good enough as he was, wasn't worthy, reared its head, and for the first time, instead of acknowledging the possible truth in his feelings, he got just plain pissed instead.

"I'm not a damned kindergartner, El. I'm older than you are and quite versed in the ways of the world. And while, yes, I do have a tendency to like to take care of others, I also am quite proficient at taking care of myself. I've survived just fine for thirty-six years."

"Life is about a lot more than surviving. I want to see you with someone who adores you. Who cares more about you being happy than her own happiness."

The way Elaina and Peter had felt for one another.

"Point taken," he said and looked back to the movie that had played on without them. "For the record, Cassie and I have decided, together, not to pursue a relationship between the two of us. I am not on the verge of being hurt. Now eat your popcorn."

Wood went to bed that night without sending Cassie a picture of baby furniture. He did text to tell her goodnight, though.

Then he lay in the dark. Tossing and turning. Aching for a woman who made him happier than he'd ever been, and who, at the same time, left him feeling as though he'd never be enough.

Yeah, their situation was fraught with emotional upheavals that had nothing to do with dating or sex or romantic love. Yeah, it would be a bad time to start something.

But the bottom line was that Cassie didn't trust herself to love him. Didn't trust that what she felt might become love.

And he didn't trust her to love him, either.

Wondering how in hell, when all he'd ever wanted to do was look out for those he cared about, his life had twisted so far out of control.

Chapter Twenty

Cassie looked forward to birthing class like she used to look forward to Christmas. Not only did it make the fact that she was actually going to have a baby of her own seem more real, and she was going to get so much information that would all be part of the process, all like little presents to her, but she was going to get to spend the entire day with Wood.

Their first ever.

She'd be happy with a healthy baby and days with Wood as her only gifts for the rest of her life.

She'd scheduled them for the first Saturday in September. She was roughly thirty-two weeks along, according to her latest scan, and everything was looking good. They'd done another impromptu ultrasound in the office just to confirm. She'd texted Wood as soon as she'd found out it was happening. And again when it was done. He'd responded in spite of the fact that he'd been on the job.

He still texted every night. They still met once a week for a meal. He was great when he was with her, but there was something different about him, too. She couldn't place it. It wasn't like before, when the tension between them had been building. But telling herself to quit borrowing trouble, and being thankful for what she had, she soaked up all of him that she was allowed to have.

She'd been gone for a weekend, too, to see her mom and Richard, and on another overnighter to San Diego when the monthly Sunday friend brunch was down there. Her workload was as steep and satisfying as ever, and her paralegal had made plans to throw a baby shower for her. Her college friends were throwing another. And her mom was having one at home, too, for everyone she'd known growing up.

All in all, life was better than she'd imagined it would be when she'd first set out on her quest to have a family on her own.

And still, her heart ached in a way she hadn't known it could.

On her darkest nights, she cried some, wishing Wood could be with her. But she knew, even before the light of day came, that she didn't have the right to upend his life when hers was in such flux.

She'd been told to dress comfortably for the birthing class and chose a pair of black yoga pants with a black tank and an oversize, lightweight white T-shirt on top. She'd debated about her hair the most, not wanting to lie back and have a ponytail knot to contend with, and ended up with a loose bun. Packed a bag with extra snacks and bottles of water, though the clinic was providing a lunch, and still she was ready to go fifteen minutes before Wood was due to arrive.

They didn't talk much on the way there.

For the moment, it was enough. She was with him. And they were going to spend a whole day learning about the birth of their son.

A few seconds in the classroom, though, and Cassie wasn't feeling anywhere near as calm about things.

"I'm by far the oldest one here," she told Wood as they picked a spot to settle in.

"You look better than half of them," Wood whispered, and she smiled, as she figured he'd meant her to. She didn't really believe she looked better than anyone else in the class. But maybe…she looked as good as half of them. She'd never been a pretty girl. Interesting, people always said about her features. She'd never cared overly much. Until she sat in a classroom filled with pregnant women and their coaches with Wood beside her, wanting him to be glad she was the one of them he was with.

Don't sweat over the things you can't change, her

father used to say to her. Save your energy for the things you can.

What those were at the moment, she wasn't sure, but if the waves were giving her this day with Wood, then she was going to accept the gift. They'd bring bad along the way, but the way to deal with that was to enjoy the good.

So she would.

Halfway through the morning, Wood sat with Cassie on their floor mat, helping her practice different positions while in labor. The latest involved sitting on a rubber ball. Couples were laughing and talking. Cassie had chosen a mat on the end, so they only had someone on one side of them, two twenty-something women who'd been married a couple of years and were having their first child. They'd used some new technology at the Parent Portal that had enabled one of them to gestate the baby and then have it implanted in the other, allowing both of them to have grown it inside them.

As the women next to him laughed again, Cassie's ball rolled, and she slipped. All the information he'd learned in class fled Wood's brain as he grabbed for her before she took a fall to the floor. Lessons didn't matter—keeping Cassie safe did.

Instead of falling, she settled back down to the ball with his hands planted firmly on her back and lower stomach, on the downward slope of the baby she carried, steadying her.

And just like that he was touching her in a way that made him hungry for things he didn't want to want. An unforeseen rainfall.

He waited one last second to make sure she was good, and in that one second Alan said hello to him. Quite clearly, with a push right against his hand. Their first-ever high five.

"Did you feel that?" Cassie asked and then met his gaze. Apparently, the look on his face told her he had. Tears sprang to her eyes. She blinked them away, and the teacher gave the class further instructions.

Once again, without warning, he'd become someone different than he'd been. He'd become a father, biologically, legally, and now he'd officially bonded with his son.

By lunchtime, Cassie felt like she had a Christmas tree without lights, complete with presents wrapped in paper and topped with bows. Wood was there, but he wasn't, too. He was perfectly attentive, considerate, aware of her, focused, even, yet there was part of him that seemed to be absent. She couldn't explain it, so she couldn't really ask him about it.

They'd all been given boxed lunches of veggie wraps, a fresh fruit bowl and a cookie. Some were eating on their mats. Others had moved to across the room. Cassie asked Wood if they could go outside to a bench that she'd seen when they'd pulled in that morning. Off to the side of the clinic, it sat alongside a six-foot-tall fountain with flowers and greenery around it. A gift, a plaque read, from the Randolph family in thanks for Jimmy, the child they'd conceived with help from the Parent Portal.

She was happy for the Randolphs. And eager to have some time alone with Wood. She wanted to talk about him feeling the baby move.

They talked about things they'd learned in the class. He asked if she was afraid of going into labor. She was a little nervous but not nearly as scared as she was of losing him. She didn't articulate that part.

But when lunch was two-thirds of the way done, and she knew they'd have to get back, she couldn't face the idea of wasting an afternoon with him as she felt they'd wasted the morning. He wanted to be there. She knew that. But something was wrong.

"Is it something you can talk about?" she asked, leaving her cookie wrapped and in the box.

"What?"

"Whatever it is that's going on in your life."

He didn't deny that there was something. That fact hit her almost at once. If he couldn't tell her, he couldn't. She'd accept that.

"Elaina said something the other night—" He broke off. Glanced away, a frown on his face. "About moving out, mostly, but about life, too. It just got me thinking…"

Which explained nothing. And everything?

"Can I ask you something?"

"Of course." He glanced over at her.

"Are you, maybe, still a little in love with her?"

"What? Are you kidding? Not at all." The shock in his voice was evident. As was the truth in his gaze. "I love her. I'd have made the marriage work and found happiness there, but I was never in love with her. It's hard to explain... I promised my brother, while he was dying, that I'd take care of her. With him gone, she had no insurance, would have had to switch to some expensive, six-month policy...we didn't know, for a while there, if she'd ever walk again..."

He looked her straight in the eye as he told her he'd never been in love with his ex-wife, and she believed him.

Was sad, for no reason that made a bit of sense to her.

And was honestly relieved, too.

The highlight of Wood's week became their Monday nights at the little diner outside town. By the third week in September, he was almost beginning to feel like he had his new normal. Mondays with Cassie, going through his routine and text messages to send him off to sleep each night. The furniture was going to be done in plenty of time. He'd been spending his weekends in his shed nonstop, except the one time he went out with Elaina and some of her friends. And he took whatever weeknights he had free out there, as well. Retro was getting to the point of heading out her doggy door as soon as Wood got up to do the dinner dishes, and she would be waiting by the shed door when he got outside.

Days on the job hadn't changed, other than various guys he'd known over the years—electricians, inspectors, his contractor—coming up to congratulate him when they visited the site. He'd had no idea he was noteworthy enough for his news to spread so far, or so quickly. And the rest of his life…was in a state of calm. At least until something changed again. Like his son coming into the world.

Or Elaina telling him she was moving out.

That third week in September, he'd just finished off the one beer he'd allowed himself, had told the waitress she could take away what was left of his steak, and smiled at Cassie as she asked to have the rest of her chicken salad to take home with her. She'd ordered the family size and finished off more than half of it.

"What?" she asked, looking over at him. His knee had bumped hers under the table one night several weeks before, and she hadn't moved hers away. He hadn't, either. Ever since then, their knees met, and held on, for the duration of dinner.

"Your appetite seems to increase each week," he told her.

"I know, but I'm not gaining as much as the doctor wants me to gain," she told him. "I'm down about five pounds from where she wants me. But during the last month I'm supposed to gain a pound a week, and I can't imagine carrying that much more weight around everywhere."

She'd been getting a little more tired more easily, and he wished he could follow her home, rub her back for her. Do something to help her with the physical stress of carrying his child.

"It's all in your belly," he told her.

"That's what everyone says."

He wasn't everyone. He noticed every curve of her body, and...

"I have to tell you something." Cassie's pronouncement wiped all other thoughts from his brain. No good news came from a beginning like that.

"What?" Was she moving away? Had she fallen in love with someone else? How would he know? He knew her favorite color, every food she liked and didn't like, what movies made her cry, the name of her dog when she was growing up, but he didn't really know anything that she did during the week. Except work.

Had she met someone? Started dating?

The whole idea just felt wrong. From the bottom up.

"My paralegal, Marilyn, asked me why we weren't getting married. She thinks I'm in love with you."

He stared, certain that he hadn't heard her right. That the beer had been spiked and had gone to his head. The vulnerable look in those sweet blue eyes told him differently. He had no idea what to say. Wasn't even sure what he thought.

Her expression crumpled, and she seemed to sink down into herself while insisting on holding his gaze and remaining upright. The obvious battle she was fighting called for more from him.

"Are you?"

Tears flooded her eyes. She swallowed so hard he could see her throat move with the effort. "I don't let myself go there," she said. "I don't trust myself to know, for one thing. Not with everything else in my life so out of whack. But when she asked the question, my first response wasn't even about me. It was about you."

"About me?" He didn't want to be having the conversation. Waited for it to be over so he could do cleanup duty. Make things better.

She wasn't saying anything. He'd been left to get them out of it. "What did you say?"

"That you're so helpful and attentive because it's who you are, not because you have particular feelings for me. Other than this odd sexual attraction, but the more I think about it, the more it makes sense that we're just feeling that because I'm having our baby, which heightens our physical awareness and connection, and because we know we can't have sex. It's human nature to want what you can't have."

She sounded like the lawyer she was. Presented the case in the way it made the most sense.

"Am I wrong?" she asked while her words were still running through his mind.

He shrugged, needing to refute her but finding no clear evidence with which to convince her. Or himself.

She didn't trust herself to know if she loved him. He'd already known that. But...not trusting his feelings for her?

"I'd marry you tomorrow if you'd have me."

Tears sprang to her eyes. "You married Elaina, too. I don't want to lose you, Wood. To lose your friendship. I don't want things to be awkward between us for Alan's sake. We're already starting off odd, with you being my sperm donor, not my lover. I just... I don't want to lose you."

She didn't want to lose him.

Leaning forward, he looked her straight in the eye. "You aren't going to lose me," he promised her from the very depths of him. "Not ever."

Cassie was at work on Wednesday, the seventh of October, when her water broke. No warning. No cramping, just sitting at her desk at the computer, she suddenly felt the flooding sensation, like she'd wet her pants. She was only thirty-six weeks along. Still had another two to four to go until her due date. She hadn't even had her first internal exam yet. Alan had been kicking up a storm, though. Had he broken something in there too early?

Thoughts flew while her system processed, and then, still sitting there, she grabbed her phone. It was like she was frozen to the seat. Afraid to move, to make matters worse. She'd put her doctor's office on speed dial when she'd first been inseminated, was put through immediately, answered the questions like an automaton and was told to make her way to the hospital. But she was told not to worry. Since she hadn't even started contractions, it would likely be hours yet before she delivered, but…one way or another, she was going to be having her baby that day.

And then, still mostly numb, she called Wood. Didn't text him, called.

He picked up on the first ring.

"Cassie? What's wrong?" At ten in the morning, he was still looking at a full day of work.

"My water broke." She'd meant to say more. To tell him what the doctor said, but her words just stopped.

"I'm on my way."

She nodded. That was probably a good plan. "I'm scared, Wood. I know it's irrational, but I'm scared. It's too early."

"You're eight months along. A little early, but out of the serious danger zone. A lot of healthy babies are delivered at eight months."

How did he know?

She remembered the reading material they'd been

given in birthing class. There'd been something about that in there. He'd obviously read it all, too.

"Are you in your truck yet?" she asked, suddenly aware of what a mess she was. Of the fact that her hospital bag was at home. That she didn't have a change of clothes with her. And that...*oh my God*... she couldn't breathe...

"Cassie? Cassie? Talk to me." She heard his voice but couldn't get words out through the mind-boggling pain gripping her lower belly and back. She screamed instead.

And her phone landed on the floor.

The eight-minute drive from his work site to Cassie's office was brutal. He had to remain calm. To be strong. And he was shaking so hard he could hardly dial the phone.

With Cassie's line on hold, he phoned 911, getting an ambulance to the law office. If someone else had called, then there'd be two. He didn't give a rat's ass at the moment. He'd foot whatever bill resulted.

And then he flipped back to listening to what was going on in her office. Cassie was moaning, and it didn't sound good. He heard someone call her name and then heard urgent tones but couldn't make out words.

Something was horribly wrong. There were no breaks in Cassie's moans. No seconds, let alone minutes, in between contractions. If it was contractions at all.

He knew all about healthy births. But nothing in their class had taught them preparation for anything like this.

He was almost there and hoped to God that she held on, that he wasn't going to lose her. Or his son.

Sweating, he hollered, "Hello! Hello! Please pick up!"

"There's no time to move her. Lay her back!" The voice was female. He didn't recognize it, but then, other than Cassie's paralegal, he'd never met anyone she knew. Not her partners, her friends, her family.

Suddenly that seemed abhorrent. Unbearable.

"Hello!" he screamed at the top of his lungs.

"Hello? Who is this?"

"Wood. Wood Alexander..." He wasn't going to panic. He was going to be strong. And calm.

"Wood? Where are you?"

"I'm almost there." And not making a lot of sense.

"This is Marilyn. I met you the..."

"...yes," he interrupted as he pulled into the lot. "What's going on?"

He heard the siren before he saw the ambulance.

"She's having her baby," Marilyn said. "We've called the paramedics, but I don't think they're going to make it."

An almost inhuman scream of anguish came over the line.

Throwing the truck in Park, Wood grabbed the keys and ran.

Chapter Twenty-One

Memories of those next hours were going to stay with Wood forever. Marilyn had been waiting for him when he got in the door and took him back to the hallway of private offices. He hadn't even thought about the locked door between the lobby and Cassie.

He saw bodies as he ran into the room, huddled behind Cassie's desk, but wouldn't have been able to identify a single one of them. There were at least three. One, a woman in dress pants and a light-colored blouse, was kneeling between her legs. He saw Cassie's black dress bunched up around her, saw bare skin, and then saw her eyes. They were stark, glazed, like she was losing her mind.

He knelt at her shoulders, lifting her head, cradling it against him as he'd learned in class, sort of. He wasn't helping her push. Or supporting her while she did. He had to be her calm.

"I'm here, Cass. I'm right here. You're doing great. Everything's fine. It's fine. You're doing great." Over and over he said the words. As she moaned. When she screamed. He just kept repeating the words. Watching her face. Holding her gaze when she stared up at him.

He wasn't even sure she knew he was there. Knew who he was. But he held on. Gave her his strength. Because that was what he did.

Everything changed when paramedics burst into the room. He caught a glimpse of worried-looking lawyer faces in the hall when the door opened, and then saw the blue-suited first responders as they went to work. Without any sense of panic, they instructed everyone to move away.

Wood stayed right where he was. He wasn't leaving her. Leaving either of them. "I'm the father," he said.

Maybe there were shocked gasps from whoever had been assisting Cassie. At the moment, none of that mattered.

"It's going good," he said to Cassie as a young man knelt between her legs and assessed the situation. "You're doing fine," he told Cassie, who'd been groaning since they came into the room.

"Boy or a girl?" the young man asked while an associate knelt beside him.

"Boy," he said. "Alan."

A stretcher appeared at the door, was in the room.

"It's too late to move her," the young paramedic, a redhead, announced. "He's already half out. Okay, Mama, one more push and he's here," he said.

Whether Cassie heard him or just pushed because her body forced her to, Wood didn't know, but she gave one more scream and then lay still.

He saw a small body pass from one set of hands to another, and then was focused on Cassie.

She was breathing. But still. Her eyes were closed. And her gorgeous features were no longer scrunched up in pain.

For the moment, at least, she was at peace.

There was rustling farther down her body. A lot of quick movement. A sheet appeared. Some talking, too low for him to make out—he suspected so Cassie wouldn't hear.

And one thing was missing.

There'd been no baby crying.

Cassie felt herself being lifted. Heard Wood's voice telling her that she'd done great. That everything was fine. He'd been there through the worst of it. She'd heard him. Had focused on his words. They reminded her of something important.

Mostly though, she just remembered excruciating pain. So much of it. And then...numbness. She just wanted to sleep.

"I'm going with them." Wood was angry. She'd never heard that tone from him before. She opened her eyes to see his head at the end of the stretcher, but she couldn't see the rest of him. Thought maybe she was in heaven and he was on earth.

"Wood?" Her throat was dry, and she could hardly get the word out.

"I'm right here, Cass." His tone changed, was the calm in her storm just like always, and then his body was there, too. Sitting next to her. They moved. Fast. Sirens blared.

"I had the baby," she said, aware now that she was in an ambulance. And hooked up to an IV.

Wood nodded. He wasn't smiling.

"Where is he?"

"He's right here," he said, nodding toward a little bassinet-looking thing by the door, someone official-looking bending over it.

"Is he okay?" She hadn't heard a cry, but knew that you didn't always. Some babies just took their first breath without squalling.

"We don't know yet." His beautiful blue eyes looked so sad. "They think he needs a blood transfusion. Something about oxygen levels."

She closed her eyes. *Oh God. No bad waves. No bad waves. Let them bring in the good. If You never give me another good wave in my life, please let this one be good. I won't want any more. I swear to any-*

one who will listen. I won't use Wood for my own
personal gain. Just let my baby live...

She prayed all the way to the hospital.

And then she waited.

Cassie and Alan were whisked away as soon as
they got to the hospital. Wood was told to follow
Cassie's stretcher and then was asked to wait outside
a door through which they took her. He'd yet to even
get a good look at their son. No one had offered to
let him see or hold the baby. They'd been too busy
hooking him up and tending to him.

If it were possible for a human being to explode,
he was fairly certain he'd have done so.

And Cassie, other than that brief moment when
he'd first gotten in the ambulance, had had her eyes
closed. She'd lost a lot of blood. He'd seen it on the
floor of her office as they'd lifted her. But wasn't
sure if childbirth regularly produced an alarming
amount of liquid or if her life was in danger. A minute or two after they'd shut the door behind Cassie,
he called Elaina. She was in the hospital someplace.
She'd at least be able to give him some idea of what
might be going on.

She came right down and waited with him instead.

"You're shaking," she said, taking his hand as they
found a couple of chairs, pulled them across from
the door and sat. She'd told him that based on the

situation, taking Cassie in as they had was protocol. She'd be checked over. Might need some stitches.

And it could be worse. Much worse. She didn't say that, but he knew.

"You're in love with her." The nurturing tone in Elaina's words felt odd coming at him.

"I just need to know that they're okay. You should have heard her, Elaina. I've never…" Elbows on his knees, he hung his head, unable to get the sound of Cassie's wails from reverberating through his brain.

"I know." Elaina's tone didn't change. But he believed she knew exactly what he was talking about. She'd been trapped in the car with Peter as he'd been lying there with protruding bones, still conscious.

"It's all right to feel helpless, you know," she told him. "You aren't superhuman, Wood. No one is okay all the time."

He didn't want to hear that.

"This isn't about me," he said and stood as he heard the doorknob across from him turn.

"We're moving her to a room," a nurse told him. Gave him the number. "She'll be there in about ten minutes. If there's anything you need to do, anyone you need to call, now would be a good time. You can meet us at the room."

Yeah, fine, he wasn't going anywhere. "Is she okay? And Alan?"

Another woman came out of the room. "I'm Dr.

Abbot," she said, reaching out a hand to Wood. "Are you the father?"

"I am."

She glanced at Elaina, at her white coat and scrubs. "I'm a resident upstairs, nuclear radiology. I'm his sister," was all Elaina said.

"Are they going to be okay?" Wood asked again, his muscles about ready to split.

"She's going to be fine." Dr. Abbot smiled. "She did twelve hours' work in less than one and is extremely tired," the doctor continued. "But the tearing was minimal. And everything else looks great."

It sure hadn't looked that way to Wood half an hour before. But he wanted to believe what the doctor was telling him. Planned to be just fine, too, when he walked into Cassie's room in ten minutes.

In the meantime, his head was swimming, and he had to sit down.

Cassie saw Wood waiting in the hallway as she was wheeled to her room. Reaching out a hand, she grabbed his as he held it out and, attached to her, he walked the rest of the way with her.

They'd already settled her into a bed before bringing her down, and it was less than a minute before her IV pole was set and she and Wood were alone.

So much had happened, she had no idea where to begin. And was so scared, she could hardly think of anything but Alan.

"They said they'll probably be taking this out soon." She motioned toward the needle in her hand. "It's just sugar water. Precautionary. In case something more was needed."

He nodded. Stood by her bed, looking at her. Just looking. She couldn't tell what he was thinking, but he was different. Less…calm.

Almost…vulnerable as he held the rail on the side of her bed so hard his knuckles were white.

"They said Alan was in distress," she told him.

He nodded. "I called Elaina. She was down here, actually. She's going to see what she can find out for us."

Tears brimmed her eyes. She'd never been a weeper. Had cried more since her pregnancy than in the ten years prior to it. From hormones, or new levels of love, she couldn't be sure.

"He's going to be fine," he said, now sounding like the Wood she knew. The voice she remembered from the blur of memories of giving birth in the office that morning. He reached out a hand, smoothing it down her cheek, and beneath her eye. Then brushed her hair back away from her face. Sometime in the middle of everything, her ponytail had come undone.

"They said his oxygen levels were low," she said, just because she kept hearing the words in her head and needed to give them to him. As though doing so somehow made them less threatening.

"I know. But that's not uncommon in premature births. They're just doing extra tests on him because of the earlier anemia."

Which was more than she'd been told.

"Have you called your mother?" Wood held her hand, hooked a chair with his foot and pulled it closer as he asked the question.

She was so tired. And completely wound up, too. Her eyes ached as she looked at him. "Are you trying to distract me?"

"Yes. And I also think your mother would want to know what's going on."

"I already called her," she said. "A nurse helped me get an outside line while I was waiting for them to come get me to bring me here. She's getting the next flight out and will get a cab to the hospital. She's going to call when she lands. I…gave her your number."

"Good."

She sipped at the orange juice they'd left on her tray for her, and he asked how she was feeling. If she was in pain. She felt surprisingly not horrible, physically. Sore, of course, but nothing like she'd have expected, having felt as though she was being ripped in half such a short time before. Because the baby had come so quickly, the doctor had explained. She'd likely dilated from three to ten in minutes instead of hours.

She mentioned needing her things, her bag at the

house. Some underwear. Her cell phone. Her satchel, which had her keys in it. He gave her his phone to call her paralegal to see if she'd mind seeing to all of it. Marilyn had been panic stricken as they'd driven away, Wood told her, and was overjoyed to hear from Cassie and know that she was okay. And to bring whatever she needed to the hospital.

Wood wasn't planning on leaving. Cassie didn't argue. He was Alan's father. He should be there.

And he wasn't her…anything but her sperm donor. And friend. She might not remember some things about that morning, but she very clearly recalled her deal with the waves. Alan had to be okay. And Cassie had to give up, once and for all, any wayward hope that Wood would ever be more than a dear friend to her.

No matter how much she might love him. Because she did. Having him there in her worst moment… she'd known, as clearly as she'd ever known anything in her life, the man was her one and only.

She was pretty sure she'd agreed to give up any future husband as well, but she didn't see that as much of a problem.

A dietitian came in and offered them lunch. Wood insisted that they accept. That she at least try to eat.

"If you're going to be breastfeeding, you need to tend to your own nutrition," he told her. They both knew not all women were able to breastfeed or even pump to provide milk for their children. But she nodded. Ordered a cheeseburger and ate half of it.

And every thirty seconds or so, she looked from the door to Wood's face. Scared to death, and finding her calm. Her son was already a couple of hours old, and she hadn't even seen him.

A knock came on the door shortly after they finished eating. She called for whoever it was to come in, afraid she was going to lose her lunch in the seconds it took for her to see who was there. A doctor with good news?

Bad news?

How did a woman just lay there and wait to hear the fate of her baby?

Could Alan be on the other side of the door? Would they just bring him in to her if he was well enough?

And if he wasn't... The terror in her chest was blocking all air.

The door pushed open and she didn't recognize the stunning woman who came through, but she saw the white coat and everything in her clenched for the bad news. They would get through this. Her baby and her. He was alive. She knew that much. And they were strong. They'd make a plan and deal with things one at a time...

The doctor smiled at Wood. Walked up to him and put a hand on his shoulder. "Hi, Cassie," she said. "I'm Elaina, Wood's sister-in-law. It's good to finally meet you." The brown eyes were kind looking. Compassionate.

Cassie liked the woman on sight. But then, Wood had married her—she had to be an amazing person. She also felt a pang to her heart like none other. That hand on Wood's shoulder…looked so natural, like it was no big deal. Casual. Allowed.

Cassie had just had his baby, but had no right to touch his shoulder like that.

"I just wanted to let you both know…the doctor will be coming down to see you shortly. He got called in to an emergency when I was in the nursery asking about Alan, and he said I could give you a preliminary rundown until he can make it here. Because he knows you're worried…"

"And?" Wood's tone with Elaina was different than Cassie was used to. Not warmer. Or more distant. Just…different.

Elaina's smile reached out to Cassie. "He's a beautiful baby and going to be just fine," she said. "They were preparing to do a red blood cell transfusion. The red cells transport oxygen to other parts of the body, but his numbers have all leveled out. They're still monitoring him, working on him, and will be keeping him a bit longer, but he might even be in here by nightfall. If not, they'll take you to see him."

She started to cry. She was all alone, with this former couple who'd been family for a long time and, even after a failed marriage, still had each other. But she didn't begrudge them their togetherness, or feel jealous at the fact that she couldn't be a part of them.

Her prayer had been answered.

Her son was healthy.

"Can I talk to you a second?" Elaina asked Wood as she was leaving Cassie's room. She'd shared a picture of Alan from her phone to Cassie's and answered about a dozen of Cassie's questions about their son. She'd also asked Cassie if she could be recognized as Alan's aunt.

An honor Cassie had tearfully granted on the spot.

Elaina had a procedure scheduled and wanted to get back upstairs to prepare.

With a last long glance at Cassie, who, holding her phone to her chest, had closed her eyes, Wood followed Elaina out the door. "I can't thank you enough for that," he said. "You're definitely in the right profession," he added. "Your bedside manner is impressive."

She smiled but didn't look pleased. Or displeased, either. She looked…determined.

"What's up?"

"I want you to forget everything I said about you being careful not to give too much to Cassie. About your tendency to give up yourself for others."

He leaned back against the wall, staring at her. "What?"

"I was being incredibly selfish, Wood, afraid I

was going to lose you, or something, I don't know. But that woman in there loves you. And I just realized that I might be the one who's been holding you back from what you really want. Or my fear has." She glanced toward Cassie's room door.

"Cassie's not in love with me," he said, standing upright. "Or, at least, there's no way for us to know that. Not with everything that's been going on. And…" He quickly moved on. "You aren't ever going to lose me. And you aren't ever getting rid of me, either. I'm your brother, by law or not. And—" he swallowed "—believe it or not, I need you every bit as much as you need me." Because family was family.

She shook her head, tears in her eyes, but a smile on her lips. She hugged him, and then stood back. "Regardless of what you say, big brother, I think Cassie's love for you is pretty clear. All you have to do is stand back and watch the way her face changes as she watches you…" *Big brother.* It was what Peter had always called him.

"And while I've seen you with a few women in your time, I've never seen you look at a woman like you look at her. Not even me."

He stared at her.

"And…" she continued. "I also want you to know that the next time Jason asks me to spend the night with him, instead of getting up and going home, I'm probably going to say yes. Seeing the change in you these past months, as you found out you were going to be a father, and then as you got to know Cassie… I wanted that again, too. I at least want to try." She had tears in her eyes as she smiled. "And if I do stay out all night, I can't have Big Brother checking up on me…"

She was letting him go. Letting him know that she wouldn't be checking up on him, either.

"Go to her," Elaina said. "She needs you."

"I love you."

"I know. I love you, too. Now go."

He knew what was happening. Elaina was ready to move on now. To find another man to fill the void his brother had left in her heart. Wood had done his job well. And that particular work was done. Made him so happy for her. And a little sad, too, to let go.

"You tell your Jason that if he ever causes you to shed one tear, he'll have me to answer to…" he called down the empty hallway as she headed off to work. Because Wood was Wood. He'd always tend to those he loved.

And as she walked away, he had to lean a moment, to close his eyes as an onslaught washed over him, like a floodgate bursting open, as indeed it just had. The gate he'd been keeping on the walls of his heart. It could no longer keep a lock on the love he felt for Cassie Thompson.

The mother of his child. And the other half of his soul.

* * *

The rest of that day was a blur to Cassie, cataloged from moment to moment, but with each superseding the next. She was already dozing by the time Wood came back into the room and fell into a real sleep as soon as he settled on the couch he'd pulled up closer to the bed.

The door opening woke her sometime around four, and when she saw why, she sat straight up in bed. "You ready to meet your little one?" the plump, cheery woman asked, and with Wood on her bed beside her, she opened her arms to receive their son, settling him against her heart.

And crying happy tears.

There didn't seem to be any private moments after that. She had doctor's checks, vital checks. Alan, who, because he was doing fine, was allowed to stay in her room, did, too. He needed diaper changes. They wanted her to try breastfeeding right away. People from her office, the ones who'd apparently been standing out in the hallway worried sick as she screamed bloody murder in the process of giving birth, stopped in, one at a time, briefly. Once she had her cell phone, she'd called one of her college friends, and soon they were all texting her, wanting to know when they could meet Alan. Her mother also arrived. Wood ran home to get some clothes, announcing that he'd be staying the night, and Elaina stopped in at the end of her shift.

Her mother went home to Cassie's house a little after nine, and then it was just her and Wood and their sleeping baby. She had the bassinet next to her bed but didn't want to put the little guy down. Not until she absolutely had to, to get her own rest. He'd been sleeping next to her heart for months. Another hour or two wasn't going to hurt him any.

At her request Wood turned off all but a light under a high cupboard and then he settled, half lying on the couch next to her bed.

He hadn't held Alan yet. She'd offered a time or two, but there'd been so many people in and out of the room, so much going on, his refusals had gone largely unnoticed. Except by her. The closest he'd come to touching his son had been when he'd been on the bed, with his arm around Cassie's pillow behind her back as she'd held him for her mother to get a picture.

Hurting for him, for whatever was holding him back from fully embracing his son in his life, she looked for something worthwhile to say to him but couldn't find it. And maybe she was taking a step back herself, because she knew it wasn't her place to help Wood find himself.

"The reason I made such a big deal of the educational differences between us, of my lack of education when we first met, is because I've felt like I'm lacking for so much of my life."

The words were raw. Bald. Laying there in the near dark.

She felt like he'd volleyed her a live mine.

"If I've ever made you feel insignificant, or lacking in any way, Wood, I truly apologize. I hold you in the highest regard. And have the utmost respect for you. I might have given you the wrong idea about my father, but believe me, I didn't think it was possible for any man to ever measure up to him in my eyes, but you do. Why do you think I wanted you to be Alan's father after birth, not just during conception? It wasn't because of how I thought I felt about you, but because of what I saw in you that he needed."

She couldn't make out his expression in the shadows, and that frustrated her. Only the baby's weight against her held her in place. And calmed her, too.

"I haven't felt like myself since I met you," he said, as though nothing she'd said had had any effect at all. "I've been uncomfortable. Not just with you, but within myself."

Unsure where this was going, but sensing that what was happening was hugely important, she watched him, knowing she had to hear him out, no matter how much it hurt.

"I've been slowly realizing this for a while, but today...hearing you scream...when I thought I was going to lose you... I couldn't doubt what was real. And then, Elaina...she called me on it...

"Meeting you showed me that the life I had wasn't

enough. That there was so much living to do of which I was unaware. Mostly, it showed me that I didn't ask enough out of life for myself. Meeting you kicked my ass out of the safe zone I'd somehow slipped into. I will always be a worthy servant to those I love, but I can still have dreams of my own."

Wow. If meeting her had shown him that, then she was very, very glad to carry the burden of her unrequited love for him. He'd given her Alan, and she'd given him back his ability to dream bigger. To want, not just do.

As her mom had said, it was all meant to be.

He stood. Came over to sit beside her, one arm around her pillow again. They'd had a baby together that day and yet, other than a couple of hand-holding incidents, and some hugs, and knee touches, they still hadn't been physically intimate.

"So now I'm asking, Cassie." His free hand reached out to her, handing her something. She took it with her free hand and then saw what she was holding.

A small jewelry box. Ring size.

But it had to be earrings. A thank-you for having his child. It used to be a thing, men buying gifts for the mother of the child on the day of birth, and Wood was traditional like that.

Her free hand was holding their son's bottom. She couldn't get the box open.

"What are you asking?" She was staring at the

box. She couldn't help it. She'd made a deal that day, a life-and-death deal, and already, she was wanting more than she could have.

What was the matter with her?

"I'm asking for my own dream, Cassie. I'm asking you to marry me." He flipped open the lid of the box that was still in her hand, exposing the biggest solitaire diamond she'd ever seen in real life. Bigger even than her mother's, which she'd always thought huge. "Or rather, telling you that I believe I'm enough to make you happy, and hoping that you'll marry me."

Cassie held their son, aware of his warmth against her, needing it, and still holding the box, too. "But… my emotions are all in such a mess right now. I'm not going to take a chance on using you, Wood, on trapping you in a relationship that you'll later wish you didn't have…"

"Yet you'll trust your son to love me."

"I know he will."

She had no doubt about that. None.

"What if I tell you I trust you to love me?"

She stared at him. Frightened all of a sudden. Her heart started pounding.

She'd made a deal with God.

And a promise to herself, too. She hadn't thought about it in a long, long time, but sitting there, feeling completely trapped suddenly by all the things she needed so badly, just hours after she'd almost lost everything, she remembered the girl who'd sat alone at the cemetery the night they'd buried her father. Her mom and Richard had been at her dad's house, cleaning out his stuff, and she'd taken the car...

She'd promised herself that she'd never, ever let herself fall so deeply in love with anyone that she couldn't get over the relationship if it ended. As much as she loved her dad, she couldn't be like him. Couldn't spend her whole life pining for someone who'd chosen to leave.

At least he'd had her mom for a while. Had known bliss.

At least he had his memories.

Cassie didn't even have those memories of being with the one she loved. In some ways, she was more alone than her dad ever had been. But still...

"Can we at least wait a couple of months?" she asked.

She'd die a slow death if Wood married her just because she needed him.

"I'm scared," she told him.

"Because you're in love with me," he told her.

She knew she was. It all made sense now.

"You know how I know how much you love me? Because today, in your worst moments, I was the one you needed. I was the only one who could calm your heart. Because, all these months, you've put my happiness before your own," he told her. Her eyes filled with tears, she looked at him. Needing him. *Loving* him.

"Love's a scary thing," she told him. "You hear everyone talk about falling in love and you see these couples all sappy and in love and getting married, and…it scares the heck out of me. My dad, he was such a great guy…and his heart was just broken…"

"Maybe. Maybe not. Maybe he'd had what he wanted and was happiest just spending his time off with you."

She'd never thought of her father's single state being his own choice. She'd always seen it as something out of his control. Something that had happened to him that he couldn't fix.

"Love *is* scary," Wood said softly, his voice tender in the darkness. "Even with this little guy here. We both would have been devastated if he hadn't made it through today. But look at you now…beaming, holding him. Knowing a happiness beyond anything you can imagine…"

She looked up at him, saw the glow in his eyes as he gazed at the sleeping baby she held. "It is beyond anything we could have imagined, huh?" she asked him.

He looked back at her and nodded. "Would you choose not to have this experience, not to know him, to protect your heart from ever feeling pain because of him?"

"Of course not."

His gaze intent, he watched her. Waiting.

She knew what he was pulling out of her. Just as he knew it was there.

"I do love you, Wood. I want to make you happy. For the rest of your life, I want to make both you and Alan happy."

"Then take my ring, put it on your finger and say that you'll become my forever family."

Cassie dropped the box, ring and all. Wrapping her hand around Wood's head, she brought his face to hers and stopped his words. Her lips took them, her tongue took them, her breath took him. There was no first kiss, no tentativeness. She slid her tongue into his mouth, accepted his in hers and made love in the only way she could having just had a baby and having said baby cradled against her.

Wood didn't fight her advances. He actually made the way easier for her, gathering her, including Alan, against him as he climbed fully onto the bed with them, holding them against him as he kissed her back.

She would never in a million years have believed that she could feel any kind of good sensation down below after the day she'd had, but tiny spurts of desire spiraled, and she had to stop the kiss.

"I take that as a yes?" Wood asked, finding the ring box in the covers, removing the ring and slipping it on her finger. She teared up, of course, but didn't care. She'd never known love could feel like this. Never known emotion could be so intense.

Or so intensely right.

And kissed him some more.

They talked some, too. About him moving into her house, starting immediately. She asked about his dog. He said that if Elaina wanted Retro, he'd let her have her, but if that happened, he wanted to get another dog for the two of them, a friendly cousin to Retro when she came to visit. They talked about the nursery furniture that was pretty much done but still sitting in Wood's shed, waiting for her to have it picked up. He'd be delivering it himself now. Along with the rest of his stuff. He was going to sign his house over to Elaina, if she wanted it.

There was so much to think about. To be thankful for. Overwhelmed in the best possible way, she almost started to cry again.

"When did you find the time to buy this?" she asked, distracting herself by watching the ring sparkle in the dimmed light.

"I didn't. I asked your mother to do it for me on her way in from the airport."

Which explained why the ring looked like her mother's, but bigger and better. Because Susan knew Cassie so well. And wanted more for her than she'd ever had herself.

It was a mother's way.

"I thought I was losing you in the ambulance this morning... I knew then that you were my only dream. My true life..."

"I was praying," she said. "My dad used to say that the waves bring in the good and the bad, and the one thing we can count on is that when they've brought something bad, hold on, good will follow. I was making a deal that if this one wave could be good, if Alan could be okay, I'd give up wanting what I couldn't have."

"Meaning me?"

She nodded, tearing up again as she looked at him. "I love you so much, Woodrow Alexander."

"I love you, too, Cassie. And more, I'm forever in love with you." He kissed her again. More gently, with less tongue. "You are the one I want to be with forever," he told her.

And then brushed his thumb against Alan's cheek.

He was still holding back. She loved him too much to watch it happen.

"You know, Wood, something else occurs to me."

"What's that?"

"I think it's time for you to accept all your dreams coming true," she said. "You aren't just a bystander here, watching over things, tending to them—you're as much a part of this as I am. As the paperwork we sign before we leave here will show." Shifting enough to move the baby over to his body from hers, she helped him settle his son in the crook of his free arm.

She was never going to forget the look of sheer awe on Wood's face as he looked down at the baby he held. Not ever.

"I chose his first name," she told him, her throat tightening with emotion. "You should choose his second." She'd been wanting to make the offer for a while.

"Seriously?" He looked from the baby to her and back.

"Dream, Wood, dream. Ask for things for yourself." She was, after all, the lawyer in the family. The one trained to watch out for the rights of others.

"Then his name is Alan Peter."

"Alan Peter Alexander," she said, trying the name out loud. It didn't ring quite right. So she tried again, knowing she was truly opening her heart at last. "How about Peter Alan Alexander?" she asked.

And as if he had a say in things, the baby woke up.

* * * * *

COMING SOON!

MILLS & BOON

Coming next month

BABY ON THE TYCOON'S DOORSTEP
Nina Milne

Isobel headed to the kitchenette, scooped powder into another bottle and handed it to Jake, waited whilst he poured the water in from the kettle.

Took it from him and stepped closer to demonstrate. Too close—she was way too close.

Focus. But not on his body, the sculpted forearms, the swell of his upper arms, the strong thighs. Not on his smell, not on the way his hair spiked up— This was a bad idea but for the life of her she couldn't figure a way out of it.

'Put your thumb over the top of the teat, so you're blocking the hole. Then you shake.' Like this.' Her voice emerged squeaky...breathless...*ridiculous*.

He'd moved even closer to her now and his eyes held a wicked glint that ripped the breath from her lungs.

'So it's all in the wrist action,' he said dead pan and her gaze flew to meet his, in shock at the double entendre.

'I—'

Then he grinned and wiggled his eyebrows. 'Sorry I couldn't resist. Puerile but—'

'Yes,' she said, trying to keep a straight face. 'Definitely puerile.' But be that is it may she succumbed to a giggle, which morphed into a full-blown laugh. And in seconds he had joined in.

Now their gazes locked and she could feel the shift in the atmosphere, the swirl of desire, the fugue of need. They were even closer now. His scent tantalised; the warm smell of baby milk mixed with a hint of citrus clean sharp shower gel and a whiff of bergamot. Her head whirled and there was an utter inevitability about what happened next. She wasn't sure afterwards who initiated it, who made the fatal decision or whether it was a completely synchronised movement.

But one step took them closer and then she was in his arms and her lips met his and oh god it felt so good. His lips so familiar and yet so new, and her lips tingled as tremors of raw desire shuddered her body. Gentle, hesitant at first as if they both feared rejection and then the kiss deepened, intensified, sent a sear through her veins. His fingers tangled in her hair, she pressed her body against his wanting more, her pulse rate accelerated at his taste, his scent, the way his kiss could drive her to the edge of desperate need for more. Her body alight and craving more of him—of Jake—she wanted his touch, wanted the satisfaction her body knew and remembered.

Continue reading
BABY ON THE TYCOON'S DOORSTEP
Nina Milne

Available next month
www.millsandboon.co.uk

LET'S TALK
Romance

For exclusive extracts, competitions
and special offers, find us online:

MILLS & BOON
MEDICAL
Pulse-Racing Passion

Set your pulse racing with dedicated, delectable doctors in the high-pressure world of medicine, where emotions run high and passion, comfort and love are the best medicine.